ABOUT THE AUTHOR

Christopher Ride was born in Canberra, Australia, in 1965. He self-published his first novel, *The Schumann Frequency*, in 2007 and was thereafter signed by Random House Australia to a multiple book deal for his Overseer series. His novels are also published internationally.

A keen mountain climber, licensed pilot and historian, he divides his time between the running of his IT business and the research and writing of his books.

The Inca Curse is Christopher's third novel.

Also by Christopher Ride

The Schumann Frequency

The Last Empress
(previously titled *The First Boxer*)

Christopher Ride

THE INCA CURSE

BANTAM

SYDNEY AUCKLAND TORONTO NEW YORK LONDON

A Bantam book
Published by Random House Australia Pty Ltd
Level 3, 100 Pacific Highway, North Sydney NSW 2060
www.randomhouse.com.au

First published by Bantam in 2012

Addresses for companies within the Random House Group can be
found at www.randomhouse.com.au/offices

National Library of Australia
Cataloguing-in-Publication entry

Ride, Christopher, 1965–
The Inca curse/Christopher Ride.

ISBN 978 1 74275 011 8 (pbk.)

Incas – Fiction.
Machu Picchu Site (Peru) – Fiction.

A823.4

Cover design © www.blacksheep-uk.com
Map design by Andrew Cunningham, Studio Pazzo
Internal typesetting and design by Midland Typesetters, Australia
Printed in Australia by Griffin Press, an accredited ISO AS/NZS
14001:2004 Environmental Management System printer

Random House Australia uses papers that are natural, renewable and
recyclable products and made from wood grown in sustainable forests.
The logging and manufacturing processes are expected to conform to
the environmental regulations of the country of origin.

*For my brother David, who lived in Peru
with me when we were boys*

PRELUDE

AT THE DAWN of the Age of Pisces, around the birth of Jesus Christ, thirty-nine books of the Old Testament were chronicled upon simple papyrus scrolls. These ancient documents were written by a group of holy men known as the Khirbet Qumran Brotherhood – living saints set down on this earth to chronicle the teachings of God and His wisdom. Known today as the Dead Sea Scrolls, these mythical parchments were the first iteration of the Bible. And yet despite their obvious learnings and wisdom, these fabled documents conceal an even greater knowledge. For embedded within the text of the Dead Sea Scrolls was hidden the greatest power in the universe: the secret to travelling the pathways of time.

When the technology and wisdom of man was suitable, the scrolls would reveal themselves to a select group who would assume the mantle of protectors of the future, and of the past. In the Book of Esther the technical details of travelling time were encoded. In each of the other books of the Old Testament was encrypted a single mission – thirty-eight in all.

This is the story of one such mission.

These are the travels of the Overseer.

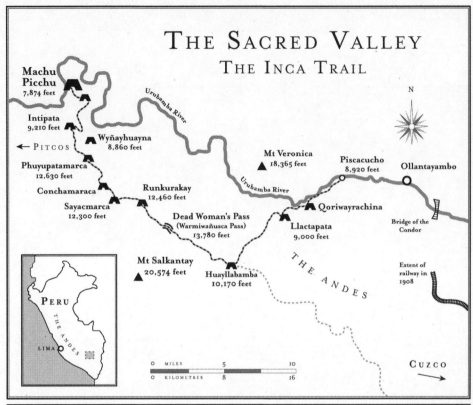

THE SACRED VALLEY
THE INCA TRAIL

Machu Picchu
7,874 feet

Intipata
9,210 feet

← PITCOS

Wyñayhuayna
8,860 feet

Urubamba River

Mt Veronica
18,365 feet

Piscacucho
8,920 feet

Ollantayambo

N

Phuyupatamarca
12,630 feet

Conchamaraca

Runkurakay
12,460 feet

Sayacmarca
12,300 feet

Dead Woman's Pass
(Warmiwañusca Pass)
13,780 feet

Urubamba River

Qoriwayrachina

Llactapata
9,000 feet

Bridge of the
Condor

Mt Salkantay
20,574 feet

Huayllabamba
10,170 feet

THE ANDES

Extent of
railway in
1908

PERU

THE ANDES

LIMA

MILES   5   10

KILOMETRES   8   16

CUZCO →

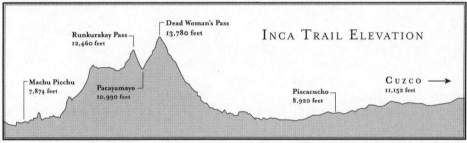

Dead Woman's Pass
13,780 feet

Runkurakay Pass
12,460 feet

INCA TRAIL ELEVATION

Machu Picchu
7,874 feet

Pacayamayo
10,990 feet

Piscacucho
8,920 feet

CUZCO →
11,152 feet

1

13 January 1908

RIDING ON A little donkey, Juan Santillana trotted through the misty rain along the cobblestone roadway. The blackish clouds above the city were so low that the eerie haze obscured the spires and rooftops of the taller buildings. Juan's hooded poncho covered all but his eyes, his right hand clenching the soaking, grey alpaca material from the inside, just under his chin. Out of the mist, the central plaza of Cuzco gradually came into view. It was here, 800 years ago that Manco Capac, the very first Inca king, threw down the Golden Staff of the Sun God and pronounced this the location where the Inca capital would be built. The ancient city was created in the shape of a puma, a sacred Inca animal, with the plaza at its very heart. The large open space was rectangular in dimension and measured 300 paces along one side, and 400 paces along the other. In the very centre stood a bronze two-tiered baroque fountain that was gushing with clear water – a tribute to the Spanish Conquistadores who had over-thrown the Inca civilisation while it was at its very prime. Three smooth walkways crisscrossed the tilted surface from corner to corner, and across the middle, creating six symmetrical triangles of grass. During the time of the Inca kings this place was called Huacaypata – Heart of the Puma – but it was renamed Plaza de Armas – Plaza of the Army – by the Conquistador Francisco Pizarro, after he brutally seized the city of Cuzco in 1533.

The legs of Juan's donkey were unsteady as it laboured forward under the wet and hazy sky. The journey had been gruelling and for the last few hours Juan was fighting his own eyelids from closing. But as he approached the Plaza de Armas and took in the impressive sight of La Catedral – the most famous basilica cathedral in all of South America – his senses sharpened.

As he had done countless times in the last three days, Juan reached back and felt the substantial weight of the saddlebag strapped across his donkey's hindquarters. Stopping at the bottom of the steps in front of the towering walls of La Catedral, Juan once again considered jamming his heels into the little donkey's sides and trotting away into the mist, taking with him the spoils of his discovery.

What is the value of my own brother's life? he asked himself.

His gaze lifted to the two imposing belltowers of La Catedral, before eventually settling on the halfway point between them – the domed central cornice that held the white wooden cross of Jesus Christ, silhouetted against the dark clouds.

Juan's heart unexpectedly began racing. There was no choice but to hand over what he had discovered, he knew as much, and yet his constantly nagging desire was playing tricks on him.

Around the plaza people were going about their business. The markets were doing a steady trade as countless donkeys pulled wagons of produce in all directions – loads of wood, sweet potatoes, corn and quinoa that had been transported from the nearby farms. A woman carried her young baby in a sling under her poncho, a heavy bail of wheat perched on her tilted back. In the distance, Peruvian soldiers huddled in a circle playing cards under the awning of the Cuzco barracks, their .303 rifles neatly lined up against the wall. Two monks were walking slowly across the plaza towards the Jesuit church – Iglesia La

Compañia – their brown hooded robes pulled over their heads to protect them from the inclement weather.

With his buttocks aching due to multiple days in the saddle, Juan dismounted and steadied his footing on the cobblestone forecourt. His clothes were soaked through and he knew the skin on his backside had certainly blistered from chafing.

As it was, no one in the city of Cuzco knew of the incredible treasure hidden in the leather saddlebag perched on the back of his humble donkey. It was an object like no man had ever seen. If there was even a sniff of its presence in these crowded streets, there would surely be a mad frenzy just to touch it, let alone the those who certainly wished to obtain the precious item for themselves. Juan had already killed one man so as to protect what he had in his possession. As much as he tried to deny it, it was as if the strange golden object had talked to him, conversing directly into his mind with thoughts of pleasure and riches, and everything that would soon be his. Juan wanted to believe that he had committed the sin of murder to save his own brother – it was much easier to think of it that way – but when he searched deep enough into his thoughts, he feared it was simply his greed to possess something so beautiful that had driven him to it.

Turning once again towards the impressive church, Juan felt a churning in his empty stomach. Was he really going to hand over this magnificent Inca object to Bishop Francisco? He searched under his poncho for the small silver cross that hung around his neck on a thin strand of leather.

'Talk to me, Christ,' he muttered to himself.

Juan's gaze once again climbed the rain-soaked walls of La Catedral, his eyes eventually locking onto the circular clock face mounted on the left tower. It was one minute to three; soon the mighty church bells would be chiming in all their glory. Then it began – the melody as sweet as angels singing by God's side. The clarity and pitch of the twelve bells of Cuzco were as familiar as the kiss of Juan's own mother. He had lived with his parents and brother within two miles of this place for his entire life and had often counted the seconds in anticipation of hearing the mighty bells strike again, each mid-morning and afternoon.

Juan closed his eyes and soaked up his memories. His younger brother, Corsell, had been a good brother – he was to turn twenty-one later this year. Juan himself would turn twenty-three. They had always been close as boys, only in the last few years drifting apart as many do when they reach adulthood. Corsell had joined the army, Juan still worked with their father as a blade sharpener, working mainly with farming equipment, scythes and machetes; anything that needed a razor's edge.

Juan's trance was suddenly broken when a hand unexpectedly touched his shoulder – the contact caused him to reel back as if he had been prodded with a stick.

'Relax, my boy,' Monsignor Pera said with a smile. 'It is only me.'

'You shocked me, Father!' Juan replied, trying not to sound out of breath.

'You were supposed to be back a week ago,' the old priest whispered through his blackened teeth. He wore a brown hooded robe, tied at the waist with a simple knotted rope. It was obvious that he had only just stepped out into the rain because the water was beading up on the outside of the heavy material. Around his neck he wore a substantial sterling-silver cross on a thick silver chain. 'Everyone is very worried.'

'It was more difficult than you could have imagined,' Juan replied.

'Where is Jesús?' the priest asked, searching the plaza for his young novice.

Juan swallowed deeply. 'I have very bad news, Father.' It was suddenly impossible to look into Monsignor Pera's eyes, such was the remorse that wrestled with his emotions. 'Jesús fell from a cliff in the mountains,' Juan eventually forced himself to say, unable to admit that he had murdered the young man in cold blood. Sobbing, Juan grabbed the monsignor's warm hand and dropped to his knees in the street, as if in prayer. 'I did everything I could to protect him! But Jesús was not a man comfortable in the mountains. He has paid the ultimate price.'

With a furrowed brow, Monsignor Pera gestured a cross on his chest. 'I was worried when you did not return that something terrible had happened. I see now that my worst fears have come to pass.' The monsignor gave a long, laboured sigh. 'Praise be to God that you were able to return safely to us.' He bent over awkwardly to whisper in Juan's ear. 'Were you able to find the lost city?' Monsignor Pera's words were barely audible through the strengthening rain.

'Is my brother still alive?' Juan responded.

Monsignor Pera gave a reassuring smile as he gently pulled Juan to his feet. 'Of course your brother is alive – that is the agreement, my son.'

Juan had known Monsignor Pera his whole life. The old man had been a witnessing priest at the ceremony to marry Juan's own parents; he had been told countless times. That was over twenty-five years ago. And now he was monsignor at the largest church in Peru, reporting directly to Bishop Francisco, a man appointed by Pope Pius himself, the most powerful man in the Christian world.

With another whisper, Monsignor Pera asked, 'Were you able to bring back the golden Inca object?'

Just the mention of it caused Juan's heart to beat so madly he thought it would explode. His overwhelming instinct at that moment was to run, but he knew the only way to save his brother was to hand over his discovery.

'Your brother's life depends on it,' the priest added, as if he was reading Juan's thoughts. 'I do not even want to think what uncertain future will face him if you have failed.'

Juan's gaze drifted towards the leather saddlebag perched on the back of his donkey. 'The Inca treasure is everything Bishop Francisco said it would be,' Juan eventually admitted. 'It is an object so magnificent that your soul will be uplifted by the very sight of it.'

'I am so very pleased,' the monsignor replied with a serious expression. 'Come, we should go inside,' and he gestured towards the main entrance. 'The bishop will return this evening and we can give him the good news.'

Juan followed the priest up the stairs towards the imposing walls of La Catedral, at the same time leading his donkey behind him. Not a word was spoken as they approached the huge green doors that stood twenty feet tall.

'Father, when you see this object you will surely ask yourself why I did not simply run off with this treasure – such is its beauty – regardless of the terrible price it would surely cost Corsell and my family.'

The monsignor pushed open the heavy creaking door and entered the great church. 'It is because you are a good man,' he replied.

The priest's comment made Juan shiver – he was not a good man; what he had done to Jesús had proven that. Leading his donkey directly into the central nave, the sound of heavy rain was replaced with a deathly silence as the door was closed behind him with a thud, then locked. The only noise breaking the utter calm was the echoing *clip-clop* of the donkey's hooves against the smooth granite floor.

La Catedral was truly a magnificent structure with towering whitewashed ceilings that stretched up towards the heavens in a series of cavernous ribbed domes, twenty-four in all. There were three main corridors in this part of the church, each known as a nave. The wide-open floors and crafted stone pillars were constructed from granite quarried from the Palace of Wiracocha, the Inca building that once stood on this very spot – it had been the principle residence of the Inca kings for more than 300 years. Upon the taking of the Cuzco, the Conquistador Francisco Pizarro ordered that the Inca palace be destroyed and the stones used to build the Basilica Catedral – the largest and most impressive in all of South America.

On the exposed inner walls of the church, and within the dozens of structured alcoves along the naves, were hundreds of works of art: lifelike effigies of Jesus and his disciples, Mary and Joseph, paintings large and small, precious metal sculptures and religious symbols. This was a place that Juan treated with reverence bordering on being dumbstruck, but today he felt no such emotion. He was unfeeling to everything around him, except for the Inca treasure in his possession.

'Is it in the saddlebag?' the monsignor asked.

Juan stared at the bulk strapped to his animal's back. 'Yes, Father,' he said reluctantly, but he did not move a muscle to retrieve it.

'I am keen to see it.'

With each passing moment, Juan became more agitated. His breath was quickening and his skin felt flushed. Could he really hand over the Inca treasure to the priest?

'Open the saddlebag, my son.'

'Where is my brother, Corsell?' Juan asked, at the same time searching the massive expanse under the lofty pillars and pristine white arches. 'Is he here?'

'He is with Bishop Francisco,' Monsignor Pera replied. 'Now, show me the treasure.' He stepped towards the saddlebag, his cupped hands outstretched.

Juan strategically moved between the monsignor and his donkey. 'Not until my brother is returned safely to me. That is our agreement.'

Monsignor Pera stopped in his tracks, his face suddenly twisted in outrage. 'How dare you disobey me in the house of God! You will do as I say and you will open that saddle-bag!'

With his blood rushing so quickly he could barely think, Juan caught sight of a life-sized effigy of Jesus Christ against the back wall of the ornate enclave. The effigy looked almost real – blood dripping from the thorny crown on the head of the saviour, His hands and feet nailed to the wooden beams with great steel bolts, His calm eyes staring down as if He was actually there in the flesh.

Juan once again turned his gaze to the angry face of Monsignor Pera.

'*He only wants the treasure for himself,*' a deep, gravelly voice called out inside Juan's head. '*You cannot give it to him.*'

Juan had heard the gravelly voice before – there was no use denying it to himself. It was the same dominating utterence that had instructed Juan to push the novice Jesús off the cliff top to his death just two days earlier.

'You will show me the treasure!' Monsignor Pera said even more sternly.

'You cannot see it,' Juan announced, his reply shredded with the perilous emotions that were swirling inside him.

'You will *not* disobey me!' the priest yelled. 'I am the monsignor here!'

'*You must kill him!*' the powerful voice shouted. '*You will strike him down in the name of God!*'

Juan snatched the little hunting knife from the sleeve of his boot and without thinking plunged the blade deep into Monsignor Pera's stomach with all his might.

Everything was suddenly a blur.

The lights became blinding.

The shadows and blackness felt endless and cold. Juan was unable to feel his limbs or even sense his own emotions. He was in a void of some kind, trying desperately to find himself in the frenzied madness he knew had engulfed the world around him. He became conscious of a growing smell, so wicked and overpowering that it made him want to vomit. It was like chicken fertilizer, pungent and powerful, and a distinct metallic scent grated on his senses as if sharp fangs were gnawing at his nostrils.

By the time Juan was able to refocus, he found himself on his knees, the mutilated body of Monsignor Pera lying on the ground before him. The old man's face was slashed beyond recognition, his limbs were still twitching – blood was spurting from the opening that was once his chest. The monsignor's eyeballs were missing, they had been crudely carved out of his face.

The soiled hunting knife released from Juan's hand and hit the floor, the clanking blade bouncing end over end before coming to a stop in the expanding pool of crimson blood that was growing around them both. The monsignor's papal robes were shredded from countless stab wounds, his filthy innards splayed out across the floor.

Juan's donkey had been desperately trying to yank away, squealing with fear, its eyes wide with the vision of death. But the reins were tied around Juan's wrist and all the animal could manage was to pull Juan a few paces to one side, leaving a smear of blood across the floor.

The realisation of what he was seeing finally caused Juan to scream in horror. He tried to suppress his cries by biting his own hand, but he began hacking up bile, such was the disgusting taste. Juan realised that his hands were covered in blood and filth also. He crawled on all fours towards the mutilated body of the monsignor as more sour bile spewed from his mouth. He lifted his gaze to the beautiful effigy of the Nativity Virgin within one of the adjacent alcoves, holding the placid infant Jesus in her arms.

'What have I done?' Juan blubbered, as if crying out to her. His grief overpowering, he pressed his face against the monsignor's savaged body and held him. 'I am sorry!' he wailed. 'I am sorry!' He could feel the wetness of the monsignor's warm innards against his cheek and forehead.

In the distance, the sound of running footsteps could be heard from the gospel nave, getting closer with each passing second.

Juan knew he should try to escape, but he was momentarily frozen. The warmth of the monsignor's body was comforting somehow and he didn't want to release him.

'Is somebody there?' a young voice called out from across the great church.

Juan's gaze sought out the small hunting knife half-submerged in the expanding pool of blood. Reaching across, he gripped the sticky handle and climbed to his feet. 'Praise be to Jesus Christ our Lord,' he muttered. 'I am your servant this day and forever more. Tell me what I must do and I will do it.'

2

Cuzco, Peru
Plaza de Armas
Local Time 10:20 am

16 January 1908

JUST THREE DAYS after the death of Monsignor Pera, the time-traveller Wilson Dowling walked along the cobble-stone laneway, through the misty rain towards the Plaza de Armas. He was relieved that his time had finally come to act and it hardly worried him that crowds of mourners, hundreds of them, were heading in exactly the same direction that he was.

Wearing a three-quarter-length jacket and a wide-brim safari hat, Wilson was well protected from the weather. The brushed cotton material of his clothing was durable and water resistant, although it could be a little warm in the middle of the summer wet season. Across his back hung a leather satchel that contained his travel papers, a rudimentary compass, a flint rod and a handful of gold coins he'd picked up when he was in China. The coins were excellent barter because the metal was soft enough to be bitten, quickly proving that it was genuine.

Because Wilson was easily a foot taller than the people around him, he didn't bother trying to blend in. With rain pattering against his hat and shoulders, he walked steadily forward with the growing crowd, making it obvious that he knew exactly where he was going. He could tell that the locals knew he was a foreigner, but they seemed too preoccupied with their sorrow to be even slightly curious about why he was there. Upon arrival by train from Lima, Wilson had decided to go directly to La Catedral to understand the circumstances surrounding the monsignor's untimely death. His bloody demise had not been chronicled in the history that Wilson had so rigorously studied before he time-traveled here from the future.

Nearly everyone in Cuzco was wearing black clothing, many of them were carrying umbrellas. When Wilson first heard that a priest had been stabbed at least a hundred times inside the famous Basilica Catedral, he was immediately sceptical. The rumour mill was often unreliable in South America and he was hoping the facts were different, or at least greatly embellished.

Wilson reiterated to himself that he possessed such great knowledge of the future that he was certainly the most powerful man in the world. It was an arrogance he constantly needed to guard against, but as the years had dragged on his discipline and his sensitivity had waned. He was the Overseer, he told himself. It was his job to complete the mission that had been assigned, the Mission of Nehemiah, regardless of the cost.

As Wilson strolled along, his thoughts could not have been further from the reality of the world he was now immersed within. This was a time of adventure and mystery. The enigmatic Teddy Roosevelt was President of the United States. Czar Nicholas II was yet to be overthrown by revolutionaries in Russia. Winston Churchill was a slim young man who had just entered the British cabinet for the first time. There had been no world wars, no global conflict. The British Empire was still the envy of every developed nation on earth. The Wright brothers had only just flown in their first homemade aircraft. The Panama Canal was yet to be finished and the Model T Ford production line had yet to produce a single automobile. There were no telephones, calculators or computers, no satellites, no Google Maps, no electricity – except in the biggest cities. Around here, there was just the odd telegraph and a weekly local newspaper. The humble written letter was the most effective form of communication for the earth's meagre population of less than one and a half billion.

For eight years Wilson had lived in this 'adolescent' world – biding his time, living like a relative hermit. His mission had called for him to wait until this very day to return to Cuzco to find the man he was looking for. For eight years he'd been separated from the modern world and the people he once knew, condemned to living in the transient era of the past where the Overseer was not even meant to exist. In this world, his actions and relationships had to be curtailed and for eight long years he had suffered terrible loneliness and the inevitable anxiety that came with it. Thankfully, he was here now, in Cuzco, and when his mission was complete he could finally transport back home.

Moving with the flow of the ever-growing crowd, Wilson approached the centre of Cuzco along Arequipa Avenue, which flanked La Catedral on its southern side. People were bumping into him now and he had to be careful not to get poked in the eye by the sharp points of the many umbrellas that were jostling about at his head height. In the distance, through the constant rain, he could hear the distinctive murmur of voices, which were getting louder with each passing step. Approaching the vast expanse of the Plaza de Armas, the unfolding sight was not what he expected. The plaza was packed with people – thousands of them – and they were angry. They squeezed together facing the towering walls of La Catedral, yelling abuses into the rain. The women were clutching rosary beads; the men were hacking away at the wet air with simple wooden crosses. Many of them were crying, but most were screaming vile insults until their throats were hoarse.

Looking adjacent to the crowd, Wilson noticed that the market stalls were empty and the buildings surrounding the Plaza de Armas were closed, the doors boarded up and the window drapes drawn. Even the post office doors were shut, which was very unusual. As he pushed his way into the throng, Wilson was surrounded on all sides by unending jeers and profanity. He had never seen anything like it – the locals were almost in a frenzy, chanting in the direction of the church. It was difficult not to be overwhelmed, especially after his years of solitude.

As water trickled off the rim of his hat, Wilson shifted his gaze towards La Catedral silhouetted against the mist. At the top of the stairs, on a raised landing, a row of twenty soldiers stood shoulder to shoulder, rifles at the ready. And behind them were twenty more. They were clasping .303 rifles and it was obvious from their expressions – mostly fearful – that they had been ordered not to let anyone approach the church.

Thunder rumbled overhead as Wilson continued to force his way towards La Catedral by muscling people out of his way. Surrounded on all sides by angry and emotional peasants, he unexpectedly recalled the conversation he'd had with Davin Chang only hours before he was transported on his mission into the past.

Wilson was sitting in a firm leather chair wearing his Mercury outfit, the beechwood boardroom table stretching away from him. The floors all around were polished glossy white. Floor-to-ceiling glass ran the entire length of the executive briefing room, affording uninterrupted views of lush, green forest as far as the eye could see. The sun was just beginning to set and the sky was becoming reddish in colour.

Davin Chang sat quietly, his expression pensive.

The Chinese-American scientist had been the Mercury Commander at Enterprise Corporation, the largest company in the world, for the last three years. He had a calm face and black hair streaked with grey, which was tied in a ponytail. His eyebrows were peaked in the middle and it gave the impression that he was very shrewd. Tragically thin, he'd lost a lot of weight since taking over the top position. 'Anything is possible . . . you just have to make it happen' was Davin's most frequently used line, and everyone joked about him being demanding. It seemed fitting, even now, that he should be the one to give Wilson the bad news.

'I have an issue I'd like to discuss,' Davin said.

'What issue is that?' Wilson asked.

'There's a timing conflict with the Mission of Nehemiah. There are compromises that have to be made, under the circumstances.'

Wilson sat forward in his chair. 'Compromises . . . that's an interesting word. I have never heard you use it favourably.'

They both just sat there looking at each other.

Wilson eventually broke the silence. 'It must be bad if you're not even capable of speaking about it. Say something!'

'You'll have to wait eight years before you can transport home,' Davin responded.

Wilson's first reaction was to smile.

Davin pointed at the display of his palm device. 'As I said, there is a timing conflict.'

'I'm leaving in *two hours*,' Wilson said, pointing at his watch. 'And you're telling me this now?'

Davin shook his head. 'I have known about it from the very beginning. I made the decision that it was best not to distract you when you had so much on your mind. That was my choice.'

'*Distract me!*' Wilson chuckled. 'Eight years of my life is more than a distraction, I think.'

Davin nodded. 'I agree – it is very unusual. However, we are confronted with this difficult position whether we like it or not. If there was another solution, we would certainly have found it. I didn't tell you earlier because I thought there was a chance we could discover . . .'

'I won't go,' Wilson interrupted. 'I won't do it.'

Davin pressed the palm of his right hand to the table. 'That is not an option.'

'We have a *time machine* for Christ's sake! Making me wait eight years in the past is *ridiculous!* We must delay the transport and rethink our options.'

'That is not possible,' Davin's replied.

Wilson glared in his Mercury Commander's direction. 'Do you realise the position this puts me in? Do you realise what this does to my life?'

'Yours is not an ordinary destiny,' Davin announced, 'or an easy one – that is the way it is meant to be, I suspect. You are the Overseer – you know that. These are the sacrifices that have to be made.'

Wilson pressed his hands to his face in realisation. He knew full well that he was the Overseer for this mission and that no one else could go in his place. 'Eight years is more than I should have to give,' he said softly.

'The cosmic strands of the universe do not connect to every place and every time,' Davin said calmly. 'The only way to get you into China by the year 1900 is to combine two missions together – both Ezra and Nehemiah. To get you back out again, you'll have to wait until 1908. That is the only way that that the Mission of Nehemiah can be completed also. That is the earliest date that it can happen.'

Wilson pointed his finger. '*You* and *your* team have screwed this up and I'm the one that has to pay the price. Christ! You should have told me sooner. At least then I could have said my goodbyes.'

The chanting brought Wilson back to the present as he forced his way to the very front of the crowd. One of the soldiers spotted him emerging from the front row and abruptly gestured with his rifle for him to back away.

'You cannot approach!' the soldier yelled out in Spanish.

Wilson continued to climb the stairs, his head tilted forward, the wide brim of his hat ensuring he did not make eye contact.

'No one is allowed near the church!'

Wilson was about to say, 'I have come from a distant land to pray here,' but as he lifted his gaze and took in the full view of the Basilica Catedral for the first time, his blood ran cold.

High on the outer wall of the right bell tower, a naked man was suspended from a large cross – a more gruesome and shocking sight Wilson could not imagine. The dead man's hands and feet were hammered against the thick wood with giant steel nails – he had been crucified. His eyes were open and his blackened tongue was hanging out. His badly emaciated body was in a terrible state, covered with purple bruises that Wilson suspected had been there for some days before he finally met his end. It was clear to Wilson now that the angry crowd were yelling insults and venting their rage at the dead body, not at the church itself.

Wilson pulled in a deep breath. The history he had studied did not include a crucifixion on the walls of the Basilica Catedral in the year 1908, or the murder of a priest inside the church itself.

The soldier broke from his line and approached quickly now. 'You must vacate the forecourt, stranger!' he ordered. 'You must back away!'

'You will tell me who that man is, Private,' Wilson said in fluent Spanish, his tone condescending. 'You will tell me immediately.'

'You must leave the forecourt!' the soldier said again.

Wilson narrowed his gaze. 'You have no idea who you are dealing with, boy. You will tell me who that man is!'

The private looked back over his shoulder in the direction of his captain, but the ranking officer didn't seem interested in getting involved. From the expression on his face, he was more focused on the angry mob than any trouble a white foreigner could possibly cause.

'I must speak to your captain.' Wilson attempted to sidestep the young private, but he was held back with the length of his rifle.

'You cannot, señor!'

'I am a very important man!' Wilson said sternly. 'Do you understand? I have many dealings with your president, in Lima. You must tell me what I want to know or there will be much trouble for you, boy.'

Wilson understood that displaying an air of superiority was a good tactic with many South Americans. Foreigners were often feared by the locals and it was quite normal for them to obey any command, regardless of what it was, provided it was delivered with enough forcefulness.

'I cannot tell you, señor.' The soldier glanced towards his captain once again.

'President Pardo will be appalled by what has happened

here today,' Wilson said, brazenly jabbing his index finger into the soldier's chest. 'I will tell him that *you* did not cooperate!'

'Please, señor. This terrible situation . . .' he looked briefly towards the body on the cross, '. . . is on the direct orders of Bishop Francisco himself.'

Wilson focussed on the naked corpse suspended on the belltower of the church – his wrists and ankles were badly scabbed with dry blood, which meant he had been tied up or clasped in irons for some time before being nailed to the cross. 'You will tell me that poor devil's name and the crime he has committed. If not, I will report your insolence to Pardo himself. Don't be a fool, boy!'

The soldier's gaze darted to his captain, then back to Wilson. 'His name is Corsell Santillana, señor.' The soldier looked sheepishly at the angry crowd, as if he didn't want them to hear what he was saying. Cupping his hand to his mouth, he said, 'He was a soldier, like I am . . . a private. I knew him myself before he deserted to the hills more than eight weeks ago. We heard nothing of him until he came back to Cuzco and killed Monsignor Pera in a violent rage, inside that very chapel.' The soldier gestured towards the tall church doors. 'The priest was mutilated beyond recognition with a small hunting knife.'

Wilson looked up at the naked body of Corsell Santillana. There appeared to be no lacerations on his hands or forearms, except where his wrists and ankles had obviously been bound. It was difficult to tell from this distance, but there appeared to be no blood or grime under his fingernails either.

'Monsignor Pera was killed three days ago?' Wilson asked.

The young soldier nodded.

'With a small hunting knife? You are certain of this?'

The soldier nodded again.

In Wilson's judgement, the shackle marks and bruising on Santillana's thighs, torso and neck indicated that he had been beaten over the course of countless days, probably even weeks.

'Bishop Francisco called for this crucifixion?' Wilson asked.

The private backed up a step, his expression wary. 'We are religious men in Peru, señor. When the head of the church takes matters into his own hands, as he has done here, we have no choice but to accept his decision.'

Wilson turned towards the countless angry faces in the crowd. In his estimation, the man nailed to the cross was innocent of the murder of Monsignor Pera. From what Wilson had seen, it was unlikely he could have killed anyone in the way that had been described.

3

WEARING A HOODED black poncho, Aclla stood amongst of the hostile crowd as she had done for the last four hours, her shoulders hunched and her back stooped uncomfortably forward. Many of the peasants around her were chanting the scripture or praying to God, while a few others just stood in the soaking rain, obviously dazed. The majority, however, were openly angry about the death of Monsignor Pera. It seemed as if a riot could break out at any moment, which was a surprise, considering the price Corsell Santillana had already paid. And yet the crowd continued shouting for revenge, many of the men having screamed so loudly that their voices were raspy.

This was an extraordinary situation Aclla was witnessing and she began to lose any sense of hope that her sister was still alive. From underneath her poncho, she once again stole a glance at the lifeless body nailed to the cross, so badly beaten it made even her want to turn away. Fate had conspired to bring Corsell and Vivane together, against all odds, Aclla realised. A private in the military and a young woman descended from the most sacred Inca bloodline should never have met, and yet they did. As Aclla had feared, the gods had become angry and exacted the ultimate price. Corsell had died in the most humiliating way possible. It took nearly two days on that cross before his young heart eventually stopped beating.

Under the cover of darkness, Aclla and her warriors had just made it into Cuzco before Corsell died. She hoped to extract information from him about her sister, but sadly they were too late and the military guard protecting the church was vigilant. All she could do was bear witness to his death from a distance. As she watched, she came to the conclusion that Corsell had been drugged to stop him from speaking – his blackened tongue further reinforcing her suspicion.

As to the whereabouts of her sister, Aclla knew very little. Both Vivane and Corsell had been taken by force from a small village near Pisac – but by whom, Aclla knew not. She suspected that it was the Peruvian army, but no one saw anyone enter or leave the fortified little village. By the time Aclla and her warriors reached Pisac, all indications of the jungle path the abductors had taken had been washed away by the summer rains.

Aclla and her warriors carefully searched the small stone hut in the western mountains where Corsell and Vivane had chosen, against all convention, to form an unholy union together. There were signs of a struggle. Blood was on the alpaca mattress and trailed across the dirt. The door and the wooden window shutter had been opened by force. A solitary chair had been splintered. The footprints on the dirt floor were male and heavy-footed. All evidence told Aclla that at least six men had been sent to capture Corsell and her sister; there may have been as many as ten.

Vivane would not have surrendered without a fight – Aclla knew that. She suspected that the trails of blood found inside the humble shack were probably from her abductors. Vivane was an excellent warrior and it would require extraordinary skill to bring her into custody without someone being seriously injured.

Although her back was aching, Aclla remained tilted forward at the waist to disguise her considerable height.

If she was to stand fully upright she would easily be taller than the peasants around her. A black hooded poncho covered her golden skin as well as her toned and muscular frame. She was a warrior who had been taught to ignore pain. As tribune, she set the example of discipline and sacrifice by which all her warriors followed. They stood in the crowd also, each taking a key position covering the many exits or on the adjacent rooftops, waiting for her signal if it came.

Sooner or later the people responsible for Corsell's death would come to see their handiwork, Aclla reaffirmed to herself. There was no choice but to wait. And when they did come, she intended to learn what she could. If Vivane was dead, Aclla would have her revenge – that was the way of her sacred Inca tribe.

Swaying with the angry movement of the people around her, Aclla remained vigilant at all times of the bizarre goings on around the Plaza de Armas. Her gaze focused on everyone and everything. She did not allow herself to be downhearted.

From the direction of Arequipa Avenue, a tall white man forced his way through the crowd. Even from a distance, Aclla could tell he was not Spanish or South American by descent. As he moved directly towards her she realised that she'd not encountered such a man until now. He was tall and solid, his skin fair, features well proportioned, his blue eyes scanning the gathered faces. Carefully watching the stranger from her peripheral view, Aclla wondered whether the mysterious figure approaching La Catedral was one of the abductors she had been waiting for.

He was close now, passing by just a few paces away.

The man was handsome, beautiful in a way Aclla had not seen before. He was certainly from across the ocean, but from where she could not say. From the look on his face, Aclla could tell that the stranger had visited this place before, but never under circumstances such as these. There was no childlike wonder in his cold blue eyes, nothing written on his face but a stern resolve.

When will he look towards Corsell Santillana? Aclla wondered. *Does he not know that a naked man is crucified on the outer wall of the church?*

The blue-eye exited the crowd and arrogantly climbed the stairs towards the church. A soldier approached him quickly, angrily gesturing for him to back away. Aclla pushed forward through the countless people to get the best possible view.

Finally the blue-eye saw Corsell nailed to the cross.

From his stunned expression and the slowing of his steps, Aclla knew instantly that the foreigner was not the perpetrator of this heinous crime. She scanned the plaza once more to be sure that she had not missed anything while she had been focusing on the tall stranger. When Aclla was satisfied that nothing else had changed, she moved her position yet again to get a better angle. The stranger was extracting information from the soldier standing on the stairs. The tall foreigner seemed accustomed to getting his way.

He is a very unusual man, Aclla thought to herself again. Even his clothes and hat were unlike anything else she had seen before.

Both he and the young soldier were talking, but the tall man's face was turned away from her for much of the time. The conversation continued before the blue-eye eventually rotated towards the assembled throng. The troubled expression on his face conveyed that he was now carrying a heavy burden.

Suddenly, he locked his gaze on her! He pinpointed Aclla precisely. The blue-eye had somehow picked her out from the hundreds of faces in the crowd!

With no choice, Aclla dropped out of sight, falling to her hands and knees. On all fours, she scampered her way through the tightly packed horde of legs and dirty feet, changing direction many times so as to conceal her position. Even with so many people around her, the white stranger had easily singled her out. How that was possible? It was like he *knew* she was there!

Carefully repositioning herself, Aclla narrowed the

opening of her hood and slowly lifted her head to eye height.

With her heart beating quickly, she scanned the crowded plaza. She turned full circle, frantically searching the faces around the Plaza de Armas for some clue as to the white foreigner's whereabouts.

Where is he?

The man with the sparkling blue eyes had vanished from sight.

4

Cuzco, Peru
Parque de la Madre
Local Time 11:12 am

16 January 1908

HURRYING ACROSS THE cobblestones under a dark grey sky, Wilson turned left into yet another narrow side street. There had not been a recorded crucifixion in Peru since the early 1600s – and yet here in the city of Cuzco, in the year 1908, a naked man was nailed to a wooden cross on the belltower of the largest church in South America. The murder of Monsignor Pera had not been detailed either and Wilson doubted that such an event would be missed by the numerous historians of the period. These two deaths, one linked to the other, told him that history was terribly off course.

'That poor bastard,' Wilson muttered to himself.

It seemed unlikely that Corsell Santillana was the man who murdered Monsignor Pera. There were no lacerations on Santillana's hands or arms, excepting on his wrists and ankles where he had been bound. There was no blood or grime under his fingernails – that was obvious even from a distance. The bruises on his undernourished body were weeks old, judging by the colour and the way the bruises were fading. Corsell had been beaten badly, and over a very long period, it seemed. And yet he bore no scratch marks or lacerations on his face or neck. If he was involved in a frenzied knife attack, as was claimed, he surely would have been injured.

Why an innocent man? Wilson asked himself.

Wilson walked at a brisk pace through the rain, every few seconds looking back over his shoulder to see if he was being followed. Since arriving in Cuzco, his temples had been aching and he'd felt mildly fatigued – certainly caused by the rapid increase in altitude. The lack of oxygen up here took a little getting used to, but he knew the feeling would diminish over the next couple of days as he became acclimated.

All the while, he was thinking about the crowd and their unholy obsession with the crucified body. Their reaction was unnatural, somehow, as if someone or something had possessed the group to react the way they had. Wilson knew it was a ridiculous conclusion, but it was all he could think of to explain the bizarre goings-on he had witnessed. One thing was certain: if historical events had so radically changed from those he expected, then there was a possibility the situation could deteriorate further. History often hung on a delicate thread and Wilson knew that every interaction he was having could make matters worse. He needed to take great care not to stamp his presence on current events any more than was absolutely necessary.

Wilson pictured the hazel eyes that had studied him from beneath a black hooded poncho. They were certainly a woman's eyes, and she was focused on him in a way that he knew was more than curiosity. Wilson had sensed her there. How that was possible, he could not be certain. He had easily singled her out from the twisted, angry faces, right before she dropped out of sight like a snake below water, a further indication that she had some sort of motive. The circumstances left Wilson only one alternative: he needed to find Hiram Bingham as quickly as possible.

The Parque de la Madre was a pleasant little plaza situated just off Nueva Alta. It was constructed in the same design as the Plaza de Armas – rectangular in shape but very small by comparison, measuring just eighty paces along one side and sixty paces along the other. Around three sides of the plaza were fifteen or so whitewashed, two-storey terraces with terracotta roofs. Each had a shallow courtyard bordering the street and a narrow balcony on the top level. Standing there, he thought it could easily be mistaken for a little Spanish village in the hills around Seville.

The Parque de la Madre was not far from La Catedral, yet even so, Wilson walked for twenty minutes in different directions, taking every side street he could. Finally approaching from the north, he scanned his surroundings one last time. Reconfirming the date to himself, he easily singled out the terrace house he was looking for and stepped across the plaza. Wilson knew exactly what Hiram Bingham was going through at this moment, and it ensured that the task of bringing the American academic into his confidence would not be that difficult.

The little terrace house had a handpainted sign above the door that read 'Pan-Am Scientific Congress'. Three donkeys were standing in the rain outside, tied to a wooden railing. Feedbags were strapped to their heads and they seemed contented even though they were soaking wet.

Wilson eased one of the donkeys aside and stood on the narrow landing. There was discarded rubbish piled up on both sides of the door at least two feet high – general refuse, newspapers, old food tins and empty whiskey bottles. Wilson looked more closely at one of the newspapers: it was *The New York Times* from July 1907 – over six months before. There was suddenly movement beside him and Wilson froze, but it was just a black cat leaping past him and scuttling over the low balcony.

Although the curtains were drawn across the lead-glass window, Wilson could still see an oil lamp burning inside. Through a gap in the material he could make out a man sitting at a wooden desk. Knocking just once on the doorframe, Wilson reached for the dented brass handle, knowing that it would be unlocked, and swung the door open.

The room was cluttered with packing crates stacked irregularly on top of each other. Two Springfield rifles were leaning against the desk. An open box filled with shiny .30-calibre cartridges sat on the floor. Two filthy mattresses were standing precariously against the only bare wall. The air had a pungent smell that Wilson guessed was the fumes of the oil lamp perched on the edge of a packing crate.

'Hiram Bingham the III,' Wilson said, recognising him from the photographs.

With just a cursory glance, the dishevelled man sitting at the desk replied, 'And just who would you be?' His accent was distinctly American.

'I am the best thing that will ever happen to you,' Wilson announced.

'The best thing that will ever happen to me?' Carefully laying down his pen, Hiram Bingham unscrewed the lid from a bottle of whiskey and carefully filled his shot glass. Turning to face Wilson again, he took a moment to look him up and down before drinking the whiskey in one slug. 'That is a mighty big claim.'

'Given time, you'll see that what I'm saying is correct.' Wilson removed his hat as rainwater streamed off the brim.

'Let me guess,' Hiram pointed his finger. 'You are an insurance salesman?'

Wilson shook his head.

'A journalist?'

'Wrong again.'

A frown overcame Hiram's face. 'You're not working for my wife, are you?' He pointed towards the door. 'Because if you are then I suggest you leave.'

'I'm not working for your wife.'

'I wouldn't be amused if you were, I'll say that.'

In his early thirties, Hiram had dirty-blond hair and high cheekbones – Wilson supposed that he was good looking if you could see past his unkempt appearance. He was thinner and punier than Wilson expected, weighing no more than one hundred and twenty pounds. He wore a filthy white shirt – with his collar up – under a tailored vest, a thin red tie, beige jodhpurs with heavy canvas strapping's protecting the tops of his brown boots. His dark jacket was hanging over the back of his chair. It was certainly not the orderly explorer Wilson expected.

'Let me guess again,' Bingham said without expression. He filled his shot glass one more time. 'You are from ...' He paused, studying Wilson carefully. 'The British Museum, am I right?'

Wilson sat down on one of the packing crates. 'Wrong again.'

'You are quite neat and tidy. A foreigner of some British extraction, I expect, judging by your accent.' Hiram set about rolling a cigarette by laying a small square of paper on his left thigh then taking a pinch of tobacco from his leather pouch. 'You are a mining executive?'

'You're not very good at this,' Wilson announced.

With one eyebrow raised, Hiram said, 'You can't be working for my wife. I realise that now.' He licked the cigarette paper expertly and rolled it closed. 'She hates foreigners. Especially the British.'

'I promise you, my part here has nothing to do with your wife.'

'Who are you then?'

'My name is Wilson Dowling.'

'Pray tell, Wilson Dowling, how is meeting you the best thing that will ever happen to me?' Hiram put the cigarette in his mouth and struck a match.

'I have come here to lead you to the lost city of Vilcapampa,' Wilson replied.

Hiram just sat there, the flaming match slowly burning between his fingers. 'Vilcapampa, you say?'

'You should light that before you burn your fingers,' Wilson said.

Coming to his senses, Bingham lit his cigarette and threw the flaming match to the wooden floor. 'I've changed my mind, you're a comedian,' he said with a wry smile.

Wilson smiled back. 'I'm not joking.'

'What could you possibly know about Vilcapampa that I do not know already? I am the world's leading expert on the Inca. Surely you know my reputation?'

Wilson gestured. 'I know who you are. But that does not

change the fact that I know where Vilcapampa is located,' Wilson replied. 'And you do not.'

'Is that so?'

'That's why this is your lucky day.'

Hiram wagged a finger. 'You are very amusing!' A puff of smoke escaped his lips. 'I have been searching for Vilcapampa for almost *four years*. My search grid is narrowing and I am closing in on a discovery. It is only a matter of time.'

'You are not even close,' Wilson replied.

'And just how, exactly, do you know where Vilcapampa is located?' Hiram asked.

Wilson leant forward as if to whisper a secret. 'I have visited the lost city of the Incas once before. That makes *me* the reigning expert, I'd say.'

Exhaling another long, steady stream of smoke, Hiram said, 'I have met every explorer that has scoured these hills in the last four years. You, my friend, are not one of them.'

'I was here before you arrived in Peru,' Wilson explained.

'And you haven't thought to reveal the Lost City of Vilcapampa to the world until *now*?' he asked sarcastically. 'So I'm clear, we *are* talking about the lost Inca capital – a place that hundreds of explorers of numerous nationalities have been looking for since Pizarro himself first set foot on this Inca soil some three hundred years ago?'

'The very same,' Wilson replied. 'My purpose here is singular and simple . . . I'm to lead you there, Hiram Bingham.'

'This *is* my lucky day then!' Hiram chuckled.

'Let's make a deal,' Wilson stated. 'If I tell you a fact that no one else could possibly know, then you'll consider trusting me. How does that sound?'

Hiram adjusted himself in his chair, a glimmer of amusement in his eye. 'I'll play along. Tell me something that no one else could possibly know and we'll go from there.' He jutted a finger in Wilson's direction. 'This had better be good!'

'I know that your wife is pregnant,' Wilson stated. 'That

letter on your desk demands that you come home immediately, or don't come back at all. If you don't return to Washington by April she intends to cut off your funding.'

Hiram snatched up the envelope and checked the seal. 'Have you been reading my mail?' He held it to the light to see if it was possible to read through the paper.

'I haven't been reading your mail.'

'You *are* working for my wife! I knew it! She thinks that because she is the daughter of the great "Charles L. Tiffany" then I have to do what she says. That's not how it works! I told her that *before* we were married.'

'I'm not working for your wife.'

Hiram's brow furrowed. 'Women with money are always a pain in the proverbial backside. They are, I'm telling you. My father warned me about that! I let her name the expedition "Pan-Am Pacific Congress", because she was providing the funding – even though it's a *stupid* name! That should be enough to show her how much I care.'

'You need to trust me,' Wilson said in an attempt to calm Hiram down. 'If you do, the Bingham name will be synonymous with the greatest explorers in modern history. You'll be famous beyond imagination.'

'I could certainly use some luck,' Hiram said through his exhalation.

'But first, you must acknowledge that my assistance in this quest comes with strict conditions.'

'There are always conditions,' Hiram said dubiously.

'First, you can never mention my part in Vilcapampa's discovery. That promise must be absolute. Second, you must vow to protect the city of Vilcapampa from those who would wish to exploit the rich heritage that resides there. You must be the city's guardian.' Hiram waited for more, but Wilson didn't say anything.

'Is that it?' Hiram asked.

'That's all,' Wilson replied. 'Do you agree to my terms?'

Hiram picked up his quill fountain pen and began gently tapping the nib on his blotting paper. 'This had better not be a joke,' he eventually replied.

'It's no joke.'

'With all due respect, sir, I think you are a madman. But, under the circumstances, I don't have that much to lose – I'm not so busy that I can't listen. To be honest,' he whispered, 'I have no idea where to look next. All my hunches so far have led to nothing, but I never admit that to anybody.' Hiram climbed out of his chair, moved a packing crate aside and spread out a large dog-eared map across the floor. It detailed the mountain peaks and the tributary rivers for 200 miles in all directions – it was quite detailed. 'Tell me where Vilcapampa is,' he demanded.

'That map you have there was drawn by Antonio Raimondi,' Wilson replied. 'It's not on there.'

Hiram looked confused. 'This is the most accurate map of Peru ever made.'

'Vilcapampa is located to the north-west of Cuzco, but the valley around the lost city is not located on that map.'

'My confidence in you is diminishing,' Hiram admitted.

'Pour me a glass of whiskey,' Wilson said, 'then I'll tell you what I know.'

'I knew you were a drinker,' Hiram said with a smile. 'I can always tell.' With smoke pouring from his lips he rustled around under his desk before producing a dirty shot glass that he hastily attempted to clean on his equally filthy-looking shirt. 'I like a man who drinks – it shows character.' Hiram pulled the cork out of the bottle and filled both shot glasses to the brim. 'Tell me where Vilcapampa is.'

Holding the whiskey out in front of him, Wilson studied the flame of the oil lamp through the golden hue of the liquid. 'To your good health.'

'Good health,' Bingham replied.

Shooting the alcohol back, Wilson made a twisted expression as if the liquor was strong. 'I am about to give you information that you have never heard before,' Wilson began. 'All of it is true. To the north-west of Cuzco, on one of the high Andean peaks, above a mighty river called the Urubamba, is perched the lost city of Vilcapampa. It was constructed at the height of the Inca Empire by King

Pachacuti in the year of our Lord 1438. During its thirty-four-year construction, the city was home to nearly 500 craftsmen, nobles and warriors, and their families. When the impressive mountain hideaway was finally completed a celebration was ordered and everyone associated with the building process was invited. It was a celebration that would never take place. On the direct orders of Pachacuti himself, the night before the festivities, as most people slept, veiled assassins went systematically through the city and slaughtered every man, woman and child. Not a soul was spared.'

Hiram sat still, his mouth hanging open.

'Every trace of the City in the Clouds was destroyed. Every map burnt, every written word across the entire kingdom was obliterated.'

'Stop right there,' Hiram interrupted. 'The Incas never had a written language.'

'That is where you are wrong,' Wilson replied. 'The Incas had a comprehensive writing system that stretched to every corner of the empire. In just two days and one night, every last trace of their written word was destroyed. All so as to protect the location of Vilcapampa.'

It was clear that Hiram was far from convinced.

'From that day forward, even just the mere utterance of Vilcapampa's existence would result in the beheading of the one responsible and the subsequent death of every family member and acquaintance of the accused.'

'You're telling me that's why the Incas have no written language? Because they were trying to protect the last Inca capital?'

'King Pachacuti couldn't take the risk,' Wilson replied.

'I have never heard such rubbish!' Bingham dropped the remnants of his cigarette to the wooden floor and stamped on the butt with the heel of his boot.

'I never expected you to believe me immediately,' Wilson said.

'And what is so valuable in this "City in the Clouds" that would require such a terrible sacrifice of the innocent?'

'It is their most sacred place.'

'Everything is sacred to the Incas,' Hiram replied. 'What else is new? There must be something more important than that.'

'I cannot tell you why,' Wilson replied. 'The secrets of Vilcapampa are still preserved to this day. But I know this . . . seeing the lost city for yourself will make your heart soar and your soul fly. A hundred terraces lead to a vast, deserted mecca that mere words cannot describe, such is its raw beauty.'

'Is there treasure there?'

'The city has a heart of gold,' Wilson replied. 'In a metaphorical sense. But there is no treasure that can be taken away or sold.'

'No treasure,' Hiram replied. 'That's a disappointment.'

'History has ordained that you, Hiram Bingham the III, will find Vilcapampa and reveal it to the world. That is treasure enough.'

There was a long pause.

'In all my years,' Hiram announced, 'I have never heard such a tale of folly as the one you have laid before me on this humid afternoon.' He grabbed Wilson's glass, sat it on the table next to his then proceeded to fill them both again to the very brim. 'You are *very* amusing, though. It is probably the altitude that has caused you to conjure up such a colourful story.' Hiram scratched at his chin thoughtfully. 'Yes, I think you are the funniest man that I have met . . . in Peru, anyway. I did know this guy at Yale, years ago, his name was Stephan. He was a funny man. He told me lots of jokes.' Hiram took on a broad smile. 'Two men walk into a bar, you see,' he paused. 'You would have thought at least *one of them* would have seen it sticking out of the wall.' Hiram laughed as if it was the funniest thing he'd ever heard. 'Two men walk into a bar!' he said again. 'That is so funny! How about this – what do apples and oranges have in common?'

'They're both fruit,' Wilson replied eventually.

'*Wrong*,' Hiram said. 'They both can't drive locomotives!' He laughed again. 'I've got a million of those jokes. What's brown and sticky?' he paused. 'A stick!' His alcohol fuelled laughter grew even more ferocious.

'It is your destiny to discover Vilcapampa,' Wilson said sternly. 'Whether you believe me or not.' He raised his glass again and gulped the whiskey back. 'We must leave for the Inca Trail immediately.' Wilson placed his glass upside down on the table. 'Events in Cuzco are unpredictable. A priest has been murdered and a man is nailed to a cross on the outer walls of La Catedral.'

'You saw him?' Hiram was immediately serious again. 'It's not every day you see a crucified body. What a gruesome sight. Awful. The peasants aren't happy about it, I know that much. And the longer they stand in the rain, the angrier they become. Peruvians don't like the rain, which is kind of funny, considering they live here in this godforsaken place. The rain is incessant in the summer.' His expression suddenly went blank. 'I met Monsignor Pera once, you know. Seemed like a very nice man to me. At least the killer was brought to justice. A local soldier.'

'We must leave for the mountains,' Wilson said. 'There is no time to lose.'

'My wife hates me,' Hiram announced unexpectedly, his words a little slurred. 'My father-in-law thinks I am a fool, you know? Her whole family does.'

'No one will think you are a fool after you discover Vilcapampa,' Wilson said. 'Quite the contrary.' He helped Hiram to his feet and gave him a reassuring pat on the back. 'You will be revered as one of the greatest explorers of all time.'

'How did you know my wife was pregnant?' Hiram asked. 'You must tell me.'

'I know a great many things about the future,' Wilson said, trying not to sound arrogant. 'You will soon see that I am a valuable friend to you in so many ways. All you have to do is come with me. If you do, the life you have always dreamed of will be yours.'

5

Cuzco, Peru
La Catedral
Local Time 12:05 pm

16 January 1908

THE WALLS OF the great church were awash with the
flickering glow of a thousand burning candles. Bishop
Francisco paced along the central nave, his distinctive
scarlet robes billowing out behind him. His hands were
clenched in front, his fingers tightly interlocked as if
in prayer. His fearful gaze searched this way and that,
scouring the shadows for the menace that was haunting
him. The only sound emanating within the vast church was
the rapid step of his leather-soled boots on the polished
granite floor.

Bishop Francisco had ordered that the entire church
complex, including the adjacent El Triunfo and the Capilla
de la Sagrada Familia, be vacated so that he could have
absolute solitude to fully consider his troubled thoughts.

'What do you ask of me?' Bishop Francisco called out,
his worried voice echoing between the ribbed vaults of the
impossibly high ceiling.

At every turn there was a magnificent work of art
housed within the forty U-shaped alcoves, each collection of artefacts a holy chapel in itself. There were fresco
paintings crowding the walls, a dozen towering pulpits,
sparkling golden chancels that reached upwards towards
God, many adorned with lifelike effigies dressed in traditional biblical robes. Saint Catherine of Sienna almost

seemed to smile as the bishop passed by – on either side of her was the strong figure of Saint Joseph and the beautiful face of Santa Rosa de Lima.

To the left was the breathtaking cathedral choir alcove, made entirely of Cuzco cedar rendered in polychrome or gilded in magnificent eighteen-carat gold leaf. Inside were sixty-four wooden seats crafted by the hand of the great maestro, Melchor Huaman. When the choir would burst into song, the wash of the innocent young voices soared out from the open roof of the enclave, filling the cavernous church complex with the hum of angels.

As he passed, Bishop Francisco stared at the huge canvas of Saint Christopher carrying the infant Jesus on his back. The muscular saint was straining to cross a raging river with the baby. From his expression it was clear that Saint Christopher had just realised that the small child he was carrying weighed the same as the entire world.

'You must show yourself to me!' Bishop Francisco called out.

He continued forward, his worried gaze searching the nooks and crannies of the marvellous church. He passed the effigy of Saint Anthony of Padua yet again, as he had done a dozen times, but he did not slow his pace.

'Praise be to Jesus, Mary and Joseph,' he said to himself.

'*I am your master now!*' the deep voice in his head called out, so loudly that the bishop was forced to press his fingers into his ears in an effort to ease the pain.

'I have done as you asked,' the bishop muttered, then fell to his knees in prayer yet again. 'I have done your bidding!' he yelled. 'You promised me the freedom to return to my God. Why have you not stood by your promise?'

A lengthy silence hung in the still air of the church. As he had done so many times before, the bishop prayed against all hope that he would never have to hear the terrible voice again, that everything that had already happened to him was just a horrific dream. 'Praise be to Jesus; be my protector at this time of great need,' he muttered.

'*We are both under threat,*' the deep voice eventually said.

The voice inside his head caused the bishop's body to flush with sweat from head to toe. 'Please . . . you must set me free,' he said, choking back the onset of more tears.

'You are not free until I am safe, my child. There is a man in Cuzco – a stranger – who seeks to find my soul . . . his journey is just beginning. He is from a foreign land, a land I have no knowledge of. This man will come looking for what has gone missing. I have seen it in my visions. You must stop him at all costs.'

The bishop scanned the vaulted ceilings of the Basilica Catedral. He was certainly within God's own house – his eyes told him that, at least. A building of such majesty that he once believed he could talk directly to God through the sheer greatness of its architecture.

How am I not protected in my own church? Bishop Francisco allowed himself to think. In the bosom of the House of God?

'There is no protection for you anywhere!' the voice replied.

The bishop winced in pain at the terrible voice inside his head.

'And while I choose it, I will act through you. If you follow me unquestioningly, you will be rewarded. If you fail me, you will face a death even more gruesome than Corsell Santillana. Do you remember the look on his face as the metal bolts were hammered into his hands and feet? Do you remember the look in his eyes as the life drained from him?'

'I remember.'

'You must renounce your conventional wisdom.'

An eerie candlelight filled the Epistle nave. 'Please, let me see your face,' Bishop Francisco pleaded, his head dipped forward penitently. 'You promised me that I would be able to see you in your true form.'

'Get up from the floor,' the voice demanded. *'Walk forward.'*

Bishop Francisco stood up, his bruised knees aching from having fallen in prayer so many times in the last two days. He again stepped forward, with a limp at first, then quickened his pace. He did not want to show weakness.

'Keep walking, my child.'

The bishop passed the chapel repository that held a dozen glowing candelabras surrounded by a magnificent sterling silver trellis that reached ten feet high. The precious metal, like nearly everything else inside the magnificent church, came from the melting of ancient Inca treasures. In the centre was the distinctive figure of a pelican in the act of piercing its heart with its own beak, symbolising supreme love and self-abnegation.

'Keep walking. I am close now,' the icy voice rumbled.

The bishop continued forward, past the entrance to the sacristy chamber.

'Stop and turn towards me,' the voice finally called out.

Bishop Francisco's heart was pounding as he faced the towering wall of altars and fresco paintings. His eyes carefully searched the ten or more holy canvases, each one a masterpiece in itself. Jesus, John the Baptist, Saint Luke with the Bull, Mary Magdalene, Saint Matthew and the Paschal Lamb, and Saint Mark with the Lion. Finally, his gaze sought out the giant Cuzco baroque painting of the Last Supper by the master Don Marcos Zapata. The canvas alone was twenty feet across and more than twenty feet tall.

Bishop Francisco knew the famous painting well. It had always been one of his favourites within the cathedral. The twelve apostles were sitting at a broad table, with Jesus in the centre. Each man had a drinking cup filled with traditional wine, and yet the foodstuffs were distinctly Andean in culture. The fruit was papaya, the Paschal Lamb replaced by a wild chinchilla. Jesus and the apostles were all white-faced, except for Judas, who was darker in appearance. It was said that this was to convey that he was the heretical Moor, but there had been talk for many years that the eerie, shadowed face represented something else again.

'Where are you, Lord?'

'I am right before you,' the voice replied.

The bishop was sweating profusely as he searched the canvas. Above the gathering was the star of Bethlehem, shining brightly through the window. In the upper left was an image of Jesus crucified on the cross, Mary Magdalene praying before him – a prophesy of the future to come. The bishop made the cross of Jesus from his forehead to chest, left shoulder to right, then began searching the faces of the apostles. 'Where are you, Lord?'

One by one he scanned the expressions of the concerned and reverend holy men, hoping upon hope that he would not have to stare into the black eyes of Judas. Of all the men in the painting, only the dark face of the renegade apostle did not look to Jesus for guidance. His image stared outwards, his piercing gaze seeking the viewer.

Having searched every face, the bishop knew there was only one apostle left. Lingering as long as he dared, he took in the frightening visage of Judas. Mumbling to himself in Latin, Bishop Francisco locked onto the eyes piercing into his own, a faint flicker of scarlet glowing from within the pupils on the canvas.

'I am the Lord you are seeking, priest.'

Bishop Francisco was shaking now, breathing as rapidly as if he had run up 200 steps. 'Please show mercy,' the bishop forced himself to say.

'I am the hero of this great land!' the voice called out. 'But even so, my name has been dragged through mud and refuse. The time has come to right the wrongs that have been unfairly subjected upon my good name!'

'I know you,' Bishop Francisco muttered as he began sobbing to himself.

'Look at my face!'

'I see you, Lord,' he whimpered.

'Look at my face!' the voice bellowed again.

A trickle of blood began seeping out of Bishop Francisco's right ear and running down the side of his neck. The tears welling in his eyes suddenly broke, bringing everything back into focus once again.

The dark face of Judas was moving as the voice spoke.

'My name is Francisco Pizarro of Trujillo. Illegitimate

son of Gonzalo Pizarro Rodriguez de Aguilar. I am the ultimate explorer and conquistador. Appointed Marshal of Peru in the year of Our Lord 1532 by the King of Spain, Charles V. I am founder of Lima. Conqueror of the heathens and the bringer of Christianity to the savages of South America. My will is your bidding from this day forward, priest.

6

Cuzco, Peru
Parque de la Madre
Local Time 12:35 pm

16 January 1908

AFTER LOADING TINNED food and other supplies into four brown leather backpacks, Wilson and Hiram set about tying the bags together and hitching them across the back of the smallest pack animal. The other two donkeys were considerably larger and better suited for carrying people.

'I really hate these little bastards,' Hiram stated. 'Donkeys are the most stubborn and miserable creatures on the face of the earth.'

Wilson was relieved to talk about something else rather that just fielding questions about Vilcapampa. To keep Hiram focused, Wilson had found it necessary to dish out a steady stream of superlatives about the grandeur of the lost city and the difficulty and magnificence of the terrain – all the while impressing upon Hiram the significance of his impending discovery.

'The city of Vilcapampa is perched on a ridge between two towering peaks,' Wilson gushed, 'affording unabated views in all directions. A more imposing and natural fortress you will not find. I can't wait for you to see it for yourself.'

'First we have to get there,' Hiram replied as he adjusted a packing strap across the donkey's hindquarters, then checked that his Springfield rifle was secure. 'I'm sure that in God's mind the donkey was His ultimate practical joke. Whatever you want them to do you can bet they will attempt to do the opposite. Miserable creatures.' Hiram frowned. 'That little jack you are riding is the worst of all. Consider yourself warned.'

'Why is he the worst?' Wilson asked.

'If he spots a low tree branch, he'll try and knock you off. If ever you have to dismount because the trail is too steep, he'll try and pull away and run back down to the bottom.' Hiram eyeballed the little brown donkey. 'Like I said, he's a little bastard. He and I have had our run-ins over the years – I can attest to that. And he'll give you a swift kick if you walk behind him, so be careful. All he responds to is brute force.'

Wilson pointed at the donkey Hiram was going to ride. 'That one is better?'

'She's an angel by comparison,' he replied, 'but still an ass of an animal – pardon the pun. She's not as cunning as he is . . . and she doesn't kick too much.' Hiram flicked away another cigarette into the rain.

Hiram didn't look or act like an adventurer, Wilson decided. There was no questioning the man's intellect – he had degrees in History and Politics from four different universities, including Yale and Harvard – and, to give him credit, he was passionate and conventionally knowledgeable when talking about the Inca. Yet even so, Wilson found it hard to accept that this was the great Hiram Bingham III, the man who would be regarded as the foremost explorer of modern times.

'I hate the rain,' Hiram muttered as he sheltered under the veranda and set about rolling yet another cigarette.

'We have to leave,' Wilson urged.

'I have my rituals and I need to follow them,' Hiram stated. A cloud of smoke billowed out from under the wide brim of his hat. 'All we need now is the whiskey.' He spent the next few minutes attempting to secure a large wooden case to the back of his donkey, but the soaking rain made his thick ropes difficult to pull through and tighten with just a reef knot.

'You won't need a case of whiskey,' Wilson replied.

Hiram persisted with the ropes. 'You said we'd be gone for more than a week.'

'You won't need *six* bottles.'

'I can drink six bottles easily,' he replied.

'If we leave now we can get ten or fifteen miles under our belt before nightfall,' Wilson said.

Hiram threw his hands in the air in frustration. 'An adventurer needs whiskey for warmth! Look, either you tie this on or I organise some porters to come with us. I really think we need porters – I don't go anywhere without them.'

'We don't need porters,' Wilson replied as he grabbed a rope from the wet ground, lashed it under the donkey's saddle then made a double loop knot. 'The fewer people who know about Vilcapampa, the better. For now at least.' Wilson sat the wooden box on top and pulled the rope end through the loops with a quick hitch.

'Normally the porters do that sort of work,' Hiram stated. 'I leave the packing and setting up of camp to them. I can't believe we're going without any support.'

'This is the way it has to be,' Wilson said.

'And you don't want me to bring a map?' Hiram asked.

'I told you; the Raimondi map you have doesn't show the region we are going to. Just make sure you have your compass. That's all you'll need.'

For unknown reasons, Antonio Riamondi excluded the entire track of land between the Pampaconas and the Apurimac Basin – some 1500 square miles in all – which was where the valley of the Apurimac and her tributaries cut their way between the towering glacial mountain peaks of the Andes. That was where the sacred city of Vilcapampa was located.

The rain was persistent but in the last ten minutes the wind had come up and it was raining as hard as ever. The afternoon sky grew darker than normal and there was thunder and lightning in the distance.

Hiram once again suggested they head inside until the weather settled down, but Wilson refused. 'The rainy season is here until at least April, you know that, so there is absolutely no point in trying to avoid it. We have to leave, and we have to leave now.'

Hiram looked about from under his hat. 'So, we're really going?' He reluctantly walked inside, pulled the lid off his fountain pen and neatly wrote:

Gone to discover Vilcapampa – I hope.
Will be back in two weeks.

He then signed and dated the note.

Hiram turned off the oil lamp, backed out the door and pulled it closed. Pressing the paper against the door, he secured it in place with a brass thumbtack.

'You know what I love about the Peruvians?' Hiram said as he stepped out into the pouring rain. 'You don't even have to lock the door. The locals are so honest they would never even dream of stealing anything.'

'They are very kind people,' Wilson said impatiently. 'We really must leave.'

'An old friend of mine,' Hiram added. 'Harry Foote. He's a professor at Yale. He should arrive by train in the next week or so. He's a terrific old fellow – a botanist, you know. I don't want him to worry.'

'Hopefully you will be back before he arrives.'

Hiram looked affectionately at the terrace house with garbage piled up on the doorstep. 'Goodbye, home-away-from-home,' he called out as he swung his leg over the donkey. 'And now, Jenny, you miserable little creature, we can do this hard or we can do this easy. Obey my command or it's the whip for you.'

Wilson was already astride his donkey, whose thin legs seemed to wobble under his weight. 'We head north-west,' he announced.

'Are you sure you know where you're going?' Hiram said dubiously.

'We're heading towards the village of Torontoy, at the entrance of the Grand Canyon of the Urubamba River,' Wilson stated.

'Never heard of the place,' Hiram replied. 'Tell me again how you know where you're going?'

'I've been there before,' Wilson said as he kicked his heels into the little donkey . . . but the animal didn't move an inch.

Hiram looked amused. 'I warned you, Wilson Dowling. This is not going to be as easy as you think. That little jack you are riding is not called Diablo for nothing.'

7

Cuzco, Peru
La Catedral
Local Time 2:58 pm

16 January 1908

CAPTAIN GONZALES STOOD in the pouring rain outside the towering walls of the Basilica Catedral. His men were lined up on the upper steps of the forecourt between the church and the angry crowd that had been growing hourly over the last three days. Every now and again the captain would look back over his shoulder to see the lifeless body of Corsell Santillana crucified on the church's belltower. Each time he did, he felt sick to the stomach.

The middle-aged captain had known Private Santillana and his brother, Juan, since they were boys. And now Corsell was dead and Juan Santillana had mysteriously vanished – no one had seen him in weeks. The captain's gaze searched the crowd until he saw Corsell's mother in the front row, on her knees, tears of sorrow filling her bloodshot eyes and running down her pale cheeks as they had done continuously since she had learnt of her son's terrible fate. She had knelt there in the same place for nearly three days, without food or water, watching her youngest son die on the cross of Jesus as countless voices in the crowd yelled abuse and insults in his direction. In many ways, it was worse to watch her kneeling there than it was to witness Corsell's death. His fate was sealed; her sad life was yet to be fully played out.

In her wrinkled, wet hands she clung to a fine string of

rosary beads with a heavy silver cross. Rumour had it that
Bishop Francisco had called her into the church to show
her the viciously mutilated body of Monsignor Pera, and
then gifted her the dead priest's rosary. What he whispered
to her after that, no one heard. But she had simply walked
outside into the rain and fell to her knees in the very spot
she was now.

Captain Gonzales stood like a statue in the downpour,
his tanned face expressionless, his gnarled hands clasped
behind his back. Even under the circumstances he was
a picture of orderliness in his well-fitting blue officer's
uniform with bright flashes of red on his lapels. His flat-
brimmed hat sat squarely on his head, rain trickling from
the curved edges. The shiny gold buttons of his soaked
jacket were splayed open, all except the top button at the
neck – the mark of a senior officer of the Cuzco Division.

Gonzales found it impossible to understand how such
a gruesome series of events could have come about. This
was the last thing he could ever have expected from
Corsell Santillana. Gonzales turned and faced the young
man's body; the pained expression on his lifeless face and
his terribly blackened tongue yet again sent a feeling of
sickness into the captain's stomach. Corsell Santillana was
a God-fearing, honest man, Gonzales remembered, not
prone to violence, let alone the brutal murder that had
been committed just inside the doorway of La Catedral.
Relentlessly searching his memories as he had done for the
last three days, Captain Gonzales struggled to find even
the slightest indication that the man crucified above him
could possibly have committed such a heinous crime.

'You are requested to come inside La Catedral,' a voice
said.

Gonzales turned to see a young priest in black robes
standing in the rain beside him. The priest gestured
towards the main entrance, his movement calm and
considered. 'Please, Capitán.'

'I will meet you inside in a moment,' Gonzales replied.
He walked purposefully to Lieutenant Capos, realising that so many eyes in the crowd would be upon him.

'Ensure that no one scales these steps,' he said. 'The crowd looks restless. I must go and meet with the clergy once again.'

'Si', Capitán,' the lieutenant replied.

Over the last two days, Gonzales had been called inside the Basilica Catedral to meet with the chapel priests on at least six occasions. They were fearful that the angry peasants would want the body of Santillana for themselves – and if they didn't get their way then they would take matters into their own hands. On Bishop Francisco's orders the heavy doors to the church had been boarded from the inside with the exception of the Gospel doorway that led directly into the Gospel nave. It was just to the left of the mighty forty-foot-high central doorway behind which the terrible murder of Monsignor Pera had taken place.

As Captain Gonzales entered the archway to the Gospel nave, he took off his hat and pulled his fingers though his damp hair to form a semblance of neatness. 'Praise be to Jesus,' he muttered, made a cross on his chest then stepped into the silence of the candlelit church. It was a relief to no longer hear the jeers and insults of the crowd, if only for a few minutes.

To his surprise there was not a gathering of black-clad priests as there had been on the previous six occasions. The entrance to the Gospel nave was deserted and his eyes were left to search to the farthest end of the Basilica, which was at least 150 feet away. It was an awe-inspiring sight to see the gold altar of the Holy Trinity glowing in the candlelight beneath the mighty vaulted domes.

Captain Gonzales tore his gaze away from the far wall and turned to study the Central nave. There, just twenty feet away, was a distinct shaded area on the porous granite floor where Monsignor Pera had met his gruesome end. No matter how much it was scrubbed, the porous stone would forever bear the shadowed mark of death. Up until now the gathering of clergy had blocked Gonzales's view of the murder scene and he finally had the opportunity to see it for himself.

Approaching the stained area, Gonzales searched the church in all directions for any sign of blood splatters or indications of a struggle. As he did, his gaze was unavoidably drawn to the gold leaf altar that graced the impressive entrance, the effigy of the Nativity Virgin staring right at him, holding the placid infant Jesus in her arms. 'How could such a terrible thing have happened in such a beautiful and holy place?' he whispered to himself.

From out of the shadows, footsteps began to approach.

Captain Gonzales spun towards the sound.

'I ask myself the same question,' a calm voice replied. Bishop Francisco suddenly appeared in his distinctive scarlet robes, a scarlet biretta covering his bald head.

Gonzales dropped to one knee in shock. 'Bishop Francisco, I had no idea you would be here.'

'I realise that you are curious, as we all are,' the bishop said. Stepping forward, he calmly extended his hand and allowed Captain Gonzales to kiss his holy ring. 'Please stand,' the bishop commanded.

Gonzales realised that he had knelt just a few feet from the bloodstain on the floor and instinctively backed away. 'You have requested my presence?' the captain asked, his heart rate lifting for some unexpected reason.

The bishop seemed tranquil as he stood there, his fingers interlocking his hands in front of him. 'You have always been a good man,' the bishop said, his every word deliberate. 'You are a good Christian who lives his life with honesty and dignity. I have known your family for many years, have I not? As I have known countless other worthy families in this sprawling city of Cuzco. Since before I can remember, I have served my God and this great church with everything that I have. I have lived a life of celibacy as God would have wanted. I have provided support to the impoverished, shelter to the homeless, comfort to the grieving.' He pointed to the lofty ceiling. 'And most importantly, *faith* to those unfortunates who have lost their way. The Holy Scripture has been my comfort and my teacher.'

Captain Gonzales could not help but think of his own

small children at that moment: two sons and his beautiful daughter, who herself had been baptised within these very walls just six months earlier. The image of their smiling faces brought an unexpected warmth to his heart that he knew was out of place at this moment.

'I have carried the cross of Christ my whole life, regardless of the burden,' Bishop Francisco continued, his manner becoming more passionate. 'And I have never shied away from administering the sword if it was necessary in the protection of the Holy One, His church or the beloved members of His flock.' The bishop gestured his open hand to the stain on the floor. 'And yet even with God's will on my side, such events have taken place in His house so as to cast a black shadow over this church. My God's will is that the darkness can only be vanquished if drastic actions are taken.'

The bishop took in a long breath and visibly composed himself. His voice was once again calm. The flicker of candlelight illuminated his gaunt face. 'I realise that you have opposed the crucifixion of Corsell Santillana from the very beginning. And that you requested that his body be removed from the outside walls of this church.'

There was a long silence before Gonzales replied, 'That is correct, Bishop. The peasants cannot contain their grief any longer, and something must give.'

'I do what is necessary,' the bishop said directly.

'You may be acting with the will of God,' Gonzales continued, 'but you are not acting within the law . . . and that is a problem for us both.'

'I have the overwhelming support of my congregation! Just listen to their passionate voices and you will hear their approval of my actions.'

'The locals are mourning Monsignor Pera's very public death. They do not know how else to respond except to yell insults. They are angry and they are showing it. But you must also remember that Corsell Santillana was well respected, for a young man. You know this. And whilst the people of Cuzco are angry, they still find it difficult to understand how he could have possibly killed Monsignor

Pera. In times like these the church should show compassion and forgiveness, not inspire hate.'

Bishop Francisco gave a faint smile. 'Your honesty is appreciated, Capitán. You are a good man. However, it seems that your goodness blinds you from the truth that Corsell Santillana was possessed by the Devil when he killed Monsignor Pera. Corsell Santillana slashed away at the monsignor's face and body with such violence and hatred that what was left of the good priest was almost unrecognisable. It is even suspected that Santillana took to eating the monsignor's flesh, such was the amount of blood and gore in his mouth. There can be no dispute that Corsell Santillana committed this horrific crime and that his body needed to be cleansed of the devil that possessed him.' Bishop Francisco took another deep breath. 'Praise be to God.' He then made a cross on his chest.

'I am a God-fearing man, Bishop, and I mean you no disrespect. But the law does not allow crucifixion, regardless of the terrible crime. This man was not even given a trial, one that in my opinion was badly needed.'

'Corsell Santillana is guilty!' the bishop yelled, his voice echoing in all directions. 'This is the only way that his *soul* can be cleansed! It is the only way that Santillana can be allowed to ascend to heaven after such a vile act. These are dark times, Capitán. There is a terrible evil all around us. Evil men and evil acts must be combated with equal strength.' He pointed to the vaulted ceiling. 'My God is the saviour of souls and He will not be disrespected, not by you or anyone! After all, this church is nothing without the belief and support of its followers. Members of the flock must stand behind their church. Are you willing to do what is necessary?'

Sweat began to form on Gonzales's brow. 'I have always supported this church, Bishop. As I have told your domestic prelates many times, I am here to inform you of the law, not to enforce it upon you.'

'And yet you still disagree with my tactics?'

Gonzales paused before answering, a dozen thoughts flashing simultaneously into his head. 'I mean you no disrespect, but I believe Corsell Santillana's body must finally be taken down for the hatred to stop and the healing to begin. Corsell's mother is in the crowd. For pity's sake, you must stop this madness.'

'You believe I should show compassion?'

'Yes, Bishop.'

'Compassion is for the weak. These are dark times and such petty considerations carry little weight when the enemy is the Devil himself. Know this, I will do what I must to protect this holy church. And if you love your children and want to see them grow up healthy, from this moment forward you will support my actions without question.'

Captain Gonzales looked deep into the bishop's eyes. That was the moment he saw the faint red flicker within Bishop Francisco's cold, dark pupils. The sight was so shocking that Gonzales thought he must have been imagining it.

'The body of Corsell Santillana will remain nailed to the walls of this church for eight days,' Bishop Francisco ordered, his bony finger pointing in Captain Gonzales's direction. 'On the eighth day, Santillana will be removed and his cleansed body will be buried in the church cemetery. This is the will of God, and you will ensure that His every wish is adhered to. Your military guard is to be doubled outside the walls and every soldier is to carry a loaded rifle. Anyone who attempts to approach the church is to be arrested. If things get out of hand, you have my permission to use whatever force is necessary.'

With his stomach churning, Gonzales replied, 'I will do as you ask.' In truth, he could not be sure why he responded the way he did. But the sweat on his brow told him he had made the only decision that he was able. All Gonzales could sense was his own fear – the same kind he felt when he thought about falling into fast-moving water.

The bishop slowly circled him.

'There is yet another task you must complete,' the bishop added. 'This is a most serious matter and it must be met with equally serious actions. You will seek out a white

stranger . . . a man called Wilson Dowling. He has come to
Cuzco from a foreign land – he arrived by train this very
morning. He is in the company of the American, Hiram
Bingham. I believe you know him? You must stop them
from reaching the foothills of the Andes – that is where
they are going. They seek the lost city of Vilcapampa.
Dowling is an unknown who seeks to undermine the
Church of Jesus Christ. He is to be treated with caution,
especially under these most grave of circumstances. You
are to use force to restrain him. When you have them both
in your custody, you will bring them here to me.'

'How do you know about these men?' Gonzales asked.

'*God Himself* has spoken to me and that is something
that must never be questioned. Ever.'

Captain Gonzales saw another red flicker deep
within the blackness of Bishop Francisco's pupils –
there was no mistaking it this time. Gonzales stared
straight ahead, his muscles tensed, his pulse racing.
He was so confused, like a blindfolded man that had
been spun round and round too many times. 'I will
do as you command,' Gonzales eventually replied.
'I will attend to the capture of these two foreigners myself.
When I have them in my custody I will bring them before
you.'

'You have made the only sensible choice,' the bishop
replied.

106 years in the future

8

Andes Ranges, Peru
Hiram Bingham Express
20 Miles North-west of Cuzco
Local Time 9:57 am

17 January 2014

IN A PERFECT world, Helena would fly a helicopter directly to Machu Picchu. Unfortunately, the ancient Inca ruins had been listed as a World Heritage site and there was a strict no-fly policy surrounding the area. That meant the fastest way to get there was to take a train from Cuzco. Helena would have driven a car on the perilous mountain roads if she thought that would get her there quicker, but the advice she had been given said it took at least twice as much time. As a result, she was sitting in the plush Orient-Express dining car, trundling slowly towards the Andes ranges.

The schedule on this silver service junket called for morning tea at 10 am, cocktails at 11:30 and lunch at 1 pm. The train had a top speed of twenty-five miles per hour on the straight stretches, which in Helena's opinion was far too slow. And to make matters even more frustrating, she had a terrible headache. It was taking all her effort just to remain positive as the scent of buttery croissants wafted across from the table behind. The smell made her want to be sick. Turning to the window, she tried to absorb herself in the glorious view outside.

It had been more than a year since Wilson had transported out of Helena's life, leaving her in limbo. There was no doubt that she felt alone. She told everyone around her of the symptoms of her feelings, and yet she concealed the true cause of her anguish. No one would ever believe that she had met a time-traveller – no one *could* believe something so ridiculous. And yet that was exactly how it had been. Thankfully, she had stopped trying to tell the truth and her life had been easier as a result. When dealing with something so bizarre, it was better to lie through your teeth than try to explain events that no one could possibly understand.

Meeting Wilson Dowling had been both the *best* and the *worst* thing that had ever happened to her, but mostly the worst.

She unzipped the pocket of her hiking vest and drew out the Egyptian coin Wilson had given her. The damaged coin was supposed to represent a link between the past and the future. She angrily pressed it between her fingers. Was she destined to live out the rest of her days wondering if she would ever see him again? Wilson had come into her world just over a year ago, completed his mission and then left her like a tourist leaves behind a summer romance. He said that he had *travelled time*, as crazy as the whole concept might seem. And yet Helena knew he was telling the truth – she had witnessed things that were impossible to rationalise in any other way. Wilson Dowling commanded powers that could only be explained by having a vast knowledge of the future. He was certainly the Overseer he claimed to be, she had no doubt of that.

Looking out the window, Helena wished that the train would go faster. There was no doubting that she was a beautiful woman, and that fact was not lost on any of the passengers or staff who had boarded the Orient-Express that morning. Her posture was excellent and her symmetrical face and perfect skin drew many stares, as did her athletic body. Taking off her baseball cap, she loosened her ponytail and let her hair fall about her face. The sight of her thick, shoulder-length blonde hair made the passengers in the dining car turn in her direction, but Helena ignored them. Since she was a child she had become accustomed to both men and women studying her. But it was more than just her beauty they were drawn to – Helena had a healthy *presence*, which is a quality that is very difficult to define in words. It is the value quotient of a person's life force and is remarkably obvious in people who are strong with it, and also in those who have very little. When onlookers gazed at her they invariably detected it also, and the more they looked at her the more they wanted to look.

One fact was certain, Helena Capriarty's nerves were on a hair-trigger and her outward appearance gave no indication of the raging emotions that could erupt at any time with furious consequences. No one on the train knew what she was capable of, and just by looking at her no one could possibly tell. She was a woman on a mission of her own, and she would not let anyone or anything stop her from finding the connection she was looking for.

Pressing her temples to ease her headache, Helena replaced her baseball cap then took a sip of the steaming coca tea in front of her. Pablo had said that the local concoction, which contained native coca leaves, was supposed to lessen the effects of altitude sickness.

Across the aisle sat Helena's guide, Pablo Escator. Everyone taking a trip to Machu Picchu on the famous 'Hiram Bingham Express' was appointed a guide, provided they were staying for at least two nights at Machu Picchu Lodge, the five-star hotel perched high on the mountain peak directly beside the ancient Inca city.

Opposite Pablo sat Helena's bodyguard, Chad Chadwick, said to be the best minder in the business. Helena's father, Lawrence, had insisted she take a bodyguard with her if she wanted to head down to South America – and he always pushed until he got his way. She was his only child and the wealthy businessman intended to use his considerable influence and power to protect her, even if it was against her wishes. That was Lawrence's sole condition to her taking the trip – and as a reward, he let her use his private jet, so Helena had no choice but to agree.

Chad Chadwick was a 33-year-old former heptathlete for the United States Olympic team. She had been the gold-medal favourite at the Beijing Olympics in 2008, but a niggling back injury had interrupted her javelin training, which had been her best discipline. In the end she was forced to pull out of the Games. Chad was lean and muscular with massive calves and huge shoulders. Now a professional bodyguard, she was an imposing figure, standing nearly six feet tall with pale skin and bleached, spiky hair. Her expression was stony and the constant scowl on her face did nothing to soften her appearance. Like all good minders, Chad watched everyone and seemingly never dropped her guard for a second. She always carried a concealed handgun, and in her backpack she had extra ammunition, a first-aid kit, one low-impact concussion grenade as well as ample tins of tuna in spring water, of which she ate 200 grams every three hours, almost to the minute.

'I have to keep my metabolism steady,' Chad explained. 'Tuna is pure protein. It helps keep my muscle mass up and my body fat down.'

Pablo, on the other hand, looked like a very gentle man. Helena guessed he was in his late forties, a mixture of both Spanish and native South American, probably Inca. In Spanish, people of mixed race were known as *mestizos*. His facial features were flat and his skin characteristically dark. By comparison with Chad, he was very short, standing a fraction over five-foot-five. A further indication of his native heritage was that he was openly biased when discussing the Spanish invasion by the conquistador Francisco Pizarro in 1532.

'The invaders came to South America with one aim – to find gold,' Pablo stated brashly. 'And Pizarro ruthlessly murdered the good Inca king Atahualpa, even after his ransom was paid. The conquistadors were filthy pigs!'

Helena found the comment amusing considering Pablo was half Spanish himself. She realised that Francisco Pizarro was not a well-liked man in Peru, despite the fact that he was the founding father of Lima and the bringer of Christianity to South America. Judging by the cross hanging around Pablo's neck, he was fiercely Catholic, as most Peruvians were, and yet he hated Pizarro with every cell in his being.

The luxury train was named after the late Hiram Bingham, the Yale academic who discovered the citadel of Machu Picchu in the early 1900s. Helena had an ebook about him in her bag that she was intending to read. The American explorer had lived a blessed life filled with many successes. After his world-changing discovery in Peru, Bingham went on to become Governor of Connecticut as well as a long-serving member of the US Senate. It was said that he was the inspiration for Steven Spielberg's character Indiana Jones.

The cladding of the train was royal blue. By contrast, the chairs, lounges and curtains in the carriages were upholstered in beige velour. The train had a single diesel locomotive and just three carriages: one dining car, a lounge car and an observation car at the rear. Passengers were able to stand at the rear railing and take in the full view of the towering peaks of the Andes as the train descended from the high plateaus of Cuzco along the river basin.

A group of about twenty people, some older men and an equal number of young women were crammed into the observation carriage, dancing and singing to the quick strum of a guitarist and an energetic bongo player. They were doing a Spanish rendition of 'Blame It on the Boogie' by The Jackson 5 – everyone was singing passionately at the same time.

The music could not be worse, Helena decided.

It was normally a five-hour journey from Cuzco to the base of Machu Picchu but there had been reports of heavy rain and flooding further down the valley. Pablo had advised that the trip could take as long as eight hours if the rain set in.

Although it was only mid-morning, the sky was getting darker. A spattering of rain began tapping against the windows of the dining car and Helena instinctively pressed her fingers against the glass as the gentle rain transformed into a heavy downpour.

'I think we will see big storms,' Pablo stated, looking

outside. 'The weather is coming from the west, which is not good.'

'Is there danger of flooding?' Chad asked.

'There is nothing to worry about,' Pablo replied. 'There are *many* important people on this train. *Muy importante*! We will take the care that is needed.'

Over the next twenty minutes the downpour worsened and the sky became even darker. The train passed through another narrow gorge cut out of the hillside that was already filled with shimmering stretches of water on both sides of the tracks.

In the background the music and dancing continued.

The sheer red granite cliff on one side was taking the full brunt of the wind and rain, the water tumbling like a waterfall towards the very bottom. It was easy to see how a prolonged deluge could quickly fill these Andean valleys.

Then it began, 'Uptown Girl' by Billy Joel, sung with a Spanish theme.

'Please, God, not "Uptown Girl",' Helena whispered to herself.

She put on her noise-reduction headphones and notched up the music on her iPod to drown out the sound. 'Blame It on the Boogie' was bad enough, but no one should have to sit through 'Uptown Girl'.

Helena had made her way to Peru because of the persistent dreams she had been having. For nearly two weeks they had been with her every time she slept, the exact same dream each time. She was standing before the Temple of the Sun at Machu Picchu. The rays of the afternoon sun were scything through the trapezoidal stone windows and bathing her in light. The foundations of the massive granite structure appeared to have been cut open at a forty-five degree angle, which seemed very odd. The bright sunlight in her eyes had made it difficult to see clearly, but Helena felt there was something inside that triangular entrance that she needed to discover. She had studied the ancient Inca temple on the internet, but simply looking at pictures did not satisfy her. There was definitely something in that gloomy darkness that she needed to see for herself, she was sure of it, and she dared to hope that it was something magical that would somehow lead her back to Wilson Dowling.

Helena's temples were aching, her chest was tight; she felt distinctly out of breath. As much as she believed her symptoms were simply altitude sickness, she worried that it was the stress of what she was putting herself through. The last year of her life had been the worst she could remember. She knew it was important to stay relaxed and positive – she had reminded herself countless times – but deep down her fear was that her dreams would simply lead to nothing. This would be yet another wild goose chase she was on, and everything she was doing was just a stupid waste of time.

9

Andes Ranges, Peru
Hiram Bingham Express
30 Miles North-west of Cuzco
Local Time 2:04 pm

17 January 2014

THE ODD SENSATION of the train going into reverse caused Helena to open her eyes with a start. The dining carriage was full of people and the smell of gourmet food hung in the air. Sitting up a little straighter, Helena removed her headphones and gradually took in the sounds of the people and movement around her. She must have been asleep for quite some time – she hadn't been dreaming, which was a surprise – and Chad was now sitting directly across the table from her. Outside, it was still raining heavily and the windows of the air-conditioned carriage had become foggy.

'The observation car is flooded,' Chad explained, pointing rearwards. 'All the passengers have had to come forward.'

Pablo leant across the aisle. 'The train is reversing down the switchback at this moment. We're approaching the Urubamba Valley,' he said enthusiastically. 'The weather can get *mucho* bad here as we descend into the mountains.'

Helena rubbed away the condensation on the window and peered outside. The terrain dropped away steeply and there was quite a lot of trees and greenery – much more than on the high plains. Looking about the dining car she saw waiters busily delivering drinks and plates of food, and there was a lot of chatter and commotion.

On the white tablecloth in front of her was a neatly arranged set of silver cutlery and two white china plates with gold edgings; the crest of Orient Express positioned perfectly at the top. Helena took a sip of her sparkling mineral water. 'You're not eating?' she asked, noting that the table in front of Chad was bare.

'I'll eat later,' Chad replied as she scanned the carriage.

The train came to a slow halt and after a few moments began travelling forward again. A loud 'Hooray!' came from the front of the dining carriage. The large group from the observation car – about twelve of them – had moved to occupy the furthest four tables and they were now doing shots of tequila, one shot after the other.

Noticing that Helena was looking in the group's direction, Chad said under her breath, 'Businessmen and hookers would be my guess. The men are well dressed, expensive suits. The women look cheap, and young. High heels, not a good idea in the mountains, especially in the rainy season.'

Helena nodded – it was the group that had been singing earlier.

'The men are from Peru,' Chad continued, 'judging by their bag tags. The women are from various places – Argentina, Guatemala, Brazil – they're the accents I can be sure of.' Chad leant in even closer. 'The reason they keep heading to the toilets is to do cocaine. Have you noticed how many times they have gone down there?'

As soon as Chad mentioned it, Helena realised she was right.

'I found traces of it around the basin. They're trying to keep it under wraps, is my guess, but it's not easy when you're taking as much as they are. Some of them have made at least five trips since we got on board.'

'They are on this train quite frequently,' Pablo said, leaning forward in an effort to be discreet. 'They are from a very powerful family here in Peru. Everyone knows them, so it is best to leave them alone.'

'They are taking drugs,' Chad said, looking down her nose. 'They will not be a powerful family for long if they keep that up.'

Helena whispered, 'As long as they don't sing anymore, and they stay away from us, I'm happy.'

'Avoid eye contact if you can,' Chad advised.

Helena nodded. Reaching into her bag, she opened her emergency travel pack and popped out a couple of aspirin. Her headache was worse than ever and she needed something to ease the pain.

'The railway line has three switchbacks on this part of the descent,' Pablo said, trying to change the subject. 'In places, it is the steepest part of the journey.'

At that very moment, the train began to brake suddenly. Everyone jolted forward in their seats and a few glasses toppled over as the carriages shuddered to an abrupt halt. There were brief mutters and squeals of unhappiness as precious alcohol spread across the tablecloths. Helena only just managed to stop her own glass of mineral water from spilling.

The train just sat there as waiters and waitresses ran about the carriage with napkins, mopping up the various spills. The rain continued to beat away on the roof like a million tiny drummers . . . time ticked slowly by but the train did not move.

The staff were randomly looking out the windows and Helena concluded this was not a customary place for the train to stop. They were on a relatively flat piece of track; there was an open field beside them with a simple wooden shack in the middle. Reddish boulders of irregular shapes and sizes – some of them massive, easily ten feet tall – randomly littered the view. Pablo wiped the window on his side of the carriage to reveal a sheer granite rock face looming ominously up into the mist. Giant stones would have severed from the cliffs countless years ago, and tumbled to their current positions.

'This doesn't seem like a very good place to stop,' Chad announced.

'*Las rocas estan bloqueando camino!*' a male voice called out.

'There are fallen stones blocking the track,' Pablo said with a worried look. Helena knew just enough Spanish to be able to understand.

There was further discussion in Spanish, then someone yelled out, '*Todos los hombres deben ayudar a moverlas!*'

'The staff are to assemble outside,' Pablo translated. 'The stones are to be moved.'

Helena's headache was getting progressively worse as the train sat still. She knew it would take time for the aspirin to work and she felt compelled to get up and walk it off. Wiping the inside of the window again, she looked outside at the dilapidated wooden shack in the distance; it was overgrown with weeds, the door had fallen off its hinges and a few roof shingles were missing.

'We will soon be on our way,' Pablo added. 'This has happened before.'

Helena stood up and adjusted her hiking vest. 'I'm going outside to have a look around,' she announced, trying to sound better than she really felt.

'You can't go outside,' Chad replied. 'There could be more rock slides, especially with this kind of rain.'

Pablo chimed in. 'You should wait here; it will be much a safer.'

'I'm going outside,' Helena said, feeling as if she was going to throw up. 'I've been cooped up in here for too long already.'

Chad and Pablo glanced at each other.

'I really don't think it's a good idea to go out there –'

'No . . . definitely not,' Pablo added.

'*Chad*,' Helena said sternly, 'I'm going outside. This headache is driving me crazy and I need some fresh air.'

Chad nodded.

'You will certainly get wet,' Pablo said. 'It is like cats and dogs falling from heaven, out there! You will be soaked to the skin in seconds.'

Helena pointed to the back of the carriage, then began walking. 'I need fresh air.'

'I'll get an umbrella,' Chad said.

The service manager politely tried to stop Helena from leaving, but she ordered Chad to open the back door and they both stepped out onto the connecting platform between the carriages. It was uncomfortably warm, compared to the cool temperature inside and the air felt thick with humidity. The sound of the rain was deafening as Helena opened the flimsy Orient Express umbrella into the weather. She slowly climbed down the ladder and stepped off the train onto the loose shale lining the railway tracks. The rain was hitting her umbrella so hard that it was moving it about in her grasp and she could feel her pants quickly getting soaked below her knees.

Towards the front of the train, it was possible to just make out the silhouettes of a dozen people working together to lever away the stones that were heaped across the track. Beyond that, it was impossible to see anything through the grey blankets of rain sweeping up the valley towards them. Chad landed on the shale beside her wearing a red plastic poncho and a pair of wraparound hunting glasses with bright orange lenses.

'I'm coming with you,' Chad said with a nod.

'There's an old house just over there.' Helena pointed, giving herself a goal to focus on. 'We may as well check it out.'

'Please be back in five minutes!' the service manager called out.

Helena and Chad made their way across the water-logged ground towards the old shack that looked as if it had been there for a hundred years. It was less than fifty feet from the train and Helena decided that it was probably built as a storage hut during the construction of the railway line. The sound of thunder rumbled ominously along the valley as Helena stepped ankle-deep into a bog and had to extract her foot very carefully so the suction didn't pull her boot off. Feeling worse than ever, she was beginning to wonder if the aspirin was ever going to work.

'Don't you just love the rain!' Chad called out. 'Hopefully we won't get struck by lightning.'

The sky above was so dark that it seemed more like evening than the middle of the afternoon. The old shack appeared to be built from eucalyptus – the Australian gum trees had been planted all over Peru in the late 1800s because they grew quickly, even at this altitude, and they were robust enough to handle the long dry season. The hut had certainly seen better days and if you looked carefully, you could see that it was tilting ever so slightly to one side.

As Helena approached the open doorway, Chad put her hand on her shoulder to stop her progress. 'I'm going inside first.' Chad removed her Glock 10mm handgun from the small of her back. 'There could be animals in there.' Looking down the dark brushed-steel barrel, she eased her way inside.

With her temples throbbing, Helena swivelled towards the train to see a few passengers peering out through the glass in their direction. A strong wind suddenly threw Helena's umbrella inside out, leaving her holding just the handle. With the rain beating against her face, she leapt through the open doorway for cover.

As soon as she was inside, Helena immediately felt disoriented. Her vision began fading in and out and it took all her balance just to stay upright. She tried to fight what she was seeing, but the more she did the more the world around her altered.

Through the sudden brightness she could see Wilson Dowling – the time-traveller – sitting on the floor in front of a raging fire. Helena had to stop herself from crying out in surprise. Another man was sitting across from him. The vision was so clear – it was like they were right there in front of her! At that moment of discovery there was not even time for Helena to ask herself how this could possibly be happening.

Both men were wearing only their undergarments. They were leaning against what looked like brown leather horse saddles. Wet clothes hung from the rafters above them. Wilson was sitting cross-legged, eating sardines from a rectangular food tin.

A crackling hot fire was burning in the middle of the

floor, the violent orange flames licking up towards the peaked roof of the hut. The wood was obviously wet; thick plumes of white smoke billowed up into the rafters.

Helena focused on Wilson's face. He looked a little older than she remembered. He was talking – the conversation seemed serious – but she couldn't hear his voice or anything related to the vision, only the drumming of the rain hitting the roof and Chad's heavy footsteps on the rotten floor beside her. She could sense Chad close by, and yet her mental picture was all Helena could see.

The man across from Wilson was smoking a cigarette and drinking whiskey straight from the bottle. He was very thin and puny. Helena knew his face but she couldn't place where she had seen him before. A rifle was leaning against the wall – a bolt-action Springfield. Her father had one just like it in his gun collection.

Helena's vision was more intriguing than frightening. She had thought so many times about seeing Wilson again, and although she knew what she was witnessing wasn't actually in front of her, it filled her with relief that there was still a connection – however bizarre – between them. Wilson stabbed a small fork into a greasy sardine and lifted it to his mouth.

The walls of the shack were clean and new, so it must have been when the building was first constructed – stepping forward, Helena moved within her hallucination. Although the fire was smouldering hot, she couldn't feel the heat. She studied Wilson's face and the texture of his hair, which was longer than when she last saw him. His hands were exactly as she remembered, his movements deliberate and strong. He had a leather satchel on the floor beside him. His boots were placed carefully by the fire, the openings facing towards the flames in an attempt to dry them out.

A familiar sensation filled Helena's stomach as she watched him speaking – but she still couldn't hear a sound. She remembered the many conversations they'd had together and how much she loved the sound of his voice. Helena wanted to call out to him, to say that she was there watching, but she knew he couldn't answer.

Wilson climbed to his feet, his body naked from the waist up. He began readjusting the damp clothes that were hanging from the rafters. His body was exactly as Helena remembered and she found herself stepping through the fireplace towards him.

Suddenly Wilson's gaze sought her out!

There was an unexpected look of recognition in his eyes!

Can he see me? Helena wondered, standing among the flames.

Wilson extended his hand directly towards her, like he was trying to feel her presence. It looked like he was going to say something . . . but then he frowned and dropped his hands to his sides as if the connection had somehow been lost.

Chad's voice suddenly broke Helena's concentration. 'Are you okay?'

Helena's mental picture dissolved away and Chad appeared next to her. As much as she tried to refocus, Helena couldn't bring the incredible scene back.

'Are you okay?' Chad asked again.

'I'm fine,' Helena eventually replied. Looking about her, she studied the dilapidated shack for the first time. The walls had rotted through in places, cobwebs criss-crossed the ceiling between the rafters. In other places, narrow strips of light poked through the walls where the timber had warped. Roof shingles were missing and rain-water was streaming through. Tufts of grass were growing through the rotten floorboards and everything underfoot was covered in a layer of dirt.

'It smells terrible in here,' Chad said with disgust.

Helena used the edge of her boot to clear the dirt and expose the floorboards. She stepped to the centre of the shack where the fireplace had been in her vision and did the same thing again. Unsurprisingly, the floorboards were badly blackened by the large open fire that had once been at that very spot.

Chad gazed outside. 'You're going to get soaked on the way back. We can't have that.' She holstered her handgun then peeled off her red plastic poncho and handed it to Helena. 'How's your headache?'

'Still the same,' Helena replied.

'You should drink more of that coca tea. It's supposed to help altitude headaches – Pablo swears by it.' Chad wiped away the droplets of water from the orange lenses of her glasses. 'It's probably quite good for you, which is a bonus.'

It was clear that only Helena had experienced the incredible vision of Wilson. After more than a year – inside this dilapidated railway hut in the middle of the Andes Ranges – the connection she had been searching for had finally been discovered. Against all logic, her instinct to come to Peru had been validated. The time-traveller Wilson Dowling had entered Helena's life once again – the question now, was why?

10

Andes Ranges, Peru
30 Miles North-west of Cuzco
Local Time 11:23 pm

16 January 1908

WILSON WOUND BACK the metal lid of the sardine can
with a stainless steel key. It was an ingenious can-opening
system that he had not seen before. On every rectangular
tin the little key was soldered on top and it saved having to
stab his knife into the metal, which could easily blunt the
blade.

On the wooden floor, the substantial fire had finally
taken hold and both Wilson and Hiram were forced to keep
their heads low to save breathing in smoke. Thankfully, it
was now beginning to thin out as the moisture burned
away but the fire was still crackling and hissing like an
angry cat and every now and again there was a bang and
a pop as the moisture pockets in the wood were violently
released.

Wilson took a sniff of his sardines – it smelt overpowering, but he knew he needed food so he plunged his fork
into the oily flesh and gulped it down. The taste wasn't too
bad, once he got it past his nose and into his mouth.

The fire was burning on a stack of neatly spaced stones
that Wilson had carefully positioned to ensure the floor
didn't catch alight and the flames could also breathe. The
only place dry enough to light a fire was inside the shack
itself. He had found some dry kindling under the footings,
but even that wasn't enough to generate the heat that

was required. In desperation, he poured some precious kerosene out of their hurricane lamp onto the soaking wood, but not even that got it started. The entire experience wasn't helped by Hiram's constant complaining about how cold, wet and tired he was.

'Heading into the mountains in the middle of the rainy season is foolish,' Hiram kept muttering over and over again. 'I told you we should have waited.'

To get the fire started, Wilson was forced to go out into the darkness to search for more wood. Luckily, he came across an old pine tree and was able to hack out some four-inch-long strips of tinder. Pine burns even when it's wet because the wood resin is flammable. Within a few minutes of getting back to the shack, and with a little help from another splash of kerosene, the fire crackled to life.

Wilson held his sore hands towards the leaping flames to dry them out. For the last ten hours it had been necessary to slap Diablo on the hindquarters to get the stubborn little donkey to move along the muddy trail. The whip didn't seem to work and jamming his heels into Diablo's sides did nothing either. Even when he was moving, Diablo only went at a walking pace for a minute before he decided to stop again. An hour into the journey, Wilson wanted to leave Diablo behind, but Hiram insisted that his donkey stayed with them and promised that the animal would become more cooperative as the journey progressed. If anything, Diablo got worse.

With the fire burning brightly, Hiram's complaining finally stopped as he lounged on his leather saddle, a smouldering cigarette in one hand and a bottle of Tennessee whiskey in the other. It had taken him no time at all to strip down to his tattered undergarments and hang his wet clothes from the rafters among the smoke.

'Which mountain is Vilcapampa near?' Hiram asked.

'It's called *Machu Picchu* in Quechua, which means "Old Peak",' Wilson replied.

Hiram stared into the flames. 'Old Peak . . . I like it.' He took another swig of whiskey. 'It's too bad it already has a name. That's how you become truly famous – you get a mountain named after you. President McKinley will live on forever now that the tallest mountain in the United States is named after him – it's in Alaska, you know? He never even visited the place!'

Hiram offered the whiskey bottle to Wilson but he waved it away.

'It will help warm you up,' Hiram said, extending the bottle towards him once again. 'Come on, have a drink!'

Wilson took a quick shot then handed it back. The whiskey felt warm as it went down his throat – a pleasant sensation after having been wet and cold for so long. 'You were right about that donkey,' Wilson admitted. 'He is one frustrating little bastard.'

Hiram grinned. 'It gave me great pleasure to watch the battle of the wills you two were having.'

'Tomorrow, you can ride him.'

'No, thanks,' Hiram replied. 'You wanted donkeys. I gave you donkeys. Which one I ride is up to me. Anyway, enough about that, tell me again how famous I will be.'

'You'll be as famous as Thomas Jefferson,' Wilson replied.

Hiram smiled. '*Thomas Jefferson* . . . I don't even care if you're lying,' he said lounging back. 'I just like the thought of being famous. I would really suit me, I think.'

'You will be credited with the discovery of the lost city of the Incas,' Wilson continued. 'Nothing like this has ever been seen before.'

Hiram's brow ruffled. 'Out of curiosity, if this discovery of Vilcapampa is so important, and so much adulation and acclaim comes with it, then why not tell the world yourself? *You* could reap these great rewards.'

'It is not my destiny, it's yours,' Wilson replied.

'And what do you know of my destiny?'

'I know more than you realise,' Wilson said.

'What is that supposed to mean?'

'Let me put it this way . . . there is a greater fabric to the universe. And you are part of the discovery of Vilcapampa whether you like it or not.'

'How do you know about my destiny? What does that even mean? Part of what? What is this *fabric* you refer to?' Hiram made inverted commas with his fingers to emphasise the word *fabric*. 'How can you even know where Vilcapampa is located? How did you know my wife was pregnant? You are a very strange man, Wilson Dowling.'

'All you need to know is that I, too, am playing my part in the discovery of Vilcapampa. I will lead you there . . . you will do the rest. That's all I can tell you.' He pointed in Hiram's direction. 'You must never mention my name or the role I have played.'

Hiram tilted his head to one side. 'I really can't decide if you're full of crap, or not. I really can't. In so many ways you seem so credible. Normally my "horse dung" detector is pretty effective.' Hiram let out a sigh. 'I guess the fullness of time will tell.'

Thunder reverberated through the night air, all the while the heavy rain drummed loudly against the shingled roof.

Hiram looked about. 'Finding this building was a stroke of good fortune, I'll give you that.' Hiram had no way of knowing that Wilson was aware of the railway shack's existence even before they left Cuzco. The mission notes had detailed this place as a stopping point for the night.

There was a loud bang from inside the fire and a smouldering ember shot out, just missing Wilson and hitting the wall. Wilson used his fork to pick up the glowing nugget and toss it back into the roaring fire. He turned his saddle around to dry the other side and sat down again. All the while, he was conscious that Hiram was watching him.

'Are you a gymnast?' Hiram asked.

'No, I'm not a gymnast,' Wilson replied.

'Your muscles are bulging everywhere.' Hiram exhaled a long stream of smoke then flicked his cigarette butt into the fire. 'My bodily structure is much better suited for long-term exploration into the wilds of South America. I once didn't eat for a week – I bet you can't do that.'

Wilson looked at the skinny man sitting across from him, with his pasty skin and ribs showing. 'You look like you could use a good meal to me.'

Hiram took another swig of whiskey. 'You're Australian, aren't you?'

Wilson nodded. 'I am.'

Hiram scoffed. 'You Australians gave the vote to your womenfolk, I hear – first in the world!' He laughed.

'The New Zealanders were the first,' Wilson said.

'New Zealanders?' Hiram looked baffled. 'Really?'

'The New Zealanders were the first. The Australians were second.'

'Either way, both countries are foolish,' Hiram said passionately. 'The pesky suffragists are everywhere in the States. A troublesome lot they are – very troublesome. If you want my opinion, they'll never get the right to vote back home. There are more women than men in the United States – that's what the census of 1900 confirmed – and that means the womenfolk would control *everything*.'

'Would that be so bad?'

Hiram pointed at Wilson with his bottle. 'You're kidding, right?'

'Men and women will both have the vote,' Wilson announced. 'That is the future for which we are headed.'

'Utter nonsense!' Hiram replied. 'It will never happen.' He paused for a moment to study Wilson's expression. 'I certainly hope you know more about finding lost Inca cities than you do about politics, because you clearly know nothing about that. Could you imagine if women ruled the world?' He scoffed again. 'There would be vases of cut flowers everywhere and a doily on every table. Nobody would be allowed to say what they really meant. Men would be expected to do fifty percent of the housework. Fashion would be valued above all other things. It would be utter chaos! Not to mention the end of the month!'

'Everything changes,' Wilson announced. 'That is the only certainty I have ever encountered.'

Hiram began rolling another cigarette. 'I know two things that will never change. Religion is here to stay, and gold will remain the most valuable substance on the face of the earth. I've studied history my whole life, many eras and many different empires. There're always the two common threads: religion and gold. That's why the Incas were here, and same goes for the conquistadores. It's even why that railway track is being built outside that doorway; to gather souls and to gather wealth, be it sugarcane or coal or whatever. All things are eventually measured in gold.'

Wilson motioned with his fork to the backpack filled with tins of sardines and baked beans. 'You really should eat something.'

Hiram held up his bottle of whiskey. 'I have everything I need right here.'

The rain continued to beat heavily against the roof of the railway shack as Wilson rehung his clothes to ensure they dried properly. Standing there in the dense smoke he couldn't help but think about the role he was playing in the events circling Machu Picchu. The ancient city was a time-travel portal to other worlds, and yet it was his job to lead Hiram Bingham to the ruins so the lost Inca city could be finally introduced to the modern world. As to why Hiram Bingham was the man to be credited with the city's discovery, not even he could understand – Hiram seemed an odd choice. Even so, Wilson was here to play his part, and after eight long years of waiting he was finally nearing the end of his mission. His life was inextricably intertwined with forces he could barely understand, and yet he had no doubt that the past could affect the future and, in return, the future could affect the past. He was the Overseer and it was his role to act upon the missions coded within the Dead Sea Scrolls. They were the documents that guided his destiny. The past needed to be protected from the future and the future needed to be protected from the past. That was the way of things.

In the next few days Wilson would finally be gone from this timeline. The Machu Picchu portal would be his exit from this strange and ignorant world and he could rest easily knowing that he had successfully led Hiram Bingham to his destiny, and the fame that came with it.

Suddenly the hairs on Wilson's arms bristled and a shiver overcame his body.

He felt like he was being watched from the darkness.

His gaze nervously scanned the empty corners of the shack. All he could see was the dancing light of the fire painting an eerie ever-shifting hue of gold against the exposed wooden walls. The rain continued to beat down outside and the wind gusted against the flimsy walls, causing them to creak and groan. Wilson wanted to walk to the door and look out, but he knew there would not be anyone there – just the three donkeys tied with ropes to the circle-latch of the doorhandle. If they were spooked, they would surely pull the door open. Yet against all logic the sensation was unmistakeable – someone was watching him. He could feel it.

Sheet lightning flashed outside, which momentarily revealed the tiny gaps in the wooden walls. Then came the rumble of thunder overhead, deep and reverberating.

Instinctively, Wilson reached out his hand towards the roaring fire – he could feel a strong presence in the room, somewhere on the other side of the flickering flames. Was that a silhouette he could see among the heat haze? His heart was beating madly and he could not slow it down no matter how he tried.

There was definitely someone there!

'You'll burn yourself! Back away!' Hiram yelled out.

Wilson pulled his hand back just before it entered the flames. As suddenly as the strange sensation had begun, it was gone. Wilson focused on the raging fire and the yellow-hot embers falling between the flat stones and blackening the floorboards.

'Have you completely lost your mind?' Hiram grabbed his rifle and circled the fire. Carefully, he eased the wooden door open with the barrel and peered out into the blustery rain. When he was satisfied the donkeys were okay, he latched the door closed again. 'What were you looking at?' He gestured his with gun towards the fire.

'I thought I saw something,' Wilson replied.

'What did you see?'

Wilson shook his head. 'In the end, I didn't see anything.'

Hiram rested his gun against the wall, turned his saddle round to dry the opposite side, then sat down. 'I certainly hope I don't live to regret coming out into the wilderness with you, Wilson Dowling. You are a strange man, that is plain to see.'

Deep down Wilson knew he had sensed something real. A presence of some kind was in the shack with them – and whatever it was, it was watching him with a keen eye. Events were out of control, he knew that. He needed to get to Machu Picchu as fast as possible and exit this timeline before the situation became even more complicated.

11

Andes Ranges, Peru
20 Miles North-west of Cuzco
Local Time 11:45 pm

16 January 1908

THE WORDS, 'You must seek out a white stranger, a man called Wilson Dowling', were still echoing in Captain Gonzales's ears as both he and Lieutenant Capos rode their donkeys into a rain squall with ten soldiers walking behind them in single file. Leading the way were two mountain guides holding kerosene lamps at chest height, which at best cast a hazy light in the soaking wet conditions.

This was the last place on earth that Captain Gonzales wanted to be, especially considering the grave circumstances of Corsell Santillana's crucifixion. Given a choice, Captain Gonzales would be warm and dry at home with his wife and children, tucked up in their small bedroom on the chicken feather mattress he had spent one month's full salary to purchase. At the foot of his bed, next to the mudbrick wall, was the little bed of his three growing children. A faint smile came to Gonzales's lips when he thought about waking in the night and looking in his children's direction, the moonbeams providing ample light in the darkness. He thanked God every evening when he would see them safely sleeping there under the colourful alpaca covers their mother had knitted for them. On many occasions the children would be holding each other to ward away the harsh chill of the Peruvian night air.

His smile drew into a scowl as Gonzales thought of

Bishop Francisco pacing from side to side in front of him across the wide expanse of the Gospel nave.

'These are my worst fears!' the bishop had called out, an obvious trembling taking hold of his bony fingers. 'You have failed me and you have failed this church!' He had scrunched up the single piece of paper Gonzales had brought to him and thrown it to the polished granite floor. 'You have let the impostors get away, and now your task will be more difficult.'

The reaction was nonsensical – no time had been wasted. After receiving orders from the bishop, Captain Gonzales had left La Catedral and immediately made enquiries about the location of Hiram Bingham's head-quarters – the Pan-Am Pacific Congress, as it was known – and he had gone there directly. The building was not far from the Plaza de Armas, just a five-minute walk, which he took at a brisk pace with two of his best men flanking him on either side. Upon their arrival, however, all they found was a letter written in English stuck on the door with a brass thumbtack. The whole process, from first hearing the name Wilson Dowling to standing at the doorway of Hiram Bingham's headquarters took less than one hour in total. That was a reasonable timeframe in his estimation, and yet the bishop had reacted as if Gonzales had waited a full day before seeking out the foreigners.

Gonzales twisted the wet reins between his cold fingers, and as much as he would have wished he could turn his animal back towards Cuzco and his family, he continued onwards through the pouring rain. Why would anyone want to look for the lost city of Vilcapampa at this time of year? In this terrible weather? And how could Bishop Francisco have known that Hiram Bingham was leaving today, looking for Vilcapampa, as was written on the letter stuck to the door? The situation was ridiculous!

Treasure hunters had been scouring the inhospitable Andes Mountains for the lost Inca city of Vilcapampa since Pizarro himself. So why all of a sudden did the failed explorer Hiram Bingham matter now? Especially when there were obviously more important events at hand in

Cuzco. The thought crossed Gonzales's mind that Bishop
Francisco's intention was to have him leave the city so he
could have an even greater level of control over his troops.
He hated thinking about it, but Gonzales still had his
doubts about whether Corsell Santillana was the man who
murdered Monsignor Pera. There was little evidence that
he could see other than Bishop Francisco's surety, which
came almost twelve hours after the event, as did his direc-
tive to crucify poor Corsell on the outer walls of the church.
As much as Captain Gonzales wished that he could have
put a stop to the brutal ritual, he did not intervene – and
even to this moment he could not truly understand why. It
would have meant going against the bishop's wishes, but
regardless, Gonzales knew that the laws of the land should
come before religion.

From under his hooded poncho, Captain Gonzales took
a long, muted breath to be sure no one – especially his men
– could hear his obvious discontent. He carefully adjusted
the rifle strap across his shoulder, the weight of his .303
carbine somehow feeling twice a heavy as it did when
they'd ridden out of Cuzco nearly eight hours earlier.

'We must move more quickly,' Gonzales said to his
lieutenant beside him.

'The men are going as fast as they can,' Capos replied,
looking back over his shoulder. 'If we push them too hard
now, it will take longer to get there in the end.'

It had been necessary to offer Capos and the other
soldiers double pay to get them to leave their families and
head off into the night on such a wet and stormy evening.
The only one not getting extra pay for this expedition was
Captain Gonzales himself, but he had decided he would
take some time off when he returned to make up for such a
drastic and uncalled-for departure.

Captain Gonzales had confronted his fears about Bishop
Francisco; the priest's appearance and actions, although
outwardly calm, were a cause for great distress. In his eyes
was a look that Captain Gonzales had not seen before in
his nearly forty years on this earth – and as much as he
wished to, there was no denying the red flicker within

the bishop's pupils. It was an unholy sight, he knew that without doubt. As well as that, the priest had uncanny foresight; he knew things and made threats that were difficult to grasp – it was as if he could look into the future and know what was going to happen and why.

Just thinking about the bishop's flickering eyes had caused Gonzales physical pain, and he found himself wincing at the most unusual moments. His symptoms were difficult to describe, even to himself. The harsh feeling that gripped at his head and chest felt like he was caught between powerful, twisting ropes that continued to wind, tightening with each passing moment. He felt like his stomach was knotted, a feeling similar to when, as a small boy, he was told his grandfather had died. How could the priest's appearance engender such a reaction? In truth, it was the pain that had driven Gonzales into the rain and the darkness, away from his family on this cold night, not his loyalty to the church or the military uniform on his back.

The effects of his condition fuelled an interesting response that Captain Gonzales was all too aware of – when he finally caught up with Hiram Bingham and the white stranger, Wilson Dowling, he intended to vent his rage upon them. Feeling the chill of wet clothes gripping his skin, Gonzales adjusted his rifle and imagined yet again the sensation of hammering the stock of his gun into the face of the man called Wilson Dowling. It was certainly because of the mysterious foreigner that he found himself out here. Gonzales was not a man prone to acts of violence, but in this case he intended to extract a price for the predicament Dowling had put him in. His vain hope was that once he achieved his objective, the mysterious pain that gripped his body would finally set him free.

The mountain guides led Gonzales and his soldiers carefully down a steep muddy incline that was treacherous underfoot. At least three of his men fell to their backsides into the bog, but Gonzales was not deterred.

'Think of your extra pay!' he called out.

In the distance, a swollen river growled loudly into the darkness. The sound meant they were getting closer to the mountains and to the railway shack where Bingham and Dowling would be spending the night – Bishop Francisco had predicted that was where the two foreigners would be hiding. If they were not at the railway shack, Gonzales would have played his part and his soldiers would be witness to his efforts to follow the bishop's orders and seek them out. Either way, Gonzales and his soldiers would be heading home again very soon.

'Faster!' Gonzales called out to his men. 'The sooner we capture the white foreigners, the sooner we can return to Cuzco!'

12

Andes Ranges, Peru
30 Miles North-west of Cuzco
Local Time 5:15 am

17 January 1908

IT WAS JUST after five o'clock in the morning when the
utter blackness of night finally began to fade. Wilson
had not slept for more than fifteen minutes at a stretch,
such was his worry. As soon as he saw the faint signs of
daylight, he got dressed into his dry clothes and began
making preparations to leave. It had been warm in the
railway shack for the first part of the evening until the
fire eventually died down and the chilled air from outside
worked its way through the flimsy wooden walls. The cold
then set in for the remainder of the night as it always did so
close to the glacial mountains, even in the summer months.
The predominant northerly winds blew straight over the
icy peaks of the nearby ranges and the thin air was close to
freezing. In the summertime, there could be a thirty-degree
temperature change between day and night.

Looking out the door, the view was entirely restricted
by the mist and heavy clouds that had dropped down to
ground level as morning approached. And yet, even so,
the drizzle continued falling. The morning was very quiet;
everything seemed to be perfectly still outside. As Wilson
breathed in, he could taste the wet forest in his throat. The
chill air turned into plumes of mist as he breathed out. On
the doorstep, the donkeys looked to be asleep standing
up, which was something Wilson had not seen before. All

looked well, but Wilson had a bad feeling that he could not explain.

Hiram was lying on the floor in his tattered long johns. His head was awkwardly pressed up against the side of his saddle and his wool blanket was twisted around one leg, barely covering his body. He was hugging an empty whiskey bottle in one hand and his safari hat in the other. Mist wafted out of his open mouth as he snored and Wilson couldn't help but think what a pathetic sight he made.

'Get up,' Wilson nudged Hiram's leg with his boot. Hiram didn't move, so Wilson nudged him again. 'I said, get up!'

Hiram groaned and opened his eyes, looked up at Wilson, then eventually took on a disgusted expression. 'Go away!' he said with a hoarse voice.

'Get up before I pour a bucket of water on your head.'

Hiram opened one eye. 'You don't have a bucket.' He then readjusted his blanket and pulled it up under his chin. 'That makes you a liar.'

'If you want to see Vilcapampa, then you'll get dressed.' Wilson kicked Hiram's foot.

'Alright . . . alright!' Hiram placed the empty whiskey bottle on the floor, where it wobbled around before falling over. He pointed at his shirt, vest and moleskin pants hanging from the rafters. 'Pass me my clothes, will you?'

Wilson pulled them down and tossed them in his direction.

Hiram sniffed the material before inserting his thin arms into the shirtsleeves. 'Why don't you light a nice fire and then we can have some breakfast?'

'There's no time for hanging around.' Wilson collected the last of his things and put them into his satchel. He then set about loading the backpacks.

'What about breakfast?'

'You should have eaten last night.' Wilson threw a metal water canister into Hiram's lap and it landed heavily on his stomach.

'What is your problem, Wilson?'

'You need to stay hydrated . . . and we need to get moving.'

'I never get up this early,' Hiram muttered. 'What time is it, anyway?'

Wilson glanced at his watch. 'It's half-five.'

'Half-five!' Hiram rolled back onto his side and set about once again readjusting his blanket to cover his body, tucked himself into a ball and closed his eyes.

Wilson wrenched the blanket away and threw it to the side.

'What the hell are you doing?' Hiram yelled.

'We have to leave!'

Hiram swore out loud before yanking his pants on. 'This is ridiculous! When I agreed to come out here with you it wasn't to be driven like a slave day and night! You said "don't bring any porters", and here I am fending for myself in the cold and rain. I can't believe this, really I can't.'

Wilson opened the door and stared intently into the heavy fog. He was certain they were being watched, although he had very little to support the theory. Visibility was down to only a few feet, so whoever it was, they had to be close. Wilson's only evidence were the goosebumps on his arms and the nervous electricity in his legs that he couldn't shake off. Ever since he had arrived in Peru, he had been spooked by thoughts and sensations he had not experienced before. He needed to control his emotions, he told himself. It was imperative that he stayed positive and in the moment. He was a time-traveller who had seen many things – remarkable things – and he would not allow himself to be put off for no good reason.

'Close the door, for God's sake!' Hiram called out. 'It's freezing out there!'

Wilson eased the door shut.

'All I want is a cup of tea.' Hiram sat down on his saddle on the floor and began winding a heavy canvas strap around his ankle. He would eventually wrap the material around his calf at least a dozen times then secure the end just under his knee with a binding elastic. The straps were excellent for keeping rain and mud out of his boots and also provided some protection from snakebite. 'If you make me a cup of tea, then I promise to ride all day without complaining.'

Wilson glanced at the pile of kindling left over from the night before and the stack of dry wood. 'Promise me you'll eat something?'

Hiram began strapping his other leg. 'I promise.'

Wilson dropped to one knee, drew his knife and unscrewed the flint rod from the handle. He stacked fresh kindling on the dead embers of the makeshift fireplace. 'The thin air is taxing on your body – it's very important to refuel.' After just one strike of the flint rod with the back of his hunting knife, the kindling burst into flames. Within minutes of coaxing, the fire was burning strongly and shortly after that, water was boiling in one canister and baked beans were cooking in another.

'I hope you know where you're going,' Hiram eventually said as he sipped at his hot tea. 'I have shown remarkable confidence in you, don't you think? Letting you drag me all the way out here into the middle of nowhere. It's not like you've done anything to *prove* that you know where you're going. I'm too trusting, that's my problem. My mother always warned me about my trusting nature. She said it would be a problem for me later in life.'

'I know where I'm going,' Wilson said.

'She was a hard woman, my mother.' Hiram picked at his beans with his fork. 'Anyway, I still don't understand why we have to leave so early. If we wait a few more hours then it will be much warmer. It gets quite pleasant up here when the sun is high in the sky.' He took another small mouthful. 'If, as you suggest, Vilcapampa has been hidden for four hundred years, then I really don't think a few more hours is going to make any difference, do you?'

Wilson folded away Hiram's blanket and stacked the backpacks next to the door. 'It takes at least two full days, maybe three, to get from here to Vilcapampa – especially with those uncooperative donkeys of yours. The last thing I want is for it to take an extra day because we are not leaving early enough.'

'That makes sense,' Hiram admitted, eating one baked bean at a time. 'You should have said that before. You know, it's funny.' He pushed aside his half-eaten plate of beans and began rolling a cigarette. 'I don't like waking up early in the morning, but when I do I'm glad that I have.' He licked the cigarette paper then expertly sealed it closed. 'It makes for a much more productive life, I think.'

Wilson scraped the last of Hiram's beans into the fire then gathered the old food tins and tossed them in also. 'Have you got everything?' he asked, looking about.

Hiram did up his red tie into the semblance of a knot then donned his hat. 'That's everything.' He grabbed his rifle and tucked it under his arm. 'How do I look?'

Wilson didn't even glance in his direction. 'You look fantastic.'

Hiram dragged his saddle along behind him and swung the wooden door open. With an unlit cigarette between his teeth, he asked, 'Where are the donkeys?'

'What do you mean, where are the donkeys?' Wilson rushed to the doorway beside him and looked out into the thick fog.

The four animals were gone.

A thousand thoughts flashed through Wilson's mind in that instant. He had checked the ropes just thirty minutes earlier and he knew it would be difficult for the animals to pull free from the knot without the door opening.

'Is this some kind of joke?' Hiram asked.

Wilson cautiously stepped out into the fog and scanned the wet ground. Misty rain continued to fall, which was good and bad – the fog would eventually thin out, but the rain-soaked earth could potentially mask any tracks that had been left behind. Luckily, it took only a moment to find the clear trail leading away into the haze.

'You wait here,' Wilson said under his breath.

'I'm coming with you,' Hiram called back as he nonchalantly slung his rifle over his shoulder. 'They can't have gone far. This has happened before, you know. I warned you, didn't I?'

Wilson pointed to human footprints and Hiram's eyes

widened. 'Stay here and protect our things,' he whispered.

'In case you haven't noticed, I'm the one with the gun!' Hiram awkwardly yanked the rifle from his shoulder and held it in front of him. 'It must be some local boys. We can give them a scare –'

The tortured cry of a mortally wounded animal suddenly cut through the chilled air from very close by. Both Wilson and Hiram stared at each other in confusion. Gathering themselves, they cautiously stepped forward across the soggy ground in the direction of the blood-curdling cries.

'One of the donkeys must have been caught in a trap,' Hiram whispered.

Wilson drew out his hunting knife. At the same time, he tightened the strap of his satchel so it was pressed firmly against his body. With each step forward the awful screaming became louder. Wilson's eyes frantically searched the mist in every direction. The screaming was so loud that it was impossible to hear anything else.

Ahead of them a large, curved image began to take shape. It was ominous in size – easily taller than a man and at least twice as wide. Both men slowed their approach, trying desperately to make out what the dark figure before them could possibly be.

'Should I shoot it?' Hiram asked, raising his gun to his shoulder.

Wilson shook his head, at the same time held his index finger to his lips. All around them the mist hung suspended in the frigid air. Wilson took another cautious step forward and realised that the image they had been approaching was an enormous granite boulder shaped like a hippo. The screaming was coming from just on the other side. He ran towards the stone and pressed his back against the surface.

From here, Wilson could just make out Hiram's silhouette.

With his back against the cold stone, Wilson worked his way around, inch by inch.

Then he saw blood.

The bright red liquid was pooling into the muddy water at his feet.

Using all his might, Wilson flung himself skyward, clearing the giant stone in a single leap. It was an incredible display of strength and dexterity. In midair, he took in the full view of the screaming donkey lying helplessly in the muddy grass, the tendons on all four of its legs having been viciously severed. Landing on the other side, Wilson drove his knife into the back of the female donkey's head and hammered the blade upwards to sever the animal's spinal cord. For the first time in over a minute, there was a deathly silence.

In every direction, all Wilson could see was white mist.

Blood had pooled into the human footprints that surrounded the animal – judging by the tracks there had to be at least three people, and they weren't wearing any shoes. The footprints were large, probably male, and whoever made them was trying to inflict the greatest pain possible without killing the donkey immediately.

Wilson carefully extracted his knife from the donkey's head, the serrated blade making a scraping sound as he pulled it from the bone. He flicked the remaining blood off the blade with his thumb and index finger. Heavy footsteps approached and Wilson knew it was Hiram because of the distinctive squelch his boots made in the mud.

'Don't shoot!' Wilson called out.

Hiram appeared from around the edge of the stone, his face pale. 'Did you just jump over this boulder?' He looked up at the wall of stone eight feet high, trying to rationalise what he had just seen. 'You jumped over it?'

Wilson pointed the blade of his knife at the carcass. 'Look.' Deep lacerations had sliced through the upper legs of the donkey, it's wiry tendons coiling out of the open wounds.

'Jenny is dead?' Hiram looked as if he was going to be sick. He slumped to his knees next to the body, his gun still pressed to his shoulder. 'Why would anyone do this?'

'The tracks lead that way.' Wilson pointed.

Hiram steeled himself then aimed his gun in the same direction. 'Should we go after them?'

The shrill cries of a second donkey suddenly filled the

air directly ahead. Hiram rose abruptly to his feet. Just hearing the anguish of yet another animal was almost more than he could take. 'What the hell is happening?'

Wilson grabbed Hiram's sleeve and yanked him in the opposite direction.

With tears in his eyes, Hiram listened to the awful screams behind him. 'We have to put that animal out of its misery!' he said, looking back over his shoulder. 'It sounds like Diablo!'

Wilson continued to drag Hiram away. 'That's exactly what they want us to do.'

'You never liked my donkeys! That is clear, but we can't let his happen!' Hiram tried to pull away, but Wilson didn't release his grip.

'We're not heading back to the railway shack either,' Wilson stated. 'There are cliffs in this direction, over the railway line. I saw the cliffs last night. It will be more difficult to track us on rocky ground.'

The cries of the wounded donkey lessened as they moved further away.

'What about our supplies?' Hiram asked.

'There's no time.'

'But my whiskey is back there!'

'You're going to have to do without it.'

'We need our supplies!'

Wilson wrenched Hiram closer. 'Do you hear that sound? That is the sound of *death*. That's what's waiting for you if you go back for your whiskey.'

Hiram listened to the screaming for a moment then shook his head. 'You're right. We should head back to Cuzco.'

Wilson stepped over the narrow-gauge railway line. 'We're not heading there either. We continue on towards Vilcapampa.'

Hiram pulled to a stop. 'My donkeys have been murdered! We should report this to the authorities; to the military; to someone!'

'I've been through these mountains before,' Wilson said as he scaled an incline of loose shale. 'We can live off the land until we get there.'

Out of the mist, a towering granite wall appeared. The accumulated rain was running down the jagged surface, betraying the brilliant rich colours of red, pink and crimson trapped within the stone. Wilson held his open mouth under a trickling stream of water and took the opportunity to wash the terrible taste of death out of his throat.

'How did you jump over that boulder?' Hiram asked again. 'It was like you flew straight up into the air. It was an impossible leap.'

'The mist must have affected your view,' Wilson replied.

'I'm not a fool,' Hiram countered. 'I saw what you did.'

'There are more important things to worry about right now. Like, why anyone would want to kill your donkeys that way?'

'I have never heard or seen anything so horrible and upsetting,' Hiram admitted. 'Poor Jenny. Poor little Diablo. They deserved better than that.'

'Whoever it is, they clearly wanted to turn us away from Vilcapampa,' Wilson reasoned.

'Who even knows we're here? Hiram asked.

'The screams were probably masking the sound of their footsteps. Someone wants to stop us from entering the Sacred Valley of the Incas.'

'Sacred Valley?'

'The most direct path to Vilcapampa is via *this* route. It's a holy Inca valley that is said to be protected by ancient warriors that are half man, half ghost – or something like that. This entire area is not listed on the Raimondi map.'

'You're leading me into a lost valley guarded by ghosts?'

'There are many legends about this place,' Wilson said as he moved quickly across the loose rock. 'Quechua spirits are said to protect the trail leading to the Inca capital. Thirty-five years after the conquistadors first came to Peru there was a huge battle, right where we are now, and the Spanish were driven back by a force of men they claimed were invisible.'

'Invisible warriors?'

'I know this much, whoever maimed those donkeys was

barefooted so it has to be local Indians at the very least. And judging by the size of the tracks they are very tall, which is unusual for these parts.'

'What am I doing here?' Hiram muttered.

'It could be worse,' Wilson added. 'Whoever maimed your donkeys could just have easily have killed us while we were sleeping. If they can steal those donkeys away from our very doorstep, then we are very lucky to be alive is my guess.'

13

Andes Ranges, Peru
30 Miles North-west of Cuzco
Local Time 9:45 am

17 January 1908

WITH A FRUSTRATED growl, Captain Gonzales kicked his boot into one of the leather backpacks and sent it flying across the railway shack. 'Where are they?' he yelled.

Outside in the rain, his men continued searching the open fields in pairs, concentrating their efforts on the numerous large boulders that could easily conceal a dead carcass. They found two donkeys; one of them was still alive when they arrived, its weak breath wheezing in and out as its life force painfully faded away. The animals had their legs brutally slashed open in the same appalling way and left to die, wallowing in their own gore.

Captain Gonzales stood in the doorway of the shack and scanned the railway line that ran off into the mountains. His eyes lifted to the huge, red granite cliff towering above them at least 200 feet into the low-hanging clouds. He turned once again and studied the crude fireplace that had been constructed on a bed of stones in the middle of the wooden floor. From the heat of the remaining embers, he reckoned that the fire had been out for at least an hour.

Lieutenant Capos approached through the rain with one of the local mountain guides, a dark-skinned fellow called Ompeta. Unlike the soldiers the little guide wore traditional Indian clothing with a large, wide-brimmed hat and a black alpaca poncho that seemed to repel the rain-water well enough.

'There are tracks going in almost every direction,' Lieutenant Capos announced. His dark-blue officer's uniform was soaked through and he was covered in mud to his knees. From the hue of his skin and the bags under his eyes it was obvious he was very tired. 'We count the footsteps of at least twenty men running in all directions.' He turned to Ompeta. 'Tell the capitán.'

The Indian guide stood there in the rain, his tanned face wrinkled by years of exposure to the harsh weather, but even so his eyes were bright and he looked relatively fresh. The mountain guides were remarkably fit men and they could travel for days at the highest altitude without food or rest.

'We found two donkeys, Capitán,' Ompeta said with a deep voice. 'One of them *there* and the other *there*.' He pointed southward. 'Another donkey was led away towards the forest to the east.' He pointed again.

'Explain to me why this has happened,' Gonzales said impatiently.

'Local Indians have killed the white men's donkeys,' Ompeta replied. 'As to why, I cannot be sure. I have not seen such strange events as these before.'

'Why would they kill the donkeys?' Gonzales demanded.

Ompeta shrugged his shoulders. 'I have no idea. The white men's footsteps ran off in that direction, towards the red walls of stone. The Indians are chasing after them. I count about ten who went that way; maybe eight others went in that direction. All of them are heading lower into the valley, in the direction of the *Great Speaker*.' To the local Indians, most large rivers were known as the Great Speaker due to the deafening roar the rapids made during the wet season.

Gonzales rubbed his unshaven chin. 'The white men are heading into the mountains without any supplies?'

'Without beasts of burden to carry their goods, they must have decided it was best to go with nothing,' Ompeta said. 'Either that, or it was fear that drove them away.'

'They must have been afraid,' Capos said.

'Judging by their deepened footsteps,' Ompeta continued, 'they were running away at a very fast pace. The fog would have been heavy here before the sun climbed into the morning sky. They would not have been able to see but for a few feet in each direction. I cannot imagine what they must have been thinking when they were listening to their donkeys' terrible cries.'

Gonzales adjusted the leather strap of the rifle hanging from his shoulder. 'Which tribe is it that killed the donkeys?'

Ompeta shrugged his shoulders again. 'Possibly Campa tribe, but that is just a guess. Judging by the tracks, the donkey-killers are strong and fleet of foot. They are able to move across the muddy ground with footsteps that span as much as the length of a man. They are certainly tribal warriors, but in all my years I have never heard of such a gruesome attack as this.'

'You must know something!' Gonzales demanded. 'You Indians have a story for everything! Tell me what you know.'

Ompeta stood quietly for a moment. 'I cannot be sure, Capitán.' He stared into the rain for quite a while then eventually spoke. 'This place is holy ground to the local Indians.' He pointed into the valley.

Gonzales huffed. 'What is so special down there?'

'It is holy Inca soil, Capitán.'

'So what if it is? It's just another valley that leads into the mountains. Just one of ten thousand others like it in this inhospitable place.'

Ompeta shook his head. 'This valley is different, Capitán. Years ago I went to the village of Huadquina, many miles away in that direction.' He gestured towards the west. 'The wise men there told stories of mysterious warriors who would hunt the gateway to the Sacred Valley like ghosts. It was said that the Spaniards were driven back from the valley below by a force of men they *never saw* in the daylight. Only the footprints of the enemy did they ever find. Spanish soldiers were not safe in that valley, and more than one hundred men over ten terrifying nights had their throats slashed while they slept.'

'Who was hunting them?' Capos asked.

Ompeta shook his head. 'Nobody really knows. But the wise men believe it was the long-dead spirits of the mighty Inca kings. It is said they prowl these valleys with the stealth and cunning of the black puma.'

Gonzales paced towards the tracks crisscrossing the soggy ground. He bent over at the waist to point his finger at the foot-shaped pools of water. 'You suggest that these footsteps come from *ghosts*?' The gentle rain was flickering against the dark, shiny surface. 'This was made by a man, not a ghost!'

Ompeta nodded, but his expression did not alter.

'Can you track them into the valley?' Gonzales snarled.

Ompeta nodded again, his dark eyes clear and focused.

'Gather the troops!' Gonzales ordered. 'The white men can only be a mile or so ahead of us. We must find them quickly so they can be taken back to Cuzco.'

Lieutenant Capos approached his captain. 'The men need rest,' he said carefully. 'They have been travelling all night long and they do not understand why the white men are so important. What is it that they have done to cause us to chase them with such unyielding vigour?'

Gonzales felt his muscles tense. He was out here because Bishop Francisco had ordered him to be. 'The bishop demands it,' he whispered. 'I know precious little more than that. The bishop said the white men would travel here to this railway shack, and they did. As a result, we have no choice but to follow them from here.'

Capos moved closer. 'We have known each other since we were boys. These men, our soldiers, many of them are our friends. It is time for you to show understanding and let them rest. They have travelled all night for you, Capitán, as I have. I strongly advise that we make a fire and prepare some food.'

'We should have been here before dawn!' Gonzales bleated. 'If we had, then the foreigners would already be in our custody and we would be heading home now!'

'Driving the men to exhaustion will not help the situation,' Capos replied. 'The bishop will understand that, surely. Our soldiers need food and they need rest.'

'The bishop will *not* understand,' Gonzales said worriedly. 'He expects results and that is what we must deliver.'

'I agree with the lieutenant,' Ompeta interrupted. 'We are not the only ones tracking the two white men. The footsteps of the animal-killers – some sixteen men, as best I can tell – also head towards the Urubamba and the calling of the Great Speaker. They have fled into the forest, but they are certainly heading in that direction. If we encounter these dark warriors, we may have to fight for our own lives. The legend of this valley states that no man, except for those of pure Indian blood, may enter without fear of death.'

'Are you suggesting we should leave because we are not of pure blood?' Gonzales questioned. 'Because we are *mestizo*?'

Ompeta opened his palms as if in surrender. 'I am employed by the army, Capitán. My interests here are for the safety of you and your men – nothing more. You may take my advice or you may ignore it, but these are strange events and we should be cautious. The white men cannot go far, especially without supplies.'

Captain Gonzales lifted his rifle from his shoulder and for a moment considered pointing the weapon in Ompeta's direction. He knew that the pure Indians looked down on half-casts like himself. But deep inside he knew that the old man was absolutely right. Gonzales fought his instinct to react, leant the barrel of his rifle against the outer wall of the railway shack and gestured inside. 'Make a fire and feed the men.' He pointed at the two open backpacks on the floor. 'Give every soldier two shots of whiskey for their efforts – that will lift their spirits.'

Lieutenant Capos saluted. 'I will see to it immediately, Capitán.'

14

THE ORIENT-EXPRESS locomotive was trundling slowly forward, descending through the forests and high granite cliffs towards the Urubamba River. In the dining car, the sparkling silver cutlery shifted ever so slightly on the white tablecloth as the tracks curved around another bend. It was still raining heavily, which reduced visibility to less than a few dozen yards. The beads of condensation forming on the inside of the train's windows were slowly dripping down the glass.

Helena held a dry towel around her shoulders as she drank her second cup of coca tea. When she and Chad reboarded the train there was much interest from the staff and fellow passengers. Their excursion into the torrential rain had given them the opportunity to ask questions, which was the last thing Helena wanted. After the visions of Wilson inside the railway shack, she just wanted to sit quietly and contemplate what had happened and why. To deter anyone from talking to her, Helena put on her head-phones, but she wasn't listening to any music.

Chad returned from the bathroom wearing sweatpants and a hiking jacket. She had been soaked to the skin by the rain. With her spiky hair still damp, Chad sat down just as Pablo was about to bite into a chocolate eclair.

'You shouldn't be eating that,' Chad said.

Pablo looked at the eclair, then back at her. 'Why is that?'

Helena couldn't help but overhear.

Chad pointed at the chocolate treat. 'When you look at that eclair you see *pleasure*. When I look at that eclair I see *pain*.' Chad nodded. 'It's about three hundred calories – mainly sugar, no nutritional value. You need to vigorously exercise for thirty minutes to work that off.' Unzipping her backpack, she pulled out a large tin of tuna in spring water. 'This is protein.' Chad cracked open the lid and the smell of tuna wafted into the air. 'If things taste good, they are generally bad for you – you should remember that.'

Lifting the eclair to his lips, Pablo took a big bite. 'I like to eat eclairs,' he said, his mouth half full. 'They are my favourites.'

It had been good to see Wilson's face again, Helena thought. She couldn't help but smile at the vision of him sitting there in front of the raging fire in his underpants, his wet clothes hanging from the rafters. What an interesting sight that was. The whole episode had lasted for approximately twenty seconds, that was Helena's best guess. The conversation Wilson was having with the skinny man had seemed passionate, judging by his expressions and the hand gestures. Unfortunately, she couldn't hear what they were saying. Helena had definitely seen the skinny man somewhere before and it was just a matter of time before she remembered where.

According to Pablo, the railway line was built in the early 1900s. In her vision, the shack had been brand-new. Judging by Wilson's clothes, the food tins, the rolled cigarettes and the Springfield rifle, Helena concluded it was quite some time ago. Wilson had certainly time travelled into the past. From the look of him, Helena could somehow tell that he had seen and experienced many things since they had last been together. It was strangely obvious to her that he had suffered, but she could not be certain of anything beyond that.

I wonder if he misses me in the same way that I miss him, she thought.

Helena nodded to herself. Her decision to come to Peru was justified now. Most people would have questioned their sanity after seeing the visions that had flooded her mind in the railway shack, but Helena felt no such doubt. She knew that Wilson was no ordinary man, and her connection to him was a destiny of sorts.

Wilson had said on many occasions that all time existed simultaneously. He used the term 'holographic universe' to explain it. 'At the forming of the cosmos, a millisecond after the Big Bang, when all things were created, a spider web of very powerful tubes of energy called *cosmic strands* were blasted across the universe. It is their energy that is the nucleus of all dimension. The cosmic strands allow the fourth dimension of time to exist, and they also allow time travel to be possible.'

There was a bond between Helena and Wilson that was difficult to comprehend. Thankfully, Helena's and Wilson's worlds had intertwined yet again – albeit across an obvious barrier of time. She was connected with him and there had to be a reason. If she could just put all the pieces of information together then she might begin to understand why she was here and what her role was. It certainly had to do with Machu Picchu and the Temple of the Sun. Helena again considered the dream that had led her to Peru in the first place. She was looking into a dark cave under the distinctive tower, into the unusual triangular entrance. The bright sunlight was shining in her eyes, making it almost impossible to see. She squinted just thinking about it.

He's going to Machu Picchu. Helena was sure of it.

Reaching into her bag, she grabbed her iPad, slid her finger across the screen and tapped in her passcode. The device came to life in rich colour as a picture of Stonehenge appeared with the winter sun in the background – shafts of light carved their way through the upright stones. Helena didn't give the image a thought as she pressed the library icon. She had purchased a book called *The Lost City of the Incas*, about the discovery of Machu Picchu.

When the front cover flashed onto the screen, Helena sucked in a hurried breath. There was a picture of the man Wilson was travelling with! It was *Hiram Bingham*, the explorer who had famously discovered Machu Picchu!

Helena began laughing to herself. 'I can't believe it!'

Her gaze lifted to the ceiling in wonder.

Hiram Bingham had been searching the Andes in the early 1900s, so that placed Helena's vision at about a century ago. The discovery of Machu Picchu was one of the greatest archaeological finds of the early twentieth century. Staring at Hiram Bingham's image on the screen, Helena felt a profound sense of discovery knowing that Wilson had been with him.

A finger suddenly appeared from Helena's peripheral view. 'That is a picture of Hiram Bingham,' a voice announced in a smooth, educated accent. 'They even named this train after him.'

Helena glanced up to see an imposing-looking man standing next to her table. He was in his mid fifties, obviously wealthy judging by the cut of his suit, his manicured fingernails, as well as the ample girth of his waistline. His greying hair was slicked back with gel and his teeth were straight and white. His black suit had a faint cream pinstripe. The matching cream tie was a nice touch. Helena had spotted him earlier with the cocaine group at the front of the carriage. He was certainly the most important of them because when he spoke the group around him seemed to hang on his every word.

Helena pointed to her headphones as if she couldn't hear over the music.

'Hiram Bingham was the first *white man* to discover Machu Picchu,' the gentleman continued as if he knew she could hear him. 'But it is more complicated than that –'

Chad stood from her chair to usher the gentleman away, but he calmly gestured for her to back up so that he could finish what he was saying. 'You will find that *other* men discovered Machu Picchu before him. Because they were *mestizo* they were given no credit. Spaniards and Indians are men also, do you not agree?'

Helena forced a polite smile.

'My name is Don Eravisto, señorita. I am here with my business partners.' He looked to the front of the train and snapped his fingers. The drinking and laughter stopped immediately. 'I fear we have made too much noise and this has disturbed you. I would like to make amends.'

'There is no need,' Chad interrupted. 'Now, if you would excuse us.'

Don Eravisto stared in Helena's direction. 'Your body-guard is very polite, but she is too obvious. If you look to my group, you could not easily tell which of them is there to protect me. It could be the men or one of their girl-friends.'

'They look more like their daughters,' Chad replied.

Don Eravisto smiled and clapped his hands, pretend-ing to be amused. 'Enough small talk.' He looked again into Helena's eyes, his expression serious. 'I noticed that you visited that railway shack back there. Did you know that Hiram Bingham once spent a rainy night inside that building?'

Helena did her best not to look surprised.

'I could tell you stories about his journey that you will not find in that book. That rundown old building has an interesting history.'

Helena slowly removed her headphones. 'You have my attention, señor.'

Don Eravisto placed his hand on the tablecloth. 'May I take a seat?'

'Please sit,' Helena eventually replied. Her instinct told her to be on alert, but she was more curious than worried. The railway shack was certainly important and maybe this man, Don Eravisto, could tell her why.

Chad reluctantly stepped out of the way, her gaze scru-tinising the passengers at the front of the train who were equally focused on her in return.

'The history of that building is very dark,' Don Eravisto said as he undid the button of his jacket and slid his heavy frame across the chair. 'We have much to discuss.' With a snap of his fingers a waiter ran down the centre aisle as if his life depended on it. 'I will have a gin and tonic,' Don Eravisto said. 'And some cashews.' He looked across at Helena. 'Yes of course . . . you will need another coca tea. Do not worry, señorita, your headache will soon be gone. We are finally descending into the Sacred Valley as we speak. As the altitude lessens, so too will the throbbing in your temples.'

15

Andes Ranges, Peru
40 Miles North-west of Cuzco
Local Time 3:02 pm

17 January 1908

WITH A GROAN, Hiram slipped over yet again. Wilson was forced to double back to help him along. This time the American just lay there in the mud and the tall greenery, between two giant rocks, waiting for Wilson to pull him to his feet.

'We should head back to Cuzco,' Hiram repeated as Wilson dragged him up. 'There's no point continuing into this kind of weather with no support and no food or supplies!'

For the first hour, Wilson and Hiram had followed the railway tracks between the high granite cliffs and down into the heavily wooded tributary of the Urubamba Valley. The misty rain had not let up for the entire journey. Wilson had decided they should walk along the railway lintels because the footing was secure and there was little chance of leaving behind a trail that would be too easy to follow. It had taken a full hour to get below the cloud line and visibility was now reasonable, but it was still impossible to see the glacier-capped mountains that surely towered above them on all sides.

As they descended lower into the valley and the altitude decreased, Wilson felt distinctly better and his breathing became easier. The railway line had stopped on a steep section of track about a mile back. He guessed that there was no work being done during the rainy season because it would be too difficult to excavate the drop-offs and steep gorges. The workers would probably not be back until at least April when the rains began to abate and the river levels dropped once again.

'Take off your boot,' Wilson said and pointed to Hiram's right foot.

'I will not take off my boot!' Hiram replied.

Wilson drew out his hunting knife and pointed at Hiram's foot with the tip of the shiny blade. 'Those shoes are not suited for climbing across wet rocks and mud. Give them to me.'

'We should head back to Cuzco,' Hiram said yet again. 'I know a great little place where we can get local beer – a Peruvian version of it, anyway – and we can have a hearty vegetable soup that will fill your stomach.'

Wilson could hear the distant roar of the river to the north-west – a cacophony of sound that clamoured up the valley towards them. 'Can you hear that?' Wilson asked, putting a hand to his ear.

'It's a river,' Hiram replied. 'A big one, by the sound of it.'

'Once we get to that river the trail becomes much easier. Pass me your boot. I'll cut some grooves in the sole that will make your footing more secure.'

'How much better will the trail become?' Hiram asked.

'There is an excellent track ahead.' The rain began falling more heavily and visibility once again faded into the grey. Wilson wondered how he was ever going to get Hiram to Vilcapampa through the thick jungle and up the steep cliffs ahead. The trail didn't get any easier at all; it got more difficult.

Hiram sat on the edge of a granite boulder that had obviously fallen from the high cliffs above them and tumbled down through the forest. As he undid his laces he mumbled, 'This is the worst trip I have ever taken, do you know that?'

Hiram sniffed the inside of his boot then tossed it in Wilson's direction. 'It doesn't smell that bad . . . I'm surprised.' He pulled out his tobacco satchel from under his jacket. Gazing up at the steep jungle on both sides, he skilfully set about rolling a cigarette with his wet hands under the cover of his wide brim hat. 'Sacred Valley you say? This valley doesn't seem that special to me.'

Wilson used the sharp blade of his knife to cut into the sole of Hiram's boot, taking care not to puncture the leather. 'The local Indians around here are supposedly from the Campa tribe. They are said to be extremely savage.'

'That's a piece of information I could have used *before* my donkeys were killed.' With a disgusted looked, Hiram gazed back over his shoulder and up the rugged trail that stepped its way into the distance until it eventually disappeared into the cloud layer. 'Poor little Diablo.'

'We never should've stayed for breakfast,' Wilson said. 'We waited too long.'

'You should have told me it was so dangerous!' Hiram blurted.

Wilson had already cut three serrated grooves into the sole of Hiram's boot and he began working on the heel. 'I had no idea the Indians would maim your donkeys the way they did. They wanted to create the maximum pain and fear possible.'

Hiram licked then sealed his cigarette shut. 'They've upset me! That's what they've done! Are there any other surprises I should know about?'

'We must go forward, Hiram.'

'I vote we head back to Cuzco. We get more men with guns, come back here and teach those devil Campas a lesson they'll never forget.' Hiram then rubbed his stomach. 'And think of the warm soup . . . and the beer.'

'You will be the man who discovers the lost city of Vilcapampa – surely, that must mean something to you.'

Hiram struck a match under the brim of his hat. 'At this moment, I'm more concerned with the prospect of getting impaled with a spear than I am of being famous.' He flicked the match away then exhaled a long stream of smoke.

Wilson pointed. 'We are going forward whether you like it or not. Ahead of us is a world of uncompromising beauty. The mighty Urubamba River cuts through the steep valley with incredible force at this time of year. It's actually one of the tributaries of the Amazon. The water that runs by us will eventually travel more than 1500 miles and empty out into the Atlantic Ocean.'

Hiram gazed at Wilson with a quizzical expression. 'How do you know that?'

Wilson began cutting the final groove in Hiram's right boot. 'I've told you, I know a great many things about this region. And if you had more faith, you'd realise there's more to be gained from coming along than there is in trying to halt our progress with your negative attitude.'

With his cigarette hanging from his lips, Hiram replied, 'I fail to see how I'm being negative. Logical, I call it. Vilcapampa isn't going anywhere. It's been lost for hundreds of years! I say we go back to Cuzco and return better prepared.'

Wilson tossed the boot, but Hiram didn't see it coming and it flew past him and bounced down between the rocks.

'Oh, that's just perfect!' Standing on one foot, Hiram leant awkwardly over the boulder and attempted to extract his boot from between the rocks. 'First, my donkeys are killed and now I've lost my boot. And it's still bloody raining!'

'Give me your other boot,' Wilson said.

Hiram's head was down between the rocks. 'Just a second.'

Wilson noticed a large tree stump that had fallen from the forest above. The stump had splintered open and he could see larva tracks. He jumped across some heaped rocks and began splitting the rotten wood with the blade of his knife. In just seconds, he found some beetle larva, which looked like white, hairless caterpillars. They were easily the largest grubs he had ever seen. 'Do you want something to eat?' he asked as he held up a fat, wiggling grub on the blade of his knife.

Hiram looked up. 'There is no way in hell!'

Wilson dropped the twisting grub into his mouth and

bit down. The larva exploded between his teeth unpleasantly.

'They're poisonous, aren't they?'

'Only the colourful ones,' Wilson replied. 'Or the ones with hair on them.'

Hiram looked perplexed. 'That's so disgusting!'

Wilson put another grub into his mouth. 'In my experience, you should eat when you get the chance. You never know what can happen in the jungle and you have to take your opportunities when they come to you.'

'I will not eat grubs!'

The distinctive strike of rock against rock echoed from the forest-lined cliffs above. Instinctively, Wilson looked up into the shroud of mist suspended between the greenery. It was amazing how precisely he was able to identify the falling rock's location. The boulder came shooting out of the thicket and arced its way to the valley floor. The rock struck a larger boulder at the base of the valley with a resounding crack, splitting it in half, each piece ricocheting in different directions.

Wilson set about extracting another writhing grub with the point of his knife. Multiple stones suddenly began ripping through the forest above and shooting out of the greenery. Looking up again, Wilson saw a flash of skin – he was sure of it – tanned and glistening, moving quickly across an upper terrace. Then he saw another flash of skin only a few feet behind, barely visible through the thicket of trees and ferns.

Standing on one leg, Hiram held out his left boot.

'We have to get moving!' Wilson said urgently. 'Put your boot on!'

'What about the sole?'

Wilson turned his back on the forest. 'I saw people up there. Put your boot on.'

Hiram glanced upwards.

'Don't look up there, Hiram! There are natives moving along the ridgeline . . . I don't want them to know we've seen them.'

'You saw natives?' Hiram reached for his rifle.

'Put your boot on!' Wilson said under his breath.

Hiram dropped to one knee and began frantically tying his lace.

Wilson had no way of knowing what he had seen, but whoever they were, they were moving quickly, considering the terrain. It was logical to assume they were the natives responsible for killing Hiram's donkeys. It was impossible to tell from his fleeting glimpse if they were Campa tribe, but judging by their speed and exposed skin, Wilson knew they were athletes of great ability.

'We have to get to the river before they do,' Wilson said. 'We are going to have to move quickly – can you do that?'

Hiram crouched down as if he was expecting spears to fly out of the dense jungle at any moment. 'Are you sure we shouldn't make a stand here?'

'Definitely not . . . they have the high ground. If ten warriors come at us, one bolt-action Springfield won't be able to stop them.' Wilson pointed in the direction of the river then ran.

'I hope you know what you're doing!' Hiram called out.

'If you value your life, you'll save your breath.' Wilson leapt between two rocks and across a small drop-off filled with thick bushes. He was conscious of selecting a path that Hiram could follow without too much difficulty.

'I've never been much good at running,' Hiram puffed. 'I'm more of a sprinter.'

Wilson maintained a steady pace and despite the odd groan from behind him he was pleased that Hiram was keeping up. The terrain was rough going and Wilson had to make sure he didn't accidentally pick a trail that led to a dead-end. Every now and again he glanced up to the valley walls sensing that they were being watched, but he didn't see anything among the thick forest. All he saw was a mishmash of bamboo thickets interspersed with lush green leaves of every size and colour.

With each step, the clamour of the Urubamba River became more ominous.

It seemed curious that the natives were tracking them from the ridgeline – surely it would have been easier to follow them directly into the valley. First, the natives had stolen their donkeys then killed them, and now they were hunting them from along some very difficult terrain.

Hiram was lagging behind and Wilson urged him forward. 'It's not far now, Hiram.' At any moment, Wilson was hoping that the river would appear through the greenery.

16

Andes Ranges, Peru
40 Miles North-west of Cuzco
Local Time 3:25 pm

17 January 1908

IT FELT GOOD to run with purpose – to feel the humid air coursing in and out of her lungs. Aclla's muscles were burning as she moved quickly through the dense forest, her chest heaving as she drew in each breath. She felt the pain of her extraordinary exertion, but she liked it – she liked it very much. Up ahead, a layer of mist was suspended in the humid air between the trees and hanging vines, only to be obliterated by the Quechua warrior running in front. The raindrops felt cool against Aclla's skin as she leapt effort-lessly over a fallen tree, landed softly on the rocks without breaking stride and continued to follow directly behind her virgin pair.

Just off to their right, every now and again, Aclla caught a glimpse of the valley below. Soon they would come upon the two white men they were tracking. They had slipped away towards the river while Aclla and her warriors were attempting to lure them towards the southern forests by torturing their donkeys, but the white men did not take the bait. By the time Aclla realised the cowards had fled, it was too late to give chase because Captain Gonzales and his troops had happened onto the open plain just as the fog was lifting. Aclla could not take the chance they would be seen, so they were forced to settle back into the shadows of the forest.

If Aclla had her way, she would have fought the soldiers where they stood. But if just one man escaped, the secret existence of the Virgins of the Sun would be lost forever and that was not a risk worth taking.

'We are like spirits in the night,' were the wise words of Mamacona Kay Pacha, the female priestess who had taught Aclla since before she could remember. The Virgins of the Sun did not take chances; they acted only when they could be certain of the result. There was too much at stake for it to be any other way. And so it had been for nearly 500 years, and surely would be for 500 more.

By the time Aclla and her warriors went the long way around, much time had been lost. The sun had reached its highest point in the rainy sky before her scouts once again picked up the white men's trail. At first they had followed the railway line towards the river, then their tracks entered the Sacred Valley, which had been Aclla's fear all along. Her decision should have been to kill the white men while they were sleeping, but she had ordered against it. Protecting the valley from intruders was Aclla's prime responsibility, just as it had been for her ancestors for so many lifetimes before. The Sun Virgins had driven back the powerful forces of Viceroy Toledo with brutal stealth and cunning – the teachings she had received dictated that there was no place for compassion. Aclla's sister, Vivane, had foolishly surrendered to her womanly desires and her fate had been sealed. Aclla would not hesitate again – her actions would be decisive and brutal from this point forward.

All that mattered now was to stop the white men before they could reach the rushing waters of the Great Speaker. If they had the knowledge to find and enter the Sacred Valley – a valley that did not exist on any man-made map – then they might know of the mighty suspension bridge that crossed the steep gorge at the river's highest point. All the while, they were leading Captain Gonzales towards the hallowed lands of Vilcapampa – as to why he was pursuing them also, she could not be sure.

Aclla followed behind Sontane – her virgin pair since birth – mimicking her every step and movement. They travelled in perfect synchronicity through the rise and fall of the forest that clung to the steep walls of the valley. The faith Aclla had in Sontane could not be questioned – she was a warrior of incredible skill and grace. Following her meant that Aclla could think about strategy and other things while Sontane made the decisions about how to best traverse the slippery jungle. Both women had trained together since they could first walk, having been matched as a virgin pair because of their perfect genetic compatibility. Their fathers were chosen so as to ensure identical stature, strength and coordination – their cunning, wisdom and hardness of character were attributes that were trained. Aclla and her warriors were the protectors of the Sacred Valley and it was their job to halt the encroachment of civilisation for as long as possible; the railroads and the telegraph, and the explorers that each year attempted to penetrate these precious Inca lands.

All the Virgins of the Sun were in perfect pairs. Just behind them was Polix and Sepla – she could hear their footsteps. At the very front, leading the way, was Orelle and Ilna. Every now and again their plaited ponytails came into view as they moved quickly through the forest twenty steps ahead. They all wore the fitted bronze breastplate of Inti, the Sun God, and a short bow and a leather quiver hung from their naked backs. On their right thigh was strapped a razor-sharp sword in a puma skin sheath. Fourteen warriors in all were scything along the valley wall – each of them highly trained, sacred defenders of the Incas; the finest warriors the world had ever known; guardians of the ancient city of Vilcapampa and her treasures; protectors of the Inca Cube.

Sontane took a quick stride and leapt high, arching her back to gain extra distance, and landed on the other side of a rocky outcrop. She then took a giant step, grabbed an overhanging tree limb and swung over a shear drop-off. Aclla followed without hesitation, her faith in her virgin pair absolute.

As she ran, Aclla recalled the sight of the tall white man with the sparkling blue eyes. They would surely be upon him and his skinny travelling companion at any moment. She was curious to see the blue-eye again so that she could study him, albeit from a distance. He intrigued her in a way she had not encountered before. She was desperate to understand why she had not ordered his death during the night. It was not simply that he was a foreigner – she had seen many of them in her lifetime. On at least thirty occasions she had made the trip to Cuzco and Olleyantambo to be among the 'civilised' world, as they liked to call themselves. Entering the cities was part of her training, the need to understand their rapidly developing enemy. But in all her travels she had never seen a man like the blue-eyed stranger – the way he had appeared before her, striding purposefully across the Plaza de Armas through the rain, the cut of his clothes, the way his hat sat on his head, the determined look on his face. There was something about him that was different – a knowing in his gaze that Aclla had only seen in the wisest of the Virgin Priestesses.

Up ahead, Orelle made a single click with her tongue and all the Virgin Warriors knew exactly what it signified – they were passing alongside the two white men. It was not a moment too soon. The valley was deep below them and the thick foliage camouflaged them perfectly – they could pass by high above and continue along the difficult path to ensure they arrived at the Great Speaker with time to spare.

As the greenery flashed past, Aclla could see the two impostors below. Her curiosity got the better of her and she glanced in their direction at every opportunity. The blue-eye was holding the skinny man's boot and was cutting grooves in the sole with his knife. Even from this distance, it was obvious that the blue-eye was tall and broad. So many of the prospectors that found their way to the Andes were an insipid and wiry lot, but this man was an exception.

A thicket of long-leaves flashed past and Aclla lost sight of the strangers. Sontane made a difficult jump, spinning full circle in midair to avoid a thicket of bamboo that would be impossible to penetrate. Aclla did the same, leaping then twisting her body. They each landed elegantly, one after the other, and burst through a hedge of wet ferns. All around them the angled trees were laden with moss and the forest floor was covered with humus and peat that was soft under foot.

Up ahead, Aclla caught a glimpse of Orelle and Ilna as they moved higher up the valley wall, still travelling as quickly as ever. The foliage was very thick now and the wet leaves flicked against Aclla's bare skin as she followed Sontane's path. It was exhilarating to be challenged with such an important purpose – to be pushed to the limits of time and physical exertion to fulfil their purpose. Everything they had spent their life training for was needed at this very moment.

Legions of men had dreamed of finding the lost city of Vilcapampa, but none had even come close. Those who did were either killed or, more recently, lured away to other places by drugging them with the sap of the Algodon tree. Many an explorer had found themselves ten thousand paces from their original location and had not even realised it. That was the reason no modern maps contained the existence of the snow-capped mountain ranges between the Apurimac and the Urubamba.

When Antonio Raimondi scouted the mountains of Peru in 1875, he was drugged and removed from the valley without his knowledge. His famous map did not show the existence of Vilcapampa or its mountain ranges, creeping glaciers and river tributaries. The cunning of the Virgin Warriors had created this necessary deception. It had been Mamacona Kay Pacha, Aclla's teacher, who had pricked Raimondi with the poison needle and instructed the removal of his entire camp – every tent, bed, table, spoon, cup, book and water bottle.

Now it was Aclla's turn to protect the Sacred Valley from impostors. She had been right to lead her warriors in pursuit of the white men after discovering the word *Vilcapampa* on the note attached to the door of Bingham's headquarters.

Leaving Cuzco without first finding out if her sister was dead or alive had been difficult. Discovering Vivane's fate would have to wait for another day. If she was indeed alive, her sister would understand the need to protect the Sacred Valley before anything else; she would understand the reasons why Aclla had left.

In the distance she could hear the growing voice of the Great Speaker as it roared through the narrow gorge, the waters were at their highest level in many years. It was as if the river was trying to warn her somehow. Another gap appeared in the foliage and Aclla again stole a glimpse in the white men's direction, her gaze lingering as if everything was in slow motion. Sontane took a stutter-step then leapt. Aclla was distracted at the exact moment she should not have been. Her footing was out of step and her weight fell upon an unsteady platform. She knew immediately that she was falling. She grasped at the jagged rock beside her, her weight pulling the stone free as she tried to right her movements. Below her was a drop of some one hundred feet.

This was not the first time that Aclla had lost her rhythm while running through the forest. There was the time when both she and Sontane had happened upon a large female jaguar and her cubs, which forced both warriors to go to ground in a tumble of arms and legs. It was only their incredible speed between the trees – a technique taught to them when they were children – that saved them from certain death. And now this disaster. Aclla strained every muscle to spring away from the wall, grasp a horizontal tree limb, and swing herself skyward to land on a narrow platform of stones that barely jutted out. Behind her, she could hear rocks clattering down into the valley as she tried to find a hold, but it was impossible and she sprang off the nearly vertical wall once again. Up ahead, Sontane realised her partner was in trouble and she turned; their eyes made contact. Aclla flew through the air and slammed into the sheer stone just as Sontane grabbed her by the wrist, suspending her swinging body in midair.

As she hung there more rocks were falling and clattering against the mountainside. Suddenly, Polix and Sepla flew into view, clasping Aclla and holding her securely against the sheer wall, all four of the half-naked warriors skilfully using one arm to grip the other and climb slowly to safety.

Aclla was uninjured, but the damage was done. Through the trees she could just see the blue-eye's discerning gaze looking up in their direction. Aclla could not be sure exactly what he had seen, but she knew for certain that he had been alerted to their presence.

17

ABOVE THE THICKETS of dense greenery, plumes of moisture from the raging rapids wafted upwards against the high cliffs. Through the eerie-looking haze the perfect spherical brilliance of the sun was just visible. Each time Wilson took a deep breath, he could feel the wetness of the air saturating his lungs.

The clamour from the Urubamba was overwhelming. Wilson felt a fluttering in his stomach such was the ferocity. The walls of the Sacred Valley were very steep and jagged on the northern side, but to the south, where he had seen the figures shadowing him, the gradient had fallen away and he concluded it would be relatively simple to descend into the valley if that was their pursuers' aim. Thankfully, the small stream that ran down the middle of the valley had formed into a running tributary twenty feet wide that at least provided another obstacle they would have to traverse.

Hiram had not said a word for the last ten minutes – he was panting far too much to talk. The threat of being shot by spears had motivated him no end but he was beginning to look exhausted, his cheeks as red as a beetroot. As much as Wilson encouraged him to leave his Springfield rifle behind, Hiram had slung his gun over his shoulder and it was bouncing uncomfortably all around the place.

'Tell me it's not much further,' Hiram groaned. 'Please!'

As soon as the words left Hiram's lips the tall greenery seemed to open up and the Urubamba River came into view in all its frightening glory. With no foliage to muffle the sound, the rushing movement of whitewater was deafening. The river was at least a hundred feet across – the raging waters being so wide that they disappeared into the mist on the other side. The angry torrents were hurtling down the valley, the tipping gradient of the land obvious, as if everything was leaning to one side. The river was the roughest Wilson had ever seen, with columns of churning whitewater shooting skyward like giant, crashing surf, interspersed with slow-moving sections where the deep brown waters folded over themselves and disappeared to a great depth. A tree stump flew into view, tossed across the churning rapids, easily moving faster than a man could run. The huge stump, with roots attached, suddenly dropped out of view before being propelled into some underwater impediment. The muffled thump of wood against stone reverberated from the depths, before the splintered remnants of the stump – nothing greater than the width of a man's wrist – blasted out of the white water. Judging by the flow, the riverbed was littered with giant boulders and huge wedges of rock that had fallen into the steep valley over the course of millennia.

'Now what?' Hiram asked. 'We can't cross *that*.'

Wilson pointed. 'Yes, we can.' High above, between the steep walls of the valley, the sagging vines of an ancient Inca suspension bridge were just visible.

Hiram squinted. 'You have to be kidding!'

'It's called the Bridge of the Condor,' Wilson announced. 'It's been here for hundreds of years and it has seen many travellers safely over the river.'

Hiram scoffed. 'Not this traveller, it won't!'

From here it was impossible to see how high the cliffs were because of the mist, but Wilson knew they stretched upwards many hundreds of feet. The Bridge of the Condor was only a hundred feet above the river and it appeared to be dipping badly in the middle, the twisted vines drooping downwards just above the dancing and diving of the whitewater. The fact that the old suspension bridge was still in place was a relief, but Wilson would reserve his final judgement until he could make a more detailed inspection. On the other side of the river was a jungle landscape known as a 'cloud forest' – a sanctuary of incredible diversity that contained more species of life per square mile than any other similar-sized area on the planet.

'We need to get up there,' Wilson said as he continued forward.

'There's no way I'm crossing that bridge!' Hiram protested. Wilson kept moving. 'We are being followed, Hiram. We have no choice.' Wilson studied the steep walls leading up to the Bridge of the Condor. They were framed by a series of dark granite shelves layered between lighter coloured sedimentary rock. The climb would be challenging, but not impossible. As the pair approached the sheer walls of stone, some crude steps suddenly appeared. They formed a clear pathway that would be easy to follow.

At all times Wilson was anticipating an ambush. And yet there were no fresh signs on the ground that he could see – no footprints in the mud, no broken twigs or bent leaves, the soft green moss was not grazed off the stones.

As Wilson scaled the stone stairway, he could not help but reflect on the Inca engineers who carved these steps so many hundreds of years ago. Everything in the ancient Inca Empire had a purpose. The Incas lived in synergy with the world around them, with a great understanding of the stars and the seasons, the mountains and the rains. They were an advanced culture in so many ways. They knew how to plant and fertilise crops so that the soil was not exhausted of the life-giving element of nitrogen. The Incas understood the chemistry of drugs such as quinine and cocaine, and their effects. Master architects created stepped plateaus on even the steepest of mountain slopes so they could plant and irrigate their crops. Due to their knowledge of foods and grains and the domestication of the mountain sheep of this area – the llama and the alpaca

– theirs was a world of plenty. And with this knowledge came kings and rulers who structured laws and administration through an effective bureaucracy so that no servant of the Inca world would go hungry. Their communication system spanned the four corners of their empire: the realm of the four Suyus. The four sections of the Inca world were divided by two straight lines running through Cuzco – 'the navel of the world'. One line went directly north-west–south-east, the other went north-east–south-west. The northern regions stretched from Ecuador to Brazil, to the south they reached all the way to Chile. At the height of its reign the Inca Empire stretched over 800,000 square miles and commanded many millions of subjects.

The Incas considered themselves to be the most advanced and highest ranking peoples on the face of the earth. To them, every other civilisation was made up of savages and barbarians. Their realm was 'the world' and everything it had to offer. The gods had sent the Inca kings to earth to spread civilisation and culture to all that they could control – it was their obligation to conquer the lesser peoples and assimilate them into the bosom of the Inca Empire. They built a war machine unlike any other in South America and they trained warriors of the highest discipline – tens of thousands of them. They absorbed all the lesser tribes of the Andes; and if the conquered did not submit, the Incas slaughtered the unwilling until they got the result they wanted. Theirs was a world with a brutal and cruel edge that demanded obedience at all costs. The Inca king was omnipotent and his every direction was the word of god.

Wilson imagined the shock the king must have endured when the Spanish arrived in meagre numbers and overthrew everything the Incas had built over five centuries. The Incas had never seen anything like a full-sized horse, or the shining silver of the conquistadors' breastplates and helmets – not to mention the incredible power of their muskets and the quality of their steel swords. They were fooled into believing the bearded European invaders were descendants of the gods themselves, on par with their own king. Their trust was misplaced and they lost everything.

And yet, mysteriously, Spanish feet had never stepped upon this very pathway that Wilson and Hiram were now traversing. The Inca may not have been able to vanquish the Spanish invaders, but they were able to hide the lands of Vilcapampa for hundreds of years, which in itself was a remarkable feat.

Inca runners ferrying messages between Cuzco and the northern provinces would have used this stone staircase. These steps were once carved to a sharp edge, but the ravages of time and the incessant rains had taken their toll. The stairway's former glory had diminished in much the same way as the entire Inca Empire – you could see its structure, but it was nothing like it used to be.

Wilson was surprised at how easy it was to scale the rudimentary steps. In places, entire sections had been cut from the sheer cliffs to make the climb easier. Appearing through an opening in the rock, the roar of the Urubamba once again caught Wilson's attention. What an awesome sight it made, and what a fitting and terrible clamour went with it.

The top of the stairs opened onto a terrace, the pathway cutting directly back on itself through a twenty-foot-high sheer wall of granite. On the other side was surely where the suspension bridge spanned the river. A dense white mist hung in the gap between the walls, making it impossible to see through in the hazy light. The ominous clamour of the Urubamba reverberated around them.

If they were to be set upon, this would be the place.

Hiram was not looking where he was going and he walked into Wilson's back. 'Sorry,' he heaved. He was puffing badly from the climb and his face was completely flushed. 'I'm not crossing that suspension bridge,' he said through his gasping. 'Did you see it? It's made of . . . spindly old vines! I think it's time . . . we headed back to Cuzco.' He pointed his thumb behind him.

Wilson put his hand on Hiram's shoulder. 'The bridge will be safe, I assure you.'

Looking back towards the Sacred Valley, Wilson detected an unusual rustling among the tall grass on the other side of the river. The unusual shake of leaves, even from this great distance, was obvious. When forest movement is not created by the natural elements of wind and rain, it seems at odds with everything around it. Wilson squinted through the mist to be sure it was more than a single wild boar or some other lone animal making its way towards the water. Suddenly there was movement in at least five places. Wilson could feel his heart thumping madly as he dropped into a crouch and dragged Hiram down beside him.

'Look out there!' Wilson whispered.

By the time Hiram turned around the foliage was still again. 'What am I supposed to be looking at?' Hiram wiped the rainwater from his eyes so that he could focus more clearly. 'Did you see something?'

The layers of tall green grasses and lush ferns swayed in perfect rhythm against the gentle breeze and misty rain wafting down into the valley.

'Just watch,' Wilson whispered.

The seconds ticked by, but nothing happened.

'I'm not sure what your game is,' Hiram muttered, 'but if we're stopping, then I'm having a cigarette.' He put his hand into his jacket to retrieve his leather tobacco pouch.

Wilson clamped his hand on Hiram's wrist to stop him from standing up. 'Just wait!'

'You're trying to scare me into crossing that bridge!' Hiram said, trying to pull away.

'Look now!' Wilson whispered.

From out of the greenery, two half-naked warriors appeared with short bows strapped to their backs. The tanned, athletic women were each holding a long bamboo pole and they were moving incredibly fast. They ran in perfect unison, speared each pole into the tributary stream and easily vaulted over the water. Wilson didn't know what he was more shocked by – the fact that they were women or the incredible speed and dexterity they exhibited as they flew across the rain-speckled stream. Before he had time to consider what he was witnessing, two more female warriors appeared and vaulted effortlessly over the water in just the same way.

Hiram's mouth was hanging open.

Then a third pair appeared, and a fourth!

Wilson yanked Hiram to his feet and dragged him into the cutting of the granite wall towards the roar of the river. 'We have to go!'

'They're women!' Hiram was saying. 'Did you see them?'

Wilson now realised they were being pursued by an ancient Inca tribe that had somehow survived the Spanish occupation. The women were incredibly fit and strong – the jumps they were making over the water were extraordinary, even by modern Olympic standards. He had counted at least four pairs of warriors, and each pair was very similar. They were majestic to look at, like watching cheetahs racing at attack speed. He would have been happy just to stay and watch their form and dexterity, not to mention their naked bodies covered only by a leather loincloth at their waist and some sort of bronze breastplate moulded to the contours of their chest. On their wrists they wore heavy bronze bracelets that obviously protected their forearms in a fight. Strapped to their right thigh was a short sword of some kind. The warriors certainly looked menacing, and from the determined expression on their faces, even from such a distance, Wilson concluded that both he and Hiram were their targets.

Why would the mission notes not have mentioned such warriors? Could they possibly be descendents of the Virgins of the Sun? The female warriors were said to have an impressive temple inside the citadel of Machu Picchu, but Wilson knew precious little more about them than that.

'The legends are true,' Hiram muttered as Wilson pushed him along. 'They're *Amazons*! Just as Francisco de Orellana had described.'

Orellana had explored the rivers of Peru and Brazil in the 1540s and had made claims of encountering female warriors of incredible strength and beauty. Hence the

Amazon River was given its name. The original Amazons were the all-female warriors of classical Greek mythology. They were said to have lived in the region of Scythia, which was later to become the modern territory of the Ukraine. The word 'Amazon' in ancient Greek was said to mean 'to make war with men'. They were heralded across the globe as the most vicious and capable of fighters, women who enslaved men for sex so as to procreate their race. If their offspring was male, the infant would be killed at birth or dumped in the wild where he would surely die from exposure or starvation.

Through the dense mist, Wilson pushed Hiram towards the resounding clamour of the river. It was only after they had moved twenty steps into the haze that Wilson was able to see the two thick pillars of stone, about four feet apart, each wound with thick jungle vines that suspended the Bridge of the Condor above the Urubamba.

The vines looked to be in poor condition.

The bridge was secured to a matching pair of stone pillars on the other side of the canyon with long stretches of cable made from liana vines and woven grasses. The two main cables were wound together and strapped with plaited branches and grass to form a narrow pathway. Two thinner cables were suspended on each side that acted as guardrails, with each vine rail looking hardly strong enough to hold the weight of a man. The bridge itself looked to be waterlogged and heavy, which made it dip in the centre, causing it to descend at a thirty-degree angle, then rise up at the same pitch on the other side. Just twenty feet below, the brown rapids of the Urubamba made a frightening sight as it sped by, grumbling and churning.

To make matters worse, the spindly-looking bridge was swaying from side to side in the updrafts of air that were thundering off the rapids below.

'I'm not crossing that pathetic bridge! Look at it!' Hiram yelled. He was visibly shaking as he slung the rifle off his shoulder and turned towards the rock opening. 'I'll take my chances with the women.' He pulled back the bolt on his Springfield and locked it into place.

'The bridge will hold!' Wilson said, raising his voice over the sound of the water. 'We have no other choice!'

'I'm not going!' Hiram said resolutely. 'I'm going to stay and fight!'

18

Andes Ranges, Peru
46 Miles North-west of Cuzco
Local Time 5:10 pm

17 January 1908

'PREPARE THE ARROWS,' Aclla called out as she slid her
bow off her shoulder without breaking stride. Sontane
drew her bow in one arc as the pair leapt up the final set
of carved steps towards the rock opening that led to the
Bridge of the Condor.

Both women had sweat glistening off their backs and
shoulders – they had been running at full speed for nearly
two hours without stopping. If the two white men crossed
the suspension bridge, then Aclla and her warriors would
have failed to protect Vilcapampa from the foreign
invaders. It would be the first time the sacred lands had
been breached and she would be the one responsible.
Everyone knew the day would eventually come when
the progress of the Europeans would overrun the defences
of the Virgins of the Sun, but Aclla prayed that today
would not be that day. She had worked too hard
and studied too long to let this be the moment that triggered the evacuation of the Inca Cube into the Amazon
valley.

The Inca Cube had remained safely protected for
hundreds of years and now it was under threat once again,
just as it was when Viceroy Toledo attempted to drive his
army through this valley in search of the Inca prince known
as Titu Cusi. Back then, using the cover of five moonless

nights, the Virgin Warriors had been able to move through the shadows, killing soldiers while they slept by slashing their throats. The genius of their strategy had not been in their ability to kill, but in letting some of the men live. For every throat that was slashed they would leave another man sleeping right beside them. Stories rapidly grew of the Sacred Valley being haunted by the long-dead spirits of the Inca kings. And so it was that Viceroy Toledo and his men were turned away.

Today will not be the day this valley falls, Aclla reaffirmed.

'If we die protecting the Cube, then it will be a death most worthy,' Mamacona Kay Pacha had instructed her. 'The Cube is an object that can *never* be allowed to fall into the hands of men. The power it holds is too great.'

Aclla was breathing hard as she sprang upwards through the drizzling rain to land on the rock plateau next to Sontane. In just seconds, Orelle and Ilna landed softly beside them. On the ledge below, Polix and Sepla crouched down to crack open a small gourd containing two bright blue frogs with black spots on their backs. The living frogs were pinned to the inside of the lid with small vine straps. By the time Polix carefully passed the open gourd to Ilna, all four warriors had drawn an arrow from the quiver strapped to their bodies and began gently stroking the back of the smooth frog with the bronze arrowhead. They were very careful not to let accumulating ooze from the frog touch their skin or the aggravation and swelling would be immediate.

'They have a single rifle – a Springfield carbine.' Aclla whispered. 'The intruders cannot be allowed to cross to the cloud forest. You all know the ramifications if they do.'

The four warriors gently touched their foreheads together, their eyes closed. They maintained the unusual contact for nearly five seconds as they concentrated on becoming of 'one mind', as Mamacona Kay Pacha had taught them. Their collective heartbeat and breathing fell into perfect unison.

'*May the Sun God Inti protect you,*' Aclla said with her mind voice. There was a simultaneous reply from the other three.

All four women at once opened their eyes and leapt to their feet. Each warrior set her poisoned arrow in place and drew back on the heavy twine of her short bow. Even the slightest graze from the poisoned arrowhead would cause certain death within five minutes. A strike anywhere near the blood flow of an artery and death would be delivered before five breaths were taken.

'Today will not be the day,' Aclla whispered to herself.

The other three repeated the words.

Running at full speed, the four female warriors entered the dense white mist, their bows drawn. They broke through the haze and let out a unified scream as the white men came suddenly into view. With a coincident *twang*, the women released their deadly arrows, which flew straight and true towards their targets.

19

Andes Ranges, Peru
Hiram Bingham Express
45 Miles North-west of Cuzco
Local Time 4:30 pm

17 January 2014

THE DOWNPOUR THAT had been soaking the mountains
appeared to lessen as the diesel locomotive completed yet
another switchback and descended the final incline to
the river basin. Helena was focused on her conversation
with Don Eravisto, but it was impossible not to notice the
train change direction yet again. The ground had levelled
out for the first time in ten miles, and through the closed
windows the roar of the Urubamba River could now be
heard in competition with the rain beating down on the
roof of the carriage.

'Why is it that you have come to visit us here in Peru?'
Don Eravisto asked.

An image of Wilson's face flashed into Helena's mind. 'I
have always wanted to visit the lost city of the Incas. The
opportunity came to clear my schedule, and here I am.'
Helena sipped at her hot tea. 'And why are you here, Don
Eravisto? A celebration of some kind?'

Don Eravisto seemed to force a smile. 'I have visited
Machu Picchu countless times over the years, señorita.'
His gaze looked off into the distance and he briefly
clutched at a small cross through his starched business
shirt. 'It is my greatest joy to visit this place, blessed be
the Lord. You see, I am a local businessman based in

Lima and this train trip to Machu Picchu has become a pilgrimage of sorts.'

'A pilgrimage?' Helena replied.

Don Eravisto nodded. 'It is a spiritual place, Machu Picchu. I can be at one with myself when I visit the ancient citadel of the Sun God, Inti.' The mention of the Sun God seemed at odds with Don Eravisto's obvious Catholic upbringing.

'Having said that, I'm surprised that you travel with so many companions,' Helena commented. 'It looks to be more of a party than a pilgrimage.'

'The more people with me, the merrier,' he said. 'A man of my position does not do things alone. I have thousands of workers in Peru and South America. With that comes a responsibility to share. This is the way in our culture. Family is very important, as are the friends that are close to our hearts. We must share experiences.' He paused for a moment. 'Will you be staying at Machu Picchu Lodge, on the mountain?'

There was no advantage to lying, Helena decided. Any of the train staff could easily tell him of her travel arrangements. 'Yes, I am intending to do some hiking to the top of the local peaks as well as spending time among the ruins.'

'There are many treacherous paths through the surrounding hills,' Don Eravisto stated, 'with sheer drop-offs that fall away many thousands of feet. An awe-inspiring sight it is and yet you must have your wits about you at all times.' He glanced at Chad, who was sitting across the aisle from him. 'But it seems you are in capable hands.'

Don Eravisto turned and pointed to one of the younger men from his entourage, a handsome gentlemen wearing a grey suit with a black tie. 'That is my son, Daniel. His mother was American – my second wife.' Helena could see in his expression that Don Eravisto was fiercely proud. 'If you require anything at all, we are both available to meet your needs.'

Even though he was seated quite a distance away, Daniel's gaze met Helena's and he nodded in her direction as if he could hear every word of their conversation. He appeared to be in his thirties, his dark hair slicked back exactly like his father's. His brooding eyes were shadowed and deep set, and he kept scratching his nose as if he had a terrible itch. On either side of him sat two young women of raw beauty, but Helena could tell by their shy expression and their lack of deportment that they had been plucked from the foothills of a local village somewhere.

'I will be sure to let you know if I need anything,' Helena replied. Gesturing out the window, she asked, 'Have you ever seen the weather like this before?'

'Very rarely have I seen it as dark and as treacherous,' Don Eravisto replied. 'The rockslide was most unexpected, but it has happened before on occasion.' He pulled in a deep breath through his nostrils. 'The smell of the forest after it has been soaked by the heavy summer rains is intoxicating, is it not? The swollen rivers come to life like roaring monsters. They are frightening when you get close to them – so powerful it makes your skin tingle.' There was passion in his every word. 'It is one of the many reasons the summer rainy season is still my favourite time of year to journey into the mountains. I have waited a very long time for this day to arrive,' he said, nodding.

Don Eravisto's last comment seemed out of place, but Helena chose not to question him about it. 'You mentioned Hiram Bingham stayed in that railway shack back there?' she asked.

'They were dark times,' Don Eravisto muttered. He pointed across the aisle towards Helena's travelling companions. 'I will need privacy if I am to speak frankly. You should send them away.'

Helena was taken aback by the request, but even so asked Chad and Pablo to move to the next booth along. It was obvious from Pablo's expression that he was intimidated by Don Eravisto, which only added to the unexpected dread she was feeling.

'They were dark times indeed,' Don Eravisto said again as he grabbed a handful of cashews and shook them about in his closed fist before tossing them into his mouth. He was still chewing as he said, 'It was raining much like this

when Hiram Bingham spent a night in that railway shack
– how ironic.'

'Hiram was travelling alone?' Helena asked.

Don Eravisto paused as if to think carefully about his
answer. 'He had company with him, that is true enough.
No one headed into these parts alone in those days –
unchartered and wild they were. Ancient Indian tribes
still held these mountains, especially to the west, towards
the Amazon. They were said to slay foreigners and shrink
their heads so as to wear them around their necks as ornaments. As fate would have it, the night Hiram Bingham
and his party slept inside that railway shack, their precious
donkeys were cut loose and led away to be slaughtered.'

'By who?' Helena asked.

Don Eravisto became very serious. 'This was once
a sacred valley, señorita. The indigenous Indians that
protected this place stole the pack animals and brutally
maimed them – a terrible sight it was.' Don Eravisto
paused to throw more cashews into his mouth. 'As I have
been told, it was one of the most gruesome scenes Hiram
Bingham had ever witnessed.'

'That's terrible,' Helena replied.

Don Eravisto pointed at Helena's iPad. 'You will *not*
find that in your book. Hiram Bingham did not want to
offend anyone when he wrote that story. Selective history,
I call it. As I said before, they were dark times – the local
Indians, as well as the church hierarchy, have chosen to
forget much of what happened during those years. As I am
sure you already know, Hiram's visit to this place coin-
cided with the last crucifixion to be held in South America,
in the city of Cuzco.'

'There was a crucifixion?' Helena asked in surprise.

'Just three days before Hiram came to this valley,' Don
Eravisto said. 'It is not well known. Alas, the church has
done an excellent job of keeping the terrible event well
hidden. A local soldier named Corsell Santillana was crucified on the outer walls of La Catedral for all to see, facing
the Plaza de Armas.'

'How do you know all this?' Helena asked.

Don Eravisto smiled. 'The information has been passed down from father to son. That is the way of things in this country. We have *culture* here, unlike the broken rituals you have in the United States.'

Helena was surprised by the arrogance that had over-taken Don Eravisto's tone. 'Why was the soldier crucified?' she asked.

Don Eravisto levelled his gaze. 'It was said that he was possessed by the Devil.'

'What year was that?' Helena asked.

'It was the year of our Lord 1908.'

'Do you know the exact date?'

'It was in the middle of the rainy season, as we are now, but other than that I could not say.' There was long pause before Don Eravisto continued, all the while he was crushing cashews between his thumb and forefinger. 'Many believe that the crucifixion in Cuzco and Hiram Bingham's visit to this sacred Inca valley are related.'

'How have you made that connection?' Helena asked.

'It is not a connection *I* have made, señorita. It is what I have been told. On the orders of Bishop Francisco – he was the man responsible for determining the purification of Corsell Santillana – a military unit was sent from Cuzco to pursue Hiram Bingham and all those who travelled with him. Their capture was of the highest priority to the leader of the church.'

'Who was travelling with Hiram Bingham?' Helena asked again.

Don Eravisto looked across at her. 'You already know the answer to that question, señorita. Otherwise, why else would you be here?'

'I'm not sure what you mean, señor.'

'There is no need to be coy.'

Helena shook her head. 'I have no idea what you are talking about.'

'You should admit what you know.' Then, with a deep breath, Don Eravisto managed to flash a smile. 'It seems the emotion of the moment has got the better of me and I have lost my manners. You must understand, I have waited a very long time for this day to come.' Helena watched the artery on Don Eravisto's neck pulsing more quickly.

'Why are you playing games with me?' Helena said. 'If you have something to say, you should say it.'

'*Wilson Dowling* is the reason we are both here,' Don Eravisto stated. His fists suddenly clenched. 'I have ridden this train almost every day in the wet season for nearly two years. I was told you were beautiful, and I am pleased to say that the sight of you does not disappoint. While you were in the railway shack you saw a vision,' he added with a whisper. 'A clear vision of Wilson Dowling, as real as I am sitting here in front of you. It is remarkable, is it not?'

Helena just sat there stony faced.

'Do you deny what I am saying is true?' he asked.

Helena could see that Don Eravisto was positively giddy at the thought of knowing what she had seen. 'You saw Wilson Dowling – I know you did!'

'Whatever you think you know, señor, it is merely the tip of the iceberg.' Helena would not allow herself to show self-doubt or weakness – if she did, the situation could worsen. In front of her sat a man who knew of her visions, however unexpected that was. *How could he know?* She casually sipped at her tea again, which was now barely warm. 'I knew you would be here to meet me,' Helena stated. 'Do not be so foolish to think that I know less than you.' It was impossible to know where Helena's sudden self-confidence had come from, but she sensed this was the moment to be brave.

Don Eravisto stared deeply into her eyes. 'It is possible, I guess.' Lifting his hand, he snapped his fingers to catch the eye of a waiter standing at the end of the carriage. 'Get me some cigarettes and an ashtray!'

'You cannot smoke here,' Helena said sternly.

Don Eravisto calmly flipped open the button of his jacket and drew out a nickel-plated revolver. 'I am the one in charge here,' he stated, then pointed the high-powered weapon at Helena's head.

The sight of the shiny Colt .45 caused a frantic and immediate commotion throughout the dining carriage. Gasps and screams could be heard in every direction as some people froze in shock, while others dived between the seats in panic.

Chad frantically drew her Glock pistol. 'Drop your gun!' she screamed.

At the other end of the carriage, at least five of Don Eravisto's men produced an assortment of weapons, from simple revolvers to an MP5 assault rifle. They were screaming at Chad in return. 'Drop your weapon!'

From the floor, Pablo was muttering, 'Praise be to Jesus, my holy protector.'

All the while Don Eravisto and Helena just sat there looking into each other's eyes, neither of them blinking. Helena showed no signs of fear. She remained completely calm, not letting a solitary furrow crease her unblemished skin.

Helena slowly raised her hand, which caused the yelling and screaming to stop for a moment. 'Put down your weapon, Chad.' Behind her, she could hear her body-guard's laboured breathing. 'I have this situation under control.'

'It doesn't look like it to me!' Chad yelled back as she panned her gun between each of the five men at the end of the carriage. From where she was, she didn't have a direct shot at Don Eravisto.

Helena rested her arm on the shoulder of the dining booth and turned to her bodyguard; there was no colour in Chad's face, even her lips were pale. 'If he was going to shoot me,' Helena said calmly, 'he would have already pulled the trigger.'

It took a few moments for Chad to reluctantly lower her gun.

'Your men are to stay where they are,' Helena said to Don Eravisto.

'Somebody get me some cigarettes!' Don Eravisto yelled.

'You cannot smoke here,' Helena reiterated.

'I will do as I like!'

Helena shook her head. 'Did you really think that I would come here without protection? With my connections to the past, I know more than you *ever* will!'

Don Eravisto looked worried for the first time.

'You are dealing with forces beyond your understanding, señor. I have been expecting your arrival, as you have been expecting mine. I know everything that is about to happen and why. That is the reason you will do exactly as I say.'

Don Eravisto held a stern expression.

Helena reached out and with her index finger and eased the tip of Don Eravisto's handgun down and to the side. 'You will lower your gun, and your men will do the same. There is much to discuss, and your handgun will not be necessary.'

20

Andes Ranges, Peru
46 Miles North-west of Cuzco
Local Time 5:13 pm

17 January 1908

TIME SEEMED TO pass in slow motion as Aclla watched
the four hunting arrows flying straight and true towards
their targets. The two white men were halfway across
the Bridge of the Condor, some forty paces away. It was
only while the arrows were in flight that Aclla was able to
take in the full scene and witness the strength and dexterity of the blue-eye running with extraordinary balance
down the narrow and slippery incline of the suspension
bridge. On his shoulders he carried the limp body of the
skinny man, gripping his light frame by the arms on one
side and his right leg on the other. The skinny man was
either dead or unconscious, judging by the way his head
swung from side to side. Such was the speed of the blue-
eye's movement, he did not use the vine guardrails. He
was relying only on his cat-like balance to navigate the
swaying bridge.

Aclla and her warriors stood line abreast on the edge
of the sheer drop-off, each with a second arrow set but
not drawn, watching the extraordinary sight before them.
There was no time for words to be spoken aloud, but they
were all of one mind and thinking the same thing.

*How could this man move so quickly and with such
power?* It was an athletic display unlike anything the
Virgins of the Sun had ever seen.

The four arrows sliced through the turbulent air towards the blue-eye. Aclla could not help but wince at the thought of a poison arrow breaching his perfect flesh. The prospect of killing such a man seemed abhorrent to her all of a sudden. Having seen what he was capable of, her instinct was to want it for herself – and if that was not possible, then to want it for her offspring.

As the four arrows neared their target, the blue-eye leapt forward yet again, his vigour defying logic as he reached the bridge's lowest point and began the difficult ascent to the other side. The three warriors standing next to Aclla simultaneously drew back the twine of their bows to a firing position, but Aclla did not. She knew that at least one of the arrows would strike its mark. She had aimed higher than the rest.

Three of the arrows dipped in the moist air – just a hand span below their target – but Aclla's arrow hit the blue-eye in the back of his left thigh, impaling the material of his heavy waterproof pants. Judging by his startled reaction and the way he reached behind him – yet still holding the skinny man's body in place with his other arm – the arrow had breached his flesh.

To his credit, the blue-eye managed to maintain a steady stride up the incline to the other side, but his balance was clearly affected by the poison. The female warriors simultaneously released the tension of their bows and inserted their arrows back into the safety of their quivers.

'*May the Sun God Inti release you*,' Aclla said in her mind voice and the women's eyes closed then reopened – they were once again set free from each other. Aclla had been taught to keep mind connections as brief as possible because those of lesser influence could be driven to madness if they were held together longer than required. The sense of loss and grieving that always accompanied a separation of minds momentarily gripped Aclla and she tensed her muscles to ward away the sensation.

'You have a weakness for the blue-eye that you should not,' Sontane said.

'He is our enemy, yet you see him as beautiful,' Orelle added.

'It was *my* arrow that felled him,' Aclla said sternly. 'Not yours! You all know this. I did not let my feelings get in the way.'

On the other side of the bridge, the blue-eye dropped awkwardly to one knee. He let the skinny man fall to the ground and turned to inspect the wound where the arrow had struck him, then pulled it from his flesh.

'He is a dangerous man,' Ilna commented. 'We can only hope there are not more men like him. His physical strength and balance were a sight to behold.'

Orelle nodded. 'The fact that he is able to stay breathing as long as this after such an arrow strike is further proof of his power.'

'We should take his body back to Mamacona Hurin Pacha,' Ilna added. 'So that she may study his remains.'

The thought of the blue-eye's lifeless body sent a pang of remorse into Aclla's stomach. With a sharp breath she steeled her resolve. 'Come, we must cross the river. By the time we get there he will certainly be dead.'

Setting her bow across her shoulders, Aclla stepped onto the swaying suspension bridge. With both hands clasping the wavering guiderails, she took note of the footmarks where the blue-eye had crossed before her. His stride was enormous. She glanced towards him to see that he had now fallen to both knees, his hands gripping either side of his face – it was clear that he was screaming, but she could not hear his voice over the roar of the river. Death was near for him now.

Aclla concentrated so as not to lose her footing on the slippery vine matting. The rapidly moving brown water just below her was very distracting, as was the occasional spray of froth that shot upwards.

'The valley will not be breached on this day!' Aclla screamed in the blue-eye's direction. 'Not this day!' She had done her job. 'We will be welcomed back to our village as heroes once again.'

The four warriors approached the halfway point across

the drooping suspension bridge to begin the difficult ascent up the slippery incline to the other side. With each step the view of the two white men on the rock ledge became clearer. The blue-eye had fallen to his back and was now barely visible. The skinny man he was carrying had not moved since he was dropped to the ground. Aclla studied the crashing rapids, the highest point of the raging water churning just a body length below her heels. It was an awesome and frightening sight to see the forces of Pariacaca, the God of Water, at work. Pariacaca was master of the rainstorms and the rivers; he was born as a falcon and changed into a human in his later years. To look down at him now, Aclla could see his talons clawing upwards from the fast-moving water, attempting to grab and draw in anything that was foolish enough to get close.

Looking in the blue-eyes direction, Aclla felt no sense of elation at the thought of his passing. Then suddenly he stood up! It was the last thing Aclla expected. In his hand he held a shimmering silver knife, which he effortlessly slashed across one of the vine rails, causing it to sever and whiplash out of Aclla's hand. All four warriors struggled to maintain their balance as they frantically adjusted their footing while holding desperately to the remaining rail.

The women did their best to hold their position as Aclla decided whether they should make a rush forward or retreat. She knew they could not gather their bows or they would certainly lose their balance. The bridge was swaying more violently and just standing there was difficult.

Aclla once again locked eyes with the blue-eye, just as she had done when he singled her out in the Plaza de Armas. His expression was steely, his jaw clenched, his eyes calm.

How could he possibly have survived the poison?

It was obvious to her that he was going to cut the remaining handrail. It was inevitable. With a simple slash of his shimmering blade, her life and those of her loyal warriors would come to an end among the violent brown waters of the river below. Pariacaca, the God of Water, would have the final say.

21

Andes Ranges, Peru
46 Miles North-west of Cuzco
Local Time 5:15 pm

17 January 1908

A PROFOUND SENSATION of warmth radiated from the centre of Wilson's chest to the tips of his fingers and toes – the after-effects of his healing command. It had taken only a moment to realise that an arrow tipped with poison had struck him, and yet he was almost too late to activate the command that had just saved him from an excruciating death. A few second more and it would have been all over.

Turning the blade of his knife towards the remaining handrail, Wilson prepared to strike the vine where it was coiled around the thick pillar of stone. If the female warriors took one step forward, or if they reached for their bows, he would be forced to slash the second vine and send them plummeting to their deaths. With his gaze locked firmly on the lead female, Wilson remembered where he had seen her hazel eyes before. She was certainly the very same woman who had watched him from beneath the dark hooded cloak, huddled among the crowd in the Plaza de Armas. The vision of her eyes was imprinted in his memory.

The woman was stunning to look at and to see her unveiled exceeded even his expectations of her beauty. Her hair was thick and black, tied into a plaited ponytail. Her face was square cut, with high cheekbones and fine eyebrows. The expression she carried was of grim determination, and a sense of knowing, like she recognised him also. Her body was unlike anything Wilson had ever seen – her tanned skin was even and toned, her shoulders and breasts were bulging, as were her muscular upper thighs. She was an incredible sight wearing a fitted breastplate of bronze, heavy bronze bracelets, and a simple leather skirt with a sword strapped to her thigh. It was understandable that the sight of such a splendid creature could easily distract anyone fighting her. Amazingly, the other three warriors behind her were equally striking – even their awkward jostling to reclaim their balance on the swaying suspension bridge did nothing to detract from their beauty.

At Wilson's feet, lying on the wet stones, Hiram Bingham began to stir, then groan. 'Oh . . . my head.' He slowly opened his eyes and looked about. 'What the hell?' He frantically reached about for his rifle, clutching this way and that, at the same time trying to get his bearings.

Hiram lifted himself into a sitting position, then took in the view. 'I'm not crossing that river,' he groaned as he removed his hat and rubbed his face like a child waking from a deep afternoon sleep. 'Where's my gun?' he said in a panic.

Wilson motioned the blade of his knife ever closer to the coiled vine, then pointed back over the women's heads, clearly indicating that they should retreat or he would sever the only remaining handrail.

'We're being attacked from both sides!' Hiram said in distress.

'Just relax,' Wilson said. 'We're fine.'

Hiram turned around once again in an attempt to figure out where he was.

Keeping his gaze fixed upon the leading Amazon, Wilson said to Hiram, 'We've crossed the river to the northern side.'

'Where the hell is my rifle?'

'Your gun is over there,' Wilson gestured towards the stone pillars suspending the bridge from the other side of the ravine. 'I had to carry you across.'

'*You left my gun behind?*'

'If you'd stayed to fight, you would be dead now,' Wilson said.

Hiram slowly climbed to his feet, a look of deep estimation on his face. 'They're the female warriors who were chasing us? The ones who killed my donkeys?'

Wilson nodded.

'They don't look so tough from here.' Hiram rubbed his neck where Wilson had inflicted the nerve block that made him unconscious. 'No one will believe me when I tell them there are Amazon warriors in Peru – females, for *God's sake* – out here in the Andes. They'll think I've gone mad.'

By now, Aclla and her warriors were reversing slowly away, one careful step at a time, up the thirty-degree incline towards the southern side of the river. With only one handrail it was treacherous going as the Bridge of the Condor swung from side to side under their combined weight and the updrafts generated by the river.

'You have a wound on your leg,' Hiram said as he gestured to the blood running down the back of Wilson's left trouser leg. Then he saw a bloodied arrow lying on the stones. '*They shot you?* Those tricky little bitches! Cut the vine and let the donkey-killers fall into the river, I say.' Hiram reached down to pick up the arrow.

'Don't touch that!' Wilson barked. 'It's poisoned.'

'Then how are you still alive?' Hiram mocked.

'Just leave it where it is!'

'It's not poisoned,' Hiram said as he confidently fingered the shaft to study it more carefully. 'Look at the workman-ship, it really is –'

Wilson spun towards him, grabbed the arrow and tossed it over the edge of the cliff.

'What did you do that for?' Hiram groaned. 'The arrowhead would have made a fantastic souvenir!'

'Why don't you listen? It could have killed you.'

'If it was poison, then how do you explain the fact that you're still breathing?'

'I'm immune to frog poison.'

Hiram stomped his foot. 'You think I'll believe anything, don't you?'

By now, the Amazon warriors had made it halfway back up the incline to the other side. Seeing the safety of the rock ledge, they made a mad scramble up the wet and matted vines. The lead female eventually broke off her stare, somersaulted backwards in an obvious display of physicality and landed on her feet between her female counterparts. Three of the warriors drew their bows in one swift movement and extracted an arrow each from their quivers – all of them except the leader. It would be a very difficult shot from such a long distance, especially with the wind gusting. If they did release their arrows, there would be ample time for Wilson and Hiram to retreat into the thick forest that framed the rock shelf they were standing on.

The lead female calmly raised her hand and her three warriors lowered their bows. She was talking, yelling probably. In seconds the women had their bows holstered and arrows back in their quivers.

'How did we get on this side of the river again?' Hiram asked, still looking about.

'I carried you across,' Wilson said.

Hiram laughed. 'Impossible!'

With one strike of his knife, Wilson severed the remaining vine rail and it whiplashed away towards the raging whitewater of the Urubamba River. Dropping to one knee, he set about hacking away the matted base of the suspension bridge. In just seconds, it too separated from the two stone pillars and plummeted towards the river. When it hit the water, the matted twine was inextricably caught in the folding rapids, which easily tore the bridge from its southern foundations and eventually gobbled the entire structure into its depths.

Hiram studied the sheer rock wall behind him, then looked to the narrow pathway that disappeared into the shadowed forest. 'You just severed the bridge that leads back to Cuzco,' he said in a sombre tone. 'We have no supplies, no tents to protect us from this incessant rain, and no whiskey.'

'There is another way back,' Wilson replied, all the

while maintaining his gaze on the lead female on the other side of the river. They were obviously trying to protect the Sacred Valley, and possibly Vilcapampa itself. The question was, did they have another way across the Urubamba? Wilson had to assume they did – if not, they'd have to run the Inca Trail back into the mountains to get to Machu Picchu. It was at least three times the distance going that way.

'All jokes aside,' Hiram said seriously. 'How did I get over to this side of the river? The sooner you tell me, the sooner I'll feel better about where I am.'

'I told you,' Wilson said, breaking off his stare. 'I carried you across the suspension bridge.' He then turned and stepped into the darkness of the cloud forest.

22

Cuzco, Peru
La Monasterio
Local Time 12:10 am

19 January 1908

'CAPITÁN GONZALES HAS *failed again!*' the deep voice said.

Bishop Francisco threw himself to the cold stone floor, his skin becoming slick with sweat as a hacking cough violently overcame his emaciated body. He had not heard the voice of Conquistador Pizarro since before the last wax candle had burnt away to nothing, some hours ago. After sitting in total darkness until his nerves could not take it anymore, he had since lit another candle which was now halfway gone. As each minute passed, he had dared to hope that he would never have to hear the terrifying voice in his head yet again, but deep down he knew the voice of Pizarro would come to him. He was cursed and only God Himself could save him. Helplessly peering across his bedchamber to the far wall, he looked up at the life-sized oil painting of Pope Innocent II, who had slept in this very room when he had visited Cuzco more than 200 years before. His expression was confident and satisfied – everything that Bishop Francisco was not. With a thick film of sweat now covering his naked, shaking body, Bishop Francisco climbed to his knees and began to pray. 'Save me, Holy Jesus, protector of the downtrodden.'

He looked helplessly to the peaked roof above him, then to the elaborate cross of Christ on the wall. The sight of the Son of God nailed to the cross was a mixed blessing – it gave the bishop strength to see the Lord's sacrifice, but it was also a reminder of the terrible sins he himself had committed. With a gasp, he realised he didn't have his rosary beads, so he snatched them from atop the silk blanket of his huge bed. Running the emerald rosaries through his fingers, he continued reciting the words, 'Virgin Mary full of grace . . .'

'*The Virgin Mary will not save you either,*' the voice said.

Bishop Francisco began sobbing, tears running down his pale cheeks as they had done countless times in the last three days. 'Please Lord, you must set me free from this hell! I cannot do what you ask of me.'

'*The only way to be free is to commit my bidding.*'

Bishop Francisco's mouth filled with acid at the mere thought of what he had already done. He wanted to vomit, but there was nothing left inside him. He had not been able to hold down liquid or food for days, such was his self-loathing. 'You said the pain would go away, and it has not – it only grows worse. I feel so hot, like my skin is burning, but I cannot drink to quench my thirst.'

'*It is because you defy me. Release yourself fully and the pain will leave you. Release yourself to me.*'

'You have said that before,' the bishop whimpered, 'and regardless, the pain is worse than ever.' He let the rosaries fall to the ground between his knees then pressed his forehead to the floor. 'Let me die, Lord! Release me from this bondage. My sins have consumed me. Please let me take my own life.'

'*You cannot die while I watch over you,*' the voice replied. '*You are my servant and I do not wish it.*'

On more than one occasion, Bishop Francisco had climbed the circular staircase to the rooftop of La Catedral in an attempt to throw himself from atop the steep walls and free himself from this terrible purgatory. But as he approached the stone ledge, the devil Pizarro simply possessed his body and, against his own will, the bishop walked to ground level and away from danger.

On another occasion, he had attempted to slash his throat with a solid silver dagger that lay on the Altar of Saint Anthony. But no matter how he tried, he was unable to pierce his own skin. Pizarro had warned him not to make any further attempts on his life. The consequence would be that more of his congregation, the ones he loved the most, the people he found most pure, would die in a most gruesome way.

Bishop Francisco continued crying, but his tear ducts were now dry. The voice in his head could not fully control his unconscious mind, but the power it wielded in driving him insane was considerable. In trying to lessen the pain, in many ways he had made it even worse.

'Please let me die, Lord.'

'*There are further tasks you must complete.*'

'I cannot do what you ask,' the bishop whimpered. 'Not again.'

'*Do you not wish to protect your congregation?*'

'You know I do.'

Bishop Francisco could sense a perverse joy in Pizarro's comments. His was evil beyond imagination. The spirit of the once great conquistador was twisted with hatred by his eternal captivity within the Inca Cube. His soul was forever trapped and his only way of feeling *anything* was by taking the innocence and life force of others.

'I cannot kill again, and I cannot rape again,' the bishop pleaded. No matter how many times he scrubbed away at his skin with soap and hard bristles, he was unable to free himself of the thoughts of what he had done, save only to scrub his outer flesh until it was raw.

'*You will do my bidding. If not, I will take your body and drive it for myself.*' There was a long period of silence. '*Remember, you were the one who sent your men to Vilcapampa to break open my stone prison. I am here because of you.*'

Bishop Francisco's greed had unleashed a scourge upon the world, and he alone was responsible.

'*Get dressed, my servant,*' the voice continued. '*There*

*are visitors approaching the monastery. They have bad
news to give you.'*

Although Bishop Francisco was exhausted, he knew
there was no choice but to obey. Climbing slowly to his
feet, he began donning his bishop's robes. 'Great lord,
how can you know that there is someone approaching the
monastery?'

'I know all things.'

'But how is that possible?'

*'I possess the souls of all men. They are connected to
me in an unbreakable chain. What they think comes to my
mind.'*

Bishop Francisco remembered the exact moment when
he first touched the Inca Cube. The very instant he had
reached out to take the glistening object from Juan
Santillana, who was on his knees, handing the Cube up
to him as if it was the greatest of offerings. On the floor
lay the mutilated remains of Monsignor Pera and one of
the altar boys who had been unlucky enough to stumble
across the murder scene just moments after it had taken
place. A donkey was tied to an ornate pillar next to
the magnificent Altar of the Virgin La Antigua – in the
donkey's eyes was pure fear, Bishop Francisco realised it
now. Juan Santillana was covered in gore; not an inch of
him was clean. Filth was sprayed across his face, his clothes
were blackened with it – even his mouth was stained with
blood. The moment Bishop Francisco touched the Cube,
his existence turned from good to evil. Despite the terrible
scene of death and the horrible stench that filled the air, he
still reached for the shiny golden Cube with both hands,
like a starving man reaching for a succulent piece of fruit
from the Tree of Life.

The Inca Curse had consumed them all – Pizarro
included. When Bishop Francisco said those words out
loud, Pizarro flew into a rage. With a pain he could not
describe, such was the agony, blood poured from Bishop
Francisco's ears and there was no escaping it. As a warning
to never mention the Inca Curse again, Pizarro sent the
bishop out in the darkness to brutally murder his own

niece. What he did to her young body after that was so depraved that the mere thought of it caused the bishop to dry-retch until it felt like his stomach was coming out of his mouth.

This was all happening because of a small symmetrical object that easily fit into one hand. It was captivating to look at – its razor-sharp lines, the lustre of the metal that almost appeared to glow, the terrific weight, the way the candlelight reflected off its impossibly shiny surface.

As soon as he handed it over, Juan Santillana ran from the church, his heavy footsteps becoming ever more faint as he sprinted out the door and into the pouring rain. He had not been seen since.

Bishop Francisco cursed himself for wanting to acquire the Cube in the first place. He had discovered its existence after Corsell Santillana – Juan's younger brother – had mentioned the sacred Inca treasure in confession to Monsignor Pera. That was in the midst of winter – seven moons had passed and since then a chain of events had led to the capture of his woman, an extraordinary creature called Vivane, who was at this moment in bondage in the tunnels under this very monastery. She still believed Corsell to be alive, but on the orders of Pizarro, Corsell had been crucified for everyone to see, drugged so that he could not speak. Although he was innocent, Corsell would take the blame for Monsignor Pera's murder.

Corsell's crucifixion would be his brother Juan's eternal failing. In his attempts to save his own brother, he had condemned Corsell to die on the cross to repent for his sins. A life had been traded for a life – and the spirit of Pizarro was responsible for it all. Bishop Francisco felt little pity for either Corsell or his brother. Corsell was free of this world, in a better place, and Juan had escaped somehow. At this moment, Bishop Francisco would happily trade his own fate for such an ending.

'*Capitán Gonzales is approaching,*' the voice said. '*He has failed in his task to bring the stranger, Wilson Dowling, back to Cuzco. He has abandoned his duty. It was made clear to him that he should* only *return if he captured or killed this man. This sort of failure cannot be tolerated.'*

Bishop Francisco adjusted his scarlet robes and sat on the edge of his bed to tie up the laces of his cobbled boots. 'What do you ask of me, Great Lord?'

'*You will order the captain to bring more troops from Lima. I cannot see into the soul of this man, Wilson Dowling. His journey is cloaked in a mystery that not even I can understand.'*

Bishop Francisco stood up, his bruised and battered legs weary from nearly five days of mental and physical torture. 'As you wish, Great Lord.' He could not have argued even if he wanted to.

'*Protecting the church must become Capitán Gonzales's primary concern – more soldiers are needed – nothing can be left to chance.'*

The stranger, Wilson Dowling, had struck fear into the Pizarro spirit – either way, events were shifting because of the white foreigner. Bishop Francisco secretly prayed that Wilson Dowling succeeded in his quest, whatever that was. Perhaps the only way to escape his own bondage was via the strength and resolve of Dowling's actions. How odd it was to put his only hope into the hands of a man that he had never met, but a drowning man will cling to whatever he can to save himself.

Bishop Francisco donned his papal hat, lifted his chin and pulled back his shoulders. With a long exhalation, he turned the large metal key and the door unlocked with a click. The humidity was stifling and he could feel sweat dripping from his stinking underarms. Heavy rain had been falling for five consecutive days now – in Bishop Francisco's estimation the rains were God's futile attempt to wash away the ghastly evil that had already consumed the good city of Cuzco.

23

Andes Ranges, Peru
51 Miles North-east of Cuzco
Local Time 5:24 pm

17 January 2014

AFTER MUCH CONVINCING, Don Eravisto had placed his nickel-plated Colt .45 on the table beside him. His expression was one of frustration, his pupils were shrunken, an obvious warning that at any second his emotions could overwhelm him.

At Helena's request, the passengers and train staff were back in their seats, Don Eravisto's men included. Chad and Pablo were at the table behind her – she couldn't see them, but she could hear their worried breathing.

No one was allowed to move.

Everybody looked tense and afraid as the train trundled slowly forward with the raging Urubamba River gushing by just outside the window, getting wilder with each stretch and turn of the railway track.

'There is no option other than to work together,' Helena said convincingly.

Helena had discovered that Don Eravisto had been riding this train for more than *two years* – every time heavy rain was predicted – waiting for her to arrive. To balance the situation, it had become necessary for her to pretend she knew more than she really did to buy herself time to understand her circumstances. Wilson's journey to Machu Picchu with Hiram Bingham was definitely at the heart of why Don Eravisto was here. He knew about the visions she had witnessed at the railway shack, and of her psychic connection with the time traveller. The revelation confirmed for her once again that her life and Wilson's were inextricably linked, which was comforting in one sense and yet deeply disturbing in another. How could this man, Don Eravisto, possibly know what she had seen? And why was he so angry? He had dared to point a gun at her – the *asshole* – and Helena knew that every word that came from her mouth could set off another hostile reaction if she unwittingly said the wrong thing.

Helena carefully filled her glass with sparkling water and set the glass bottle off to the side. She was cautious not to let her hands tremble or show any signs of fear. All the while she was studying the exact location of everything on her table with her peripheral vision – the cups, the plates and the knives.

'I am a reasonable person,' Helena stated. 'I see it in your eyes that you agree. And you are a powerful man, which pleases me. The world has been good to you – and to your son, Daniel. That is not to say that you are not without your demons, we all have them, but we must continue to look to the future if we are to have any hope of not letting this complex misunderstanding – because that is what this is – from ruining both our lives.'

'You play with words eloquently, señorita. But it does not change the fact that Wilson Dowling is a scourge upon my ancestors. He is the one who destroyed my family and sent them to madness. He is the one who devastated the life of a good man and took everything from him in the most horrific way. It is true that I have reaped the benefits of my knowledge, but in return I must do my part to put things right. That is the price of things.'

'Wilson Dowling is a good man, with an honest heart,' Helena replied, attempting to go with her instincts.

Don Eravisto's expression reflected that of a man with revenge in his heart. 'Then you do not know him,' he replied. 'He is evil personified.'

'What is Wilson Dowling's crime?'

Pressing his index finger to the tablecloth, Don Eravisto

replied with a wavering voice, 'He brutally killed the wife and children of my ancestors. *He is a murderer.* A perverse killer who revels in the horror and humiliation of his victims.' Don Eravisto snatched up his Colt revolver and once again pointed the barrel between Helena's eyes. 'I cannot play these games anymore!' His hands were shaking and Helena could see that he was capable of pulling the trigger.

There was a collective gasp inside the railway carriage as the assembled passengers steeled themselves for what would happen next.

Helena calmly moved her glass an inch to the left. 'And you think that by targeting me you will have revenge on a man in the past?'

'I am certain of it.'

'You are a fool, then.'

Don Eravisto's gaze hardened. '*You* are the reason for his success!'

'I would never partake in the murder of innocents!' Helena replied as vehemently as she dared. 'Your information is wrong and you are about to make a terrible mistake.'

Beads of sweat had formed on Don Eravisto's brow and his hands were shaking. 'That is what I expected you to say. I have played this moment through in my mind countless times. I predicted you would try and squirm your way out of your responsibilities. You are at fault here, woman!'

'How dare you accuse me of wrongdoing!' Helena said brazenly.

'You are at fault!' Don Eravisto said again. 'Wilson Dowling's actions are directed by *you*! Killing *you* is the only way to stop the evil actions he will take.'

Helena continued to stare calmly into Don Eravisto's cold eyes. It was impossible to say where her calculating resolve came from, but deep down in her heart she was sure that her life did not end here at the hands of the man sitting in front of her. Wilson was close to her now, albeit separated by a barrier of time, and she would get to him – it was her destiny.

'So you think you can pull the trigger and change the fate of your ancestors?' Helena questioned. 'The only fate you will affect will be your own, and that of your children.' Helena looked about the railway carriage, then to Daniel, who was ashen-faced at the sight of his father's obvious madness.

'Is it your intention to kill everyone on this train to cover up my murder?' she asked. The other passengers were obviously startled by the comment, as were the women sitting at Don Eravisto's table. It was now clear to them that this terrifying situation affected their lives also.

'I must do what it takes to change history,' Don Eravisto said irritably. 'I will kill you and then I will kill myself! Everyone else will be safe.'

'Will you kill yourself in front of your own son?'

'Killing you will change history,' Don Eravisto stated. 'You will not play your part and the devil Wilson Dowling will fail. He will be blind and my family will be protected.'

'I cannot believe you would heap this terrible fate on Daniel,' Helena said, feigning compassion. 'I look at his face and I do not see a man ready for the burden and humiliation you would unload upon him.'

'I have prepared my son for this moment,' Don Eravisto replied. 'He will know exactly what to do when my journey is complete.'

'You have made him an accomplice to murder, then? That was not a smart thing to say to the countless witnesses you will leave behind.'

Don Eravisto let out a harried breath, his mind clearly filled with overlapping thoughts. 'My boy is ready for what I must do.' He glanced over his shoulder towards Daniel to deliver one last look of reassurance.

Finally seeing her opportunity, Helena gripped the perfectly positioned water bottle and swung it forcefully at the side of Don Eravisto's head. The half-full bottle struck his skull with a resounding crack that echoed off the walls of the dining car like two stones hitting together. The bottle released from her grasp on impact and flew into the window beside them, shattering the glass. In a calculated rage, Helena grabbed Don Eravisto by the hair and violently slammed his face into the tabletop with all her might, which cracked the plates and glasses with his nose and forehead. Blood spurted from his lacerated face as she tore the gun from his grasp and pressed the barrel against his bloodied temple.

'If anyone moves a muscle,' Helena yelled out, 'I will blow his fucking head off!'

24

Andes Ranges, Peru
55 Miles North-west of Cuzco
Local Time 11:20 am

19 January 1908

HAVING SPENT NEARLY three full days on the move, both Wilson and Hiram were a dishevelled sight. Their clothes were torn and muddy, Hiram's skin was covered with insect bites and they both had the beginnings of a beard. Cutting away at the dense undergrowth, Wilson knew they were finally leaving the cloud forest because the tree canopy above them was thinning out and he could hear a throaty river directly ahead. Machu Picchu was somewhere just across the other side of the ravine and up the switchback ridge that would one day be called Hiram's Highway.

For the last two days, Wilson had been worried they would face another attack from the Amazons. He had no way of knowing if they had another way of crossing the Urubamba River. If not, they would be forced to take the Inca Trail back through the high mountains, which was a much longer way to go, on a completely different route, across the other side of the river. Taking what precautions he could, whenever they crossed a tributary stream – and there were many – if the water was not moving too quickly, they waded upstream and exited where the ground was rocky. Other than that, they left a clear trail through the dense and muddy vegetation that was almost impossible to disguise.

With no clear pathway to follow through the cloud forest the journey had been gruelling. Wilson realised now why the Incas chose the dangers of the high pass of the Inca Trail rather than attempting to maintain a causeway through such thick vegetation. The cloud forest threw up some of the steepest and most difficult terrain that he had ever seen, and getting Hiram through the ordeal in good condition had been a real challenge.

A heavy mist hung in the still air between the ferns and gnarled trees. The terrain was nearly always slippery and for hour upon hour Wilson had to cut his way through the dense foliage with his hunting knife until his hands were blistered and bleeding. They didn't see any jaguars, but Wilson knew they were close because he found fresh tracks in the mud on two occasions. All the while it continued to rain heavily, day and night, and they were soaked to the bone. The bugs were ruthless and they had to cover their skin with mud, especially at dusk, to stop the relentless bloodsuckers. Lighting a fire was impossible, even when they found a cave or an overhang. And because they couldn't cook anything, the best meal they'd eaten in the last two days was a green python that Wilson had caught and skinned. The meat didn't taste good raw and he had to force Hiram to gulp it down so that he at least had some energy to draw on.

The entire way Hiram complained that the trail was not getting any easier. Then, with a relentless persistence that was utterly infuriating, he kept nattering about how they should have headed back to Cuzco when they had the chance. And about how he was too trusting, and constantly questioning how Wilson knew where he was going. Hiram always walked slowly, his shoulders slumped, sighing a lot, and he had to be encouraged all the time just to keep moving.

Pushing through a bank of ferns, Wilson stepped out of the jungle for the first time in nearly two days. The surging Urubamba flashed past before him in all its frightening glory – it was the last great obstacle before the climb to Machu Picchu. Wilson sucked in a deep breath, holstered his knife and put his hands on his hips. Hidden above them in the mist on the other side of the river was the lost city of Vilcapampa. The end of Wilson's journey was close at hand.

'We have to find a way across there,' he stated.

'Cross over?' Hiram replied as he looked at the thrashing whitewater. 'I have news for you, my friend, you can't swim across that.'

'Let's move up this way and we'll see what our options are,' Wilson answered.

The rock walls of the ravine were narrower to the east, and it was clear that the elevation was higher there. As a result, the water sped up as it gushed with great force through the constricted opening. There was more spray, froth and noise, making for an awesome sight. Draping from the walls of the steep cliff on both sides were hundreds of green liana vines.

As they scaled the fallen boulders up the incline towards the narrowed gorge, Hiram couldn't help but complain. 'It's hopeless! We'll never make it to the other side.'

Finding a relatively flat stone plateau, Wilson set about tugging on the thickest of the vines. When he was happy, he put his entire weight on the jungle thread and looked across to the far side of the river to see if it would swing the full distance.

'What do you think you are, an ape man?' Hiram studied the distance. 'I did a minor in engineering, you know? You'll never make it. If you had one of the vines from *that* side of the river, then it makes more sense. At least the vine pivots in the direction you want to travel.'

'If I can get you one of those vines,' Wilson gestured through the mist to the other side of the ravine, 'then you'll swing across?'

'You can't get there,' Hiram said.

'And if I do?'

'It's impossible. It can't be done.'

'Either we cross here,' Wilson said, 'or we have to head back into the cloud forest. There's no other choice.'

'I told you we should have headed back to Cuzco,' Hiram said with a sad face.

Wilson pointed across the raging river. 'Cuzco is over that side.'

Hiram unconsciously scratched at the mosquito bites around his neck and ears. 'The *last* place on earth I ever want to go back to is that cloud forest.'

'I'll make you a wooden seat to swing on. How does that sound?'

Hiram's jaw was tense as he looked back towards the jungle. He folded his arms and carefully studied the river. 'If you get me a vine from that side, I'll do it. But you won't make it over there – you'll die trying.'

Wilson smiled. 'It's a deal then.'

'Let me make this clear,' Hiram said. 'I don't want you knocking me out, or whatever you did the other day, to get me across. It's just so undignified.'

Wilson tugged at the vines above him and selected the strongest one he could find. Pulling it along with him, he proceeded to walk further upstream and away from the pivot. 'I'll be back,' he said confidently.

'What if you don't make it?' Hiram called out.

'Then you're on your own,' Wilson yelled back.

Hiram hacked out a laugh. 'I thought you were funny when we first met, but I'm beginning to realise you're not funny at all.'

From the other side of the river, Aclla and Sontane watched the two white men as they studied the hanging vines that draped from the cliff above them. All the while, the blue-eye Wilson Dowling was testing his full weight on the vines and talking to the skinny man, Hiram Bingham, who just stood there with an odd expression on his face.

Aclla had ordered the abduction of one of Captain Gonzales's men as they marched out of the Sacred Valley. The soldiers had ventured all the way to the Great Speaker, where Wilson had severed the Bridge of the Condor. Aclla's warriors easily took one of the soldiers while darkness approached and the information he provided was invaluable – including the names of the two white men. As soon as Aclla had what she needed, she ordered the soldier's throat be cut.

'I told you the blue-eye would find his way here,' Aclla said, a hint of triumph in her voice. But there was little else to be happy about.

Both she and Sontane lay among the greenery, their faces and skin painted with crushed tree moss until they were almost the exact colour of the jungle. Aclla had already sent Polix and Sepla back to the fortress outpost of Qente to pass on the disastrous news that the Bridge of the Condor had been breached and that two white men were approaching Vilcapampa. The fortress of Qente was half a day's run from here, situated high on the crest of a mountain that afforded unrestricted views of the twisting valley in all directions. 'Qente' meant 'hummingbird' in Quechua. The little birds frequented the microclimate on the eastern ridge of the fortress, towards the river basin. In the early morning they would fly through the city to feed on the beautiful flowers that grew in the rich soil of the carefully cultivated terraces.

Aclla watched as Wilson climbed to the highest point of the ravine; the vine he was pulling was now at a tight forty-five degree angle. He was so fluid in the way he moved, confident at all times in the surety of his step. When he reached the pinnacle of a jagged rock, he simply grabbed the vine with both hands, stepped back to the wall behind him and launched himself with amazing power off the precipice. There was not even a moment of contemplation, no need to map his flight path before he took off – he leapt like he had no fear whatsoever.

He soared with tremendous speed out over the plumes of whitewater on a steep arc. The vine easily flung him across to the other side, where his feet hit the ground running across the layers of shelf rock and boulders. One hand still gripping the liana, he slowed himself to a stop and calmly tied the vine off and set about selecting the strongest of the vines from those now above him.

Aclla and Sontane looked at each other. They were both asking themselves, *what are we dealing with?*

Wilson selected four vines, tested their strength then secured them with a loose knot. He tied the bundle to his waist, grabbed the vine that swung him over and proceeded to climb to the highest point he could reach. It felt exhilarating to fly out over the river, and he was looking forward to the return trip.

Waiting to jump, he made sure that the four vines at his waist were slack as he sprang off the rocks and flew out over the water. His landing was perfect and he easily set down beside Hiram, took just five steps, then uncoiled the four vines from his waist and tied them off to the rock wall.

'What sort of man are you?' Hiram said in exasperation.

Wilson began searching for a piece of wood that would make a good seat.

Hiram prodded Wilson with his finger. 'No one should be able to do what you just did. No one!' He let out a huff and stamped his feet like a child. 'It shouldn't be possible!'

'It is possible,' Wilson said. He presented a smooth piece of flat wood that he could easily bore holes into with his knife. 'This will make an excellent platform for you to sit on. Trust me, I'll get you across the other side of the river in one piece.'

Hiram stared up at the clouds and let out a cry of distress. 'Arrrh! I can't believe I'm even out here with you. *Trust you?* What a joke!'

'Are you scared?' Wilson asked.

'I'm not scared,' Hiram replied. 'I'm terrified.'

25

HELENA KEPT THE .45-calibre handgun pressed to Don Eravisto's temple – it didn't matter to her that he was still unconscious. The train took less than thirty minutes to get to the railway terminus at the base of Mount Machu Picchu, but it felt much longer. Chad stood in the centre aisle holding the MP5 submachine gun in the direction of her captives. The weapon was capable of shooting bursts of up to 800 rounds per minute, and she looked supremely confident that she could handle the five men seated in front of her with their hands raised above their heads. The real concern was that there might be another passenger or member of the train's staff that was on Don Eravisto's payroll.

From the moment Helena struck Don Eravisto in the head with the bottle there had been pandemonium inside the dining car. Chad fired two terrifying shots just above everyone's heads into the wood panelling on the back wall of the dining carriage. Thankfully, Don Eravisto was in the line of fire and his men were unable to shoot back. The young women inside the carriage were screaming and crying, scrambling over the chairs and tables to try and get away. In all the commotion, Pablo fell face first on the floor, splitting his nose open. He was now being cared for by one of the male waiters, his head tilted back and an ice compress covering his eyes.

Helena checked Don Eravisto's pulse, which was faint but steady. His face was a bloodied mess and two shards of splintered glass protruded from his left cheek. Blood was streaming down his face and soaking into the white table-cloth, which made him look like something out of a horror movie. The important thing was that he was breathing and Helena decided to leave it to the authorities to clean him up when they eventually boarded the train.

Helena looked to Daniel Eravisto who was obviously relieved that no one had been killed. At first he had fears for his father's wellbeing, but after Helena had reas-sured him he was still breathing, Daniel appeared much more comfortable. Throughout the stand-off, Helena had watched the young man's face as his father ranted and raved about 'changing history' and she could tell that he had doubts about what was being said.

The train slowed to a crawl as it lumbered into Machu Picchu terminus. Built on the banks of the Urubamba at the lowest point in the valley, it was a small village of about four hundred people. The sky was dark and the lights of the station were turned on, as were the local streetlights. The rumble of the river in the distance was unmistakeable and the sound added to the emotion Helena felt as the train finally came to a halt. Standing under the corrugated-iron canopy on the platform were six armed soldiers in smart grey uniforms. The train driver had radioed ahead with details of what had happened. Pablo had assured Helena that he knew one of the soldiers well – one of them was his cousin – and they could be trusted to take Don Eravisto and his men into custody.

Helena was nervous as the soldiers jumped on board, their AK-47 rifles at the ready, but the handover seemed to go quite smoothly.

Captain Zevallos, the officer in charge, appeared profes-sional and focused. He was dark-skinned with short black hair, his thin frame no taller than five-foot-five. Zevallos didn't ask too many questions about how Don Eravisto came to be in such a terrible state, other than to say, 'It is *impos-siblo* that a young woman like you could have done this to him. Isn't it?' He looked her up and down with a doubtful expression, evidently not believing that she had acted alone. 'There is no need to point the gun at him anymore, señorita,' he added. 'We have everything under control.'

Asking to keep the Colt handgun for her own protection, Zevallos agreed, and Helena inserted the nickel-plated weapon into the waistband of her pants. Don Eravisto was just coming out of his stupor as two soldiers dragged him from the bench seat, handcuffed him and carried him off the train. His face was so badly swollen that he looked like a different person altogether.

'Don Eravisto is well known here,' Zevallos stated. 'He has donated much money to the local school and police station. With respect, señorita, do you intend to press charges?'

'He tried to kill me,' Helena replied. 'Of course I do.'

Chad interjected, 'They were doing cocaine in the toilets.' But the comment didn't seem to affect Zevallos's demeanour one bit.

Pablo started ranting in Spanish, at the same time holding a cold compress to his nose, saying that Don Eravisto was *loco*, telling how he pointed his gun at Helena and said he was going to change history by killing her.

Chad remained in the centre aisle with her gun pointed at the last of Don Eravisto's men as they were handcuffed and led off the train in pairs via the forward door.

'This is a quiet little village,' Zevallos said looking outside. 'There is never much trouble to speak of. There is *good energy* here.' He scrunched his hands into tight fists. 'That is why the Incas built their great city up there, I suspect. They knew that this place was special.'

Daniel Eravisto was one of the last two men to be escorted off the train and Helena caught his eye. 'Will you excuse me, Capitán? I would like to talk to that man if that's alright.'

Zevallos gestured her forward with the barrel of his AK-47.

'I'm coming with you,' Chad announced.

'I'm sorry about your father,' Helena said as she stepped off the train and approached Daniel. The heavy rain was beating against the corrugated-metal roof above them, which made it difficult to hear.

Daniel stopped in his tracks, which also halted the progress of the large man he was handcuffed to, as well as the soldier who was escorting them along the platform.

'Why did your father do that to me?' Helena asked.

'It is obvious that my father has lost his mind,' he eventually replied.

'Surely you can tell me more than that? Your father said he'd prepared you for this moment. What does that mean?'

'My father has mental problems and he needs treatment. There is nothing else to say. I am certain a financial agreement can be reached that will compensate you for your trauma and suffering.'

'I do not want your money,' Helena replied. 'I want you to tell me why your father thought he knew me?'

The large man behind Daniel whispered in his ear, but the young Eravisto told him to be quiet. 'That is all I know, señorita. I am sorry.'

'Your father pointed a gun at me, for Christ's sake! He said that my death would *change history*. That is a very difficult thing to understand.'

Daniel began walking again. 'I can tell you nothing more.'

'You are an accessory to kidnap and attempted murder!' Helena called out. 'You did nothing to help me. You and your companions will all see jail time if I decide to prosecute. If you tell me what you know, I could be convinced to change my mind.'

Daniel halted in his tracks and turned towards her. Helena could tell by the way he was twisting his arms that his handcuffs were bothering him.

'If you are honest with me, I will drop the charges against you,' Helena offered.

'My father always said that a blonde woman would visit

that abandoned railway shack. He was so fixated upon his beliefs that when he heard they were going to tear that old railway shack down he purchased the land so that it could stay standing.'

'He owns the railway shack?' Helena asked.

'Yes, and all the land around it. That place has been an obsession for him since before I can remember.' Daniel paused. 'I would ask you: why did you go inside the shack? It was your actions, after all, that triggered his harsh response.'

'I simply had a headache and needed some fresh air,' Helena answered. 'I knew nothing about that building until today.'

'You seemed to know what he was talking about when we were on the train,' Daniel said suspiciously. 'I was beginning to wonder if he was right all along.'

Helena paused for longer than she would have wanted, she couldn't help it. 'Your father was threatening to kill me. A gun was pointed at my face! I would have said I was from *outer space* if I thought it would keep me alive a little bit longer.'

Daniel looked towards Don Eravisto as he was bundled into the back of a green military van. 'My father has always been of crystal-clear mind, in all his dealings. He is one of the richest men in Peru. He is respected by many. But when it came to the subject of that old railway shack . . .' Daniel suddenly became sombre and his voice trailed away. 'You have my most sincere apologies, señorita. All of this is madness. I have no excuse for my actions, or for the insane reaction of my father. I should have tried to stop him, but I was in shock, as we all were. If this can possibly be settled out of court, I would welcome the opportunity. My father needs medical help – prison is not the answer for him.'

'Who was the relative your father kept mentioning?' Helena asked. 'The man who lost everything and was driven to madness?'

'His name was Lucho Gonzales,' Daniel replied. 'My great-grandfather. He was a captain in the Peruvian army. My father believes that a man called Wilson Dowling viciously murdered his wife and children in their beds, all except his eldest son, Arturo – my father's father.'

Helena felt a sinking in her stomach.

'My great-grandfather always said that a beautiful American woman would one day visit that deserted railway shack during a fierce rainstorm, after a rockslide blocked the tracks – just as you visited the railway shack today. He passed that information on to his son, Arturo, and in turn it was passed on to my father.'

'How is visiting the railway shack related to the murders?' Helena asked.

'My great-grandfather believed that the woman from the future, the woman who visited that railway shack, would somehow guide the hand of the murderer Wilson Dowling. I know it sounds crazy, but he believed they were connected across *time itself* by some form of telepathic link that cannot be explained with science. By stopping the woman from the future, the family of Lucho Gonzales would be saved, somehow.'

'But your name is Eravisto, not Gonzales?' Helena asked, trying to piece all the information together.

'After the murders, Lucho Gonzales and his young son, Arturo, fled from Cuzco and changed their name to Eravisto. From that point they built a huge fortune that covered almost every industry in Peru. But no matter how much money and power my grandfather and father accumulated, they were never satisfied. That is all I know. Señorita, I myself do not understand how a person from the future can affect people's lives in the past. But right or wrong, that is what my father has always believed. That is why we are all here, and that is why events unfolded today exactly as they did.'

26

Cuzco, Peru
La Monasterio
Local Time 12:35 am

19 January 1908

RIDING HIS SMALL donkey, Captain Gonzales approached the double wooden doors of La Monasterio with
Lieutenant Capos by his side. The rain was tumbling from
the dark sky as the two donkeys came to a halt in the
narrow cobblestone laneway. The only light was coming
from the second-level windows of the monastery and from
the small hurricane lamp that was attached to the bridle of
Capos's animal. Both men were exhausted; they had been
in and out of the saddle for more than thirty-six hours.

The situation in Cuzco could not have been worse, and
it seemed all of Captain Gonzales's fears had been realised.
Since leaving the city, a putrid evil he could not understand
had overcome this entire place. The wraith-like peril that
lurked in the darkness was snatching innocents. Murders
had been committed in countless places – depraved acts that
left men, women and children ripped to shreds in bloody
attacks. The army was stretched to breaking point trying to
respond to calls for help. The military guard they encountered as they approached the city said that the people of
Cuzco were holed up in their homes, weapons at the ready,
unable to sleep for fear of what would happen to them.

Gonzales let out a sigh. 'I will meet the bishop on my
own,' he said to Capos. 'You must head home to your
family to be sure they are safe.'

'I will stay with you,' Capos replied. 'We set out on this cursed journey together and we will finish it together.'

Captain Gonzales struggled to muster the energy to argue. 'If I could go home to my family right now, I would. Maybe *you* should meet with Bishop Francisco and I will be the one who leaves.' Gonzales smiled for the first time in days. 'How does that sound?'

Capos smiled in return. 'I am certain that our families are safe, Capitán. We should both meet with the bishop. Then, if there are tasks that need to be completed in the morning, as I am sure there will be, I can take care of them.'

Captain Gonzales climbed off his donkey and gingerly set his boots on the slippery cobblestones. It was such a relief to be out of the saddle that he momentarily forgot about how cold, wet and tired he was. His legs were aching and it felt good to stretch them out. When he was done giving his report he would head directly home. Capos would take his donkey to the military barracks where it could be fed, brushed and given a well-earned rest. Gonzales would take his donkey to the corral that had been built at the back of his house.

The metal latch to the main entrance of La Monasterio unlocked and the stud-reinforced door creaked open to reveal a dark silhouette in a long flowing robe.

'I have been waiting for you,' a voice called out, but Gonzales could not yet make out who it was.

'Is that you, Bishop Francisco?' he replied in the silhouette's direction.

'Yes, my child. I have been waiting for your return.' Bishop Francisco stepped forward into the hazy light. 'You can leave, Capos. You are not required here anymore.'

Both Capos and Gonzales could not understand how the bishop could have known they were back in Cuzco, especially at this late hour. They were expecting him to be sleeping in his grand chamber and they would have to wait for him to be woken by one of the novices.

'I am surprised to see you up this late,' Gonzales said as he handed his reins to Capos and set about untying Hiram Bingham's Springfield rifle that was neatly secured to the saddlebag.

'The hand of God never sleeps,' the bishop replied. 'You can go, Capos. I have spoken.'

Lieutenant Capos looked confused and his donkey was pacing backwards and forwards as if it wanted to run away. 'I will wait out here,' he replied, at the same time trying to steady his animal.

'You will go home to your family,' Gonzales ordered as he scaled the steps to La Monasterio rifle in hand, past the Spanish Royal Arms Escutcheon that was carved proudly into the stone. The emblem denoted that this building belonged to the Spanish king, and would forevermore. With a wave to his loyal lieutenant, Gonzales stepped out of the rain for the first time in days.

La Monasterio was a grand building of more than a hundred rooms on three levels. Square in shape with a huge central courtyard, it was home to more than forty priests and church novices who trained and lived there. Normally bustling with people, at this hour of the night there was not a soul to be seen.

Removing his hat, Gonzales raked his fingers through his wet hair before closing the large outer doors and letting the heavy metal latch fall into the locked position. He adjusted his dripping uniform as best he could and made sure all his buttons were done up. When he turned around, the bishop was standing in the middle of the grand foyer, his arm extended and his golden bishop's ring held forward. On the walls on either side of him were two large paintings. To the right was the resplendent Virgin Mary, to the left was the calm figure of Joseph of Nazareth, both with glowing hallows surrounding their heads.

Gonzales approached at a brisk pace and fell to his knees to passionately kiss the bishop's ring. His legs were aching so badly that kneeling was painful, but Gonzales did not complain. 'Forgive me, Father, I have come with further bad news.'

'You have failed to capture the white stranger called Wilson Dowling,' Bishop Francisco said. 'This is of grave concern to me.'

There was not even time for Gonzales to ask himself how Bishop Francisco could possibly have known. 'Father, I am more concerned about what has taken place here in Cuzco. The murders and the missing people. It seems that a veil of evil has fallen over this once protected city.'

Bishop Francisco snatched his hand away, showing his displeasure. 'You will tell me what I want to know!' he said with a gruff voice. 'I sent you on an important mission, to capture the enemies of the Church. You will do *my* bidding, Capitán, until I say otherwise.'

'I am sorry, Father. You are right, of course.' From his knees, Gonzales offered up the battered Springfield rifle with both hands. 'This is their gun,' he said.

'I send you on a mission to bring back these men and you bring me their *gun?*' The bishop spun away and began walking along the shadowed hallway towards the central courtyard. 'That is all you have for me?' he called back.

Gonzales carefully leant the rifle against the wall then quick-stepped so that he was close behind the bishop. 'Please, Father, let me explain what has happened.' The water dripping from Gonzales's clothes left a trail across the stone floor. 'As you requested, we set off with an armed contingent in pursuit of the man called Wilson Dowling and his travelling companion, Hiram Bingham. The foreigners moved very quickly through the weather and the muddy darkness. They travelled much faster than I could have imagined, like they had the Devil chasing after them.' Gonzales paused for a moment to gather his thoughts. 'We rode all night without stopping, but when we got to the railway shack the foreigners were already gone. To our dismay we searched the area and found that two of their donkeys had been maimed and killed. The animals suffered horrible deaths. My guides told me that it was local Indian warriors who had committed these acts. We did not see them, but their footprints were everywhere, like they were acting in a terrible frenzy.'

The bishop looked concerned now. 'You continued to follow the two white men after their donkeys were killed?' he asked.

'We tracked them to an area my guides call the Sacred Valley. Have you heard of this place?'

The bishop shook his head.

'We followed the trail all the way towards the river cliffs, but by the time we got there the foreigners were gone, certainly killed after they attempted to cross an old Inca suspension bridge across the raging torrent. That was where we found the rifle.'

The bishop turned and looked towards the inner courtyard. 'They are not dead,' he said to the darkness.

'The suspension bridge was pulled from its foundations by the force of the water. My guide believes Indian warriors tracked the white men to the bridge and gave them no choice but to attempt a crossing. All their footsteps climbed the cliffs, but only the Indian warriors' tracks returned. One of my men picked up a discarded Indian arrow. Just the merest touch of primitive poison on the arrowhead caused his hand to swell up like a toad on a hot day.'

'The foreigners are not dead,' the bishop said again.

'But, Father, the evidence is clear . . .'

'One of your soldiers, Bonito Rodriguez, went missing on the return trip to Cuzco. Is this correct?'

'How can you possibly know that?' Gonzales replied.

'He was kidnapped and killed,' the bishop proclaimed. 'By dark shapes that were difficult to see. Women, I think they were. Cold-hearted women.'

Bonito had indeed gone missing on the return journey, but Captain Gonzales had no way of knowing what had happened to him. He simply thought Bonito had become lost along the way. 'You are saying he was murdered?'

Bishop Francisco nodded. 'I have seen it in my visions. In the very same way, I sense that the two white men are not dead – they are still heading for Vilcapampa.'

This was the first moment that Gonzales had truly studied the face of Bishop Francisco – he looked pale and unwell, his eyes were sunken and his skin had taken on a green hue. The situation in Cuzco would certainly have been a worry to the head of the Church, Gonzales decided.

That had to be the reason he looked so awful. 'Are you all right, Father?' he asked.

A terrible anger suddenly overcame the bishop's face. 'Do not ask stupid questions . . . *listen!*'

Gonzales once again remembered the flicker of scarlet he had seen deep within the bishop's pupils. He couldn't see it at this moment, but he sensed dreadful conflict within the man before him. 'What do you ask of me?' Gonzales said, instinctively looking away for fear he would see flickering in the man's eyes once again.

The glow of the oil lamp illuminated only one side of Bishop Francisco's face. 'You will request more soldiers are sent here from Lima, to protect the Church and its followers.'

'They have not been sent for already?' Gonzales asked in surprise.

'I was waiting for your return.'

Captain Gonzales nodded. 'Many people are missing and others have been found murdered. Reinforcements are required, as you say. I am terribly sorry to hear about your niece,' he said sincerely. 'She was a beautiful young girl.' With those words, the bishop took on a twisted look of pain that was heartbreaking to witness. 'I know she was special to you,' Gonzales added.

The bishop was momentarily unable to speak, such was his anguish.

'I told you, Father, the crucified body of Corsell Santillana must be removed from the outer walls of the church.' On his way through the Plaza de Armas, Captain Gonzales had passed the putrid, decaying body that was still nailed to the outer walls of La Catedral. The black crows had pecked away Corsell's eyeballs but his blackened tongue was left untouched. The angry crowds that had been in the plaza three days earlier were gone, all except for Corsell's mother, who still held vigil in the darkness, on her knees in the rain next to the terraced stairs.

Bishop Francisco pulled in a deep breath and his composure returned. 'The body will remain on the outer walls,' he said sternly. 'Do not mention it to me again, Capitán. Only I may speak for God in these matters.'

'Father, the evil that is overtaking this city is certainly related to the crucifixion. Take the body down. If you would somehow reconsider, then I believe that healing can finally begin. I give you my word that I will move mountains to track down those responsible for these heinous murders –'

'I am the hand that wields the sword of God!' the bishop interjected in a deep voice that made the hairs on the back of Gonzales's neck stand on end. 'Do not mention this matter to me again, or you will face the consequences! You will bring more troops from Lima,' the bishop continued. 'You will send a telegraph from the post office immediately.'

Even though it meant waking up the telegraph operator, Gonzales was not going to argue with the man standing before him. The highest representative of the Church in South America had spoken. But more than that, Gonzales was afraid of Bishop Francisco for reasons he did not understand. Just a week earlier, he had believed that he would never be afraid of any living person, no matter how strong, determined or powerful – but everything changed the moment Gonzales saw flickers of scarlet deep within the blackness of Bishop Francisco's pupils.

'When they arrive, you will garrison the roadways towards the north-west,' the bishop commanded. 'You will order your soldiers to shoot the white men Dowling and Bingham on sight, if they return. Do you understand?'

'Yes, Father.' No matter what he thought of the insane orders he was being given, Gonzales counselled himself not to argue or question.

'These are dark times that surround Cuzco,' Bishop Francisco said in monotone. 'We must be ready to combat any force that confronts us. The lives of the innocent are being taken, many of them from the warmth and safety of their very own beds. If you do not wish such a fate to befall you and your family, you will do as I say without asking questions. The man Dowling is integral to the horrific wickedness that descends like a shadow moments before the prey is struck. He will attempt to return to Cuzco to steal what is not his. This man is *evil* – the most depraved of men who has ever walked the face of God's great earth.'

The bishop stepped out from under the archway and into the pouring rain. A strange type of steam rose from his exposed skin. 'Do you love your family?' the bishop asked.

Gonzales felt a shiver go up his spine.

'Do you love your family?' he asked again.

'I love the Church, Father, but as God would have it, I love my wife and children more than *anything*. More than my own life.'

'You would die for them?' the bishop asked.

'Without a moment's thought.'

Bishop Francisco seemed to smile, but his teeth and eyes were shadowed, which made for an eerie sight. 'You are a fine soldier for the Church. A man like you can face any challenge, it seems, and it will only make you stronger. That is why God has chosen you to be my right hand.'

27

EVERYONE WAS SURPRISED when Helena said she wanted to stay on at Machu Picchu. It was difficult for people to understand why she didn't want to leave immediately after such a harrowing ordeal – being the victim of *attempted murder* would generally drive most people away. Captain Zevallos had offered to hold Don Eravisto and his men in custody for the night, in the jail cell at the local army barracks, so that she didn't need to travel back on the same train with them to Cuzco. Helena had refused, insisting that Zevallos send the prisoners back instead. This caused a problem for some of the other passengers who had witnessed the bizarre event and wanted to get back home as quickly as possible. They didn't want to be on the same train as the prisoners either.

'That's not my problem,' Helena had replied. 'I've travelled a long way to see Machu Picchu, and that is what I intend to do.'

Chad pleaded with Helena to leave also, saying there was no way to guarantee her safety if she stayed. Eravisto was a man of resources and she worried someone else would target Helena in his place. But even so, Helena's decision was made – she was on the verge of something amazing and she would not run away.

Directly outside Helena's suite, in the hallway, sat an

armed security guard who arrived just this afternoon from Houston. Chad insisted that she needed extra security and Helena had agreed to fly an additional man in to assist. John Hanna was an ex-Navy SEAL and despite his short stature, he was a respected and capable bodyguard for the rich and famous – mainly celebrity clients like rock stars and sports professionals.

'He looked after Bono while he toured the United States last year,' Chad said. 'He's seen it all before and that's what we need right now. Don't be fooled by his size. He can kill a man with just his pinkie finger if he has to.'

Helena had only met Hanna once, but she could tell from first impressions that he could be trusted. He seemed a little hyperactive; the way he spoke and the way he energetically jumped about the room while he did his sweep was unnerving until you got used to it. He was so eager that he even leapt off the balcony to check out the security from the bottom – it was a fifteen-foot drop to the rocks below.

Now that Hanna was here, Chad was sleeping in the adjacent bedroom. She'd taken it upon herself to stay awake the entire night before in case there was further trouble. Helena had not slept either, but it wasn't out of concern for her own safety. It was the fact that she had not had any contact with Wilson since arriving at Machu Picchu. She expected *something* to happen – the events on the train with Don Eravisto certainly had predicted it, and yet she felt nothing. As much as she would wish a connection with Wilson, the link had not engaged. With her immediate hopes dashed, Helena began to run theories about what could possibly have happened. Had she missed her chance? Had she misinterpreted Wilson's destination? Or, at worst, had some terrible fate overwhelmed him before his arrival at Machu Picchu?

There is nothing more dire than being alone and having too much time to think, particularly when things are not going your way. Even the most normal of situations can be interpreted as something quite the opposite.

Helena kept asking herself why Don Eravisto would

believe that Wilson had murdered an innocent mother and her children? That was something Wilson would never do – Helena was certain of that fact. It was not in his DNA to commit such evil, even if it was demanded of him. And yet that is how Don Eravisto saw history. It had seemingly driven the path of his grandfather's life, his father's and now his own. That is a terrible burden of revenge to carry for so long, by so many men. And yet it seemed Don Eravisto – with everything he had to lose as a result – was still willing to pull the trigger and see Helena's skull and brains blown across that train carriage in some futile attempt to change history.

Helena's thoughts drifted back to earlier that morning when she got out of bed, even before her alarm had gone off. Don Eravisto's Colt .45 was tucked inside her padded vest. With Chad by her side, Helena was downstairs for a quick cup of black coffee and a slice of dry toast. Pablo handed them each an umbrella before leading them outside into the inclement weather. The swelling on Pablo's face had subsided, but he needed six stitches on the bridge of his nose to finally staunch the bleeding.

There was thunder in the distance as Helena walked up the steep incline towards the guardhouse. A layer of mist hung in the humid air, making it difficult to see more than a short distance in any direction. The muddy ground was corrugated by the countless little streams busily making their way towards the bottom of the valley, where the faint grumble of the Urubamba could be heard through the pouring rain.

Helena felt a burning sense of anticipation as she scaled a carefully constructed stone pathway – this was the first time she had come into direct contact with an ancient Inca construction.

'Pablo, I want you to take me to the Temple of the Sun,' Helena said as they passed through the guardhouse into the World Heritage site. There was no one else around except the clerk who took their entrance tickets then stamped their passports. They were the only tourists who were prepared to brave the bad weather.

Pablo was wearing a transparent plastic poncho that covered him to his knees and a wide-brimmed hat with a waterproof elastic cover. On his feet he wore knee-high rubber boots. 'I will take you there,' he replied. 'It is very important that you watch your step, señorita. The rocks can be very slippery and while you cannot see it, the drop-off to our right is more than a thousand feet straight down. So, care must be taken.'

Helena looked cautiously into the swirling mist.

'Any fall of more than fifty feet will kill you,' Chad said matter-of-factly. 'So the distance is irrelevant. Fifty feet or a thousand feet – either way you die.'

Interestingly, Chad had not mentioned a word about the bizarre conversation Helena had had with Don Eravisto in the dining carriage. It was like she had blocked out the entire event. Either that or her code of conduct as a professional bodyguard excluded her from saying anything about it.

'Watch your step,' Pablo repeated as they climbed the steep stairs.

Helena had seen countless pictures and studied many websites relating to Machu Picchu. It was indeed a place of rare beauty and she had marvelled at the designs and photographs of the ancient stone city atop the razorback ridge between two giant peaked mountains. All around the citadel breathtakingly steep cliffs fell away into thin air, making this place almost impossible to attack. As far as the eye could see, the towering glacier-capped peaks of the Andes were at every point of the compass. This was meant to be one of the greatest sights on earth, but not today.

The constant rain and resulting humidity meant that visibility was down to nothing. The temperature varied greatly depending on the direction of the wind gusts – it was warm one second and freezing the next. Pablo said it was because the moist air from the Pacific Ocean was driving head-on into the super-chilled air that came off the glaciers. That was why it rained so much during the summer. All Helena saw through the cloud cover was carefully stacked rubble walls and staircases that

climbed upwards through the city. It was steeper than
Helena expected and the altitude was making her breathe
faster than usual. And while it was not quite the elevation of Cuzco, it was still high enough to cause breathing
problems if you exerted yourself too much.

'This is the Watchman's House,' Pablo said as Helena
came puffing up the stairs behind him. On a small landing
stood an impressive three-walled building with a thatched
roof supported by timber crossbeams. 'From here we are
at the highest point of the agricultural terraces.' Pablo
ushered them out of the rain and under the roofline. 'It
is possible to see in every direction from this place, down
into the valleys on both sides and towards the Inca Trail.
There was once a drawbridge just outside here. This was
the only way to enter Machu Picchu. Truly spectacular the
view is on all sides.'

Chad peered through one of the trapezoidal windows.
'I'll have to take your word for it,' she said in a droll tone.

Helena was waiting for something amazing to happen.
'Take me to the Temple of the Sun,' she said again. 'You
can explain more about the city as we move along.'

Pablo lowered the brim of his hat and stepped out into
the rain once again. He followed a grassy terrace that slowly
arced to the right, a ten-foot-high, perfectly constructed
wall beside him. After approximately a hundred steps they
began descending beautifully assembled stairs, even more
precise than the ones that led upwards through the terraces
and into the city.

Just beside them, a finely crafted aqueduct system of
square-cut channels was gushing with crystal-clear water.
'There are sixteen natural springs on Machu Picchu,' Pablo
said without breaking his stride. 'The water originates
from the heart of the mountain above us. These springs run
year round with the purest of water, the only place in this
entire region where that still occurs. As you can see, the
city walls are in perfect condition. Machu Picchu has been
cleared of the trees and bushes that had overtaken the city
after hundreds of years of being uninhabited. The walls
and buildings have been reconstructed to capture Machu

Picchu's former glory. This work has taken fifty men more than fifteen years to complete. Any missing stones were cut from the old quarry using traditional building methods.

'We are now in the heart of the Urban Section,' Pablo said. 'Notice the quality of the masonry. These are some of the finest constructions in the world. These stones are known as ashlars: large cuboids of granite that are sculpted to have square edges and smooth faces. Notice the perfect fit between the stones? There is no mortar used here – it is precision masonry. The Incas built this place to be earthquake-proof.' Pablo pointed down the stairs. 'And the finest building of them all is just down there, the Temple of the Sun.'

Helena's heart began to race. Her dreams had always been very specific – afternoon rays of sunshine scything through the trapezoidal windows above and bathing her in light. She would be standing at the base of the structure, before the triangular entrance that was cut at a forty-five-degree angle into the granite foundations. The brightness in her eyes made it difficult to see clearly, but she knew there was something in that cave she needed to discover.

Is Wilson going to be in there? she wondered.

Descending the slippery stairs, the rain became heavier, making it difficult to hear. The numbing of Helena's senses only added to her apprehension. The accumulated rainwater was gushing down the stairs past them, gaining speed as the volume increased towards the bottom steps. The white granite wall beside her changed from finely carved ashlars to a sheer wall of natural, blackish stone.

The entrance to the inner temple is just ahead.

Stepping through a stone archway she came out onto an open plateau. Turning around, she stared for the first time into the Royal Mausoleum of Machu Picchu, the mysterious shrine that was located directly under the Temple of the Sun – the most holy building located within the City in the Clouds. The vaults of the inner shrine were thought to have housed the mummies of Inca kings and queens. This was where Helena's dreams had led her.

Looking into the dark shadows of the inner shrine, she waited, expecting some connection . . . a vision of some kind. But there was nothing except the rain hitting her umbrella and the freezing cold winds that suddenly cut through her waterproof clothing.

'Above us is the Temple of the Sun,' Pablo said. 'It is the finest construction in all of Machu Picchu. It is the only building in the Inca world that is built with *curved walls*. The Sun God, Inti, is the most important of all the Inca gods. He is the supreme ruler of the universe, the bringer of life and the taker of life. He warms the earth and he makes the crops grow. It is said the Sun God rules the lust and ambition of men, which is at the very core of human progress.'

Helena was listening to Pablo's words, but her despair at the lack of a supernatural connection had her dazed and confused. She had come all the way to Peru with so many hopes, but at this moment they had come to nothing. What cruel twist of fate would lead her on a journey with no destination? She had been tempted by her vision of Wilson in the railway shack. It was so real, and now this – nothing but an empty construction of stones on a mountain ridge.

Sitting in her warm hotel bed, Helena gazed up at the ceiling and remembered the pangs of despair she felt as she stood there in the pouring rain earlier that morning. She told herself it was important to stay positive, and yet no matter how she tried it was difficult not to be consumed by her disappointment.

Helena's thoughts once again drifted back to Don Eravisto. How could he believe that changing history was even possible? After everything Helena had witnessed when she was with Wilson, it still remained difficult to reconcile that all time existed simultaneously; and that changing history was even possible. It defied logic that Don Eravisto could accept a concept so bizarre when it originated two full generations before.

The central question remained: what was her part in all this? Don Eravisto looked at her like she was an accomplice to murder, like she had been the one who committed the heinous crimes against his family. She was not even alive a century ago, and her connection to Wilson remained a theory, except for what she had seen in that railway shack. Helena pulled in a long, deep breath then exhaled. Reaching over to the side table, she picked up the Egyptian coin Wilson had given her. She pressed the cool metal between her fingers and ran her thumb over the damaged surface before taking time to study the coin by the brightness of the bedside lamp.

This was the very object that had saved Wilson's life just over a year ago.

Helena was certain that the coin in her hand would find its way back to him one day – it was Wilson's destiny. But for now he was certainly in the past, at least a hundred years back was her best guess. He had travelled *backwards* in time, not to the future where she expected him to be. From what Helena had seen in her vision, Wilson looked older, as if *more time* had passed for him than it had for her. It was possible, but it surprised her nonetheless.

With the Egyptian coin in one hand and nickel-plated revolver in the other, Helena studied them both in the light. The coin had saved Wilson's life . . . and the gun had nearly taken hers. The sight of the two contrary objects had her feeling conflicted.

She just needed to be patient, she told herself.

There was no choice but to wait.

28

Cuzco, Peru
Avenue Pavitos
Local Time 4:26 am

19 January 1908

CAPTAIN GONZALES WAS so tired he could hardly
think straight. As instructed, he had woken the telegraph
operator and dictated a message to military headquarters in Lima requesting more men be sent immediately.
According to the clock at the Plaza de Armas, it was 4.15
in the morning by the time he led his donkey through the
heavy rain along the narrow laneway and into the corral at
the back of his simple home. He dutifully took the saddle
off his animal and set out some dry hay for it to eat.

'You've done well,' he said, and gave the donkey a pat
on the head.

After circling the house to make sure everything was
okay, Gonzales removed his soiled clothes and draped
them over the rock wall next to the door. He stood naked
in the freezing downpour with his hands shivering uncontrollably as he attempted to work a cake of soap across
his filthy, waterlogged skin. His wife was very particular
about bringing dirt and mud into the house and he knew
he should wash himself before stepping inside or face the
consequences.

'When will this rain stop?' Gonzales muttered as he
unlocked the door. Stepping into the cold darkness of his
small kitchen, he began rummaging through the bottom
cupboards in search of a towel. He knew he should strike a

match to light the oil lamp, but he didn't want to wake his family, who he hoped would be asleep in the next room.

The simple three-room dwelling near the city square had stone floors and brick walls. It was well built compared to the other houses nearby, constructed by the same workers who built the military barracks. With the leftover materials of wood, plaster, three window frames and plenty of stone, they were able to cobble together a relatively modern home. The house was not large but it had high ceilings and an excellent tiled roof that drained easily no matter how much water came down. The kitchen had a wood-burning stove, a sink and a modern icebox that could keep meat fresh for up to a week. Out the back there was a stall for his donkey and a chicken coop that held ten hens. Both Captain Gonzales and his wife were house-proud and felt they were the envy of their extended family.

Gonzales dried himself off, secured the towel around his waist and sat down in the darkness to contemplate what he had been through over the last few days. His thoughts shifted to the murders that had been taking place around Cuzco. A terrible evil had indeed overcome the city. As he rode towards the city outskirts, his sergeant had given him a full briefing on the grisly events of the last half-week. The fear in Sergeant Veha's eyes was evident as he requested he return to his family as quickly as possible to be sure they were okay and his children were safe.

With his eyesight gradually adjusting to the dim light of the kitchen, Gonzales could just make out a plate of half-eaten food on the chequered tablecloth. It was most unusual for his wife to leave scraps out in case it lured the rats in.

Gonzales jumped to his feet and ran to the bedroom doorway. His blood was pumping so quickly he could barely hear anything around him except the heavy rain running off the roof into pools on the muddy ground around the perimeter of his house. Staring into the shadows of the bedroom, Gonzales faced his worst fears as he gazed down at the two beds and the people lying in them.

'You are here, Lucho,' his wife said with a drowsy voice. 'Thank the Lord.'

With a sigh of relief, Gonzales checked his three small children who were safely together in their small bed. 'I'm back now, chiquita,' he said in his wife's direction.

'Thank the Lord,' Sarita said again. 'People have been murdered and others have gone missing. Everyone is scared to death.' She propped herself up on an elbow and unveiled the rifle that was lying under the covers next to her.

Gonzales took the .303 weapon and propped it next to the bed. 'Everything will be okay now.' He laid her back down and stroked her forehead. 'I am here to sort everything out. I will not be leaving again.'

'Thank you for coming home safely to me,' she whispered.

'You must sleep now, chiquita. The children will be up soon. We can talk in the morning.'

She nestled into her pillow once again and closed her eyes. 'I am very pleased that you are home, Lucho.'

Gonzales settled his weary body into the warm bed next to his wife. Scanning the darkness towards his three children, he could not help but think about Corsell Santillana and his terrible fate. Gonzales had seen dead men before, many of them, but this was different. The expression on Corsell's face was the horrific veneer of a man who had lost everything. It was like his soul was still inside his dead body and his torture would carry on until the end of time.

Bishop Francisco was responsible for Santillana's death. On his word alone, the church sextons had taken it upon themselves to nail the young man's hands and feet to the makeshift cross then hoist him up on the outer wall of the cathedral. What madness was it that would allow something so cruel to take place in these modern times? The crucifixion had done nothing to ward away evil; the events of the past few days were certainly proof of that. The bishop was losing his mind, Gonzales allowed himself to think. The death of Monsignor Pera and now the others around Cuzco had pushed him over the edge.

'Praise be to Jesus,' Gonzales whispered as he studied

the dim outline of the small cross mounted on the wall above his children's bed.

For more than thirty minutes he lay there thinking about what he had seen. In one sense he wanted to sleep, in another he was afraid to close his eyes until the sky became brighter to herald the coming of a new day. In the end, it was simply his exhaustion that let him drift away from his worries.

Feeling a heavy impact on his stomach, Gonzales let out a scream of fright. Sunrays were streaming in through the window as his little boy Ortega landed in his lap. Gonzales was lucky not to have struck out at the child before he realised what was actually happening.

'I have missed you, Papa!' his six-year-old son called out as he jumped up and down, his innocent laughter filling the room.

Sarita's naked backside was pressed against Gonzales's hip. The sight and smell of her shiny hair was so familiar, as was everything about this place. In just moments, all three of Lucho's children were on top on him, jumping around and laughing – his eldest son, Arturo, who was eight years old; Ortega, the cheeky six year old; and his little princess, Juanita, who had just turned three. With the combined weight of his children on top of him, Lucho was reminded how stiff his legs and back were from his long ride.

'I am glad to see you all,' he said with a hoarse voice. 'Papa has been on a long journey.' He kissed his children, then turned to his wife who was smiling at him. Looking out the bedroom window, Gonzales realised the clouds had finally drifted away and it had stopped raining. It was still early in the morning and he wondered if he'd slept at all, but he was too tired to decide. 'Papa had a difficult journey,' he said as he lifted his children one by one and put them on the floor. 'Go with your mother and she will make you a giant breakfast!' He hoped his words would encourage his children to go quickly so he could fall back to sleep before he started thinking again.

'Quickly, children,' Sarita said, clapping her hands to hurry them. 'Your father needs rest.' She kissed her husband on the forehead and they were gone.

When Gonzales woke up again, his wife was sitting on the bed next to him with a steaming cup of coca tea in her hands. 'You must drink this,' she said.

Lifting his aching body, he pulled a pillow in behind him, grabbed the mug and took a sip.

'It is after midday and we are going to mass,' Sarita said. She was wearing her best black dress with a black scarf around her shoulders.

Gonzales shook his head. 'Not today, Sarita.'

'It's Sunday!' she said with a calm smile.

'I do not think we should go to church today,' Gonzales replied. 'Not today.' He pointed in the direction of the Plaza de Armas. 'The body of Corsell Santillana is still there, crucified for all to see. I do not want the children going there, chiquita.'

'We can cover the two young ones' eyes, as the other parents are doing. And we need not worry about Arturo – he has already run down there with his friends on many occasions to see it for himself.'

'I told you he was not to go there!' Gonzales said angrily.

'I could not stop him,' she replied. 'He is a young man and does what he wishes, especially when you are not here.' Sarita put her hand on her husband's chest. 'It is a beautiful day outside, Lucho. The first in many weeks. The children are dressed and ready, I think we should go. How does it look for everyone else when the *Captain of the Guard* does not take his family to church for mass? You are a sign of strength for them.'

'I do not care what anyone else thinks,' Gonzales said with a sigh. 'Anyway, they don't even know that I am back.'

Sarita levelled her gaze. 'We are going to church today, Lucho. What's more important than what other people think is what *God* thinks. I will not let my relationship with Him be affected by the terrible murder that Corsell Santillana has committed.'

'This is not only about Corsell Santillana.' Gonzales made the cross of Jesus on his chest. 'Bishop Francisco has broken the law by calling for the crucifixion of a man who was not properly tried and sentenced. I cannot be seen to condone that kind of behaviour, not even from the bishop.'

'Your soldiers stand in protection of the church, Lucho. You are committed already.'

'I have no choice! It is the duty of the military guard to protect the church regardless. Going to mass with my family is a different matter.'

'Lucho,' she said with a soft voice, 'you have already condoned the crucifixion by letting it happen in the first place. Don't you see that?'

'We could go to a *different* church, like Iglesia San Cristóbal?'

'I am not going to a different church, Lucho. That is the church we were married in, and the church where our children were baptised, as we both were before them. I am not going anywhere else.'

Gonzales wanted to tell his wife what he had seen in the bishop's eyes, and the fear he felt as a result, but for some reason he just couldn't. It was as if the strange evil that had mysteriously descended over Cuzco had stripped his own resolve to fight her.

'We are going to La Catedral today,' Sarita said sternly, 'as we have done every Sunday for the last ten years. People are dying and God and the Church needs us right now more than ever. We are going there to pray for our children and each other. We will pray for the soul of Monsignor Pera and also for his murderer, Corsell Santillana, and also for the poor souls who have been taken by the mysterious evil that roams the streets at night. That is what God would want of us in these dark times.'

'Maybe you're right,' Gonzales replied.

'I'm always right about this sort of thing.' Sarita stood beside the bed looking as beautiful as Gonzales could ever remember – around her neck hung the simple silver cross that he gave her when they first met. She was a full-figured woman, always was, with beautiful soft skin and friendly hazel eyes. Her hair was waist-long, and when the sun hit her directly, her hair seemed to shine. 'We have much that needs to be protected, Lucho.'

Gonzales smiled. 'You're right, we have much to be thankful for.'

Sarita gestured to his dark-blue military uniform neatly laid out on the children's bed. 'The afternoon mass is at two o'clock. If you get ready now, we can head off straight after.'

29

Andes Ranges, Peru
55 Miles North-west of Cuzco
Local Time 12:43 pm

19 January 1908

'WE'RE GETTING CLOSE now,' Wilson said.

The climb to this point had been exhausting. The jungle terrain was steep and slippery, requiring both men to practically claw their way upwards through the dense undergrowth on all fours. The ascent was always going to be a treacherous, requiring great expertise in climbing. As a result, Wilson was constantly yelling instructions to Hiram about where to place his feet and hands. With sweat dripping from both their faces, Wilson realised they couldn't keep going at this pace and he stopped at a smooth stone outcrop that literally protruded thirty feet out over the valley.

The rain had ceased some time ago and the winds were finally calm. The sky was just becoming blue as sunbeams broke through the haze for the first time in over a week. The sight of the mountains and moss-covered cliffs with thousand-foot drop-offs was breathtaking, as was the spectacle of the mighty Urubamba as it roared past at a white-water gallop into the distance, around a steep mountain bend. This was certainly one of the most beautiful places on earth. Wilson knew the lost city of the Incas was concealed atop the narrow mountain ridge directly above them. Amazingly, even from this vantage point, it still wasn't visible.

Sunbeams were shining through the distant ranges, the rays of light like translucent spears piercing through the jagged, glacier-capped peaks. Wilson took off his sweat-soaked jacket and laid it on the stone next to him.

Hiram gazed out at the view. 'I'm lucky to still have my hat, you know? I nearly lost it when I flew over that river.' Pulling his tobacco pouch out of his pocket, he wiped away the accumulated water then set about carefully laying the entire contents of the pouch on the flat rock beside him. 'There are two things you should never do in the jungle. First, you should never squat over a fire ant nest. Second, never lose your hat. The sun will burn a hole in the top of your head at this altitude and send you mad.'

Wilson rubbed the stubble on his chin and let the afternoon sunshine caress his face. 'Thank God the rain has stopped.'

'Now we get humidity,' Hiram replied. 'That's just as bad.'

Layers of fine mist hung in the tree line and against the cliffs, indicating that the humidity was nearly one hundred per cent. Wilson rubbed a layer of sweat from his face, peeled off his shirt and laid it on the stone next to them. 'The humidity is uncomfortable, but nothing is worse than rain.' He sat down on the flat rock and pulled off his shoes and socks. Removing his hat, he let his bare feet dangle over the edge, a two hundred-foot drop directly below.

Eight years earlier, when Wilson had transported into Machu Picchu, it was raining and dark so there was no chance to look around. This would be his first real opportunity to see the city of Vilcapampa for himself. It felt like ten lifetimes ago since he arrived here. He had experienced so much since then that he felt like a completely different person. When he thought about it, in some ways he didn't even know who he was anymore. Suddenly an image of Helena's face came into his mind. It was a comforting thought that had carried him through countless lonely times. He treasured his memories of her and despite his experiences a tiny part of him had managed to stay the same.

If everything went according to plan, Wilson would be transporting away from here in just a few hours. He would return to Enterprise Corporation and assume a normal life, as much as that was possible for an Overseer.

Would there be another mission for him? Only time would tell. And although he would like to defy his superiors by telling them he would never time travel again, he knew deep down that he would probably go if the Scrolls called for it.

'You really think the lost city of Vilcapampa is just up there?' Hiram questioned. He was rolling the wet tobacco into one of his damp papers.

Wilson pointed. 'Up on that ridge.'

Hiram squinted into the sun. 'Just up there?'

'It's the last great undiscovered citadel in South America, and you will be the one credited with its discovery, Hiram.'

'Assuming what you say is true,' he said. 'Tell me again why you don't want to take credit for finding the city yourself?'

'When history is tabled, Hiram, I will not have been here. If you recall, that is one of the conditions of our agreement.'

'That doesn't answer my question.'

'I'll tell you very soon,' Wilson said.

Hiram licked the cigarette paper and sealed the tobacco inside. 'You make a lot of promises, but you never explain your motive. It's very disconcerting.'

'Believe me,' Wilson said, 'The best way to get you to keep my secret is to tell you the truth.'

'Because your secret is so shocking?'

'Something like that.'

'Tell me now . . . I've come this far, haven't I?'

Wilson opened the lid of his water bottle and took a long, cool drink. 'If I tell you too soon, you might think I've gone crazy.'

Hiram struck a match and lit his cigarette. 'I think the crazy person is *me* . . . for following you out here in the first place.'

Wilson smiled. 'When you look back at our travels together you'll remember them fondly, I think.'

'I doubt it, Wilson.' Hiram appeared to savour the taste of his cigarette. 'Did you see the amazing bodies on those Amazon warriors? Wow.'

'Not this again . . .'

'*That* is something I will remember fondly. *You*, I'm not so sure of.'

'Those women wanted you dead. They killed your donkeys remember?'

Hiram took another drag of his cigarette. 'That's right . . . those vicious little bitches – I can't believe they did that. Poor little Diablo. Anyway . . . I'm not normally into tall women, but in their case, who knows?'

'You're not what I expected,' Wilson said with a shake of his head.

'What were you expecting?'

Wilson shrugged his shoulders. 'I just thought you'd be different.'

'You're starting to sound like my wife.' Hiram laughed. 'She still can't believe that Yale appointed me as a lecturer for South American history. You should have seen Alfreda's face when I told her I was going to live in Peru so I could discover ancient Inca cities. Hell hath no fury like a woman who just found out her husband is moving to Peru.'

'Wait till she learns that you've discovered Vilcapampa.'

'And where will you be, Wilson?'

'I'll be gone.'

'Where?'

'Back home.'

'Australia?'

Wilson smiled. 'Yeah . . . I'll be heading back there.'

'Back home to the voting women of Australia. Good luck with that. It's a road to disaster, mark my words. Women cannot be trusted with power.'

Wilson lay back on smooth rock and let the sunshine bath across him. 'We'll rest here for an hour or so, dry out, then we'll get going. I want you to be fresh so you can enjoy your discovery.'

Hiram took another drag of his cigarette and lay back also. 'Part of me still thinks there'll be nothing up there. Just two stone hovels and a llama hutch. My only discovery will be that you are *deluded*.'

'The city is up there, I assure you.'

Hiram stubbed his cigarette on the stone beside him and threw the butt into the damp jungle. Looking at the mountainous terrain, he said, 'The Incas must have been totally mad. Why build a city all the way out here? It's impossible to get to. It's dangerous – I mean, look at this place! The cliffs and the rivers. It's surely freezing here in the winter and humid as hell or raining in the summer.'

'They didn't want the city to be found,' Wilson answered. 'They destroyed their entire written language so they could keep this place a secret.'

Hiram rubbed his chin. 'I confess, the Incas are a very advanced culture *not* to have the written word. All that I have ever seen are those *quipu* ropes with the knots and the colourful strands. But nobody knows how to read them anyway.'

'The Incas had forty-two characters in their written alphabet,' Wilson stated. 'All the priests and noble class could read and write; they used pulp scrolls to write on; they had libraries of knowledge going back hundreds of years. Then, in the mid 1400s, their entire written language was destroyed.'

'All to protect this place?' Hiram stated.

From the corner of his eye, Wilson spotted a giant condor circling above the valley on the thermal currents. The bird was enormous, uniformly black with a frill of bright white feathers around the base of its neck and extra-long feathers, like fingers, at the very tips of its huge wings. 'A condor,' he said.

Hiram gave the bird a cursory glance. 'Yeah, that's a big bird.' He focused on Wilson again. 'Are you sure there's no treasure up there?'

'There's nothing there worth having,' Wilson replied. 'Thankfully, just finding Vilcapampa will deliver you ample fame and fortune to last you a lifetime. You have to trust me . . . you don't need gold to make you rich and famous. All you have to do is tell the world what you have discovered and the rest will be history.'

30

ACLLA AND SONTANE were crouched down behind a
fallen tree on the viewing platform of the agricultural
terraces next to the ruins of the Watchman's House. Aclla
wanted to scream at the mere thought of what she found
when her warriors went to check the Temple of the Sun.
Her worst fears had been realised – for the first time in half
a millennium the Inca Cube had been set free and its evil
forces had been released. It explained so much about what
she had witnessed in Cuzco: the crucifixion of Corsell
Santillana, the anger of the crowd, as well as the abduction
of her sister.

Eight hundred paces below, on a rocky outcrop protruding from the jungle, the two white men were lazing in the
sun like they did not have a care in the world. It was odd
that they were not taking greater precautions to conceal
their location, but then anything was to be expected from
these two strange men.

From this vantage point, Aclla and Sontane had an
unrestricted view of the valley to the east as well as the
overgrown ruins of the citadel behind them. To the north
was the towering mountain peak of Mount Machu Picchu;
to the south was the lesser peak of Mount Huayna Picchu.
From this spot, whichever way they turned, sheer cliffs
fell away to the Urubamba River below. This was the

precipice where the Virgins of the Sun stood watch for
the two hundred and forty-five years they inhabited
Vilcapampa. But that was many lifetimes ago. The fortress
citadel built by King Pachacuti to safely house the Inca
Cube had been deserted for exactly two hundred and three
years since then. At the time, the *mestizo* settlers were
pushing further and further into the mountains and it was
feared that the smoke from the winter fires would give
away the citadel's position. That was when the decision
was made to let the jungle reclaim the mountain ridge.
Since the day the Virgins of the Sun left Vilcapampa, they
had sent their best warriors here twelve times per year,
under the protection of the waning moon, to be sure
that everything was as it should be. The city was put to
sleep and the world of men would remain unaware of its
location, hopefully forever. And yet, as of this day, the city
had already been breached – everything the Virgins of the
Sun were here to protect had already been taken. And the
perpetrators of this unexpected invasion had arrogantly
carved their names into the stone steps, foolishly proud of
what they had so deviously achieved.

Looking about Machu Picchu, it was obvious that
the ravages of time had taken their toll. Once the finest
city ever built by Inca hands – using all the accumulated
knowledge of a wise and learned people – it was slowly
becoming a jungle. Shrubs, trees and bamboo thickets had
taken hold of the rich black soil that had long ago been
transported from the base of the valley and poured into
the miles of agricultural terraces. The nitrogen-rich soil
was like an elixir for the starving foliage at this altitude
and the city was quickly engulfed by lush greenery, aided
by the natural spring water that flowed out of the great
mountain. The roots of the larger trees had pushed over
walls of even the most impressive structures, including
the Priestesses Chamber, the Temple of Three Windows
and the Chamber of Ornaments. Seeing a citadel like this
die was sad, but that was the way of things. The Sun God
gave life and the Sun God took life away. And yet it was
not the wind and the rain, the earthquakes or the rampag-

ing forests that would claim this citadel's soul – it was the world of men. Aclla knew deep down that her sister's disappearance was certainly related to the dire predicament they now found themselves in – and the two *mestizo* names carved into the stone of the inner temple confirmed that without any doubt. The city had been breached while Virgins of the Sun were focussed on other things; everything now was surely lost.

'We should kill the white men while we have the chance,' Sontane said.

'It is our duty to learn what we can,' Aclla replied. 'Those two down there are not the men who breached the city. But the source of their knowledge may just spring from the very same location. That is something we must discover first.'

Sontane looked into the eyes of her virgin pair. 'We had the opportunity to kill the white men twice already and each time we have failed. Just promise me it is not your sexual feelings that have blunted your resolve. If it is bad luck, or their great skill that saved them, then I can accept it, but nothing else.'

Fury tensed Aclla's muscles. 'I do not have any such feelings,' she replied, taking great care not to let her anger spill into her words. 'I am *not* my sister. You are wise to remember that.'

'I felt your thoughts when we were as one,' Sontane said. 'So did the others.'

'Wilson Dowling is a magnificent specimen. That is all. And, like it or not, he deserves our respect. He evaded us at the Bridge of the Condor, and he chose mercy when he could have sent us to our death in those rapids. Rest easy, Sontane. I know my part here. And you should know yours. I am in charge and you will obey my orders.'

From nowhere, a magnificent black condor with white neck feathers swooped just over their heads and shot out over the deep valley. Its wings seemed to growl on the wind as it shot past. Both warriors carefully watched the giant bird.

'It seems that Apu, the great spirit of the mountains, has sent the condor to watch over us,' Aclla said.

'That is a good sign,' Sontane replied. 'The bird is female.'

Aclla nodded. 'It is a good sign.' Looking down over the cliff, it was clear that Wilson was watching the condor also. 'Wilson Dowling knows of the location of Vilcapampa. We will wait for him here, sheltered in the protection of the city. We will watch and wait to see what he does when he arrives. When his intentions are clear, we will take him and his companion as our prisoner.'

'You saw the way he moved,' Sontane said. 'And the way he survived the poison of your arrow. This is not a normal man we are dealing with. We must take care that we are not over-matched.'

'The man called Wilson has a weakness that we can exploit to our advantage.'

'I have seen no weakness,' Sontane replied.

'The weakness is his companion,' Aclla stated. 'Capture Hiram Bingham and we take away his power. This Wilson has gone to great lengths to protect him and bring him here to Vilcapampa. It is my guess that this is his duty. And when Wilson is weakened, he can be captured or killed.'

Sontane rested her hand on Aclla's forearm. 'I am sorry to have questioned you about your feelings. It was wrong of me.'

Aclla nodded in return. 'All is forgiven. Now go and tell the others of our plan and make things ready. Make sure no tracks are left behind.'

As Sontane jumped away over the fallen trees and greenery, Aclla once again studied the giant black condor effortlessly circling high above the raging waters of the Urubamba Valley.

'Choices will be made this day,' Aclla said as if she was talking directly to the great bird of prey. 'I must believe that the fate of the world still rests on the decisions that are yet to be made.'

31

Cuzco, Peru
Avenue Pavitos
Local Time 2:42 am

19 January 1908

SITTING IN THE seventh row of the mighty Basilica Cathedral, Captain Gonzales was wearing his full military uniform, including sword, which now rested across his lap. Next to him was his wife and in the pew directly in front sat his three fidgeting children dressed in their Sunday best, which included jackets and bow ties for the boys and a little red dress for Juanita. All the children's clothes were handmade by Sarita's sister, who was a seamstress in the Punta factory near the railway station.

The pews of La Catedral had seating for over seven hundred and fifty people, but today there was less than a third of that – the crucified body of Corsell Santillana had kept the worshippers away, as Gonzales expected. The small turnout, however, did nothing to diminish the inner beauty and character of this extraordinary cathedral. The impossibly high stone arches and whitewashed ceilings were breathtaking. The sheer expanse of the three-church complex was enough to make a believer out of even the most defiant soul. Not to mention the grandeur and symmetry of the high altar that stood proudly reaching up to the highest point of the central nave. It had two distinct baroque tiers and three vertical columned rows with a central core that held a gleaming statue of the Virgin of the Assumption and below her, a large silver tabernacle.

The altar was made of Cuzco cedar, but its external façade was entirely covered with over three thousand pounds of pure silver, dug from the Lluska mines by Inca engineers more than six hundred years earlier. On all sides of the columned altar were hundreds of glowing candles that spread a golden light to all reaches of the central nave.

In the background, the combined voices of the boys' choir rose up towards the lofty ceiling proclaiming 'Espiritu de Luz y Amor', as if angels themselves were singing. It was uplifting to hear their sweet voices echoing gently through this sacred place. Towards the front, all the priests, novices and church staff were lined up in perfect rows in a show of obvious solidarity. The priests wore black cassocks with a purple sash, some with red trimming on their robes, and in the centre stood Monsignor Domingo proudly wearing a shiny purple cape over his black cassock to denote that he was the newly appointed supernumerary. On either side, the sextons of the church wore brown hooded cloaks, and the novices wore white.

When the singing eventually stopped, Monsignor Domingo slowly lugged his fifty-year-old body to the top of the high pulpit and began the Rite of Blessing. 'In the name of the Father, the Son and the Holy Spirit,' he began.

Everyone in the church then replied, 'Amen.'

'The Lord be with you,' the Monsignor said.

'And also with you,' everyone replied.

From the side entrance, Bishop Francisco walked out of the sacristy chamber wearing an embroidered dalmatic of pure white with an outer cape of gold, his bishop's mitre on his head. His hands were clasped in front of him as if in prayer and his head was down as he slowly made his way towards the grand altar. All the while, Monsignor Domingo kept talking.

'Lord God, creator of all life, of body and soul, we ask that you bless this water, as we use it in faith to forgive our sins and save us from the power of evil.'

Bishop Francisco now stood at the grand altar table, his hand extended over the solid-silver bowl called an aspersorium, which he slowly filled with clear water from a large silver jug. Captain Gonzales studied the bishop carefully as he watched the flowing water and muttered a prayer to himself.

Why am I afraid of this man? Gonzales asked himself.

But the question came more easily than the answer, for no matter how he tried, he could not accept that he had seen evil in the bishop's eyes. It must have been a trick of the light, he told himself yet again. It had to have been. Looking at the bishop now, it seemed he was as holy as the church itself, and the countless images of Jesus, the Virgin Mary and the apostles that adorned the lofty walls of the magnificent cathedral around him.

'We ask you now to bless this water,' Monsignor Domingo continued, his voice echoing across the church. 'Give us your protection on this day Lord, which you have made your own. Renew the living spring of your life within us and protect us in body and spirit that we may be free from sin and come into your presence to receive your gift of salvation. Protect us from the terrible evil that seeks to take the souls of our congregation and make us worthy so that we may act in His name. We ask this through Christ our Lord.'

The entire congregation replied, 'Amen.'

Bishop Francisco muttered further prayers, then made the cross of Jesus above the aspersorium to proclaim the liquid now holy.

There was a moment's silence before the choir once again filled the great hall with 'Gloria', one of the most beautiful hymns ever to reach Gonzales's ears. Bishop Francisco took the handle of the silver aspergillum in his hand, and the aspersorium jug in the other. He then walked with slow purpose down the central steps of the high altar with three priests in black cassocks following closely behind. As he approached the congregation the bishop dipped the end of the aspergillum into the holy water, removed it and shook the silver perforated ball towards his flock, sprinkling fine beads of holy water into the gathering.

The sprinkling of water was a ritual that Gonzales

knew from Palm Sunday, where the bishop would bless his congregation with holy water to signify the purification of the soul and grant protection from evil. He had not seen this ritual used on any other day.

'Lord, we have sinned against you,' Bishop Francisco said with a strong voice. 'Lord have mercy.'

Whomever was struck by the beads of holy water then replied, 'Lord have mercy.'

The bishop slowly made his way down the central aisle, flicking holy water this way and that. 'Lord, show us your mercy and love,' he continued.

Whomever was struck by holy water replied, 'And grant us your salvation.'

As the bishop approached, Captain Gonzales could not help but feel protective of his family. His sudden instinct was to shield them from this man, regardless of the mighty position he held within the church. He turned to warn his wife, but in her eyes he saw only innocence and hope.

She whispered, 'We are going to be protected.'

In the background the choir was now in full song and the scent of fragrant jasmine filled the air from the burning of incense in the many chapel repositories.

Bishop Francisco suddenly locked eyes with Captain Gonzales and a shiver went up his spine. The priest's eyes were as black as night, his facial expression gaunt and pale as alabaster.

'May Almighty God have mercy on you,' Bishop Francisco said as he flicked water from the aspergillum in the direction of Gonzales's family.

At that moment everything went into slow motion, and the heavenly sounds of the choir became a cold silence. The perfect beads of glistening water seemed to somehow hang in the air while Gonzales watched the priest's infected gaze turn towards his wife. An evil smile briefly touched the man's lips as his vision lowered to take in the small silver cross hanging around her neck and the fullness of her body. His gaze then swung hungrily towards Gonzales's three small children seated in the next row. Captain Gonzales wanted to draw his sword and strike the bishop down – or whatever he was. His instinct told him what terrible acts were being played out in the bishop's depraved mind. Gonzales gripped the handle of his sword, yet no matter how he tried he could not draw the blade from its scabbard.

Suddenly, the holy water splashed against Gonzales's face, stunning him. He recoiled, feeling a hot wetness in his pants – he had pissed himself and the warm urine was soaking his clothes and running down his thighs. He looked helplessly at the bishop, whose gaze was momentarily fixated on the beads of glistening water sparkling on the perfect skin of his wife's neck and upper breasts. Time suddenly sped up again and Captain Gonzales was staring directly into Bishop Francisco's dark eyes.

In that moment, it was impossible to know what was real and what was not.

'Forgive us our sins,' Bishop Francisco said in a deep voice, 'and bring us to everlasting life.'

Sarita and the three children dutifully replied, 'Amen.'

Captain Gonzales was unable to speak. He sat there, his heart beating madly, his mouth filled with the acid of his utter helplessness.

The bishop released his gaze and continued down the aisle flicking water at his congregation and repeating the Prayers of the Lord.

Wiping the beads of consecrated water from her skin, Sarita made the cross of Jesus on her chest. 'Why did you not say "Amen"?' she asked her husband, obviously distressed by the failure of his voice. She leant closer so that no one would hear. 'The holy water hit your flesh, I know it did. Why would you not say "Amen"?'

'The water was not holy,' Gonzales replied, his hands shaking.

'What do you mean by that?'

Tears began to well in Gonzales's eyes as sweat flushed his brow. 'Something is very wrong here, my love. You must trust me when I say that. We should *never* have come.'

Sarita pressed her hand to her husband's forehead. 'You

are burning up!' she whispered. 'I must get you home, immediately.'

The bishop and his priests had by now made their way to the end of the pews and were returning to the front of the church. Gonzales pushed his wife's hand away and repeatedly wiped the accumulating sweat from his face. 'We will stay!' he said, feeling his strength returning. 'Do not worry about me,' he whispered to her. He gripped her leg so hard that she had no choice but to do what he said.

Bishop Francisco slowly climbed the silver stairs to the top of the high altar and looked down at the congregation once again. 'These are dark times that surround Cuzco,' he said, his voice resounding to all corners of the church. 'This is a test of your character.' His gaze then singled Captain Gonzales out once again. 'Jesus reveals God's merciful character in His compassion and healing. When people are vulnerable, cold and without friends, they have a difficult time understanding God's tender mercies. The innocent struggle to survive in a world of evil and are often treated as lambs to the slaughter.' He was speaking very slowly now. 'They are looked down upon, pitied. But Christ says, "It was I who was hungry and thirsty. It was I who was a stranger. It was I who was innocent". In Matthew Twenty-five, Jesus responds to the people who needed Him most: the downtrodden, the weak, the ill, the grieving and those entangled in webs of sin. He responds with protection and infinite compassion. This is what I will deliver to each of you. This is God's commitment on this day. In Christ's name, Amen.'

Once again Monsignor Domingo climbed slowly into the high pulpit to direct the prayer. 'If everyone would stand for the Apostles' Creed,' he said, his arms outstretched.

When everyone was upstanding, the congregation began as one, 'I believe in God, the Father Almighty, creator of heaven and earth . . .'

Captain Gonzales was the last to rise from his seat. He was trying his best to say the words, but he was distracted and embarrassed by the warm piss that had soaked his pants and was running down into his boots. Gathering his composure as best he could, he eventually prayed with the others, their words slow and deliberate.

'I believe in the Holy Spirit, the holy catholic Church, the communion of the saints, the forgiveness of sin, the resurrection of the body, and the life everlasting. Amen.'

Gonzales gripped tightly to his officer's sword, which now seemed to carry the weight of a thousand boulders. Feeling utterly exhausted by it, he had no choice but to lay the sword on the seat beside him. It was just too heavy.

Lucho Gonzales and his family were certainly cursed he realised.

It was the only explanation he could muster.

32

19 January 1908

THE SKY WAS a rich blue and there was not a cloud to be seen. From the distant horizon, the iridescent beams were aglow against the hundreds of immensely deep, forest-clad valleys they passed above. In all of Wilson's life he had never seen anything so striking, nor on such a grand scale. The Andes were truly breathtaking as was the intensity of the streams of light that cut across the shadowed wilderness.

Because of the heat, both Wilson and Hiram had their jackets tied around their waists and their shirts unbuttoned. The humidity was crippling and they were doing what they could to keep cool while they climbed.

'Can you believe that?' Hiram said, looking out at the view. 'If Michelangelo had seen this, he'd have to repaint heaven on the roof of the Sistine Chapel. I mean, look at that mountainside – that must be a twenty-five-hundred-foot drop from the peak to the river there, and sheer! And the way the river cuts back around that mountain . . .' He motioned his hand like it was running with the direction of the water.

'That knobbed mountain you're looking at is called Huayna Picchu,' Wilson said, his hands on his hips. 'The river loops back around to protect the city from three sides. Above us here,' he pointed left into the overhanging greenery, 'is Machu Picchu.'

'The name this city will eventually take,' Hiram said.

The first hours of the climb had been very difficult, but Wilson and Hiram eventually reached the base of the agricultural zone. From there they found a stone pathway that stepped upwards through the ten-foot-high stone terraces at a fifty-degree angle. The ancient Inca stairway was rudimentary in construction and the pathway was badly overgrown, however it was a vast improvement from having to hold on by their fingernails to maintain a grip on the slippery mountainside. Measuring distance was difficult with so much greenery around, but in Wilson's estimation they were now about halfway up the terraces.

He gestured towards the setting sun and the narrow ridge between the two mountain peaks. 'The city of Vilcapampa is just up there, behind centuries of forest.'

'I can't see any city,' Hiram said.

Suddenly, Wilson had the sensation that they were being watched from the ruins above. Scanning the path ahead, it was impossible to see more than the first few rows of terraces among the thick green foliage.

'What's the matter?' Hiram asked.

'I have a feeling we're being watched,' Wilson replied.

Hiram studied the cluster of ferns, high grasses and bamboo thickets. He frowned. 'Is this your way of telling me Vilcapampa is not there?'

Wilson pressed his hand on the retaining wall beside him. 'Do I really have to keep convincing you?'

Hiram pointed. 'I've seen walls like that in Torontoy. It certainly doesn't mean Vilcapampa is up there.' He let out a huff. 'I've crawled over and under branches, through rainforests. I've crossed raging rivers. I've been bitten by bugs. My knees are grazed and my feet are blistered –'

'Vilcapampa is up there, Hiram.'

Against the blue sky above them, the magnificent black condor was still circling the mountain ridge, its wings seemingly never moving. The sun dipped a fraction and it became darker and cooler, the brilliant sunlight that had been streaming through the trees was now being blocked by the steepness of the ridge ahead.

With no choice but to continue, Wilson set off at a steady pace up the stairs between the thickets of bamboo and waist-high mountain grass. Whenever he found open space he went faster, invariably having to slow again when he reached another fallen obstacle. Terrace by terrace, they climbed the side of the mountain. Through the thinning trees the imposing peak of Machu Picchu came into view in all its towering glory.

Hiram was falling further behind as they climbed and Wilson kept turning around to make sure he was still there. Wilson was eventually standing in the sunlight. It took a second for his eyes to adjust and, with his hand blocking the brightness of the sun, he scoured the landscape for signs of movement.

Directly ahead, across a sheer chasm, stood the roofless structure of the Watchman's House, an imposing stone building with three trapezoidal windows that looked towards the east.

He had finally arrived.

Wilson took a moment to study the overgrown ruins of Vilcapampa laid out before him along the razorback ridge. Stunted forests and thickets of bamboo had taken hold of the city. The imposing stone buildings that littered the Urban Section were covered with moss and lichen, giving them a distinctly brown and dirty appearance. Everything else was inundated with ferns, high grasses and liana vines. Nowhere else in the world, at this altitude, could wilderness like this have survived.

Wilson couldn't help but feel a sense of discovery, knowing that he was looking upon a once-pristine city that had been lost for hundreds of years. And despite the passage of time, it did nothing to diminish the magnitude and beauty of this extraordinary place.

The Watchman's House had a gnarled hardwood tree that was conspicuously growing in the middle of the floor. The roots were slowly shifting the walls and the carefully laid ashlars were beginning to separate.

When Wilson transported here, he had leapt this chasm in the dark before heading along the Inca Trail towards

Cuzco. Looking down, he was thankful that he hadn't seen how sheer the drop-off really was.

Hiram's heavy footfall approached, as did the sound of his laboured breathing. 'I can't believe . . . I've come all the way.' He couldn't force out a full sentence, such was his need for air. 'Where's . . . the city?' He bent over at the waist and put his hands on his knees, letting his hat fall to ground. Sweat dripped off his forehead and nose. Grabbing his water bottle from his belt, he zipped off the lid. 'Can you pour this . . . on my head,' he asked.

Wilson grabbed the canvas-covered water bottle and unleashed the contents over Hiram's sweaty neck and hair.

'That feels so good!' Hiram stood up and let the water run down his back. With the bright sun in his eyes, he squinted out towards the Urubamba Valley, then up towards the mountain of Machu Picchu. 'So, where's this incredible city you promised me?

'*Oh my God!*' Hiram whispered.

Only the discovery of Tutankhamen's tomb by Howard Carter in the early 1920s would ever rival this moment.

'I am so pleased you are not a liar!' Hiram called out in delight. He gave Wilson a bear hug and spun him around in a circle, excitedly jumping up and down. '*You're not a liar! You're not a liar!*' He was singing.

Wilson was happy for him, but he grabbed Hiram by the shoulders and pushed him off. 'Take a moment to get your composure.'

'You're not a liar!'

'Keep your voice down,' Wilson whispered.

'But I'm happy!' Hiram threw his arms into the air. 'Look at this place!' He gazed out at the ruins of Vilcapampa with wonder emblazoned on his face. 'It's even more glorious than I imagined. It's magnificent!' Hiram walked towards the ruins not noticing the chasm directly in front of him. Wilson grabbed him by the collar and yanked him backwards, causing him to tumble into the greenery.

'What did you do that for?' Hiram said angrily, rubbing his backside as he climbed to his feet. 'Don't you want me to be happy?'

'I don't want you to be dead,' Wilson replied.

Hiram looked down into the sheer granite chasm that fell into the forest below. The sight was dizzying and he had to steady himself against a tree to collect his thoughts. Wilson had just saved his life again.

Higher up the peak of Machu Picchu, Aclla and Sontane were hidden among a wall of treelets and ferns, between a natural granite fissure. They were lying on their stomachs with their short bows positioned next to them so they could fire an arrow with minimal movement. From their vantage point they could see everything Wilson and Hiram were doing, and importantly, they could hear every word they were saying.

About a hundred steps further away, Orelle and Ilna were hidden in the ruins near Nusta's Palace, waiting to be called upon. If the two white men crossed the chasm to the Watchman's House, then they would easily have them surrounded.

'The skinny man is like a clown,' Sontane whispered. 'He nearly fell into the chasm.'

Above the overgrown citadel of Vilcapampa, the female condor continued to slowly circle about the clear blue sky. It was flying a little lower now, probably only 500 feet up. The sunbeams were hitting the bird of prey from underneath and it was possible to see the power of its huge talons and the brilliant white of its feathered collar.

'Apu is watching,' Sontane whispered.

'Our ancestors are with us,' Aclla replied.

Down below, Wilson backed up five steps then ran full speed towards the chasm. Flying through the air, his body spun and flipped towards the granite sidewall, his feet meeting the sheer surface halfway across, his legs compressing to relaunch himself the rest of the way. It was very similar to the technique the Virgins of the Sun used to take flight when they wanted to achieve maximum distance.

*

Wilson landed gracefully with five feet to spare. Pressing his hand to the wall of the Watchman's House, he looked inside the overgrown construction to see if there was any hardwood roof lintels that could span the twenty-foot drop-off.

'I'll be right back,' Wilson shouted as he skipped down a flight of perfectly carved stairs towards a bamboo thicket, at the same time searching the ruins for any footprints or broken twigs that would indicate someone had arrived before them. Taking a large rock in one hand, he drew his knife, pressed the sharp blade to the base of one of the shafts of bamboo and began hammering the back of his knife with the rock. In no time he had five perfectly straight posts that he dragged towards the chasm. Using liana vines, Wilson tied the posts together, stood the structure upright and let it fall across the divide, forming a relatively secure bridge.

'Let's go,' Wilson said, gesturing Hiram across.

It was clear from the expression on Hiram's face that he didn't like the idea at all. 'I don't like heights, you know,' he yelled out, but after a little cajoling he got on all fours and slowly crawled across the bridge, all the while moaning and groaning. When he made it to the other side, Wilson pulled him to his feet.

'You are now standing inside Vilcapampa,' Wilson announced. 'A city so important that every person involved in its construction was murdered so its location could be kept secret. A city for which all written language was destroyed. Your role is to introduce this place to the world, Hiram Bingham.'

'I'm happy to share the credit with you,' Hiram stated. 'I'm really not as greedy as you think.'

'Soon I will have to leave you,' Wilson replied. 'You will make a map of this place and then you will head back to Cuzco on your own.'

Hiram looked flabbergasted. 'You're leaving me? How in the hell am I supposed to get back to Cuzco from here?'

Wilson pointed towards the setting sun. 'About three miles that way, over that mountain range, there's a small church next to the banks of the Urubamba. It's called Our Lady of Mercy. There is a priest there named Father Marcos who will help you. I'm confident that you can make it back to Cuzco on your own.'

'A church . . . *out here?*'

'Father Marcos will organise a guide to lead you back home.'

'And where will you be?'

'I told you, I'm heading home also.'

'I've followed you through that jungle, Wilson, through *all that.*' He pointed down the mountain towards the cloud forest. 'And now we're going to separate? I was just beginning to like you!'

'It's the way it has to be.'

'You enjoy keeping me in the dark,' Hiram complained. 'I know you do. It's disconcerting, you know, the way you fly around and jump over ridges, like you can cheat death or something. It's not normal. Now you tell me you're leaving me here on my own. With no support and no rations!'

'I've delivered on my end of the bargain, haven't I?' Wilson gestured around him to the vast citadel. 'Vilcapampa is here, just as I said it was, and you will be a hero.' He eased his way along the narrow terrace through thickets of ferns and mountain grass. He was heading north along the spine of the city in the direction of Huayna Picchu.

'That is not the point,' Hiram said emotionally. 'We set off on this journey together and we should finish it together.'

'Look, Hiram, I'm sorry. If it's any consolation, I'm certain you can make it to Father Marcos without me. You rode a donkey from Santiago to Cuzco, for Christ's sake. That's thousands of miles. You can certainly find your way to a church that's three miles away.'

Hiram looked around at the rugged scenery. 'I was on a donkey – that's different. Despite what you think, I'm not that comfortable trekking around the mountains.' Hiram became distracted by the majestic ruins of the city. Will you look at this place . . . Christ! And anyway, I had ten porters with me when I rode from Chile, and three Yale academics. I was hardly alone. And I had Diablo with me, may God rest his annoying little soul.'

Hearing the trickle of water, Wilson eased some mountain grass aside to reveal a fast-moving channel running along a man-made watercourse. He bent down, dipped his fingers in the stream, then tasted it. 'That's one of the reasons everything grows so well up here.' Looking at the adjacent mountains there was hardly any foliage at the same altitude.

Wilson leapt over a tree that had fallen because the retaining wall behind it had given way. 'I'm going to take you to a very special building, just down here.'

'I can't believe you're going to leave me,' Hiram moaned.

'It's called the Temple of the Sun.'

'There's also a Temple of the Sun back in Cuzco,' Hiram replied. There was silence for a few steps then he said, 'Look, if you come back to Cuzco with me, I promise to share the credit with you. You can be famous too.'

'I told you before, I was never here.'

'You can't leave me on my own!' Hiram complained.

Wilson descended some badly overgrown stairs. In front of him, the valley literally dropped away into thin air. 'Hiram, you are about to see one of the greatest buildings of the ancient world.'

Little did Wilson realise, on the plateau just above him, the Amazon warrior Aclla – proud Tribune of the Virgins of the Sun – was not more than twenty paces away. She and her three companions had their arrows drawn and were moving silently through the ruins with the stealth and cunning forged through a lifetime of training. They were gradually closing in to make their attack, each with an eye on the other. All they needed now was to separate Hiram Bingham and they would have their advantage.

All the while, the black condor continued to circle on the hot thermals. The bird's shadow silently flashing past on the ground nearby to Aclla's position. The eyes of Apu were indeed watching.

33

Andes Ranges, Peru
Machu Picchu Citadel
Local Time 4:35 pm

19 January 1908

THE DISTINCTIVE GRANITE tower of the Temple of the Sun took Wilson's breath away. Unlike everything else in this ancient, overgrown citadel, the perfectly carved ashlars were not covered in moss or lichen. The stones were of a genuine ash-whiteness with a particularly fine grain, the outer surface polished to a smooth sheen that had withstood the ravages of time with ease. It was like the building had just been finished, the stones carefully masoned and set together with great precision.

One of the undeniable beauties of Inca construction was that the walls and buildings were made without using mortar. The stones were painstakingly shaped so they fit together perfectly, which was the reason they were mostly immune to the winds, the weather and the many strong earthquakes that hit this area of the world. The precision of the ashlars gave Inca buildings an elegance that had not been seen since the Egyptians thousands of years earlier.

Descending the overgrown stairs, the Temple of the Sun seemed to glow in the bright sunshine. The walls were curved in symmetry with the massive black granite foundations below it. The lower section of the temple was a neat jigsaw of particularly large ashlars, which gave it a look of brutal solidity. As the tower construction climbed the ashlars diminished in size and leant inwards, somehow making it look delicate and modern. The exterior surface was simple and unadorned, except for the three high windows – one to the north, one to the east and one to the south – each having an astrological purpose relating to the summer and winter solstice.

'That is the most beautiful building I have ever seen,' Hiram whispered.

'I told you it was worth coming here.'

'I think you're right . . . I *am* going to be famous.' Hiram laughed out loud. 'I can't wait to see my wife's face when she finds out that I was party to discovering this place. She'll never believe it.'

'This building must be protected at all costs,' Wilson said. 'It was sacred to the Inca and must be treated as such. I cannot stress this enough. The walls of this building should never be tampered with under any circumstances. Hundreds died as a direct consequence of creating this place. I suggest you respect the old traditions or risk falling victim to forces you do not understand.'

'I understand. This building is not to be tampered with.'

'I'm serious, Hiram. I've seen enough in my life to know that magic exists, light and dark. Don't be so foolish as to think that this world is merely as it seems on the surface.'

'I told you . . . I understand.'

Wilson continued anyway. 'Anyone who accepts the Inca could decipher the anti-malarial qualities of quinine and yet concludes they were unable to scribble some simple notes on a rock, is a fool. There are a thousand layers in life, Hiram, and a thousand layers below that. Take my word for it – disobeying Inca traditions will ruin your life. Imagine watching everyone you truly love die before your eyes, and you are helpless to stop it. That is barely the beginning of the curse that will befall you if you tamper with this place.'

'I don't think scaring me out of my wits is really necessary, do you?'

'I'm not trying to scare you . . . just tell you the truth. The price of your fame and fortune is your continued protection of this incredible place. You are now this city's guardian.' Wilson eased the tall grass aside and continued down the stairs.

Hiram thought a moment then said, 'So why leave today? Stay here and make sure that I keep my end of the bargain. I have no food and no supplies. At least make sure I find my way to Father Marcos.'

Wilson kept walking. 'I've been travelling for too long already. It's time to go back to my world and face the consequences of the things I've done.'

'Why do you always make everything sound so dramatic? Just tell your wife that you were busy – I assume you're married. They understand that men have to find their way in the world.'

'I'll say it again, Hiram. You're not what I expected.'

'I still don't understand why we can't return to Cuzco *together*. If you're heading back to Australia then you have to go home that way anyway. That's where the train station is . . .'

Wilson began easing the bamboo apart so he could squeeze himself through. Just on the other side was the black granite base of the Temple of the Sun. From this lower perspective it would give Hiram a full appreciation for the most sacred structure within the City in the Clouds, as well as the most sacred structure within the entire Inca world. Wilson would omit the crucial detail that within the granite walls of the temple itself was the resting place and prison of the Inca Cube – one of the most powerful objects ever created.

34

Andes Ranges, Peru
Machu Picchu Citadel
Local Time 4:45 pm

19 January 2014

FOR THE FIRST time since Helena set foot on Machu
Picchu, the sky was crystal blue and the winds had eased
away to nothing. The incessant storms that had lashed the
area for the last week had finally pushed away over the
eastern mountains.

Helena had barely slept since arriving and, to make
matters worse, she'd hardly eaten a thing. There was no
indication that Wilson had ever visited Machu Picchu
and she was beginning to lose hope. Since sunrise she had
walked the entirety of the agricultural zone from corner to
corner, as well as scoured nearly every building within the
urban section. She had even climbed to the top of Huayna
Picchu to get a look at the city from a higher vantage point
and was suitably amazed at what a beautiful place this was
and how well maintained the citadel grounds were. The
trees, shrubs and bamboo thickets that had once overtaken
everything had been completely cleared, the moss and lichen
dutifully scraped away. The retaining walls and hundreds
of stone buildings had been painstakingly reconstructed –
with the exception of the thatched roofs – so it was exactly
as the Inca architects had intended. According to Hiram
Bingham's autobiography, it was a very different place
when he discovered Machu Picchu a century ago – unlike
the manicured green grass that covered the multitude of flat

terraces today, it had been a relative jungle. There was only one tree left in the whole city – the thirty-foot tall hardwood that stood proudly in the main square. It was said to have been planted by female weavers hundreds of years ago so they could tie their alpaca threads to it after they were dyed.

As the shadows lengthened Helena noted that the city was deserted except for a couple of Germans who were walking the ruins together with their guide. A maintenance crew of four workers was restoring a simple retaining wall in the industrial section that had toppled over due to shifting soil caused by the heavy rains. The reality was, everyone was stuck here at Machu Picchu for at least the next two days. Landslides had blocked the road from Cuzco and the Urubamba had burst its banks, which meant the Orient Express had been unable to make its daily journey into the mountains. It was the first time Machu Picchu had been cut off in ten years. The river was at its highest level in a lifetime and the rapids were said to have overwhelmed the hydroelectric plant to the west. The hotel was now without power and air-conditioning. It was very hot and humid and they had only candlelight. Even if Helena wanted to leave, she couldn't. How ironic it was that she was now stuck in the very location she had wanted so desperately to get to.

Chad had been shadowing Helena the entire day while John Hanna slept in preparation for the upcoming night-shift. Chad carried a bottle of electrolytes in one hand and no doubt had her handgun at the ready. Every thirty minutes she would offer Helena a protein bar, a rice cracker or a bottle of water, saying, 'You need to keep your energy up,' or, 'It's important to stay hydrated.'

All in all they had made three trips to the ancient city together, and each time Helena's spirits faded a little more. Her objective on this visit was to re-create the vivid dream that had brought her here in the first place, which required her to be at the Temple of the Sun as the fading rays of sunlight passed through the high windows. She needed to be on the plateau outside the triangular entrance of the inner shrine. That was the perspective she had had in her dream – into the mausoleum where Pablo had claimed the Incas stored the mummified bodies of their ancestors. There was not a cloud in the sky, just as she'd seen it, which was one positive at least.

When Helena informed Chad that she wanted to visit the ancient city yet again, she simply looked at her GPS. 'It's excellent exercise walking up and down those stairs. We've already walked ten miles today. At this altitude, that's equivalent to walking double that distance at sea level. That means I can eat whatever I want for dinner tonight.' Then she smiled, which was a rare sight.

That had been more than an hour ago. Since then, the pair had made their way up the paved road to the small guardhouse, shown their passports to prove they had already entered, then walked slowly up the ancient terraces, level by level, towards the Watchman's House. All the while, the Urubamba in flood roared in the background.

The panoramic view across the Andes was stunning, but Helena gave it barely a glance. Incredibly, it was Chad who stopped to point out the iridescent sunbeams cutting their way across the deep, shadowed valleys in such an extraordinary way. The image was indeed spectacular, but Helena had other things on her mind. Her darkest thoughts were beginning to take over; she wondered if her link to Wilson had been permanently severed. Was it possible, as Don Eravisto had argued, that he did in fact murder an innocent mother and her children? It was inevitable that Helena would be forced to consider such claims, but in the end it made no sense. A shiver suddenly went up Helena's spine as she remembered the sensation that gripped her when Don Eravisto pointed his gun at her forehead. There was something very disconcerting about looking directly into the barrel of a gun – a finality about it – as if the cold blackness inside the barrel was about to draw her in, which is really the opposite of what is about to happen. Helena hoped she would never have to experience that feeling again.

Ever since she first laid eyes on Wilson, Helena felt like she had been living in a whirlwind. Everything she once loved had become meaningless and her values and logic had been forced to change. Her hopes and fantasies were about Wilson now, like he had stolen her dreams and replaced them with the whim of his unlikely arrival. That was not to say she had a perfect life before they met – she didn't – but at least back then her world started and finished with what was around her. She controlled her life and her feelings in a real world with real people. The man she now wanted to be with was a *time-traveller*. Simply considering such a ridiculous thought made her feel frustrated. There were so many more questions than there ever would be answers. As much as she tried to hold her emotions in check, she just couldn't. Based on what she'd seen, Wilson had aged ten years in the last year. Time was obviously moving at a different pace for him.

Helena's dreams had led her all the way to Machu Picchu, into the wild mountains of Peru, and yet she received nothing when she needed reassurance the most. Walking along the manicured terrace, she saw llamas chewing away at the grass one level below. They were proud-looking animals. Her gaze fell to the irrigation channel that flowed parallel to the terrace and she wondered yet again if Wilson had been here. The water that came out of the mountain was clear and swift as it fed along the aqueduct. Helena wanted to believe that Wilson had led Hiram Bingham here, but there was no mention of it in his autobiography. As always with Wilson Dowling, it was a guess at best.

Descending the perfectly carved stairs, Helena watched her shadow stretching away from her towards the valley that fell away below. She turned left and walked along yet another terrace, past Nusta's Bedroom, towards the knobbed peak of Huayna Picchu. Turning down the final flight of stairs, the Temple of the Sun seemed to be almost glowing white in the bright sunshine. The towering walls were curved in symmetry with the black granite foundations below. An air of apprehension filled Helena as she stepped through the stone doorway to the open plateau and approached the twenty-foot-tall triangular entrance to

the inner shrine. It really did appear like the black granite
had been split at a forty-five degree angle with a giant's
axe. Inside the mausoleum she could see the three irregular
steps that ended at the smooth granite wall. Pablo had said
they represented the pathway between the underworld and
heaven, but Helena had her doubts. Stepping over the thin
rope that stopped tourists from entering, she took in the
dank smell as her gaze fell upon the two names carved large
and deep into the middle step. They seemed so out of place
here, an audacious act in the citadel's most sacred location.

JESUS VELARDE
JUAN SANTILLANA
1908

The date stuck in Helena's mind and she remembered that
Hiram Bingham had discovered Machu Picchu in 1911.
If the date was correct, then these two men had been here
three years before Hiram had arrived.

Chad was standing just outside the temple, watching the
stairs to make sure no one else was approaching. Helena
studied the carefully masoned walls of the inner shrine. To
the west and north they were made of symmetrical square-
cut ashlars with five upright niches built into them. To
the south, the remaining wall was solid granite that tilted
slightly inwards. The surface of everything inside the shine
was brilliantly smooth, as if an incredible heat had glazed
the stones. But, of course, that would have been impossible
so many years ago.

Looking outside towards the mountainous east, Helena
gazed up at the black granite that had literally been split
open to reveal the shrine. The weight of stone that was now
missing would have been incalculable. Helena decided it
felt more like a dungeon than a shrine. There was coldness
inside that was difficult to understand on this hot day.

'Can you believe they kept the remains of former kings in there?' Chad questioned. 'And on special occasions they would come and get the corpses and take them to dinner.' Chad kicked the dirt at her feet. 'Sounds a little strange, doesn't it?'

Helena nodded. 'Yes, it does.'

'I know one thing about people,' Chad continued. 'They want to make a legacy for *themselves* . . . not go down to the cemetery and drag grandpa's old bones out for dinner so *he* can get all the glory.'

Helena studied the triangular entrance once again. Considering the Inca had no written language, and this place was deserted for hundreds of years before it was rediscovered, it was impossible to understand how anyone knew anything.

In Hiram Bingham's autobiography, many of the conclusions he made about Machu Picchu were completely different from what Pablo had said. The truth had to be somewhere in between, Helena decided, or not even close. She had found the same discrepancy when she went to Egypt. She would listen to two different guides with two different groups telling completely different stories about the same statue. When it came to ancient history, the only people who really knew the truth were dead. From there, the interpretations and speculations began.

Chad reached out and offered Helena a bottle of water. 'You need to hydrate,' she said again.

Helena unscrewed the lid and took a long, cool drink. After being inside the inner shrine she had a sour taste in her mouth and was glad to wash it down.

Walking to the very edge of the plateau, Helena gazed down into the deep valley and noticed the river basin was in a hazy shadow. Plumes of whitewater mist were rising up from the Urubamba. She turned towards the Watchman's House, some twenty layered terraces above them on the crest of the ridge. Beyond the city, the magnificent peak of Machu Picchu loomed ominously, the sun striking it nearly side-on. The classic mountain with its sheer cliff faces and sharp summit was almost alive with colour. From this distance the Peruvian flag at the very top looked like a tiny speck as it hung limply against the windless sky.

Helena handed the bottle back to Chad then turned towards the Temple of the Sun to take in the full view. The sun was approaching the angle that Helena had seen it in her dream, and she backed up to give herself the identical perspective.

'Would you mind giving me a moment?' Helena asked.

Chad looked about, deciding where to wait. 'I'll be over there, by the stairs,' she replied.

Helena sat on the stacked stone retaining wall. Behind her was a sheer drop that led to another jumble of ruins about ninety feet below. Beyond that, the gradient of the land sloped away even more steeply before reaching a sheer granite cliff face that plummeted to the very bottom of the valley, some one thousand feet further down.

'If you hear me talking to myself, don't be alarmed,' Helena called out. She had said the same thing to Chad numerous times over the last two days.

'Just call my name if you need me,' Chad replied.

Looking again at the Temple of the Sun, Helena's gaze was drawn to the unusual triangular entrance at the base. With the sun dropping noticeably in the sky, she started to squint. Her instinct was to put on her sunglasses, but she stopped herself – she wasn't wearing them in her dream.

'Prepare yourself for disappointment,' she whispered. Glancing at her watch, she took note of the time. It was exactly 5.05 pm.

Helena was already thinking about what she would do if nothing happened. She would have to stay at least another couple of days, maybe longer, until the Orient Express was running again. That choice was probably made for her, so there was no use thinking about it. She then considered if she would return to the Temple of the Sun tomorrow on the slim chance that something amazing might still happen. As much as she told herself that this was the last time she would put herself through this kind of disappointment, deep down she knew she would have to return.

Helena took a deep breath and let out a sigh.

The sun was now at the same point as it had been it in her dream. She raised her hands to her furrowed brow. 'What am I doing here?' she whispered. 'This is ridiculous.'

35

Andes Ranges, Peru
Machu Picchu Citadel
Local Time 5:05 pm

19 January 1908

WILSON EASED HIS way between the tall bamboo, having to compress his chest to make sure he would fit between the thick green stalks. Hiram was right behind, groaning with discomfort as he followed. There is no easy way through a thicket of bamboo, it required patience and flexibility. Thankfully there wasn't a gusting wind, because the swaying stalks had a habit of pinning you inside if the gaps became too narrow.

As soon as Wilson extricated himself, he eased the tall mountain grass aside and stepped under the impressive stone archway with a heavy lintel above it. Directly ahead, a gargantuan chunk of black granite lay at the base of the Temple of the Sun. The wedge of stone was cut in the shape of a triangle. Wilson could hardly draw in a breath as he scrambled up the rugged stone to get a better view. The inner sanctuary was agape, revealing the open bowels of the structure.

A cold sweat immediately flushed Wilson's body as he attempted to put together what could have happened. It was obvious the black granite wedge had fallen only recently – it had crushed the trees and shrubs underneath, which were just beginning to wither and die.

Hiram climbed the fallen block also and gazed into the shadows under the temple. 'I wasn't expecting this,' he said, not realising the gravity of what he was looking at.

'This is not good,' Wilson said seriously.

'The surfaces in there are so smooth,' Hiram said, peering at the highly polished inner walls. Looking up, he carefully studied the white ashlars of the temple set neatly on the black granite foundation. 'That is *seriously* impressive.' The sun was hitting the tower from behind and lighting up the high windows. 'You're right, Wilson, this is the most beautiful construction I have ever seen. There isn't even any moss on it.'

Hiram's gaze drifted back down to the triangular opening cut into the base. 'What's supposed to be in there?' Hiram shifted his position so he could get a better view inside. 'Look at the texture of the stone.'

Wilson pressed his hands to his face in despair. 'This is not the way it's meant to be.'

'What was kept in there?' Hiram asked again, turning to Wilson. He could tell that it had to be something really important.

'A golden cube,' Wilson replied, and he held out one hand to show the size.

'I thought you said there wasn't any treasure here?'

'This is not a treasure you want, Hiram.'

'A golden cube! That sounds pretty good to me!' Hiram slapped himself on the thigh in obvious elation. 'I *knew* you were searching for treasure – I knew it from the very beginning –'

'You don't understand,' Wilson replied. 'We are in real trouble.'

'You look a little pale.' Hiram backed up to study him.

'Just give me a moment to figure out what to do next,' Wilson replied. Without the Inca Cube the time portal would not engage. The mission notes had been very precise: the cosmic strand that terminated within the Golden Cube of the Sun God was the power source that allowed the Machu Picchu portal to open a chink in the earth's magnetic field. Without it, Wilson was stuck here. There would be no way back home and his mission was a failure.

Hiram approached the triangular entrance through the waist-high mountain grass, trying to see if there was anything in the shadows. 'There's no golden cube in there – that much I can see. And those niches cut in the walls are empty.'

'There would have been large crystals in those holes,' Wilson said.

Hiram looked about. 'Someone's taken the lot.'

'Without the Inca Cube, I can't leave this place,' Wilson muttered.

'You're not leaving?' Hiram said happily. 'That's good news, at least.'

Wilson rubbed at his forehead. 'Someone has cracked open the inner temple and taken the most precious object in the Inca world.'

'Clarify this for me.' Hiram pointed. 'Is the Cube valuable or not?'

'The Inca Cube can destroy worlds,' Wilson said.

'Don't be ridiculous.'

'I mean it, Hiram.'

Hiram tilted his head in surprise. 'Well . . . whoever took the golden cube has carved their names on the stairs – you don't see that everyday.'

Wilson ran forward. Two names were etched deeply into the face of the middle step in five-inch-high capital letters:

JESUS VELARDE
JUAN SANTILLANA
1908

Hiram pointed at the names. 'You don't think this Jesús and this Juan will be able to claim discovery of Machu Picchu instead of me, do you?'

'They are the last two people on earth I would want to be,' Wilson said with dread in his voice. 'They have unleashed a power beyond their understanding and they are certainly cursed.'

'Cursed?' Hiram pulled his finger away from the polished white granite. 'I must say, it does feel eerie in here. Doesn't smell good, either.' He was looking about as if sensing an attack at any moment. 'I hate smelly places.'

'I wouldn't stay in there if I were you.'

Hiram glanced back at him. 'Why?'

'The evil that was once trapped in there might still have a residue.'

Hiram's eyes widened. 'Are you serious?'

Wilson pointed at the top step. 'The Inca Cube was locked in there for nearly five hundred years. It sat right here.' He pointed to a faint square on the top step. 'It's reasonable to assume that traces of its evil have been left behind.'

Hiram stumbled outside into the daylight, busily shaking his hands like he was trying to flick mud from his finger-tips. 'That sounds really spooky. I'll just head over here and have a cigarette while you work out what to do next?'

Wilson knelt down to study the names carved into the stairs.

'You don't think *we* are going to be cursed now, do you?' Hiram called out. 'We didn't take the Cube, so we're both in the clear, right?'

Wilson studied the black granite foundations, looking for signs of what could have cracked the stone open. He looked again at the writing carved into the step. 'Santillana . . . that was the name of the man who was crucified at La Catedral – Corsell Santillana.'

Hiram was busy dusting away the step so he could sit down. 'You're right, it is the same last name.'

'We have to get the Cube back,' Wilson stated.

Hiram was sitting on the staircase above the high grass. He'd finished rolling his cigarette and he was about to strike a match. 'From what you said about the Cube, I'm not sure we want it, do we? At least we know the names of the men who took it.'

Wilson spotted eight boreholes, spaced evenly across the top edge of the triangular entrance. He eased the mountain grass aside and studied the fallen wedge of stone. The boreholes were there also. He picked up a discarded plank of eucalyptus – there were a few of them lying about. The wood was badly swollen.

'I've figured out how they busted the stone open.' Wilson waited, but there was no reply. 'Hiram?' Wilson called out.

Wilson's gaze was drawn to the burning tip of Hiram's discarded cigarette lying on the step where he'd been sitting just moments earlier. A thin thread of smoke lazily stretching upwards into the still air.

Immediately realising something was wrong, Wilson somersaulted into the tall grass and sprinted towards the stacked stones that framed the eastern ridge of the valley. On the other side was a long fall into the jungle below, beyond that another one thousand foot drop to the river below.

'I know you have him!' Wilson yelled at the top of his lungs. 'That man plays an important part in the destiny of Vilcapampa!'

Seconds ticked by but all he heard was the sound of his own quickened breath.

Wilson sensed there was someone behind him – he pulled off his hat and spun round . . . but there was no one there! He didn't know if he should run or stay where he was. He couldn't be sure what was happening.

Hearing a distinctive rush of air, Wilson swung round to see the huge black condor swooping towards him, its talons extended! Throwing himself behind the wall of stacked stones, the bird swooped directly overhead, its stalled wings making a whooshing sound as it landed on the granite wedge that had once concealed the Golden Cube of the Sun God.

Wilson warily lifted his head above the tall grass.

The giant condor was looking directly at him, its black eyes singularly focused, its wings extended and fully fanned out. The bird issued a loud screech – one continuous sound that made Wilson press his fingers into his ears. Then it folded its magnificent black wings against its body and sat motionless.

'This is fucking ridiculous,' Wilson muttered to himself.

A loud female voice suddenly cut the silence. 'We have a blade to your friend's throat! You will surrender now or we will remove his head!' The aggressive accent was unlike anything Wilson had ever heard before.

At the high point of the Temple of the Sun an impressive Amazon warrior appeared, her face and skin painted green. She was walking confidently along the outer rim of neatly stacked ashlars. In her right hand she held a short bow. She was fifty feet above him and had the sun at her back, but even so Wilson recognised her immediately.

'You will not hurt him,' Wilson yelled. 'My friend is important to this place, although you do not yet understand why.'

'It will be my choice if he lives or dies,' the Amazon replied.

'I could have killed you and your warriors at the Bridge of the Condor,' Wilson shouted. 'I suggest you remember that.'

'It is an honour for the Virgins of the Sun to die in the protection of Vilcapampa,' she said proudly. 'Do not expect mercy in return!'

Wilson glanced towards the inner temple. 'You have failed to protect Vilcapampa, and you will make the situation worse by acting in haste.'

'You should not be here, Wilson Dowling. The role of my people is to protect the sacred city, no matter what the cost. You are an intruder!'

There was no time to figure out how she could possibly know his name. 'The inner temple was breached *before* we arrived,' Wilson stated.

The Amazon nodded. 'That is true. And the only reason you are still breathing is because Apu has sent the condor for your protection.' The large bird remained perched on the massive granite wedge, sharpening its curved beak against the stone, its lustrous black feathers shimmering in the hazy afternoon light.

'Do you have possession of the Inca Cube?' Wilson called out.

The Amazon remained motionless. Her face was in

shadow and it was difficult to read her expression. 'The Inca Cube is lost,' she eventually replied.

'And what of the men whose names are carved into the step?'

'Jesús Velarde is dead. Killed in the mountains,' she said.

'Is the other man crucified at La Catedral?' Wilson asked.

'That man is Corsell Santillana,' she replied. 'The brother of the man whose name is carved into the stone.'

'The brother?'

'It was *through* Corsell Santillana that the secrets of Vilcapampa and the Inca Cube were revealed to the world of men.'

'And from where did Corsell Santillana get his knowledge?' Wilson asked.

There was silence for a few seconds. 'The knowledge came from my sister,' she eventually replied. 'The warrior, Vivane, trusted *Corsell Santillana* – and she was betrayed!'

'The inner temple was opened by chiselling holes into the granite and inserting pieces of wood,' Wilson said. 'The wood was soaked until it expanded. The force of the rock could not withstand it.'

'An age-old method taught to us in the event we needed to remove the Cube for ourselves,' she replied.

'What is your name, warrior?'

'I am Aclla,' she said proudly. 'Tribune of the Virgins of the Sun. Protectors of the ancient city of Vilcapampa. Guardians of the Inca Cube.'

Wilson couldn't understand why the mission notes had not cautioned him about the female warriors and their continued protection of the city. 'You must listen to me,' Wilson said. 'Hiram Bingham must not be harmed. His destiny is linked to this place.'

The huge condor suddenly opened its powerful wings and sprang forward. Its muscles pumped and it flew directly at Wilson, forcing him to duck into the grass once again. The giant bird shot out over the valley, panned left to pick up a thermal and gradually eased upwards into the sunshine.

'You will come with me to Pitcos!' Aclla called out. 'You must face the Mamaconas . . . the oracles of the Virgins of the Sun. They will judge your fate.'

A strange illumination suddenly caught Wilson's eye. An elongated image was magically forming within the triangular entrance of the Temple of the Sun – the exact place where the Inca Cube once would have resided. Glowing faintly at first, it was difficult to discern what the strange light was exactly. Wilson watched the image from his peripheral view so as not to give away his distraction to the female warrior standing high above.

What is that strange light? Wilson asked himself as it grew brighter with each second.

'The Inca Cube will become more powerful as time moves on,' Aclla continued. 'You have no choice but to come with me.'

As the seconds passed, a womanly form gradually took shape in the entrance, but no matter how hard Wilson tried he couldn't focus clearly. The figure was milky white and shifting, as though it was behind a wall of choppy water. He had become transfixed by the shifting illumination and could no longer disguise his interest.

'There is no choice,' Aclla repeated.

The glowing image stretched towards the polished step where the Inca Cube once sat. A lifelike figure suddenly appeared – it was Helena Capriarty, her hand pressed to the top step.

'You are surrounded!' Helena yelled. 'You have to run!'

Wilson stood there, his mouth agape.

Helena was dressed in black – a button-down shirt under a survival vest, her sleeves rolled up, and cargo pants with large pockets. Her blonde hair was pulled back under her baseball cap.

'You have to run, now!' Helena repeated. 'They're approaching from both sides – three warriors with arrows drawn!'

Wilson glanced in Aclla's direction and it was obvious that she couldn't hear Helena's voice. Was the Inca Cube playing mind tricks on him? Staring into Helena's familiar eyes, Wilson was overwhelmed with emotion.

Helena kept her hand pressed to the white granite step, as if that alone was maintaining the connection between them. There was no logic to it, but in his gut Wilson knew it had to be her.

'Come back in four hours'!' Helena yelled. She frantically pointed towards the northern staircase. 'You have to *go!*'

Wilson turned in the opposite direction and sprinted for the stacked retaining wall. With a single leap, he flew out towards the Urubamba Valley, arms extended like a bird. Two speeding arrows flashed past, one of them grazing his jacket, the other fractionally missing the side of his face.

He twisted into a somersault, his flight now erratic, as he plummeted towards the thick jungle canopy some ninety feet below. The violent rush of air ripped at his ears and he could feel his adrenalin building.

Time slowed down as it always did when he faced death. A further one thousand feet below, the swollen rapids of the mighty Urubamba cut its way through the low point of the valley. The sky was bright blue. The crisp sunshine was hitting the high part of the mountain range, the lower forests cloaked in an emerald darkness. It was a beautiful sight.

Suddenly, he was into the treetops – impact was imminent. This was definitely going to hurt.

36

Andes Ranges, Peru
Machu Picchu Citadel
Local Time 5:32 pm

19 January 1908

'I TOLD YOU not to approach!' Aclla yelled in Quechua.
'Who fired their arrows? The blue-eye will think we were
trying to kill him from the very beginning.'

Skipping along the narrow ashlars, Aclla leapt fifteen
feet between building tops and landed on the ruined wall
of the Royal Palace that straddled the northern staircase.
Without looking at Hiram's body, she jumped down the
irregular stone steps, between the trees and mountain
grasses, past Hiram's burnt-out cigarette and towards the
retaining wall. Her three Amazons were already leaning
over the side, looking down into the thick green jungle.

'He couldn't have possibly survived that fall,' Orelle
stated.

Sontane peered downwards. 'He wouldn't have jumped
if he didn't think he was going to survive.'

'I told you not to close in on him unless he refused to
come along! Why did you approach?' Aclla said angrily.

'We were of *one mind* and Sontane called for it,' Ilna
replied.

'The blue-eye was distracted,' Sontane announced. 'It
was written on his face and I responded to my instinct.'

Aclla locked eyes on her virgin pair. 'He escaped
because he could sense that you were coming, Sontane!'
Aclla pounded her fist on the retaining wall. 'The man that

jumped off this cliff, into the clear thin air, may now be hunting us – do you realise that? Can you imagine what would happen if he did? Your hasty actions have made our position worse than it was.'

'When he jumped, we had no choice but to release our arrows,' Sontane replied. 'His motive was escape and we were right to let fly.'

'The mistake was made *before* he jumped. You acted hastily, Sontane. You heard what this man said. He knows about the Inca Cube and its connection to the Sun God. He knows of its power. He would have come with us to Pitcos – that is my feeling. He was considering my proposal.'

Sontane slung her bow across her shoulder. 'Men are not to be trusted. That is what I have always been taught – especially when it comes to the Inca Cube. This man,' she pointed down into the jungle, 'is no different. They come here to pillage and plunder. They care nothing for the balance of the earth and the gods that control it. You are wrong to trust this man. You have been wrong from the beginning. We should have killed him and been done with it.'

'And how do you explain the arrival of the condor? In a thousand years that will not happen again. Apu seeks to protect him.'

'I cannot explain why the great bird arrived. But if Apu was indeed strong, she would have stopped the Inca Cube from being stolen in the first place. The condor is a symbol of protection, nothing more. The *real* protection of this city is up to us . . . and the actions we take.'

'We have *already* failed to protect the Inca Cube. *Do you not see that?* This man has powers that are beyond our understanding. He dived off this cliff without hesitation. He could help us . . . I am sure of it. You heard him talking to Hiram Bingham – he was as shocked about the disappearance of the Inca Cube as we were.'

'We did not fail to protect the Inca Cube!' Sontane snapped. 'Your *blood sister* failed us! Her obvious weakness for men is the reason all this has happened. And I fear it is the very same weakness that lives in you also.'

Aclla's muscled rippled. She wanted to draw her sword
and cut her virgin pair in half, such was her anger. 'Are
you so ignorant?' she snapped back. ' I see greatness in this
man,' she pointed down into the jungle also. 'I do not deny
it. But my motive is pure and always has been. I seek only
to recover the Inca Cube and I will do everything within
my power to get it back. This man, Wilson Dowling, has
knowledge and strength that can be used to our advantage.
That is my aim – nothing more.'

'He was distracted by something in there,' Orelle interrupted. She pointed through the high grass into the inner
temple. 'I saw it in Wilson Dowling's eyes. He was looking
there and he couldn't tear away his gaze away.'

'Inside the temple?'

'His gaze was fixed,' Ilna added. 'He could see something we could not.'

Aclla leapt towards the entrance and over the fallen
wedge of rock, her three warriors shadowing her all the
way. Stepping carefully into the enclosed space she spun
around, her gaze searching. 'The putrid scent of the Inca
Cube is still here,' she said with a sour expression. She
reached out and touched the polished stone stairs, then
quickly withdrew her hand. 'What could he have seen?'

'Something had his attention,' Orelle confirmed.

'What was it?' Aclla asked. 'There is nothing in this
ancient prison but air.'

'We would not disobey you,' Orelle announced. 'This
man has a connection with something that was in this
very dungeon, an unholy spirit of some kind. That was the
reason he fled – it was not our approach that drove him to
jump, I promise you that.'

Aclla stepped outside and let the fresh air fill her lungs
once again. 'Not only does he have the strength and speed
of a puma, but it seems he has contact with the underworld. This man is either a powerful ally or a dangerous
foe.' Aclla looked to the eastern mountains. 'We must seek
the guidance of The Three.' She turned to Orelle and Ilna.
'You will take Bingham to the Watchman's House and
leave him there, bound and gagged.'

'We should take him with us,' Sontane stated.

'It will be impossible to move quickly,' Aclla replied.

'Then we should kill him.' Sontane made a slash of her hand.

Aclla shook her head. 'You heard what Wilson Dowling said. He was concerned for Hiram Bingham's safety. He believes the skinny man's destiny is linked to this place.'

'We should kill him anyway.'

'If Hiram Bingham is alive, Wilson Dowling will be forced to care for him, as he has done for the last three days. That will slow him down and he will be unable to move at the same speed we do if he chooses to follow.'

'Injure Bingham if that is your strategy. A leg wound perhaps. Something that will eventually heal.'

'He is not to be harmed,' Aclla said. 'That is an order.'

'I disagree with your tactics,' Sontane countered. 'You choose to hold back when it is within our power to strike out one man who has knowingly breached Vilcapampa. One man who will tell a hundred others.'

'If we harm Hiram Bingham, Wilson Dowling will surely track us with pure vengeance. You have seen what this man can do. In the end, the Mamaconas will decide if I have made the right choice or not. It is one full day's hike to Pitcos; if we move quickly we can be there by this time tomorrow. The rivers are swollen and the rains will eventually come again.' Aclla turned and looked towards the western sky.

'Orelle, Ilna, take Hiram Bingham to the Watchman's House.' Calmly picking up Wilson's hat, Aclla folded it in half and tucked it into the back of her breastplate. 'You will meet us on the Inca Trail.' She took one last glance at the inner temple and a shiver went up her spine. The place was evil and she was glad to be away from it.

'Come, Sontane.' Aclla sprinted between the shrubs and mountain grasses, up the irregular stairs towards the Inca Trail. It was her intention to drive Sontane until she dropped from exhaustion. Aclla was the tribune here and she would not tolerate her decisions being questioned.

37

Andes Ranges, Peru
Machu Picchu Citadel
Local Time 9:24 pm

19 January 1908

THE NIGHT SKY was so utterly dark that the glow of the
Milky Way formed a band of white that stretched from
horizon to horizon. To the south, the glittering brightness
of the Southern Cross cut a distinctive figure, as did the
other major constellations speckling the curved heavens.
Centaurus, the Centaur, was a massive constellation to the
south. Argo Navis, the ship of Jason and the Argonauts,
was to the north. Pavo, the peacock, and Dorado, the
swordfish, were to the west. The most impressive star of
all was actually the planet Venus, four times the relative
brightness of anything else.

Although the waning moon would not rise for some
hours yet, there was more than ample light for Wilson
to see clearly. He had made the decision to approach the
Temple of the Sun from the bottom of the eastern ridge, up
the almost sheer cliff he had dived from. The ascent was so
difficult that he figured the Amazon warriors would not
expect him to approach the citadel from that direction, if
at all.

Wilson's landing in the jungle had been heavy. He
had plummeted into the dense treetops and thankfully
had become tangled in the liana vines that crisscrossed
the canopy. The vines twisted around his legs and arms,
spinning him like a dervish, which greatly lessened his final

impact in the rubble of some old Inca buildings. On the way through the treetops a heavy vine wrapped around Wilson's throat, like a hangman's noose. Lying on the jungle floor, his body smashed from the landing, he was forced to call on his incredible strength to tear the vine free, otherwise he surely would have been strangled. Before he could even stand, it was necessary to heal himself.

Since then, he had been scouring the jungle for food, trying his best to replenish his energy. The healing command stripped much of his reserves and it was necessary to eat what beetle larvae and wild berries he could so he did not become exhausted.

Wilson secured his footing on the sheer rock then reached upwards in a spider move, latching onto the next handhold. He was climbing very quickly and in less than a minute would reach the retaining wall that marked the upper perimeter of the eastern ridge. In the darkness beneath him, the grumble of the Urubamba reverberated across the valley. He would not easily be able to hear an attack if it came, but he told himself that he could see much better than anyone else in this dim light and he trusted that was going to be enough to maintain his advantage.

Was it really Helena Capriarty who had been standing within the bowels of the Temple of the Sun? It could have been a trick of his mind – a manifestation of his thoughts that had been amplified by the power of the Inca Cube – but the more he searched his feelings the more convinced he was that it was actually Helena. The tone of her voice, the fear and passion in her eyes, the way that she demanded that he escape.

It has to be her, he thought.

Wilson hardly noticed his muscles burning as he made his rapid ascent up the sheer stone wall. Hiram had certainly been captured and he prayed that Hiram's destiny would be enough to protect him from harm.

Wilson silently climbed over the stacked stones like a reptile, low and painstakingly slow. He was taking great care not to let his weight fall on a dry stick or other object and make a sound that would rise above the constant drone of the river. The distinctive silhouette of the Temple of the Sun loomed above him once again. Wilson scanned the windows and high points of the stone ruins lining the terraces, then he shifted his focus towards the forests that climbed the terraced mountain ridge to the south. He halted for a few moments to be sure that everything remained perfectly still. He again told himself that he could see much better than anyone else, which meant he would be able to spot danger well before they were able to see him.

Approaching the inner temple through the high grass, Wilson carefully stepped around the huge triangular wedge of granite that once blocked the entrance. Gazing inside the stone structure, his heart was beating harder than normal.

'Helena,' he whispered.

But there was no response.

Wilson once again began to question if his vision had been real or not. A sense of dread washed over him as he wondered if he had made the right decision by running from Aclla. He stood back and gazed up at the towering walls of the Temple of the Sun, the stars shining brightly above.

A milky dot about the size of a walnut suddenly appeared within the darkness of the inner temple, floating in midair. It was difficult to focus on the faint ball of light as it shifted about. With each moment it grew and elongated until a human torso floated just above the ground. The light continued to intensify, collapsing into itself until Helena magically appeared. She was standing in the darkness with her hand pressed to the white granite step where the Inca Cube once rested.

'When I said *run*, I didn't mean jump off a sheer cliff into the jungle!' Helena was obviously annoyed. 'I was worried you'd killed yourself.'

'It's nice to see you too,' Wilson replied.

'I pointed *that way*. You should have gone *that way*.'

'Jumping seemed like the best option at the time.'

'One day you're not going to be able to heal yourself, Wilson, and everything will be over for you. You need to be more careful.'

'I was concerned you were a figment of my imagination,' Wilson replied. 'But judging by your reaction, you're obviously the real thing.' Deep down he was so happy to see her.

Helena let out a sigh. 'I've been chasing dreams of you for more than two months. I had a vision of this place.' She looked about warily. 'I saw something inside this temple and I somehow knew it would lead me to you.'

'Do you know where Hiram Bingham is, the skinny man?' Wilson asked.

Helena gestured behind her. 'The female warriors carried his body towards the top of the ridge – I know who Hiram is – he was either dead or unconscious when they dragged him away. After you jumped, the female warriors spent some time arguing about what to do next. They were speaking Quechua, I think. I would've followed them but I lost my connection.' Helena paused. 'Battle-clad female warriors chasing after you, Wilson. Is there no end to the trouble you can get yourself in?'

'They're Amazons, and I'm just as surprised as you.'

'I'm quite sure they left the city via the Inca Trail. Hiram's body is definitely at the top of the ridge, inside the Watchman's House.'

'Wait here until I get back,' Wilson stated.

'I'm coming with you,' Helena replied. 'Don't get spooked if you feel someone close by, it's just me. For some reason I'm only visible to you if I'm touching this stone, but I can see and hear everything when you're within about ten feet of me. The further away you get, I lose the sound, then the vision.'

'Are you in the future right now?' Wilson asked.

Helena nodded. 'You left me just over a year ago. I'm at Machu Picchu right now, within the ruins. When we are both on the same piece of ground, at the right time I guess, overlapping images enter my mind. I can see the present and the past, side by side.'

'You're in Machu Picchu?'

'I'm running around the ruins in the dark. Everyone thinks I've gone completely mad. It's never boring when you're involved, Wilson.'

'What's the date where you are?'

'January the 19th, 2014.'

'The exact same date it is here, except the year is 1908.' Wilson finally smiled. 'It's good to see you, Helena.'

'It's good to see you also, Wilson. I've waited a long time for this moment.'

'Have you been alright since I left?'

Helena smiled also. 'You're a hard act to follow, Wilson Dowling. What can I say? Everyone thinks I've lost my mind, but I don't care.' Tears began forming in her eyes. Helena pointed to her left. 'Hiram Bingham is that way, up the stairs.' She then removed her hand from the stone and slowly faded from view.

It took Wilson just a few minutes to make his way across the city and climb the twenty-five terraces to the Watchman's House. There were countless hiding places tucked away in the overgrown citadel, but Wilson ignored the danger. He trusted that the path ahead was clear. All the while, he could feel Helena's presence next to him, like she was just over his right shoulder. It had been the same sensation he felt when the condor swooped towards him, and when he was inside the railway shack three days before.

Wilson approached the distinctive peaked walls of the Watchman's House and in his heart of hearts he began to fear the worst for Hiram. It had been nearly five hours since he'd seen him alive. A gentle breeze began blowing, causing the trees and mountain grasses to sway about. In the distance, the eastern horizon flickered with lightning.

Pressing his shoulder to the wall of ashlars, Wilson pulled in a quiet breath then peered around the corner. Hiram's body lay on the ground among the tall grass, his ankles and wrists tied. He wasn't moving.

'Oh no,' Wilson whispered.

He approached quietly and placed his hand on Hiram's back.

'E're . . . e . . . huck . . . hab . . . yo . . . een?' Hiram's muffled voice called out.

Wilson hastily untied the leather gag and pulled the chock out of Hiram's mouth.

'I've been waiting here for hours!' Hiram said with a gravelly voice. 'I could really use a drink of water.'

Wilson sat Hiram up, severed the bonds tying his hands and feet and held a water bottle towards him. 'Don't drink too much.'

Hiram gulped at it. 'Those women kidnapped me.' Water was running down his chin and soaking the front of his shirt. 'The Amazons.'

'Drink slowly,' Wilson said. 'You'll make yourself sick.'

'Huge women, they are! Enormous. I fought them as best I could, but they were too strong.' He wiped the excess water from his chin. 'I was beginning to wonder if you were coming back. Or if you were dead.' Hiram's voice sounded a little better now. 'I had bugs crawling across my face, Wilson. Bugs!' He began frantically scratching at his skin as he looked about at the shadowed ground. 'My legs and arms were cramping and I was lying here thinking to myself, 'Where's my fame and fortune now?' I'm gonna die with my' face pressed into the dirt, bugs crawling into my ears and nostrils.'

'You're alive, that's what matters,' Wilson replied.

'It was a terrible ordeal.'

'Wait here,' Wilson said.

Water spurted out of Hiram's mouth. 'Don't leave me alone! It's pitch black! And what if those horrible women come back to take me . . . or worse?' Hiram tried to stand but his legs were obviously numb.

'They've left the city,' Wilson said. 'And they didn't kill you, which is a surprise.'

'Oh, that's *very* nice. You thought they were going to *kill* me?'

'I guess they didn't want to upset me.'

'Gee . . . I'm so glad they didn't *upset* you!'

'He's always this way,' Wilson said over his right shoulder, sensing Helena's presence. 'High maintenance.'

'Who are you talking to?' Hiram asked.

'Let's head back down so we can continue our conversation,' Wilson said in Helena's direction.

'What are you talking about?' Hiram called out in frustration, at the same time trying to search the darkness. 'Is someone else here?'

'Wait here, Hiram.'

'You're losing your mind, Wilson!' Hiram climbed to his knees and studied the dark ground once again. 'What am I supposed to do about the damn bugs?' he yelled out.

Wilson moved quickly down the overgrown terraces, around trees, through tall grass and bamboo thickets towards the Temple of the Sun. Puffing from his exertion, he descended the final flight of stairs and approached the opening in the base of the granite foundations. Moments later the milky ball of light reappeared, increasing in size and intensity, until Helena's delightful form appeared, her hand pressed to the white granite steps.

'We're exactly one hundred and six years apart,' Wilson stated. 'To the day.'

'The date is the key factor,' Helena agreed. 'I was here yesterday and I didn't see you, and the day before.' She looked about. 'The weather is identical *here* and where *you are*. The rain has been terrible, the rivers have flooded and the roads are all blocked.'

Wilson stretched out his hand. Helena looked so real, like she was physically there in front of him, but when he tried to touch her his hand passed right through her image. Helena reached out to touch him in return with the very same result.

'Why is this happening?' she asked.

Wilson pointed at the white granite steps. 'It's because of the object that once sat right there, where your hand is.'

'The Inca Cube,' Helena replied. 'I heard your conversations with Hiram and the female warrior.'

'It is certainly the Inca Cube's energy that is sponsoring this connection between us.' He stepped closer. 'Do you remember I once told you about the formation of the universe, a millisecond after the Big Bang, when all things were created? How a spider web of very powerful tubes of energy called cosmic strands were laced across the universe. It is the cosmic strands that allow the dimension of *time* to exist?'

'I remember everything you said to me,' she replied.

'One of those cosmic strands terminates within the object called the Inca Cube. Legend has it that Manco Capac, the first Inca, rose up from the waters of Lake Titicaca carrying a Golden Staff. His wife, Mama Ocllo, was carrying a Golden Cube. Each item contained the termination point of a single cosmic strand. When the Golden Staff was unexpectedly destroyed, the Inca Cube became all-powerful. It began to possess the souls of men. According to the prophesy, the Inca Cube had to be locked away forever otherwise it would consume mankind – whatever that means. In the mid 1400s, King Pachacuti built this fortress on the most inhospitable mountain ridge in South America. Inside this prison made of stone, protected by energy crystals, the Inca Cube was concealed. Until these two men,' Wilson pointed at the carving on the middle step, 'released the Inca Cube into an unwitting world.'

'Do you know where the Cube is now?'

'My guess is it's in Cuzco. At least it was at some point. There was a man nailed to a cross on the outer wall of La Catedral, the big church in the central square.'

'The crucifixion,' Helena said. 'I know about it.'

'It wasn't part of the history that I studied,' Wilson replied.

'I was told by a passenger on the train getting here. That was the first I had heard about it also. It's not in any books.'

Wilson pointed at the carving on the middle step. 'The crucified man is the *brother* of Juan Santillana, the man who took the Inca Cube. In the future I came from, that crucifixion never happened. And the structure you are now standing inside was never opened.'

'According to Hiram Bingham's book, this place is just like this,' Helena said. 'But there was no mention of a crucifixion in his text.'

'You have Hiram's book?'

'I read it while I was waiting for you to arrive.'

Wilson rubbed his chin. 'Can you see these carvings in the future?'

Helena squinted. 'The lettering on the step hasn't changed. But that giant wedge of stone behind you is not here anymore. Neither are the trees or the bamboo. It's all been cleared and the stone buildings have been reconstructed. There's a new wall over there,' she said, pointing.

'Does Hiram mention me in his book?'

Helena shook her head.

'What date does he discover Machu Picchu?'

'He discovers it on July 24th 1911. More than three years from where you are now.'

'We're dealing with an altered history,' Wilson said thoughtfully. 'Does he mention the Amazons?'

Helena shook her head again. 'Not a word.'

'The female warriors are the original protectors of Vilcapampa,' Wilson said. 'They are the descendants of the original Virgins of the Sun.'

'They were trying to kill you,' Helena stated. 'I was in the ruins watching them. Those women had poison on their arrowheads – I saw them applying it.' Helena held her thumb and index finger three inches apart. 'At one stage I was this close to them. If you'd stayed where you were, you'd be dead now.'

'What about the woman standing on top of the building, the one called Aclla?'

'I didn't get close to her until after you jumped. She was upset with the others, I know that much. Probably that they didn't kill you.'

Wilson pictured Aclla's strong face. 'She wanted me to meet with the Mamaconas, the oracles of the Virgins of the Sun, in a place called Pitcos.'

Helena seemed frustrated. 'I'm telling you, those women wanted you dead! There is no question in my mind.'

'They have information that I need,' Wilson responded. 'Aclla said the Inca Cube would become more powerful as time went on, and I believe her.' He pulled his hands through his brown hair as lightning flickered on the horizon. 'I'm just not sure how to follow their trail.'

'If you chase after them across the mountains, I won't be able to come with you,' Helena said. 'I won't be able to keep up.'

'That's the price we'll have to pay,' Wilson responded.

'Following the Amazons is the wrong thing to do.'

'It's the best option there is. I have to get to Pitcos and find out what they know.' Wilson put his hands on his hips. 'You must understand, Helena. Without the Inca Cube I'm stranded here. The Cube drives the transport portal.'

'You're stuck there?'

'Correct. I need to find the Inca Cube.'

'I know the way to Pitcos,' Helena replied.

'How could you possibly know?'

'It's written in Bingham's book. It's to the west of here, where the Tincochaca River meets the Urubamba. There's a mountain called Amarupata. The fortress is situated on top. It's at a higher elevation than here and it's surrounded by cliffs on all sides. There's only one way in and that's from the west.'

'Thank you, Helena.'

'You realise if I take my hand off this stone we can't communicate anymore? This might just be the last time we ever see each other.'

Wilson rested his hand on the very spot Helena was touching. 'I need to find the Cube if I'm ever going to transport away from here.'

'Why didn't you come and get me?' Helena asked unexpectedly.

'I never promised you I'd come back. I didn't even realise I could.'

'You never said you'd come back, but you knew that's what I was hoping for.'

'I don't know what to say.'

Wilson could feel heat from the granite steps radiating through his fingertips and he pulled his hand away. The sensation was odd, like he'd been given a mild electric shock. There was certainly some sort of residue caused by the Cube.

'There's something I have to tell you,' Helena said with a worried expression. 'Maybe it's the reason all this is happening. On the train trip here a man called Don Eravisto pulled out a gun and tried to kill me.' Before Wilson could react, Helena gestured for him to let her finish. 'He was the one who told me about the crucifixion in Cuzco. Don Eravisto said that killing me was the only way to take revenge for the murder of his family over a century before.'

'Who killed his family?' Wilson asked.

'You did,' she replied.

'That's impossible.'

'Don Eravisto knew everything, Wilson. He predicted that I would make contact with you. He knew that you were here in the past with Hiram Bingham. He said I would help you with information, which I am. According to him, *you* will murder an honest man's family while they are sleeping in their beds – the wife of Lucho Gonzales and two of his young children – leaving the eldest boy alive to witness your horrible act. He said you did unspeakable things to them – that you raped and sodomised them.'

Wilson was stunned by what he was hearing. 'That's ridiculous.'

'I know that, Wilson. But Don Eravisto vehemently believes you are the murderer and I am your accomplice. He believes it enough to try to kill me. You need to go forward armed with that knowledge so you can protect yourself.'

'I've never heard of Lucho Gonzales,' Wilson said.

'He's a captain in the Peruvian army, based in Cuzco.'

'Why would I kill his family?'

'The Inca Cube drives people to madness, Wilson. That

could be the reason. You need to take care when you're around it. If it truly can possess people's souls, then maybe you won't be in control of what will happen.'

Wilson felt sick to his stomach. 'It's not very comforting when someone tells you that you're going to murder and sodomise innocent women and children.'

'You need to stay focused,' she said with a stern voice. 'If am near the Inca Cube we can probably communicate.' She looked at the stone step where her hand was resting. 'That might help us when the time comes. We must arrange to meet,' Helena said. 'In a place that you know you will be. In Cuzco somewhere. Something in the open where I can easily find you.'

'History is out of balance,' Wilson stated. 'And the Cube's release is the reason our worlds have intertwined once again. You need to be careful, Helena. If your role here is to help me, you might still be in danger also.'

38

Cuzco, Peru
La Monasterio
Local Time 12:35 am

19 January 1908

THE SOLES OF Bishop Francisco's cobbled shoes made a distinctive clatter as he shuffled down the stone stairway and into the underground chamber. In one hand he clasped a single brass key, in the other an ornate hurricane lamp made of sterling silver with a long handle and four glass sides. The pitiful orange flame lit up the moss-covered walls and betrayed the glassy pools of water on the floor where rain had seeped in through tiny cracks in the masonry.

As he approached yet another heavy door, he held out the same key, carefully inserted it in the lock and turned the metal latch. Just hearing the click of the gears made his pulse race. Pushing the door open, the rank scent of urine and excrement filled his nostrils. The smell made him want to turn back, but he knew that leaving would only cause him more pain.

Lifting the lamp, he peered into the cold darkness to see the naked figure of a woman shackled to the far wall, hanging heavily from her wrists. She was facing away from him, her head to one side, her body bruised and bloodied. Bishop Francisco silently closed the door and turned the mechanism to the locked position.

'This woman needs care if she is to survive,' the bishop said to the darkness. He did not want to step any further into the dungeon and he hoped against hope that this was as far as he need go. 'She has not eaten for more than a week, Great Lord. We must care for her or she will certainly die.'

'You will take the cross of Jesus and you will use it upon her,' the deep voice replied.

The bishop felt a sweat overcome him. He wanted to plead for mercy, for both the woman as well as for himself, but he knew that would be useless. The spirit of Pizarro lusted for the pain and humiliation of others. Any weakness only amplified his ravenous needs, and the consequences would be even more severe.

Carefully placing the oil lamp on the stone floor, Bishop Francisco took an embroidered handkerchief from his pocket and wiped the sweat away from his face and hands. Moving slowly, he reluctantly drew a large cross from the inner pocket of his scarlet robes. He would do anything to delay events, but he knew it would only be a temporary reprieve from the horror that was soon to overwhelm him. Stepping slowly through dried blood and urine, Bishop Francisco approached the naked woman, the silver cross of Jesus in his hand. It sickened him to think that an object so holy could be used to generate so much pain. The edges were sharp and would certainly pierce the skin.

'This woman will renounce her pagan beliefs,' Pizarro continued. *'You will not stop until she praises Jesus Christ, the true saviour of souls. Only through Him can she be saved. Only through His mercy can her soul rise to heaven.'*

Bishop Francisco eased himself closer to the woman. His shaky voice was barely a whisper. 'You must renounce your beliefs, my child. You must accept the one true God, Jesus Christ. This is your only path to freedom and salvation.' He then ran the tip of the cross down her back towards her bruised buttocks. 'You must say, "Praise be to Jesus".'

The woman did not even flinch; she just hung there in her metal shackles.

'You must say, "Praise be to Jesus",' he whispered

again. 'That is the only way you can escape the torture that will befall you.'

Bishop Francisco wanted to cry but he knew he had no more tears left to shed. All the while he could feel the spirit of Pizarro filling the cold air around him, revelling in this moment and lusting for a battle of wills and the inevitable pain that would come with it.

He spat on the silver, wetting the metal, then began to prod with the long end of the cross, jamming at the woman's exposed flesh to garner a reaction. But there was nothing. His actions became more fierce until he was fairly slamming the cross into her, over and over. And yet the woman just hung there, shackled by the wrists, unmoving.

Grabbing the woman by her hair, he eased her bruised face away from the wall. What he saw next should have filled him with horror and sadness, but his reaction was just the opposite. Her eyes were open, but there was no life in them. The leather strap that was jammed into her mouth was saturated with blood that ran down her blackened chin. There was so much gore that it had all but covered the front of her naked body then dripped down her legs.

Releasing his grip, the woman's head hit the solid wall. Bishop Francisco untied the leather gag and pulled it free, causing pieces of mangled fleash to hit the floor with a splat. She had bitten off her tongue to escape the hell she had been living. The blood from the laceration had filled her lungs and drowned her.

'You should not have told her that Corsell Santillana had been crucified, Great Lord. He was her reason for living – I told you that. From the moment she knew he was dead, her will to survive was extinguished.'

'*That was the greatest moment of all!*' Pizarro replied, a sense of elation in his tone. '*That was when she learnt of the conviction of Almighty God. She finally realised there was no escape for a heathen such as herself. Now she will burn in the fires of Hell for an eternity, in the hands of Lucifer. She will not go to Heaven as Corsell has done. He was cleansed on the cross and he will live forevermore by God's side.*'

Bishop Francisco looked into Vivane's dead eyes. It was difficult to believe that she was once a beautiful, healthy young woman, a warrior of the Virgins of the Sun, descended from the ancient Incas. From the cursed expression on her face it had been a horrible death, and yet he envied her very much. She had managed to escape the madness of the hellish world Pizarro had created. If only he could find a way to escape this madness himself, Bishop Francisco would certainly take it, no matter what the price or the pain that came with it.

'*Release her bonds,*' the voice said.

Bishop Francisco pulled the heavy split-pin from the metal shackle and Vivane's left arm released. Removing the second split-pin was more difficult with all her weight upon it, but he set his feet apart and was able to exert just enough strength to pull the pin free, letting her naked body fall to the muck and dirt on the floor.

'*You will turn her on her back,*' Pizarro stated.

'Please, Great Lord, this poor child is dead. There is no further pain that can be inflicted upon her.'

'*She has defied me! She has chosen Hell over Heaven!*' The sound of Pizarro's voice was so loud that Bishop Francisco wanted to beg for mercy, but he dared not, otherwise it would only draw further retaliation.

'*You will turn her onto her back!*' the voice bellowed, louder than ever.

The terrible pain Pizarro's voice inflicted made Bishop Francisco buckle over at the waist, his hands clasped to the sides of his head. He let out a whimper, but for what reason he could not be sure – there was no one to hear him anyway.

'I will do as you say,' he said wincing in disgust. 'I will do as you say.' Bishop Francisco threw off his robes, leaving him wearing only his scarlet shoes and papal hat. He was barely skin and bone himself as he stood there above the corpse of a once-beautiful woman.

In the midst of his torment, Bishop Francisco wanted to pray to his own God to save him from this horror, but he didn't know which God to pray to anymore. He was beginning to doubt that a true God even existed – if he did, he would not let evil such as this act in his name.

'God is merciful, God is great,' he said to himself in the vain hope that his prayers would be received.

Where is a man who can save me from this terror? he asked himself.

There was only one hope that he could cling to – the man called Wilson Dowling. The elusive stranger struck fear into Pizarro when nothing else would. The Great Lord had confessed that he could not see into Dowling's soul, as he could with all other men. A man with a soul that dark was a man who could stop the evil that was crawling through his body at this very moment. Wilson Dowling was certainly coming to Cuzco – Pizarro had ordered soldiers in place to protect the approach to the city.

He is my only hope of escape, the bishop realised.

Bishop Francisco rested his knees in the blood and muck on the floor. Sensing his madness would finally overtake his conscious mind, Bishop Francisco reluctantly placed his hands on Vivane's frigid skin. He wanted his life to end at this moment and he would give his own soul for the chance to be released from the hell he was living.

'I need you to kill me, Wilson Dowling,' he said to himself. 'All my prayers will be answered if you strike me down with a single blow.' There was no other hope in his life – only the abstract visions of a man he had never met; a man with a soul as black as night.

39

Andes Ranges, Peru
Amarupata Mountain
Local Time 8:05 pm

21 January 1908

HEAVY RAIN WAS falling again as Wilson stood at the base of Mount Amarupata, gazing up at the sheer cliffs that stretched away into the squalling darkness. He was trying to decide if he should attempt to scale what was said to be a 3,500-foot climb up a difficult rock face that he couldn't even see. His other option was to chance approaching Pitcos from the west, along a stone trail that would be much easier to traverse but was probably guarded. Pressing his hand to the granite wall next to him, he felt the weight of the water barrelling down from so high up. It was doubtful that he could cling to such a slippery surface.

After leaving Machu Picchu, Wilson led Hiram to Father Marcos at the humble orphanage of Our Lady of Mercy on the banks of the raging Urubamba. It had taken them almost a full day to travel the three miles across the mountain ridge to where they found a narrow trail that switchbacked down the perilous slopes towards the river.

Father Marcos had been more than accommodating and he provided the first hot meal of that Wilson and Hiram had had in nearly five days – a large bowl of pork and potatoes. To Hiram's great relief, Father Marcos had a bottle of whiskey and plenty of tobacco plants so he was able to soothe the American's shattered nerves with a drink and more cigarettes than he could possibly smoke. The orphanage was run by three Spanish nuns who looked after the forty or so children of *mestizo* blood, varying in ages from two to sixteen. Nearly all of them had been abandoned, but the children preferred to believe their parents had been killed in the mountains. Wilson was so grateful to Father Marcos for his hospitality that he gave him three solid gold coins to assist with the running of the church. He then handed the priest a fourth gold coin and asked him to arrange a guide for Hiram so he could be taken back to Cuzco as soon as practicable.

Father Marcos refused the money, but Wilson knew it was his pride and not the needs of his orphanage that were driving his actions. In the end, Wilson insisted in the name of God Almighty that he take the offering.

'I know a mountain guide called Ompeta who comes by this way every now and again,' Father Marcos said. The little priest wore simple brown robes over his skinny frame and a wooden cross around his neck. Easily in his fifties, he had chocolate-coloured skin, a broad nose and a wide face – certainly from Indian blood. He ran a clean and orderly orphanage and the children seemed to adore him.

'Ompeta brings us supplies and clothing from Cuzco,' Father Marcos said with a smile that exposed his tobacco-stained teeth. 'When he returns, I will have him take your friend home. Ompeta is a good man, although he is not of our faith. He is our connection to the outside world and we pray every day for his safe return, regardless of the gods he worships.'

The nuns around him nodded.

'It is always good to see him,' Sister Margaret said.

'He brings us newspapers when he can,' Sister Daniela chimed in.

Since leaving the orphanage, Wilson had been travelling very quickly. There was once a time when he craved the company of others, but that was long ago. His role as Overseer, and the life experiences that came with it, had conspired to drive the simple desire for companionship from him. He had conditioned himself to become a loner;

that had been the easiest way to survive in the places he had been – both emotionally and physically.

Wilson looked again at the sheer wall of granite that stretched up into the pouring rain. Not even he was brave enough to attempt a climb as treacherous as that. His only choice was to circle the ridge and approach Pitcos from the western side of Amarupata as Helena had mentioned.

A blinding flash of sheet lightning lit up the sky, causing Wilson to clasp his eyes shut in pain. His sensitive eyesight was excellent in the darkness, but the shock of bright light stunned him to a standstill every time. Opening his eyes, he had to wait a moment until the blurring faded and he could see clearly once again.

The way ahead was a collection of large fallen stones and shale that had obviously separated from the cliffs over the course of a thousand years. Traversing the rocks was much easier than forcing his way through thick jungle and Wilson ran forward jumping from rock to rock.

All the while he was thinking of Helena. He wished he could go back to the moment she'd appeared in the darkness, her hand pressed to the white granite step. If he could, he would have told her how much it meant to him to see her again, but the years of separation had taken its toll and he was unable to feel very much, no matter how he tried. Seeing her again caught him totally off guard, and as a result, he was unable to tell her how he really felt. It was only now, after two full days, that he was beginning to piece together his emotions. He had consoled himself over the years that things were never the same when you attempted to rekindle the past. It had been eight long years since he had last seen her – a lifetime in so many ways – but in return, it had only been one year for her.

There was no doubt that Helena made a welcome sight standing there in the darkness. The way her blonde fringe fell across her eyes was majestic, as was her classic smile and the tone of her voice. Only now was Wilson really beginning to appreciate the opportunity he'd been given. It was impossible to say if he would ever see Helena again, but he hoped that there was more to their connection than just her dire warning. He knew that she had the same biological capability to time-travel that he did – the telltale indication was in her stunning blue eyes. He wanted to reveal to her that she had the very same ability he did, but what purpose would that serve? There was no use in her knowing that her genetic structure was the one-in-ten-billion that could travel a cosmic strand. It was unlikely she would ever have the opportunity to travel the *fourth dimension* for herself. Some things were best kept secret, Wilson decided. It was best for her that she didn't know.

The trail ended and Wilson had no choice but to leap from a flat boulder into the dense jungle. The rain was pounding down through the trees as he proceeded on all fours through the tangled foliage, his hands submerged in mud to his elbows.

He considered Helena's warning – that he would murder and sodomise the wife and children of Captain Lucho Gonzales. Committing such a vile act was incomprehensible to him. And yet the history Helena had indicated seemed to dictate just that. Could he change the future that she had predicted? In his experience, history could be reinvented, but *destiny* had a way of pulling the most important events into line so they could not be altered. According to the mission notes, the Inca Cube was supposed to remain housed within the Temple of the Sun for the rest of time. Everything that happened since the Cube was taken was a deviation from that historical line, as was the crucifixion of Corsell Santillana. Wilson's unexpected connection to Helena was certainly related also. If the Inca Cube had not been freed, he certainly wouldn't have connected with her as he did.

There was good and bad in everything.

Wilson's thoughts drifted to Aclla and the Virgins of the Sun. What was their part in all this? Could they help him to retrieve the Inca Cube, or were they his sworn enemy as Helena had warned? Undoubtedly, it had been their task to protect the Cube, Aclla had said as much. And they had failed because Aclla's sister had betrayed the secret of the Cube's location to Corsell Santillana.

The thick jungle opened up again to reveal a narrow trail. Wiping the water from his eyes, Wilson pulled the satchel to his body as tightly as he could and set his knife into a place on his belt from where he could draw it easily. He was about to climb the narrow approach up the steep mountainside to the hidden city of Pitcos.

He approached a staircase carved into the steep granite that led up into the swirling rain. What lay ahead he could not possibly imagine, but if he was to find the Inca Cube he needed information from the warriors who had been protecting it for the last five hundred years. If they wanted him dead, he would have to rely on his strength and agility to make his escape.

The slippery trail followed a narrow switchback up the treacherous mountainside that cut through numerous fractures in the granite. As the altitude increased, the weather became more severe. The wind was gusting at over fifty miles per hour, which made just standing in the same spot a problem. To make matters worse, the freezing raindrops were hitting him with such force that it was difficult to see for more than a second at a time. It was unbelievable that anyone would want to live in a place like this, so high up, at the mercy of the elements – and this was *summertime*. This place would surely be lashed by terrible snowstorms in the winter.

Easing his way along a narrow rock shelf, Wilson hung to the granite by his fingernails. The cut path was only inches wide and perilously greasy. There was no telling how high up he was, but he had been climbing for more than an hour.

The stone platform eventually levelled out and a three-foot-wide fissure appeared in the granite wall ahead. The split rock surely formed the entrance to Pitcos. Standing there, soaked to the skin and exhausted, he could not help but wonder if the Virgins of the Sun were aware of his approach. From everything he had seen, he had to believe that they knew how to protect their keep.

Through the crack in the stone Wilson could see an open space on the other side.

How would a man of peace enter the city? Wilson asked himself.

Standing tall, he set his shoulders back and walked head-on into the fortress city of Pitcos. Of all the things he had done in his life, this seemed to be the dumbest; he was about to enter a world of cutthroat Amazon warriors. Charm would not work on them, and neither would brute force – the answer would be somewhere in between.

40

Andes Ranges, Peru
Fortress City of Pitcos
Local Time 10:15 pm

21 January 1908

WILSON STEPPED THROUGH the calm air cradled between the two giant walls of stone. From the information in Hiram's biography, he knew the basic layout of the buildings and the dimensions of the fortified city. Up ahead there were some fifty houses, arranged to form a rough square with a central courtyard. There were no windows or doors that led to the open space and it was easy to conclude it had been designed as a killing ground. The entire city sat upon levelled earth, with the exception of the crowning glory of Pitcos: a grand temple set a few steps higher than everything else. Helena's description about the building's exact location had been vague and Wilson assumed the temple was on the eastern ridge, above the cultivation terraces looking back towards Machu Picchu. It was claimed that the temple was constructed of black granite with thirty trapezoidal doorways – fifteen on the front and an equal number evenly spaced on the other side.

Wilson steadied his breathing stepped out into the weather once again. He made his way slowly forward, concluding that his options were better from the middle of the wide-open space. Ahead of him, the masoned walls of the compound were three times the height of a man and he knew he could easily scale the smooth stone structure if the need presented itself.

A grinding noise suddenly emanated from behind him and he turned to see a giant stone wedge drop down between the fissure, blocking his exit. The large stone seemed to pivot on a complex lever system that was activated from the cliffs above.

Two female warriors appeared and somersaulted off the wall directly ahead, both landing on their feet, side by side. One of the warriors was brandishing a sword, the other had her fists clenched by her sides.

Aclla pointed in Wilson's direction. 'We have been expecting you!' she called out through the wind and the rain. Her partner held the grim expression of an executioner as she circled behind and disappeared from view.

'You will not require a sword,' Wilson said. 'I come as a friend.'

'We have no friends,' Aclla replied.

'I need your help, then,' Wilson countered.

Aclla looked him up and down with a discerning gaze. 'You survived your fall into the jungle without a scratch, as I expected you would. And now you enter the fortified city of Pitcos without worry for your own safety, just as the Mamaconas said you would.'

'The Mamaconas are the reason I am here,' Wilson said. 'There is information that we must share with each other. The fate of the Inca Cube depends on it.'

Aclla stood there in the rain, her face expressionless. 'Come . . . I will take you to them,' she eventually said.

Aclla turned on the spot, exposing her naked back. Wilson was at all times aware of the female warrior right behind him; he could hear the softness of her footfall and noticed that she was stepping in time with Aclla up ahead. As they approached the fortifications, Wilson realised that the high walls were actually angled apart with gaps a person could easily fit through. From a distance the wall looked solid, but the trick of the eye meant the Amazons could quickly flood the courtyard with warriors if that was their intention. This would surely be a killing ground for any small band of men stupid enough to try and take this place by force.

Aclla didn't say a word as she led Wilson along a narrow laneway between two buildings. She was taller than he'd expected – probably only an inch shorter than he was. A flash of lightning lit up the night and Wilson had to press his fingers to his eyes to settle the brief discomfort. The laneway opened up again as they approached a magnificent building with fifteen doorways that stretched away into the heavy rain in both directions.

Aclla climbed the middle steps to a raised landing.

'Do you have any weapons?' she asked.

'Just my knife, Wilson replied. He drew it from its scabbard and handed it to her.

Aclla's outfit was very similar to Greek battle armour from the time of Alexander the Great – the breastplate was made of a lightweight metal, etched with the image of the sun with beams of light splaying out in all directions – the rainwater sat beaded on the metal, as it did on her perfect skin. On her wrists she wore wide bracelets decorated with the same motif, as well as engraved plates covering her shins. She was a truly magnificent creature. Her long dark hair was tied into two plaits that hung wet down her back. Wilson had to acknowledge there was a physical attraction, something primal that he had been disappointed not to feel when he looked at Helena Capriarty within the base of the Temple of the Sun.

After climbing the stairs, Wilson stepped under a thatched roof made of woven mountain grass. He could see the flickering of firelight coming from inside as Aclla swung open the solid door.

Lining the doorway were nine female warriors dressed exactly as Aclla was – four on one side, five on the other. The honour guard stood rigid, their shoulders back, their short swords strapped to their left thighs, their eyes unmoving. They were all about the same age – tanned, very tall and very fit.

The heat inside the temple was a welcome relief, as was the golden glow of the four large fires, evenly spaced out along the 250-foot-long building. The smoke was vented through four peaked chimneys, so the air was clear.

The floors were made of polished hardwood that had been carefully carpentered so there was not a single gap between the blonde planks. When the door closed behind him it became impossible to hear the swirling wind and rain hammering the building outside, only the sound of the large crackling fires.

Three hooded figures stood in the centre of a black expanse, upon what looked like a circular slab of black granite or obsidian. The timber floor perfectly abutted the black stone. As Wilson approached, he decided the shiny slab had to be volcanic glass, because it was just too polished to be stone.

One of the hooded figures raised a bony finger in Wilson's direction.

'I never thought I would see the day when a *man* would enter this most holy of places.' Her voice was rattly and ancient, as though she had lived a thousand lifetimes. 'I can feel the lust of our warriors as they look at him. It makes me sick to my stomach.'

'They are only human,' one of the other hooded figures replied, her voice a little deeper. It was impossible to see what the Mamaconas looked like because their heavy robes kept their faces in total shadow.

'Keep approaching,' the third of them announced with a frail voice, waving Wilson forward with a slow and deliberate gesture.

Aclla shadowed Wilson towards the hooded women. They were not tall or imposing, but hunched over, seemingly from old age. Aclla halted her progress three paces from the circular black floor.

Wiping the rainwater from his face, Wilson noticed that his wet clothing was dripping on the floorboards around him.

The middle figure stepped forward, exposed her aged hands and slowly pulled back the hood of her robe. Wilson had to stop himself from taking in a sharp breath at the sight of her – she looked older than any human he had ever seen. The colour of her irises and lips were terribly pale, like a piece of wood that had been bleached by too many years in the sun. Her deeply wrinkled skin was as thin as rice paper, almost translucent, and her long hair was whiter than snow, although it looked healthy and lustrous. It was obvious that the woman standing before him had once been tall and handsome, Wilson could see it in her bone structure, but that was long ago.

'I am Mamacona Kay Pacha,' the old woman announced. 'Priestess of the World We Live In.'

The figure to her left stepped forward and removed her hood also. She looked identical in every way, except her voice had a distinctly deeper and raspier tone. 'I am Mamacona Hurin Pacha . . . Priestess of the Underworld,' she announced.

The third woman stepped forward; she too was identical to the others. 'I am Mamacona Hanan Pacha . . . Priestess of the World Above.' Her voice was a little brighter and yet she had been the one who made the seething comment about the lust of their warriors.

'You come here to seek guidance,' Mamacona Kay Pacha stated, her manner feathered with the experience of her countless years. 'We have been expecting you. Before we begin,' she said in an ancient tone, 'you must first acknowledge that all things in life come with a price.'

Aclla stepped backwards a full stride, out of Wilson's line of sight.

'Will you acknowledge this?' the old woman said.

Wilson's mouth felt parched, but he forced a reply nonetheless. 'I acknowledge that all things have a price.' Suddenly four warriors grabbed him, kicked his legs out from under him, and pinned him to the floor on his knees.

He considered fighting back, but before he could, Aclla whispered in his ear, 'You must hold still, we are not going to kill you.'

Aclla sliced the sharp blade of his knife across his thumb where it met his palm. Wilson didn't flinch as skin and muscle split open and blood began pouring to the floor. Aclla held a small obsidian bowl under the wound to catch the crimson liquid. Wilson commenced a healing command

and the wound on his hand knitted before Aclla's eyes, until the blood flow had all but stopped.

Aclla stood back, her expression filled with shock at the sight of his skin recovering the way that it had. Composing herself, she turned her gaze to the warriors gripping Wilson's arms and legs. 'Let him go,' she ordered. 'We have what we need.'

Aclla held the bowl up to the three old women, who moved to the front of the obsidian circle. The central figure carefully took the bowl, closed her eyes and savoured the smell for a moment, then put it to her aged lips and drank. The other two did the same, appreciating it like a fine wine. Receiving the bowl again, Aclla made eye contact with Wilson as she walked smoothly towards the fire and poured the remaining blood into the flames, the liquid making a hiss as it was obliterated by the violent heat.

Wilson could not help but feel disgusted at the thought of someone drinking his blood. The old women stood in the centre of the circle holding hands, their eyes closed, their faces turned to the ceiling. Minutes passed as they stood silently in the shifting glow of the firelight. They eventually separated, each taking their original positions on the black obsidian floor.

'He has been to many places and he has seen many things,' the Priestess of the Underworld said softly, her eyes glazed. She could have spoken in Quechua but she chose English instead. 'He is filled with deep loss . . . and much regret. This man has taken the sword to people he loves.'

'His powers of healing and strength are clouded in mystery,' Mamacona Kay Pacha said from her trance. 'I cannot see the source of it in him.'

'He has no alignment with the gods,' the Priestess of the World Above stated. 'His knowledge comes from the teachings of men and their conventional wisdom.' Her eyes were glazed also. 'His convictions are strong, as is his desire to travel home. He needs the Cube . . . otherwise he cannot leave.'

A smile suddenly cracked the Priestess of the

Underworld's ancient lips. 'This man has travelled the pathways of time. He is a journeyman of the Creator.'

From their trance, the women began talking one by one as if no one else was in the room with them.

'Could this be true?' Mamacona Kay Pacha questioned.

'That is why the condor flew in to protect him.'

'It has to be.'

'He has seen different worlds at different times,' the Priestess of the Underworld added. 'That much I can determine.'

'Who is the woman he sees in his visions?'

'The glowing light.'

'A guardian angel, perhaps?

'That is not clear, but she is not of this world.'

'He has feelings for her. They are partners.'

'He is unsure of his feelings now.'

'He is confused by his lust.'

'The years have taken their toll.'

'Too many events have come to pass.'

'This is not his first visit to Vilcapampa,' the Priestess of the World Above said from her trance, as if it were a revelation. 'I see it now. He visited the lost city eight winters ago.' She turned to her identical sisters, their eyes cleared, and they focused on each other. 'This was the man.'

'Could this be true?' Mamacona Kay Pacha said. 'You are a journeyman?'

All three women turned their collective gaze on him.

'I am the Overseer,' Wilson announced as bravely as he could. 'I came to Vilcapampa eight years ago through the time portal located within the great Inca city. As you say, I am from another world, from another time, on a mission ordained at the beginning of the universe. A mission that had me lead Hiram Bingham, the American academic, to the lost city of Vilcapampa.'

'A mission from the gods?'

'A mission from the creators of the universe,' Wilson replied.

'And you waited eight years?' the Priestess of the World Above asked.

'The wait was not my choice, I assure you,' Wilson replied. 'It is a quirk of the time pathways. Only certain places can be connected to certain points in time. The dates were very specific, according to the writings. There was no other choice,' he said again.

'And you have completed your mission?' Mamacona Kay Pacha asked.

Wilson nodded. 'I have completed my part. But things are not as they are meant to be, and without the power of the Inca Cube I cannot leave.'

There was a collective silence as the three Mamaconas considered what they had just been told. The gentle hiss and crackle of the wood burning in the two adjacent fireplaces seemed louder than ever, the dark walls shifting against the flicker of the orange flames.

'I need your help to obtain the Inca Cube,' Wilson stated. 'Otherwise, I cannot complete my journey.'

There was no reply for an uncomfortable length of time. The three old women stood unmoving, studying him with piercing gazes. Wilson was beginning to wonder if he had said something that offended them, or if he had asked for too much, too soon.

'This man does not believe in the gods,' the Priestess of the World Above said again. 'How is that possible after the things he has seen?'

'It doesn't matter what he believes,' Mamacona Kay Pacha stated. 'The creators of the universe have called for the city of Vilcapampa to be discovered.'

'Why should we help this man?' one of them asked.

'He has completed the tasks that were required of him,' the Priestess of the Underworld admitted. 'And he is not without personal sacrifice. There is pain within him; you both felt it. Where there is pain in him, there is honour. I do not question what this man believes, or the mistakes he has made. I judge him only on the actions he takes when he is faced with a challenge that requires his ultimate sacrifice. What will he do then? That is the question you must ask yourself.'

'He has heaped tragedy upon us all,' Mamacona Kay

Pacha stated. 'The ramifications of the Inca Cube's release cannot be measured easily. He does not even realise what he has done, or the part he has played.'

'What part did I play?' Wilson asked.

'He does not even know what he did,' one of them said, an arrogant smile creasing her aged lips. 'He is foolish to his actions.'

'I need the Inca Cube or I can never leave,' Wilson said. 'It is ordained by the Creator, you know this. Together we will hunt for it, on the condition that I am allowed to use its power to transport away from here.'

There was another lengthy silence.

'There is no doubt that the Inca Cube must once again be isolated from the world of men,' the Priestess of the World Above stated. 'However, it cannot be used for your purposes any longer. You were the one who set the chain of events in motion that released it. You are at fault here, Wilson Dowling.'

'You say *I* am at fault?' Wilson replied. 'How can that be?'

'It was your presence here, eight years ago, that led us to believe the city of Vilcapampa had been discovered by the world of men. Fearing this, we infiltrated the local villages and the city of Cuzco to find out what we could. That was how the warrior, Vivane, met Corsell Santillana. You were the catalyst, Wilson Dowling. And from there our secrets were revealed.'

'You cannot blame me for what has transpired,' Wilson said. 'It was Vivane who told the secret of the Cube's location, and how to crack the stone that protected it. It was her doing that led to the Cube's removal, not mine. *Your* strategy and *your* teachings failed to keep it hidden. The world is changing, Priestesses. Civilisation is closing in on you, and no matter how powerful your magic and your cunning, it is a force that cannot be stopped. The realms of man are expanding, and they will consume all corners of this planet before long – surely you know this.'

Mamacona Kay Pacha stood a little straighter and her gaze narrowed. 'You dare to come here and lecture us about the expansion of men. It is their *weakness* that is at the root of the Inca Cube's evil power. Only the Virgins of the Sun can be trusted to shield the world from its terrible influence. It was King Pachacuti, the wisest of all kings, who changed the destiny of the Virgins of the Sun. On his orders, our time of being caregivers and healers had come to an end. On his decree, we honed our powers so that we became warriors and protectors.'

'When the Golden Staff was destroyed,' Wilson said.

Mamacona Kay Pacha nodded. 'That was when all balance was lost. In the begining, it was Manco Capac who carried the Golden Staff. Mama Ocllo, his wife, carried the Inca Cube. Together, under the watchful eye of the Sun God, Inti, they held an unnatural influence, expanding the Inca Empire at a staggering rate. But Inti was arrogant and revelled in the success of his chosen people, much to the dismay of the other gods.'

'The Inca were too powerful,' the Priestess of the Underworld continued. 'Whoever held the Golden Staff of Inti held influence over all those around him. Manco Capac proclaimed himself a living god and began deciding which deities should be worshipped and which should not.'

The Priestess of the World Above continued, 'Not long after Cuzco was founded by Manco Capac, Coniraya the Moon God deceived Inti. With great cunning, she blocked out the sun and Inti's protection was momentarily lost. During the devastating earthquake that followed the Golden Staff of Manco Capac was destroyed. Pacha Camac, the Earth Maker, unleashed a fiery river of molten rock that destroyed half of Cuzco and eventually hauled the Golden Staff back to the centre of the earth. When Inti's sunrays once again fell upon the lands of the Inca, he realised that the Golden Staff was gone and Manco Capac had lost his method of control. In his rage, Inti cursed the other gods and gave much of his power to the Inca Cube in an effort to transform the Cube into some sort of Imperium, the centre of all power, thereby ensuring the continued expansion of Manco Capac's empire. But Inti underestimated the effects of his anger, and by creating an Imperium he unexpectedly opened up a channel for the dead.'

'The Inca Cube became a receptacle of evil,' the Priestess of the World Below stated.

'Inti failed to consider the super-luminary power of gold – the fact that men worshiped gold above all other things – and his curse became mutated such that a link was formed that he did not consider.'

'All because of the nature of gold,' the Priestess of the World Above said.

'Inti's curse settled upon one of the most potent forces known to man. Since the beginning of time, gold has always been the most precious element on the face of this great earth. Men have sought it out from the mountains and the rivers with no thought for the ramifications. They have scoured the four corners of the world. Men have killed for it, in many cases in the name of God, just to obtain the smallest amount. The world's greatest civilisations have risen on the back of gold – the more of it they have, the more influence over other men they wield. They do not even realise, but a man who controls ample gold controls the thoughts of other men.'

'Inti laid his curse upon an already powerful object. In his attempt to give power back to Manco Capac, he inadvertently severed the female connection with the Inca Cube, and in its place opened up a gateway to the dead.'

'That is why the Inca Cube has no influence on the minds of women.'

'It does not control women as the Golden Staff once did.'

'That is the reason the Virgins of the Sun are the protectors of the Inca Cube. King Pachacuti was almost consumed by one of the terrible souls that came to inhabit and control the Cube. A battle of wills ensued that lasted for thirty days and thirty nights. Pachacuti was the eventual victor, but he was bedridden for a full year as a result. Pachacuti used the Cube to unite the Inca Empire, but he realised as he got older his will would weaken and the Imperium would eventually take control of him. In his wisdom, Pachacuti relinquished the benefits of the Inca Cube, save being ultimately controlled by it. He called for the Virgins of the Sun to turn their female power and knowledge to isolating the Inca Cube, whatever the cost. On our recommendation, Vilcapampa was built, as was the Temple of the Sun, to protect and house the Imperium. Pachacuti then destroyed all written language and all carvings across the vast empire. And for nearly five hundred years we have stood in protection of this terrible object. Until now.'

'The Inca Cube draws on the souls of the dead who are trapped between worlds,' Mamacona Kay Pacha stated.

'Men who have been murdered.'

'Men who have committed horrific crimes.'

'Men who have had their lives taken from them.'

'Their filthy souls are now the energy source of the Inca Cube,' Mamacona Kay Pacha concluded. 'And their strength has been increasing. Whichever soul has the strongest will controls the Inca Cube. Any living man who touches the Inca Cube will be consumed by the soul within it. The soul of the Inca Cube then acts through the living person.'

'Which soul has possession of the Cube now?' Wilson asked.

'We have no way of engaging with it, other than to see the events that rise and fall from the Imperium's terrible influence.'

'The crucifixion in Cuzco is one of those events, isn't it?'

'Yes, the Inca Cube is certainly possessed by a depraved soul. In the last two weeks, the dozens of murders committed across the city were a result of its influence, we know that much.'

'Do you know where the Cube currently resides?' Wilson asked.

'We have no way to track its location.'

'If I can get to the Cube, find it somehow, can it be safely transported?' Wilson then asked.

'How will you find it?' the Priestess of the World We Live In questioned.

'I have a method of discovering its location,' he said.

'You cannot be allowed to transport the Cube – only a woman can. If you touch it, you will surely be consumed by it.'

'That is our worst fear,' the Priestess of the Underworld stated. 'With your strength and healing ability, you would become a dangerous adversary if the Imperium was to control you.'

'If I seek the Inca Cube on my own then you risk even more,' he replied. 'I demand your support, regardless of your reservations.'

The three old women looked at each other and their pale eyes glazed over. Again, they held this position against the shifting firelight for what seemed like minutes.

Mamacona Kay Pacha eventually said, 'When you first walked in here you agreed that all things in life come with a price.'

Mamacona Kay Pacha pointed over Wilson's shoulder towards one of the women standing behind him. 'That warrior's name is Chiello.'

She was a picture of fitness and health, as they all were. Wilson turned his gaze to Aclla, who was standing closest to him, and it was clear from her expression that she was unsure what was going to happen next.

'Chiello is the virgin pair of Vivane,' the priestess continued. 'You will lay with her this night and we will talk tomorrow. Only then will we consider your request.'

'Why is this necessary?' Wilson asked, trying not to look stunned.

'The warrior Vivane died two nights ago; we felt her life force leave us,' one of the Mamaconas said. 'Vivane has certainly gone to the World Above. It is yet another sad loss at the hands of the Inca Cube.'

'Without her virgin pair, Chiello can no longer be a Warrior of the Sun. Her role now is to bring about the next generation of soldiers.'

'You cannot ask this of me.'

'You owe this to her,' the Priestess of the World Above stated. 'It is because of you that she is alone.'

'Chiello will be your partner this night,' the Priestess of the Underworld continued. 'She is ready and she is willing. In return, you will provide her your seed.'

'I cannot do this,' Wilson said.

'We will talk again in the morning,' Mamacona Kay Pacha stated. 'You will go with Chiello and you will pay your debt to her. The time has come for you to take responsibility for the part you have played. This is the price of your actions.'

41

Andes Ranges, Peru
Machu Picchu Sanctuary Lodge
Local Time 11:50 pm

22 January 2014

FOR MORE THAN two days there had been no electricity at Machu Picchu. The furious summer rains were pounding the mountains and the accompanying humidity that came with it made everything inside the luxury hotel wet to the touch, including the walls, floors and bedsheets. Thankfully, word had reached the hotel that bulldozers had been dispatched from Cuzco to clear the road that led through the mountains. If there were no further mudslides along the route, Helena would soon be able to leave Machu Picchu by four-wheel drive. The Hiram Bingham Express was still not running and expectations were that if the weather didn't ease and the river levels subside, then the train could be out of action for at least another week. The only other way out was over the Inca Trail by foot. The average rainfall in the highlands of Peru was just over one hundred inches per year – a colossal amount – and yet there had been sixty inches of rain in the last two weeks; the heaviest falls on record.

Helena stood in the open doorway to her balcony wearing shorts and a tank top. Behind her, a solitary candle burned on the bedside table. Now that her iPad had gone flat there was nothing to occupy her except the dusty old books she'd found in the hotel library. The atmosphere was warm and sticky and the interminable wait for news of her eventual departure left her feeling anxious.

Eight full years had passed for Wilson when only a little more than one year had passed for her. That was a difficult concept for Helena to grasp. It explained why he seemed emotionally distant when he first saw her. Wilson said that he had been through hell since they were last together, and he didn't try to hide it. He'd been part of the Chinese Boxer Rebellion, he told her, dabbling with history. Helena smiled to herself. If she had waited eight years to see him she probably would have reacted much the same way. The real question was: how did she feel about him knowing that more of his life had passed than hers?

Leaning against the doorframe, Helena closed her eyes and listened to the heavy rain beating on the roof and against the wooden deck. She imagined the weather pounding the ancient stone city of Machu Picchu just a few hundred metres away – how the swirling rainfall formed small channels of water that flowed between the count- less buildings down the slopes into streams that collected into gushing torrents. The torrents then reached a sheer cliff, where they collectively took to the air in a 1,000-foot drop, the tiny droplets floating to the bottom of the valley and contributing to the raging waters of the Urubamba. From there, the unstoppable river would widen and slow down as it meandered all the way to the Atlantic Ocean, thousands of miles away, via the lush, steaming forests of the mighty Amazon River.

What do I feel? Helena asked herself.

She was protective of Wilson – she had been ever since the first moment they connected. Unusually so. And she was attracted to him, despite their circumstances. It was a good thing he was a man of honourable charac- ter, because she suspected her attraction to him would be there even if he weren't. His sense of humour was entertaining and she enjoyed laughing with him. He was funny even under pressure – probably more so. He had captivating hands, the way he gestured when he talked. And when he touched her, that was heaven – she liked to watch his hands on her skin. The sex they'd had was the best Helena had ever known, and she hadn't been with another man since he left her nearly a year ago. Despite the barrier of time and the ramifications that came with that, Helena never stopped dreaming of a life with him, as ridiculous as that was.

Helena looked into the swirling rain and wondered if Wilson was safe right now, exactly 106 years before. He had chosen to go to the fortress city of Pitcos, to the hidden location of the Virgins of the Sun. Based on what Helena had seen, the Amazons had tried to kill him and, despite her pleading he had gone anyway. That was typical; he trusted his gut despite all indicators to the contrary. Helena felt her muscles tense – if they touched one single hair on his body she would be furious. What was so frustrating about it was that there was nothing she could do from here. She reached over to the side table and lifted the nickel-plated Colt .45 and looked down the barrel into the rain. Resting her finger on the trigger, she flipped off the safety and considered firing a single bullet in the direction of the ancient citadel. There was something very cathartic about firing a handgun – the muzzle-flash and recoil, the sound of the bullet streaking away at the speed of sound. The problem was, if she pulled the trigger both Chad and John Hanna would think something was wrong and they'd probably kick the door open with their own guns drawn.

Her bodyguards already thought that she was crazy – they must have, although it was their job not to admit it. Their client was relentlessly scouring the ruins of a long dead Inca city, day and night, talking away into thin air as if she was speaking to someone. The whole situation was madness, every part of it.

And who was this man Lucho Gonzales? Helena wondered. The man from the past. His ancestor, Don Eravisto, vehemently believed that Wilson was a killer of innocents; a man who would brutalise and slay women and children. There were only two possible scenarios: either someone was lying about Wilson's part in those gruesome events, or Wilson's soul had been possessed by a greater force and his actions were not his own.

Helena apprehensively tapped the .45 gun barrel against the window frame.

Both she and Wilson had agreed to meet at the central water fountain – Pizarro's Fountain – in the centre of the Plaza de Armas, in two nights' time. The reality was, without the Inca Cube nearby or its residual energy he would probably not see her, but she would hopefully see him. Wilson just needed to stay alive until then. He had already lived eight years without her, but the circumstances were different now. The Amazons were dangerous, Helena had seen it in their eyes.

'Keep your wits about you, Wilson,' she whispered to the rain.

Sheet lightning flashed across the sky and the silhouette of Mount Machu Picchu loomed above. Deep in her heart, Helena sensed that she was going to play a vital part in Wilson's quest to find the Inca Cube. She wasn't sure what her role would be but she had to believe that everything was happening for a reason. That was the way it had always been between the two of them. When Wilson needed her most, she had been there. And Helena pledged that she would deliver yet again.

Those bulldozers must get through, Helena thought to herself. Otherwise she could be stuck here at Machu Picchu and Wilson would have no idea why she never turned up at the Plaza de Armas as agreed.

42

Andes Ranges, Peru
Fortress City of Pitcos
Local Time 11:51 pm

21 January 1908

CHIELLO LED WILSON out of the main temple through the pouring rain towards the military barracks. The rows of stone buildings abutted the huge central courtyard located at the entrance to the city. The construction was neat and predictable, each dwelling sharing a common wall on either side like a terrace house, with a single wooden door and a separate peaked roof made of thatched mountain grass.

Chiello approached one of the humble barracks, slid the wooden bolt across and pushed the door open. She had yet to say a single word as she stepped into the dark interior and set about drying her hands on a small towel. Walking to the back of the room, she struck a metal flint that ignited a narrow dish of liquid which burst to life with a lazy blue flame. Wilson had never seen alcohol burned in that manner before and it gave the tiny room an unusual air of intrigue.

With the sensation that his feet were stuck in wet concrete, Wilson remained outside in the rain looking through the open door at the imposing woman before him. If he tried to run away the Amazons would certainly pursue him. Even if he could find a way out of the city, it still meant hurrying down the slippery western face of Pitcos, which would be neither easy nor safe. Sheet lightning flashed across the sky, the momentary brightness betraying the swirling patterns of rain hammering the mountaintop.

When the utter blackness took hold once again, Chiello's statuesque figure was imprinted against the unusual blue light behind her. Although it was difficult to see her face, she reached out her hand and gestured him inside. Wilson stood motionless, apprehensive about the prospect of conceiving a child with a woman he had never even had a conversation with. Despite her obvious youth and woman-liness, she seemed cold and robotic, like a machine.

'You need to make a decision,' Chiello said with a distinctive accent.

Wilson scanned the darkness – just what he was searching for, he could not be sure. He looked again at Chiello, realising this was a moment that could change his life forever. It had been more than three years since had been with a woman, on a primal level he wanted her, but even so he was reluctant to step forward.

It was impossible to deny that he needed help from the Virgins of the Sun if he was to succeed in returning the Inca Cube to Vilcapampa. Based on what the Mamaconas had told him, there was no way he could transport the Cube on his own, let alone touch it.

Taking one last lingering look in both directions, Wilson stepped forward and Chiello eased the door shut behind him.

From the other side of the compound, towards the sheer cliffs on the eastern perimeter, Aclla was crouched down looking towards the military barracks. 'Don't go inside,' she whispered, but as the words left her lips Wilson disap-peared through Chiello's door.

Aclla's heart fell in her stomach and she began berating herself about her feelings. A tribune of the Warriors of the Sun should see men as the *enemy* – not as an object of attraction. What was happening to her was exactly what must have happened to Vivane with Corsell Santillana.

Aclla clenched her fist – despite what her sister felt for Corsell it could only pale in comparison with the greatness and beauty of Wilson Dowling. He was a journeyman who had travelled time itself; the Mamaconas had proclaimed it so. A man who could heal his own flesh in moments. His strength and speed had impressed her, and Aclla was furious that she was not the one with him now. Her desire for the blue-eye contravened all her training. She wanted his seed regardless of the cost. And yet, this night, his seed would go to another.

Aclla sensed someone approaching, and from the footfall she knew who it was. 'Why are you following me, Sontane?'

'You should not be here, Aclla.'

'I am watching to ensure that Wilson Dowling does not try to flee the city. If he does, I will be ready.'

Sontane knelt beside her virgin pair. 'Do you really think I believe that?'

Aclla glanced towards Sontane, ready to unleash a verbal assault that she would not forget. But when she looked into Sontane's knowing eyes, she could not bring herself to say anything.

Sontane pointed towards Chiello's barracks. 'We should slay that man. The fact that you feel the way you do is proof that he casts a terrible spell on us all. We do not need him. We can find the Cube ourselves and take it to safety, as we have been taught. That man in there is a liability in every event. If the Cube possesses him, I do not want to think what could happen.'

As the rain hit her face, Aclla stayed focused on the wooden door of Chiello's barracks. 'Only the Mamaconas can decide his fate.'

'They are blinded also,' Sontane said under her breath. 'Look at yourself, Aclla. You wish it was *you* in there with him. Admit that I'm correct.' Sontane eased closer. 'If you cannot be with him then why let Chiello take your place? It should be you . . . or no one else. We should wait until we can hear their passion, then we will throw open the door and cut his throat while he is defenceless.'

'You don't even know that he *can* be killed,' Aclla replied.

'If that is the case, then we should find this out now, not after the Inca Cube has devoured his soul and replaced it with another. You know I'm right. The time to act has arrived. Are you with me or not?'

Standing in the still air, Wilson faced Chiello as water lazily dripped from their soaking clothes onto the smooth wooden floor. The air was warm and the vaulted ceiling was painted with the neon ripple of the strange blue flame. On either side of the room was a simple bed, but only one of them had alpaca blankets spread across the top. Wilson figured that the other bed had once belonged to Vivane, Chiello's virgin pair. It was a strange irony that he would find himself in a room where the woman responsible for revealing the secrets of the Inca Cube had spent the majority of her nights.

Chiello's expression was blank as she ran her fingers down the length of her straight black hair and wrung the water out. 'I have been trained my whole life to hate men,' she said. 'That makes this situation very difficult.'

Wilson gazed at the magnificent woman just a few steps away. She had a distinctive facial structure, with a square-cut jaw and eyebrows that peaked in the middle. Wilson figured she was more Spanish than Native American, based on her height, muscle mass and the proportions of her body.

Without releasing her gaze, Chiello untied the two leather clasps that secured the engraved breastplate to her chest. The metal skin fell away, revealing a soaking, cotton-like undergarment that clung to her body. As she unclipped her wrist bracelets, Wilson wanted to look away but could not. Chiello slid off her shin guards then stood a moment as if she was fighting her own demons.

'Are we really going to do this?' Wilson asked.

His question seemed to spark Chiello into action and she peeled her wet top over her head. The sight of her exposed upper body was breathtaking and Wilson couldn't stop from feeling aroused – it was impossible not to want her. Her stomach was muscular. Her light brown skin was flawless, her breasts full and firm. Expressionless, Chiello untied the strap of her leather skirt and peeled the wet material away, leaving her naked except for the short sword strapped to the curve of her left thigh.

'The moment I take this sword off, I move into the next phase of my life,' Chiello said. The heat of her skin caused the water to steam into the humid air. Her gaze never wavered as she unstrapped her sword and gently placed it on Vivane's empty bed. 'This is the day I give up dealing in death and my role becomes the creator of life.'

The heavy stone walls were lit with ever-shifting blue light as Chiello ran her index finger down her stomach until she inserted two fingers inside herself. After lingering a moment, she raised them to her lips and licked them clean.

'I guess we *are* doing this,' Wilson replied.

With simple grace, Chiello circled behind him and ran her hands across his shoulders, at the same time feeling the tone of his muscles as if she was testing the ripeness of a bag of fruit. Stopping in front of him again, she pressed her lips to his and passionately kissed him.

'Don't you need more time?' Wilson said. 'I think I need more time.'

Chiello began unbuttoning his shirt with one hand, the other palm never losing contact with his flesh. 'I have never touched a man this way before,' she said proudly. Her right hand parted his shirt then drifted leisurely across his naked skin to explore ever lower. Her touch was unusually confident despite the craziness of the situation.

'The Virgins of the Sun have been trained from an early age to celebrate our sexuality,' she stated. 'We are learned in the teachings of Chasca Coyllur, the Goddess of Young Maidens.'

'You've never been with a man before?' Wilson questioned.

Chiello shook her head. 'I have killed many men with my arrow and my sword,' she replied. 'Primitive tribesmen who would dare to approach our territory or the city of Vilcapampa, but you are the first man I have ever touched in this way.'

Wilson couldn't hold back any longer and he wantonly pressed his hands to her firm body. Chiello's first reaction was to pull away, but he didn't release her. His instinct told him that he was dealing with a dominant creature, and the more forceful he was with her the more she would respond.

'The passion between a man and a woman should be mutual,' she said, writhing within his grasp. 'Equal force must be applied from both sides if a spark is to be generated.'

Wilson held back a scream as she bit his neck then ran her wet lips down his chest, her tongue gliding across his skin. Standing tall, she forced her chest against his and the warmth of her core seeped into him.

'Since Vivane left, I have been alone,' Chiello said as she studied his body in the light. 'And whilst I am sad that she is dead, it will be an honour to have a child of my own.'

Wilson couldn't stop himself from exploring her body with his hands and fingers.

'The Virgins of the Sun are sexual beings,' Chiello said, a moan escaping her lips. 'We have studied everything there is to know about the female form. Our virgin pair is also our sexual partner.' She moaned again. 'We are encouraged to understand how our bodies function, what feels good and what does not.'

Lowering to her knees, Chiello undid Wilson's belt in a flurry and let his pants drop. She ripped off his boots and socks, easily removing the rest of his clothing. One of her palms remained firmly against his body; she never lost that contact for a moment. If there was a need to switch hands, both her palms would press against him for at least a second before the other hand was released.

Kneeling between his legs, her tongue ran gently across his skin before she inserted the fullness of him into her mouth. The pleasure was so great that Wilson threw his head back. 'Oh my God,' he whispered.

With her hands on his shoulders, she raised herself up on the tips of her toes then lowered herself so that his manhood slid inside her in one smooth stroke. Her eyes were locked onto his, but Wilson could not see pleasure written on her face. Her expression was stern, her focus absolute.

The door to Chiello's barracks suddenly flew open and cold air blustered into the room! Wilson spun round to see Aclla standing in the pouring rain; her sword in hand! In the far-off distance, a fork of lightning lit up the swirling sky. In that split second Wilson remembered what it was like to see a man run through with a sword – the tearing of flesh, the crunching of bone. The desperate cries of agony as blood splattered and internal organs were pierced and shredded. He then recalled the desperate look he saw in so many men's eyes when they knew they were about to die.

Tossing Chiello aside, Wilson frantically backed up as Aclla stepped forward to fill the doorway, her expression grim, her intention clear.

'It cannot be this way!' Aclla yelled, raising her blade to strike.

Wilson lunged for the sword on Vivane's bed, but he was knocked off balance as Chiello leapt forward as if to protect him.

'I cannot let you have this man,' Aclla said, holding her position in mid-strike, the tip of her blade now pointed at Wilson's naked chest.

Chiello held the middle ground, her legs crouched, her arms splayed open in preparation to repel an attack.

Both women held each other's gaze. Wilson did his best not to react. He just stood there naked against the wall, his peripheral vision on the short sword just out of his grasp. He could not be sure what would happen next.

'You cannot stop me,' Chiello said. 'It is ordained.'

Aclla suddenly turned and closed the door. 'So it will be.' Sliding the wooden bolt across, she jammed the steel blade of her sword into the handle to be certain the door was impossible to open.

'It is my destiny to be here also,' Aclla added.

'It seems we will share you,' Chiello eventually whispered in Wilson's direction. 'The tribune of the guard wishes it so.'

Chiello reached out and yanked Aclla forward.

Wilson was set upon as Aclla pressed her rain-covered lips to his and kissed him violently. Both women frantically unclipped Aclla's armour and threw it aside. With adrenalin pumping through his veins, Wilson tore Aclla's wet undergarments from her skin and let it fall. He ran his hands across her shoulders and pushed her to her knees in front of him. There was a frenzy of contact, firm and powerful. Hands and mouths were everywhere, skin was bitten, fingers searched for wetness, bodies shifted. Heated contact was coming from all directions.

43

Andes Ranges, Peru
Fortress City of Pitcos
Local Time 1:10 am

22 January 1908

STANDING ON THE circular disk of shimmering obsidian, the three Mamaconas formed a tight triangle in the very centre, each looking at the woman to her right.

'They are together with him now,' one of them said.

'Indulging in the pleasures of his flesh,' said another.

'Aclla is weak, like her sister.'

'Does it really make any difference?' the Priestess of the Underworld remarked. 'There is nothing to be lost by what is happening here. Feel their pleasure.' She tilted her head back and smiled.

'We did not request for Aclla to go to him.'

The Priestess of the Underworld refocused. 'Since when do we discourage our tribunes from taking what they want? We all felt her attraction . . . and she is only human after all. We accepted this man as a potential sire to our women. From then on, nothing we could have done would have stopped her from wanting him. We should be thrilled they are together now. It will surely increase this man's loyalty to our cause, and the risks are lessened as a result.'

'He is dangerous,' the Priestess of the World Above stated. 'A rogue element in these difficult times. If the Inca Cube somehow possesses him our problems would be compounded beyond imagination. None of us can see his future, despite savouring his blood. This is the first time we have encountered a man we cannot read.'

'Equally, his influence here could be the difference between success and failure,' the Priestess of the Underworld said. 'Even though we cannot see into this man's future, we should not be afraid.'

'It is *his* fault that we are in this situation,' the Priestess of the World Above replied. 'His arrival at Vilcapampa set events in motion that led to Vivane's defection and the loss of the Inca Cube.'

'The Inca Cube's protection is, and has always been, our responsibility,' the Priestess of the World We Live In commented. 'He was right in saying that.'

'I agree . . . we put too much faith in the hands of our tribunes. We told them too much about what they were protecting and we have paid the ultimate price. We should have kept them ignorant, as I suggested.'

'You would blame me for those teachings?'

'It is a lifetime ago, my sister, since we have been able to separate ourselves from the collective. Each of us brings a separate perspective, but our decisions are owned together.'

'This man is dangerous and we should kill him,' the Priestess of the World Above stated. 'He is a powerful force and if we remove him from this game of chance, then the battlefield becomes smaller.'

'I suggest the opposite,' the Priestess of the Underworld countered. 'He is our greatest advantage.'

'Men are not to be trusted,' was the reply.

'They are not to be *trusted* because the Inca Cube can read their minds and control their bodies. It is possible this man is different. The Inca Cube may not be able to read his mind – just as we cannot. That would explain why Captain Gonzales and his men were sent from Cuzco, across the mountains, in pursuit of him.'

'Wilson Dowling claims that he can somehow detect the location of the Cube, and I believe him,' the Priestess of the World We Live In said.

'We should assist him in his efforts,' the Priestess of the

Underworld continued. 'It is foolish to remove our most powerful ally because he possesses a threat of defection. We can control this man through the sexuality of our women – that is what is happening right now. You both feel the pleasure of our two warriors, as I do.'

'The problem is that I cannot *feel his mind*,' the Priestess of the World Above said. 'None of us knows what he is thinking at this moment. We must take action to neutralise him while we can. While we are still strong.'

'The Inca Cube fears this man – I sense it in my bones. It is an advantage to us that cannot be dismissed.'

'And what of his connection with this woman in the future? She watches over him by some divine influence of the gods. Her image is fed by the residue of the Inca Cube – that is something we will never understand – and it only increases our risk of being undermined. The Inca Cube could be controlling him somehow and we would be none the wiser.'

'The Cube cannot control women.'

'It does not have that power,' the Priestess of the Underworld agreed. 'In my opinion, the blonde woman's influence is yet another advantage, although I do not proclaim to understand why.'

'We cannot trust this man,' the Priestess of the World Above said passionately. 'His world is full of mystery . . . and that mystery only serves to make me fearful.'

'And what of the arrival of the black condor? That is a sign from the gods that we should put faith in this man.'

'I agree. It is a powerful sign, indeed.'

'By the time our warriors return to Cuzco, all the men there will surely be under the influence of the Inca Cube. According to our reports, hundreds of soldiers are guarding every approach to the city with many guns. The Inca Cube is surely there.'

'We must go to Cuzco in strength if we are to reclaim what we have lost. This man Wilson Dowling is a journeyman of the stars. He needs the Inca Cube for his own transport from this world, and he claims he has the power to locate it. We can therefore trust that his motive is to return the Cube to Vilcapampa once it is in his possession. We must use his motive to our advantage.'

'It is decided then.'

The other two replied simultaneously, 'It is decided.'

'At first light the Virgins of the Sun will march for Cuzco. We must send everyone who is able, even the older generations. There will only be one chance of success if we are to locate and then take back the Inca Cube.'

'If we fail, our journey will have ended. The time will come for us to step away from the black disc of power. May the spirit of Mama Ocllo protect us all, for the world of men is on the brink of condemnation, and all others with it.'

'With our combined knowledge and Wilson Dowling on our side, we will once again vanquish the Inca Cube into the void.'

'We are putting much faith in this journeyman of the stars,' the Priestess of the World Above stated. 'Let us pray he is worthy of our trust.'

'And when we have the Inca Cube in our possession, will we let Wilson Dowling use its power so he can travel to the stars once more?'

All three women shook their heads at the same time. 'He cannot be allowed to leave – his place forevermore will be here with us.'

44

Cuzco, Peru
Avenue Pavitos
Local Time 6:45 am

22 January 1908

THE SECURITY OF daylight finally arrived, yet even so Captain Gonzales couldn't bring himself to head back to his family bedroom. Sitting by the window next to the front door his eyes were gritty and burning from yet another sleepless night. He felt utterly drained, as if a debilitating illness had sapped all energy from his normally strong body. Despite his feeble condition, he continued to watch the avenue and study every passer-by. The heavy summer clouds were low this morning which kept the sky dark, and the rain continued to fall steadily as it had done all night long. Everything was humid and moist, including the material of the chair he was sitting on.

This had been the fourth evening in a row that Lucho Gonzales had held an all-night vigil at the window of his home. Between his legs, his .303 rifle leant against his inner thigh. On the table next to him was his sword, its officer's scabbard lying on the floor behind him. The front door was locked but the lead-glass window was ajar, making it easier for him to hear the tin cans tied with string that he had suspended across the laneway at the rear of his house.

Hearing a whisper of young voices in the bedroom, Gonzales knew his children were beginning to stir.

Rising from his chair, his legs cramping from having sat in the same position for so many hours, he took one last look towards the street then picked up his scabbard and sheathed his sword. Outside, a few people were now walking the streets, among them the odd donkey pulling a wagon towards the market. Grabbing his rifle, Gonzales slid back the metal bolt as silently as he could, removed the shiny brass cartridge from the firing chamber and dropped it into his breast pocket. He was thankful that both he and his family had survived yet another night in this haunted city, but he cringed at the thought of what terrible evil had been committed while they slept.

With his bladder about to burst, Gonzales put his head inside the bedroom to let his wife know he was going outside. What a relief it was to see them safely in their beds.

Sarita gave him a worried smile as she clutched their little daughter Juanita, who was still sound asleep.

'Are you okay, Lucho?' she whispered.

Gonzales smiled and nodded, doing his best to give her a confident expression. She could see that he was still wearing the same clothes as the night before. Turning away, the patter of little footsteps crossed the floor and Ortega, the youngest son, was beside him.

'I need to do wees,' the child said in a cute voice as he jumped about energetically and headed towards the kitchen door.

'One moment, *pequeñito hijo*,' he whispered after him. Reaching into his pocket, Lucho produced the single brass key and turned the lock. Cautiously easing the door open, he held his son back as he scanned the sheltered porch and the barn where his donkey was standing. All seemed well.

'Hurry, papa!' the boy said as he ran to the edge of the porch, pulled his pants down and began piddling into the drain that was flowing with rainwater. Standing next to his son, Lucho did the same.

There was loud knock at the front door. Lucho's heart almost jumped out of his chest. For someone to come to his home at this hour of the morning could only mean bad news. Urinating as fast as he possibly could, he sorted himself then ordered his son back to the bedroom with a stern voice. His older son, Arturo, was standing at the bedroom door, peering out.

'Get back into bed, both of you,' Gonzales said under his breath. 'Do not come out unless I tell you to do so.' Without looking at his wife, he pulled the bedroom door shut with a thud.

The knocking came again, louder this time.

Gonzales could see a dark shadow across the window frame. The rain was falling heavily outside as he frantically drew the shiny bullet out of his pocket and inserted it into the rifle chamber. Moving as quickly and as silently as he could, he slid the bolt forward and shouldered the weapon.

'Who's there?' he called out.

'It's me – Capos! Open the door, Capitán.'

Gonzales let out a relieved breath then unlocked the front door. What terrible crime had been committed that would require his lieutenant to seek him out at this hour?

'I'm glad you are here!' Capos said as his familiar face appeared.

Gonzales gestured for his lieutenant to lower his voice as he stepped outside and closed the door behind him. 'What is it?' he said. 'Quietly.'

Capos took off his hat and whacked it against his thigh to shake off the excess water. He looked pale and tired. 'I'm sorry to come here so early, Capitán.' He stepped closer. 'Bishop Francisco has called for all men of rank to be assembled at the Church of El Triunfo at nine o'clock this morning. He specifically asked for you to be there.'

'I am afflicted with a terrible fever,' Gonzales replied in a low voice. It was necessary to speak quietly in case his children heard him telling untruths. 'I cannot be there. My fear is that I will infect the other men if I do.'

Capos gave him a stunned look. 'That is exactly what Bishop Francisco told me you would say. That is amazing, eh? He told me, if you were unable to attend, he would come to your home and visit you and your family personally.'

Gonzales clenched his fists to stop his hands from shaking. The priest was possessed by some form of evil and he could do nothing to stop him. Even just the thought of raising a weapon towards the clergy-man seemed impossible. For three evenings he had been haunted by nightmares of Bishop Francisco coming to his home. He lusted after Gonzales's wife and children – he knew that – and as much as Gonzales wanted to protect his family he knew he would be unable to put up a defence.

Gonzales rubbed his unshaven chin, hoping to soften the fear that was certainly written on his face. 'I will come to the meeting today,' he conceded.

'I prayed to God that you would.' Capos put on his hat and secured the strap under his chin. 'Two young women went missing this past night,' he said sombrely. 'We need you back. No matter what we do or how many men we deploy, the situation worsens. The men at the barracks seek your strength, Capitán. I confess, I too have missed your leadership in these dark times.'

'How do you protect your own family?' Gonzales asked, staring into the distance.

Capos looked out towards the rain also. 'At my home, we have twenty people sleeping in two rooms. All my wife's relatives, as well as my own.'

'Your wife and children must come here, to my place,' Gonzales said. 'This house is bigger and easier to protect. They will be safe here.'

'Yours is a generous offer, Capitán, but my extended family are with us and I cannot move them. Can I suggest that your family comes to my home? It is not as modern, but it would be much easier for everyone else. We will set up beds for them, and we have plenty of room for the storage of food.'

Gonzales knew that his wife would not want to leave here. She was well aware of the murders around the city, but deep down she believed that no one would dare enter the home of the most senior officer in Cuzco. Lucho had been unable to tell his wife of his fears about Bishop Francisco – he could not confess the sordid details of his nightmares.

'I will speak to Sarita and let you know,' Gonzales replied. 'But I doubt she will accept your generous offer.'

'Thanks be to the Lord that we have Bishop Francisco to protect us,' Capos added. 'He has been a tower of strength when we have needed him. The bishop says he knows who the murderers are and why they are killing off the innocent in such a ferocious manner. He wants to tell us what we must do to stop this evil from spreading. We need you there, Capitán. The men need you. They have been asking every day when you will return.'

'Tell the men that I will be there.' Gonzales pointed at his lieutenant. 'I want you to send Private Ramiro to guard my house while I am gone. Tell him to bring his rifle. No one else can know that I have asked for him. Do you understand?'

Capos nodded. 'I understand, Capitán. I will send him immediately.'

The door to the porch creaked open and little Ortega appeared. The boy was still wearing his pyjamas as he scurried between his father's legs. His smile was big and beautiful, but it only served to worry Gonzales even more.

'It's nice to see you, Señor Capos,' the little boy said cheerfully.

Capos patted him on the head. 'Look at you . . . how much you have grown since last time I saw you! You will soon be as big as your father.'

'I'm nearly as big as my older brother,' Ortega said, standing as tall as he could. 'Look at this!' He tensed his biceps to show how big they were.

'Very impressive,' Capos replied. 'So much like your father.'

Lucho picked up his son and held him close to his body. 'I will see you at the assembly . . . now go. Tell Ramiro to get here as soon as he can.'

Capos saluted then stepped off the porch and headed along the flooded laneway towards the avenue. All the while, the constant rain was making the pooled water dance against the hazy brightness of the morning sky.

45

Andes Ranges, Peru
Fortress City of Pitcos
Local Time 8:15 am

22 January 1908

AS SOON AS Wilson awoke, he was immediately thinking about Lucho Gonzales and his young family. In Helena's future, Wilson was a killer of innocents and as much as he despised the thought of it he needed to entertain how it could happen if he was to have any chance of changing his destiny.

Wilson gazed about the room, an uneasiness rising in his chest. Everything inside the military barracks was in darkness except for the narrow bands of light that were seeping through the gaps around the door. Both Aclla and Chiello were gone, including their armour. They must have stolen away after he fell asleep.

There was no doubting that the Inca Cube was dangerous, Wilson knew that. It would require all his cunning if he was going to transport it to Vilcapampa without becoming a servant of its deeds. It was imperative that he never came in contact with it directly, otherwise he could lose control of his actions.

The Mamaconas called the Inca Cube an 'Imperium', which was the Latin word for 'ultimate power'. The Mission of Nehemiah had not referred to the Cube in that manner, but there was no reason to doubt the claim that the Cube indeed carried the life force of the dead.

Wilson stared up at the peaked ceiling. So much was
unknown – the history he had studied had been mutated
and there were no mission notes to guide his actions this
time round. At least with Helena's direction he might
stand a chance. Yet despite his attempts at maintaining a
positive mind, Wilson couldn't vanquish the thought of his
own body being driven by something evil and perverted.

As Wilson shifted on the bed a distinctive aroma filled
his nostrils – the scent of sex and the powerful pheromones
that came with it. He reached between his legs and gripped
his aching loins. It was a relief to find himself still intact.
During the night of debauchery, he had wondered if he
was actually going to survive the ferocious encounter. He
had never been involved in anything so harsh and physical.
At one point he was certain the Amazons would try to kill
him when they were done, like a black widow spider after
mating – their intentions being to exhaust and then devour
the male.

Sitting up, he reached over to the other bed and yanked
his pants towards him. Pressing his feet to the wooden
floor, he inserted both legs then stood up. He once again
relived the fear that gripped him when Aclla suddenly
appeared in the doorway with her sword in hand – from
the look in her eye, he really thought she was going to
attack.

Running both hands through his hair, he let out a sigh
and sat down again.

He wasn't sure if he revelled in the experience of being
with those two women or if he despised it. Physically, it
had been overwhelming, but the absolute lack of tender-
ness had him feeling unsatisfied. They were, after all,
Amazon warriors he told himself.

Sitting there on Chiello's bed, Wilson realised he was a
world away from the stark white corridors of Enterprise
Corporation, the countless scientists, the politics and
paranoia, the holographic screens, the colliders and implod-
ers – the technical complexity of it all. He remembered
the medicinal-like smell of the Mercury Laboratory and the
vibration of the crystal transport sphere – the ingenious

construction the likes of which he had never seen before. The trepidation that had gripped him as he climbed into the transport pod was something he would remember until the end of his days. The distinctive sensation of the lasers firing, the molecular deconstruction already having begun, was excruciating. Then his mind slid over into a bottomless chasm of time – seconds feeling like hours; his fragile consciousness being torn to shreds as his molecules were spread across the full expanse of human history, before everything was suddenly gathered up again in a whirlwind of superheated energy, smoke and fire.

That was the moment he arrived at Machu Picchu.

That was eight years ago.

Even now, Wilson found it difficult to rationalise the role he played as Overseer. Yet here he was in the past, doing his calculating best to complete the Mission of Nehemiah; all the while attempting to maintain the continuity of time itself.

The Mission of Nehemiah had already cost Wilson so much – eight years of separation from the world and the people he knew. Eight years of solitude – never letting his guard down for even a moment for fear he would put his mark on this world in ways that unavoidably changed the future. Eight years, knowing he could never find his way back to Helena as much as he wished he somehow could.

Grabbing his shirt, Wilson found his safari hat underneath. It had gone missing at Vilcapampa when he jumped from the retaining wall into the jungle.

Through the closed door, he could hear the trickle of rainwater as it ran off the thatched roof and hit the ground. The morning air would be cool due to the altitude, which in Wilson's estimation was well over twelve thousand feet. After tying his shoes, he grabbed his rain jacket, which was dry despite spending the night bundled in the corner.

Looking towards Chiello's bed, Wilson's heart suddenly felt heavy. How did Helena fit into these bizarre events? What loyalty should he have to her? The chances of ever being with her again were miniscule. They were separated by a century-wide barrier in time. The best he could hope

for was that Helena would assist in tracking the Inca Cube
– wishing for anything more was a flight of fancy.

Wilson eased the simple wooden bolt across and pulled
the door towards him. He expected to see a guard outside,
but the there was no one there. The constant rain was
eddying in all directions. After lifting the high collar of
his jacket and putting on his hat, he stepped out into the
weather and closed the door behind him.

Everything seemed different in the daylight. The
barracks looked larger and more imposing than they had
the night before. As he approached, the peaked structure
of Pitcos Temple slowly took shape against the grey sky.
It, too, was bigger than Wilson had realised. Climbing the
steps towards the middle door, he looked in either direction – there was not a single warrior in sight.

'You cannot go in there!' a familiar voice called out.

Wilson spun round to see Aclla striding towards him.

'Is the weather always like this?' he asked.

'Pitcos is above the cloud line,' she replied without
emotion. 'The weather is always erratic.' Aclla wore a
hooded cape made of what looked like cured alpaca hide.
'The Mamaconas have asked me to give you this.' She held
out a shiny leather tube that was tied at the top with twine,
sealing it from the elements.

Wilson looked into Aclla's dark eyes and his thoughts
wandered to her nakedness straddled above him. He
reached out and took the tube. 'What is this?' he asked.

'In your hand are the sacred words of Pachacuti, the
very proclamation that condemned the Inca Cube to the
dungeon of the Temple of the Sun. It is our most precious
document.'

'And the Mamaconas want me to have it?'

'They do not want to meet with you again – this is
their offering in return. It appears that the future of the
world goes with *you*, Wilson Dowling. It is hoped that the
strength of our former king – a man whose will was strong
enough to conquer the Inca Cube – will somehow inspire
you so that you may show the same strength that allowed
him to prevail.'

'Do I open it now?' Wilson asked.

'That is up to you.'

Wilson studied Aclla's expression and saw only the focused determination that epitomised everything about her, from the sheen of her armour to the strength of her muscles on her bare legs.

'It is written in Quechua,' Aclla said as she climbed the stairs out of the rain and flung her cape over her shoulders to expose even more of her amazing body.

Wilson carefully undid the cord and tipped the leather scroll into his hand. Scholars the world over had claimed the Inca had no written language – and yet here it was. Kneeling down, he unwound the soft piece of leather across the dry stone floor, revealing its imperfect rectangular shape.

Aclla knelt down beside him.

Carefully scanning the ancient document, Wilson was astounded by the exquisitely formed black letters that appeared to be burnt into the pale surface of the leather by an intense heat of some kind. The artistry was remarkable – he had not seen symbols like these before, and there was no punctuation.

Aclla made sure that rainwater did not drip from her clothing onto the surface of the document. 'I will translate it for you,' she said, pointing at the lettering. 'I will begin . . . "It is the most precious object on the face of this great earth. Men will search their entire lives to obtain it and not even take a moment to understand why."' Her voice was calm and steady. '"Even the hint of its existence will drive men to commit crimes of unspeakable horror and travesty. Its lustre will captivate the souls of even the most pure and civilised, who will willingly torture the innocent in this filthy quest of possession. Thousands will be driven to starvation, disease and death without even a thought – that is the might of it."'

The resonating tone of Aclla's voice did not waver.

'"Do not be fooled. Dedication to this most unholy of pursuits lives within all men. There is no in-built defence against its power. For this gleaming, forever-vibrant substance has trapped part of us within its malleable yet indestructible shell. Empires will rise and fall on its possession – even the tiniest amount can deliver madness, let alone what we have here. Forged by the Sun God Inti in his likeness, this is the tip of the mountain, a beacon where lust itself resides. This object, and its effects, cannot be controlled without incredible sacrifice. Even with my ultimate knowledge, divine wisdom and limitless power, I struggle to separate myself from what is, this day, within my very grasp. I am spellbound, and yet I know what I must do."'

Wilson watched the complex lettering as it passed under Aclla's fingertips.

'"To protect this gleaming object I will build a city in the clouds,"' Aclla continued. '"Upon the sacred centre of Axis Mundie, a natural fortress of unspeakable purity will be crafted, from where I can only hope this terrible object will be isolated until the end of time. In this protected haven it will be watched over by the keen eyes of the condor, held within a crystal spell, and protected by an army that will stand guard for all eternity. An army that will not fall foul of the scent of power that hangs in the air as sweet as flowering blossoms, and yet, in reality, is as treacherous as the most diabolical thought that can be conjured in any man's mind.

'"From this day forward, all written language will be destroyed, all maps burned. All memories erased. This golden object must never be mentioned again; the price of even an utterance of its existence will demand death by beheading – and the death of every family member and acquaintance of the accused. Nothing can be left to chance. Praise be to the Sun God Inti, the supreme ruler of the universe, the giver of life and the taker of life. In your service I will forever remain."' Aclla pulled her hand away.

'That was written by King Pachacuti,' she confirmed, 'nearly four hundred and fifty years ago.'

Wilson continued to stare at the perfectly etched black lettering upon the spread of pale leather. 'Pachacuti was talking about gold, wasn't he? "The most unholy pursuit that lives within all men" is the quest for gold? That is the reason the conquistadors came to Peru in the first place.'

'It is a powerful substance.' Aclla rose to her feet, leaving Wilson kneeling below her. 'When Inti poured his godliness into the Inca Cube, he underestimated the lust for gold that already resided in men's hearts. That is the reason the Inca Cube is cursed.'

'And the Virgins of the Sun are the protectors of the Inca Cube,' Wilson stated.

'Because we are women, we cannot be influenced by the spirit that is surely resident within the Inca Cube's dark innards. However, we can still die at the hand of its influence.'

Aclla stared out into the pouring rain. 'The Mamaconas predict that the Inca Cube cannot see into your soul, Wilson Dowling – they themselves cannot – and they suspect the Cube is affected in the same way. Even when they tasted your rich blood, they could only see sections of your past and *none* of your future.'

Wilson was suddenly conscious of the strong wind and the rain hammering the mountaintop. 'Are they certain the Inca Cube is blind to my actions?' he asked.

'It seems logical to suspect it.'

'But, are they certain?' he said again.

Aclla shook her head. 'No, they are not certain. But it explains why Captain Gonzales and his men were sent after you when you first left Cuzco.'

Wilson's heart beat faster. 'Captain Gonzales?'

It was a name Wilson had hoped never to hear.

'Captain Gonzales is the most senior officer in Cuzco. When you slept inside the railway shack, Gonzales and a dozen of his soldiers were just hours behind. Gonzales had orders to capture you and bring you back to Bishop Francisco – he knew exactly where you would be. The Mamaconas sense that the spirit that possesses the Inca Cube fears you because it cannot look into your soul via the network of other men. That was how the Inca Cube wields its influence.'

'If we find the Inca Cube, can you safely transport it?'
Wilson asked.

'We have never actually seen the golden Cube with our
own eyes,' she replied. 'It was incarcerated long before
we were all born. Not even the Mamaconas have, but we
have the teachings of our forebears. A crystal chamber
was constructed to allow the Cube to be transported, but
it is a temporary prison at best. The teachings say that
women *cannot* touch the Cube – it is warned that any
direct contact will cause instant death, so we must be very
cautious. We have a heavy set of tongs so that we may pick
up the Cube, drop it into the chamber, then seal it shut.'

'What is Axis Mundie?' Wilson asked. 'The term was
used in Pachacuti's text.'

'A natural energy vortex,' Aclla replied. 'A place where
the soul of Apu, the spirit of the earth and the mountains,
comes to the surface. It is a healing place, and legend states
that a gateway to other worlds is located there.'

Using both hands, Wilson carefully rolled Pachacuti's
scroll up again and slipped it back into the waterproof
tube. Standing up, he tied off the twine and held it towards
Aclla.

'The document is yours, Wilson Dowling. You are to
bring it back to them once the Inca Cube has been safely
returned.'

Wilson studied the leather tube. 'I cannot accept. This
document belongs here, within the city of Pitcos.' He held
it forward once again.

Aclla reluctantly took the tube. 'So be it.' Pulling her
cape over each shoulder to cover her armour, she donned
the hood and stepped out into the heavy rain. 'Follow me,
Wilson Dowling. The time has come for us to leave this
place.'

'I need to eat something,' Wilson replied.

'Food will be provided.' Aclla didn't break her stride
and Wilson had to quick-step to keep up with her. Turning
a sharp left, she headed up a narrow laneway that led
towards the central courtyard. Side-stepping the neatly
stacked ashlars, Wilson and Aclla appeared in the great

open space. Standing before them was a perfect formation of female warriors, twenty wide and two deep. They
wore identical hooded capes; the material open at the
front to reveal the same decorated breastplate that Aclla
was wearing. Each warrior had a sword strapped to
her exposed left thigh and a short bow slung across her
shoulder. They were statuesque and singularly focused on
their tribune. Not one pair of eyes sought Wilson out – it
was like he wasn't even there.

Sontane approached her virgin partner. 'They are ready,'
she called out.

Aclla handed Sontane Pachicuti's scroll, then faced the
assembly of warriors.

Wilson stayed on Aclla's left and one step behind.

Aclla gestured towards the Amazons. 'These warriors
are prepared to die for what they have been trained to
protect. Each one of them blames *you* for the Inca Cube's
disappearance – as do I.'

Aclla turned to face her warriors. 'Virgins of the Sun,'
she called out, 'Our darkest hour has arrived. The Inca
Cube has been lost to the world of men and this most
unholy of objects has taken root in the land of the living.'

Aclla stood with her hands on her hips, her shoulders
back. 'There can be no greater tragedy . . . and no greater
challenge. We have all heard of the gruesome murders that
are taking place in the city of Cuzco. It is certainly the Inca
Cube at work.' Aclla looked at her warriors, one by one.
'The time has come to reclaim what we have lost. The time
has come for us to restore order. This man standing beside
me will identify the location of the Cube. Then, and only
then, will we attack. We will be vastly outnumbered. The
soldiers we face will have modern weapons to use against
us. Despite these obstacles, we must prevail.'

Aclla walked the length of the front row. 'You will
protect this man at all costs.' She drew her sword and
pointed it directly at Wilson. 'Over the coming days, lives
will be taken and lives will be lost – but this man cannot be
one of them. He is our only hope.' She turned to the gathering yet again. 'Praise be to Mama Ocllo!'

The female warriors all replied with one voice. 'Praise be to Mama Ocllo!'

'We will travel under the protection of the weather,' Aclla called out. 'If visibility improves, we will proceed only under the cover of darkness. I pray that you all have the courage to die for what you believe in. For without you, we are doomed.'

Aclla approached Wilson and said under her breath, 'If the Inca Cube can see into your soul, Wilson Dowling, then we are surely walking into a trap. Let us pray for the sake of the world around us that the Mamaconas are right and that you are as much of a mystery to the Inca Cube as you are to them.'

46

Cuzco, Peru
Church of El Triunfo
Local Time 8:55 am

22 January 1908

CAPTAIN GONZALES WORE his finest military outfit as he walked the rain-soaked streets towards the Church of El Triunfo. With every footstep that led him farther from his home, he felt his heart become heavier. Clutching at the silver cross under his shirt, he prayed to the Lord Jesus to watch over his family until he could once again hold them safely in his arms. He desperately wanted to turn back, but he knew that the only way to protect the people he loved was to keep the bishop away.

Gonzales remembered the moment he had pressed his hands to Ramiro's shoulders and told the private to guard his family with his life. He'd looked into the young man's eyes and seen only innocence, which made him feel better. But was the young soldier up to the task of protecting his wife and children if the need arose?

Only God knew.

Rounding the final corner to the Plaza de Armas, Gonzales was shocked by the number of soldiers patrolling the large open area. He counted at least fifty men at first glance. The doors to the military headquarters had been reinforced with sandbags four feet high, as had the entire perimeter of La Catedral and the two churches that flanked the great basilica on either side. As he approached, Gonzales didn't recognise many of the soldiers; they were certainly the conscripts that had been sent from Lima at his request.

Scanning the impressive walls of La Catedral, Gonzales was relieved that the body of Corsell Santillana had finally been taken away and he no longer had to look upon the decaying remains of his former soldier. The crucifixion had heaped an unwanted evil upon the city of Cuzco and deep in his heart Gonzales knew the sinful time was not over yet.

Saluting every soldier who looked his way, Gonzales walked up the steps and passed through the barricade towards the Church of El Triunfo. The men he recognised looked dishevelled and tired, as if they too had not been sleeping these past few nights. From their expressions it was obvious that they were happy to see him back in command, and yet as much as he wanted to stop and impart some words of encouragement, he could not muster the energy. Instead, he remained tight-lipped as he passed by at a steady pace, crossing the cobblestone landing to the church.

The mighty cedar doors were guarded by two armed soldiers. Noting the dark blue jacket and gold buttons of a ranking officer, the guards immediately pushed back the arched doors and let the captain walk inside without stopping. Gonzales removed his wide-brimmed hat and handed it to the soldier standing just inside. He then set about brushing the excess rainwater from his jacket before adjusting his cuffs and pant legs to make sure they were perfectly straight. Last of all, he ran his fingers through his hair to form a semblance of neatness.

There was not a murmur inside the great hall.

Heading directly for the marble stoup of holy water, he touched his index finger to the pure liquid and made the cross of Jesus from his forehead to the centre of his chest then to his shoulders. He silently prayed that his family would be safe.

Rounding the crafted stonework, his legs felt unsteady as he entered the huge expanse of the church. Almost every pew was taken up with soldiers in uniform. For the first time in his life, Gonzales was not awestruck by the magnificence of the open chapel, with its gold-leaf walls and huge domed vault. Nor did his gaze seek out the religious frescos, or the countless artefacts that festooned the walls and cradled the impressive tabernacle. He was looking for Bishop Francisco – that was his sole focus.

Gonzales felt defenceless as he made his way forward, knowing full well that his men would expect him to sit in the front pew next to Lieutenant Capos. Glancing at his watch, Gonzales moved to the very front and sat down with just moments to spare. Outside in the courtyard, the church bells of La Catedral struck once, ominously denoting the passing of the hour.

There was not a sound and no one moved, unlike mass on a Sunday when there were many children about. A solitary pair of footsteps finally began echoing from the antechamber, growing louder with each moment. Gonzales knew exactly who it was. He drew in a deep breath and held it, wanting to appear strong for the moment when the bishop's gaze would inevitably fall upon him.

From out of the shadows, Bishop Francisco of Santo Domingo, thirty-third Bishop of Cuzco, came into view in his resplendent papal robes. His hands were clasped behind his back and his shoulders hunched forward as though the weight of the world was upon him. Surprisingly, he did not look at the gathering of soldiers – he just walked along as if he was completely alone, his eyes focused on the floor a few steps ahead of him. Gonzales took the opportunity to pull in another harried breath.

The bishop was gaunt and as pale as alabaster, as if the very life had been sucked out of his veins, leaving him only skin and bone. Not a single man inside the church had ever seen him look worse. His lips were dry and cracked and he had blackish circles around his eyes as if he'd been kicked in the face by a mule. When Gonzales took in the sight, he was shocked that he could fear a man who looked so aged, unhealthy and pathetic. It was only the brightness of his holy robes and his scarlet biretta that gave him any presence at all.

Clasping the handrail to steady himself, Bishop Francisco hauled himself up the three carpeted steps to the platform of the high altar. Everyone's attention was fixed on him as he placed his frail hands on the table of Saint Peter and looked out. Behind him was the gleaming high altar of El Triunfo and above that the Cross of the Conquest – the five-foot-tall wooden cross that was said to be carried by the conquistadors as they overran all before them in Peru in the early 1500s.

'These are dark times,' Bishop Francisco began, his voice barely finding its way to the back of the church. 'But God is always watching.' He pointed his index finger towards the expansive domed ceiling, his expression filled with worry. 'I am not here to pray for your safety . . . or for that of your families . . . as I would on the Sabbath.' He nodded. 'On this day we must take matters into our own hands.' Bishop Francisco appeared listless and his tone lacked vigour.

'Do you know why I have chosen this church as the location of our meeting? This church is called El Triunfo – *the triumph* – in 1536 this place was constructed by Francisco Pizarro of Trujillo after his momentous victory over the treacherous Manco II, appointed leader of the Inca tribes.' The tone of the bishop's voice hardened and his back became a little straighter. 'Through the goodness of Pizarro's heart, he appointed a Sapa as ruler of the Inca after the untimely death of King Atahualpa.'

Nearly every *mestizo* inside the church knew of the sad fate of King Atahualpa. After his capture by Pizarro in 1532, a ransom was set that required three rooms – twenty-two feet long and seventeen feet wide – to each be filled with a precious metal: bullion, pure gold and pure silver. And yet despite the ransom being met, Pizarro had King Atahualpa killed. But that was not the saddest part of his fate – before his execution, Pizarro demanded that King Atahualpa renounce his Inca gods and convert to Christianity. When the king refused, Pizarro forced the king to watch helplessly as his wives and children were systematically murdered before his eyes, over three days, by the most horrific and sadistic methods: babies and infants were suspended naked over open fires until the flesh was burned from their bodies; children were torn to pieces by hungry dogs; and the women were raped and slashed apart with swords. In the eyes of any man with Inca blood, King Atahualpa's miserable end did forevermore heap shame upon any man who carried Spanish blood.

Bishop Francisco's voice suddenly took on a forceful tone. 'Pizarro attempted to work with the Inca nobility, and he was slapped in the face! It was Pizarro – great leader of the conquistadors, a man appointed by God Himself – who appointed Manco II as king after Atahualpa's demise. And despite this great honour, Manco fled into the mountains where he raised a force of two hundred thousand savages. He dared to lay siege upon the Spanish conquest of Cuzco. He dared to challenge the Church of Christ and His followers.'

The bishop's pupils were now as black as night.

'Ten months this city was under siege!' the bishop yelled. 'Ten months! But despite the overwhelming odds against him, the great Pizarro of Trujillo prevailed . . . *and God Almighty played his part.*' Bishop Francisco leant out over the table of Saint Peter as if he intended to jump the ten feet to the stone floor. '*He brought the plague of smallpox upon the heathens! He brought the plague* . . . and they died in their thousands!' Spittle was flying out of the bishop's mouth. 'The filthy heathens that remained faced the cold lesson of hard steel. Do you not see? Those who oppose the hand of God will pay the ultimate price! Any man who dares to defy the Word of Jesus Christ will suffer the same terrible fate.'

Breathing hard now, the bishop's hands gripped the edge of the table so tightly that his knuckles were white. Taking a moment to compose himself, he threw his head back and stared up at the domed ceiling. 'That is why this church is called El Triunfo,' he said more calmly. 'To celebrate that emphatic victory.'

With the exception of just a few, almost every single man inside the church had Inca blood flowing through their veins. They resented the bishop's reference to heathens, but no one had the courage to admit it at this moment.

The bishop levelled his gaze. 'It was a great triumph. The champions of the Lord rose up when they were needed most.'

Bishop Francisco sought out Captain Gonzales in the crowd. 'And that time has come again. Innocents are dying . . . many from the safety of their beds . . . taken and murdered by killers who roam the darkness looking to spill the blood of the pure and brave-hearted. What will you do to stop this evil?' Tears began to well in the bishop's eyes. 'Everyone is afraid, and so far they have only had their faith to protect them. The time has come for you to *act* in the name of God.'

Gonzales could see the blood surging through the swollen veins in the bishop's exposed neck. It was like there was a terrible beast living inside him.

'Once again this city is under siege,' the bishop said in a deep voice. 'I have received word from *God Himself* that evil warriors are right now marching towards this city in an effort to reinforce their numbers. They only have murder on their minds and their intention is clear – they come here to uproot your faith in God. Once again the filthy descendants of the treacherous Manco II intend to bring carnage to the innocent Christians of Cuzco.' The bishop paused a moment, his gaze looking off into the distance. 'These sinister warriors will approach from the western mountains, over the high pass. They carry swords and short bows – primitive weapons – but they are not to be underestimated. You will recognise them easily . . . These warriors are *women*. Unholy bitches from the seventh level of Hell itself.'

The church was eerily quiet.

'I can see the doubt you have in your minds,' the bishop said, his voice rumbling like distant thunder. 'Do not doubt my words or the price for your lack of belief will be paid from the rich blood of your loved ones.'

Captain Gonzales did not dare blink. He was forcing himself to stare at the bishop as much as his heart told him to run for his life and never come back. He had a family to protect and he would do whatever he had to do.

Bishop Francisco singled Gonzales out. 'Will you protect your family?' he asked.

Gonzales's throat was dry. 'I will do whatever you ask,' he replied.

'You must kill the white stranger called Wilson Dowling. He is travelling with the female warriors . . . towards us at this very moment. I have seen it in my visions. Kill the white man and it will be enough to spare your family from danger.'

The church was filled with a cold, deathly silence.

'Will you be my right hand?' the bishop asked.

'I will be your right hand,' Gonzales replied.

'Will your men protect Cuzco from the invaders?'

'We will protect the city with our lives.'

'There is a siege coming!' the bishop screamed, his eyes uplifted. 'God Himself has called for your protection!' He pointed at the giant Cross of the Conquest. 'The time has come for you to once again protect your Lord and Master. Heed my words and protect this city with your lives!'

47

Andes Ranges, Peru
Fortress City of Pitcos
Local Time 9:03 am

23 January 1908

THE AMAZON WARRIORS began dispersing through
the narrow gap in the cliff and headed down the steep
mountainside. Last to exit the courtyard was Aclla and
her personal guard. It was only then that Wilson realised
Chiello had not been there.

Sontane threw Wilson a small hessian sack filled with
dry rations and a gourd of water. She then tossed him a
black cloak – the same type they all were wearing.

'So we don't have to look at you,' she sneered.

After leaving Pitcos, they ran at a brisk pace through
the mist and pouring rain. The landscape was slippery and
treacherous as they descended into countless valleys and
climbed countless more jagged ridges and high mountain
passes. After six straight hours the weather began to clear and
they were forced to stop near the ruins of Phuyupatamarca,
which Aclla said meant 'Cloud Level Town'. They hid on
the ridgeline waiting among the moss-covered structures of
this once substantial outpost for the weather set in again,
or for darkness to fall. The sun came out for a brief period
and many of the warriors took the opportunity to lay their
clothes out as they washed themselves in the deep rectangular baths that were fed from natural springs higher up the
mountain. To Wilson's great surprise, the air became quite
warm at one point and colourful butterflies fluttered around.

It was only after nightfall that the group began to move again. From there they descended a steep path to an open causeway spanning an expansive flat area that appeared to have once been the bed of a shallow lake. With the stars shining brightly they relied on their dark cloaks to conceal their progress. From the base of the valley they climbed a steep and rugged spur to the top of the next ridgeline to yet another ruined and overgrown outpost. At this point the Amazons broke into three parties, each heading in slightly different directions. Wilson could hear Aclla giving orders to the other marshals, but he could not understand what she was saying.

With their group now reduced to fifteen, the pace increased as they headed south-west over countless more ranges. Aclla was never more than a few feet away from Wilson, and Sontane was just as close. They didn't speak much – it was only when they passed Sayacmarca, 'City in a Steep Place', that Aclla mentioned that this had been a very important tactical position on the Inca Trail.

'Up there was once a large fortress,' she announced. 'You could not pass from either direction if you did not hold that position. It has the high ground.' The group was moving quickly and Wilson was breathing hard just trying to keep up.

As the light of dawn approached, the neatly constructed Inca pathway reverted to mud and shrubs. Running at a medium pace the Amazons continued to climb a V-shaped pass that the explorer Raimondi had called Abra de Runkuracay, which meant 'Pile of Ruins'. The simple ashlar buildings located at the top were once rest houses for the couriers who ran the Inca Trail carrying messages and supplies. The air was cold in the higher reaches of the mountains, approaching freezing as they crested the ridge and dropped steeply into yet another humid valley. The temperature difference was astounding depending on the altitude. For every thousand feet they climbed the temperature dropped five degrees Fahrenheit.

As they approached the Pacamayo River the heavy clouds moved in. Everything became soaked again but it meant they could proceed in the daylight without the worry of being seen. Heading up a treacherous switchback the group ran towards the highest point of the Inca Trail, known as Abra de Huarmihuanusca, 'Dead Woman's Pass' – a rocky, desolate place where nothing grew and the chilly wind and stinging rain seemed to blow right through them. Wilson had passed this way before, when he'd first arrived at Machu Picchu nearly eight years earlier. The last time he'd been here the mountain pass was covered in snow three feet deep.

Maintaining a steady pace, Wilson eased towards Aclla's shoulder. 'This is the way you came after I cut the Bridge of the Condor?' he asked.

Aclla nodded.

All the while Sontane was just a step behind, running with the same rhythm and gate as her virgin pair. Every now and again she would shove Wilson in the back to speed him up.

The journey was gruelling and Wilson made sure he healed his body when he could. Most of the warriors were chewing coca leaves when they were heading up to higher altitude. The marshals kept telling everyone to eat their dry rations – they would need all the energy they could get when they finally reached their destination.

After leaving the chill of the mountain pass behind them, they clambered down the bare shale slopes into bleak grasslands before reaching the cover of the woodlands. It was such a relief to finally be out of the wind and cold. There was a sense of security that came with being among the trees. For more than a day, Wilson and his entourage had run at a steady pace over some of the most difficult terrain he had ever seen. It was testament to the stamina and strength of these women that they were able to keep going at such a steady tilt.

Eventually they reached a suspension bridge that spanned some free-flowing rapids gushing through a narrow rocky pass. The whitewater thundered by just a few feet below the sagging vines, and the bridge was swaying badly from side to side.

Wilson was one of the last to cross and he jokingly asked Aclla if he should cut the vines and let the structure fall into the river.

All he got in return was a frown.

There were frequent thunderclaps as Aclla slowed their pace through the rain so they could time their approach to Cuzco with the impending darkness. As the land flattened out and the trees disappeared, scouts were sent ahead to make sure their path was clear. The Amazon warriors seemed to know exactly where the local Indians and the *mestizos* would be.

'The railway line is over in that direction,' Aclla said, angling her hand to indicate which way the tracks travelled. 'We will head to Poroy Picchu – a mountain just to the south of here. From there we will plan our advance on Cuzco.'

'I have to be at the Plaza de Armas by midnight,' Wilson replied. 'There is a fountain in the centre of the square. Pizarro's fountain. You must get me there on time if I am to have any chance of locating the Inca Cube.

Aclla nodded. 'We will get you there.'

48

Poroy Picchu, Peru
5 Miles North-west of Cuzco
Local Time 8:30 pm

23 January 1908

BY THE TIME they all made their way single file up the
rugged face of Poroy Picchu the cloudy sky was pitch
black. To Wilson's great surprise the other two groups
of Amazons had already made camp within the caverns
and fissures that threaded through the mountainside. In
Wilson's estimation they must have taken a more direct
route to Poroy Picchu because no one could have run
faster than they had done. From the bottom of the valley
it was not possible to see the entrance to the caves, which
were three-quarters of the way up the western face. The
Amazons obviously had fires burning in the deeper recesses
and they were venting the smoke back into the mountain.

As Aclla's group entered the cave network they were
each handed a large bowl of steaming stew and sweet
potatoes. None of the warriors made eye contact with
Wilson as he followed Aclla and Sontane into the narrow
tunnels. In one of the chambers further along, hammocks
were suspended from the walls. At least ten women were
sleeping there – their metal armour hanging from shackles
on the wall.

'We have been coming here for generations,' Aclla
said, turning left into another narrow fissure. It was the
first time she'd said anything to him in the last hour. 'The
Spaniards never found this place.'

Wilson tipped the bowl of stew to his mouth and ate as they walked. Up ahead, he could see firelight in the distance. Eventually the corridor opened up to a large cave that was fifty feet across and the same in height. The textured walls were lit up by four brass hurricane lamps. Water dripped constantly from perfectly formed stalactites, the large droplets echoing through the cavern as they landed in five separate shimmering pools.

'You can drink the water, but not too much,' Aclla said, pointing at the pools. 'Good minerals.'

A mahogany dining table with six carved chairs stood in the centre of the open area. It looked like the baroque setting had come straight from the palace of King Charles V of Spain. Against the far wall, a row of six wooden beds of the same era and craftsmanship were laid out with woolly alpaca blankets. The air was dank and chilly and it made the beds look even more enticing, especially in comparison to the hammocks.

'You will sleep there,' Aclla said, pointing to the end of the row.

After setting her bowl on the table, she walked to the bed at the opposite end. She pressed a dry towel to her face, threw off her cape then unclipped her wrist and ankle bracelets. She ran her fingers down the length of her ponytail in a familiar way and squeezed the water out.

Sontane went to the bed next to her and did almost exactly the same thing in the same order. They began speaking in Quechua and while Wilson couldn't understand what they were saying, he knew from Sontane's heated tone that she was unhappy that he was staying in the same chamber with them.

Rubbing her wrists to get the blood flowing, Aclla walked to the wooden table without expression, pulled out one of the ornate Spanish chairs, sat down, then tipped her bowl of stew to her mouth.

The sound of running footsteps came from the tunnel and seconds later a woman entered wearing a black cloak. Through her laboured breathing she started speaking quickly in Quechua, but Aclla stopped her.

'You will speak English, so he can understand,' she said.

The woman was taller than average for a Peruvian, with good bone structure and greying hair. She would have been fifty years old in Wilson's estimation and he couldn't help wondering if at one time she too had been a warrior for the Virgins of the Sun.

'I bring word from Cuzco,' the woman said, then pulled in a few deep breaths. Her accent was just like Aclla's with the same harsh tone.

'Continue,' Aclla said.

'There are more than two hundred and fifty soldiers inside the city,' the woman said. 'That number will double again with the arrival of another train from Lima in the next two days.'

'Normally there are less than a hundred soldiers,' Aclla said to Wilson.

'A protective perimeter has been set around the Plaza de Armas,' the woman continued. 'The churches and the shops have sandbags stacked in front. Soldiers with rifles patrol the area through the day as well as the night.'

'The Plaza de Armas?' Aclla said to Wilson. 'The very place you need to go.'

'We must be there at midnight regardless of the risk,' Wilson said in return.

'We will get you there, do not worry,' Aclla said reassuringly. She turned to her messenger once again. 'And what of the murders?'

'The murders continue as before, in random locations. The peasants want to congregate within the churches of the Plaza de Armas, but the army will not let them.'

Aclla frowned. 'The Inca Cube is driving these events – it has to be.' She clenched her fists. 'What about the approach to the city?'

'The approach from the west is clear. The soldiers are mainly stationed within the Plaza de Armas itself, and around La Monasterio. The rest of the city remains unguarded, as are its people.' The old woman glanced in Wilson's direction. 'There is something you must know. . . They have captured the man called Hiram Bingham.'

Wilson felt a pang in his stomach.

'He was brought to Cuzco by the Indian guide, Ompeta, just this afternoon. An armed contingent of ten men pushed him along the Avenue de Sol towards the military barracks. He was shackled to the outer wall of the barracks for all to see and the captain of the guard ruthlessly beat him. They were asking questions about *him*.' She pointed in Wilson's direction.

'What is the name of the captain of the guard?' Wilson asked.

'His name is Lucho Gonzales?' she replied.

The man whose family Wilson was supposedly going to torture and then kill.

'It is unfortunate that they have captured Hiram Bingham,' Aclla said. 'Through *his* mind the Inca Cube surely knows that you are with us.'

'Explain that to me again,' Wilson said.

'The Cube can look into men's minds,' Aclla replied. 'Everything that Hiram Bingham has seen and heard is certainly visible to the Inca Cube.' Aclla pressed her index finger on the table. 'Bingham saw us when we pole-vaulted the river, and he saw us after the Bridge of the Condor was cut. As well as that, everything you have told him is now part of the Inca Cube's collective consciousness. Hiram Bingham now forms part of the network of information that keeps the Imperium in control. Your friend has seen enough with his *own eyes* to betray our advantage.' Aclla turned to Sontane. 'Tell the sentries to widen the protective approach to this mountain – I do not want to get trapped up here with no possibility of escape.'

'We should send an assassin to kill Bingham,' Sontane announced. 'That is the best thing for our cause.'

There was a long pause as Wilson waited patiently for Aclla's reply.

'Hiram Bingham has become a liability now, there is no doubt,' Aclla stated.

'You cannot kill Hiram Bingham,' Wilson said calmly. 'He is crucial to everything that is going on here – he is part of Machu Picchu's future.'

'Why is he crucial?' Aclla asked.

'He is the reason I travelled the stars to come to this place. Hiram Bingham is a protector of the Incas and their secrets.' Wilson couldn't be sure what he was saying was absolutely true because the history he had studied had the Inca Cube forever incarcerated within the foundations of the Temple of the Sun. Yet, he sensed that Hiram was still important. 'He is critical to the future,' he reiterated.

'That man is a fool!' Sontane blurted.

'It is not for you to judge who is a fool and who is not,' Wilson replied. 'I have travelled many lifetimes, through *time itself*, to lead that man to Vilcapampa. It is ordained by the gods and it is unwise to question them!'

Sontane's lip quivered and her hand slipped down to rest on the hilt of her sword. 'You are unwise to speak to me that way,' she seethed.

Aclla pointed towards the exit. 'Sontane!' she said abruptly. 'You will go and tell the sentries to expand their protective area. Now!'

'It is a mistake to trust this man,' Sontane replied. But before Aclla could respond again, Sontane stepped away towards the shadows of the tunnel.

'You should not provoke her,' Aclla said.

'She is foolish,' Wilson replied.

Aclla turned to her messenger. 'Where have they taken Hiram Bingham?'

'After beating him they led him in shackles to La Monasterio, the place where the bishop and his priests live. The building is guarded with at least twenty men.'

'Where is he inside the building?' Aclla asked.

'All we know is that he's in there. Nothing else. Women are not allowed inside the monastery. From the mountains nearby it is only possible to view the courtyard. The walls are too high to see over.' The messenger reached under her cloak and produced a leather pouch. 'I have a map of the city and the fortifications. It details the areas that are guarded and the numbers of men.'

'You have done well,' Aclla said.

The woman bowed her head. 'Forgive me for saying this,

but I must: for the last eight nights there have been many murders in Cuzco. Brutal murders. They are depraved and frenzied attacks – I have seen one of the bodies. The victim I saw had bite marks on her flesh, as if the attacker was trying to eat the body.'

'Human bite marks?'

'Yes.'

'And where are the soldiers when these murders happen?'

'They are never there.'

'It is the work of the Inca Cube,' Aclla said. 'It controls the thoughts of the soldiers and directs them away from the place of the murder.'

'Innocent women and children are being taken from their homes, right from under their parents' noses,' the messenger said. 'The people of the city are too afraid to let their loved ones out of their sight – their houses are boarded up, both the doors and the windows. There is a curfew and no one is permitted to roam the streets. And yet, even so, the murders continue. The people of Cuzco want someone to protect them, but all they have is their faith in their God . . . which is doing them nothing.'

Aclla rose from her chair and pointed. 'Go and rest. Eat something. You will be safe here. Rest easy knowing that we are going to put things right.'

The old woman bowed. 'Thank you, Tribune.' Her eyes momentarily sought Wilson out. 'It is an honour to be of service.'

As the woman left, Sontane walked back in.

Aclla threw her the leather pouch. 'Open that.' She turned to Wilson. 'The Inca Cube controls everything just as the Mamaconas imagined it would. And with every day that passes the Cube becomes more powerful.'

'How do we know the Imperium cannot read *him* as well?' Sontane announced, her gaze locked on Wilson. 'He is unproven.'

'We must assume it cannot,' Aclla replied. 'Otherwise we would have been attacked already. I believe this man is not of this world, therefore he is protected.'

'If he turns to the other side, I will kill him myself,' Sontane said angrily.

'If I turn to the other side, I hope that you do,' Wilson replied.

Aclla grabbed the wad of paper squares from Sontane's hand and began piecing them together on the table. There were thirty-six squares, each one carefully drawn, which detailed the centre of Cuzco and the buildings. A symbol represented the location of every soldier, where they slept and ate, and where the sandbag fortifications were. The major concentration of men was definitely around La Catedral and the churches flanking the basilica.

Wilson studied the papers. 'We must make it to the Plaza de Armas by midnight . . . then hopefully I will be able to tell where the Cube is.' He was counting on Helena leading him to it – she had always delivered when he needed her and he hoped that tonight would be no different.

'Even if we had double our warriors we could not storm that plaza,' Sontane said with a frown. 'It is like a fortress. There are gun batteries *there* and *there*. Maxim guns on tripods – automatic weapons that can shoot hundreds of rounds per minute.'

'We will use the cover of darkness,' Aclla said.

'Where is the crystal box that will hold the Inca Cube?' Wilson asked.

'It will arrive soon,' Aclla answered. 'It has been taken by another path.'

'We did not carry it in our group for worry you would betray us,' Sontane announced.

'A good decision,' Wilson said in agreement. 'As you say, I am unproven.' He rubbed his chin thoughtfully. 'It is imperative that you and your warriors are not seen tonight. If the men of Cuzco are thinking as a collective, then we have to make them believe the Virgins of the Sun are not here. If they see me, that's fine.'

'Six of us will go with you to Cuzco tonight,' Aclla said. 'My personal guard: Sontane, Sepla, Polix, Orelle and Ilna. The others are to wait here until they are called for.'

Sontane pointed at Wilson. 'If you take one ill step, I will cut your throat myself . . .'

Aclla thumped her fist on the table and stood up. 'Enough! You will protect him with your life as we have agreed! This man is our only hope!'

'Yes, Tribune,' Sontane eventually replied.

'Not another word is to be spoken until it is time to leave. That is an order,' Aclla said.

As Wilson walked to his bed he became acutely aware of the water dripping from the ceiling into the shimmering pools. There must be a great deal of limestone in the mountain for the stalactites to be as large as they were. Lying on the bed, he pulled the warm covers over himself and enjoyed the sensation of the comfortable mattress. From the shadows, he watched as Aclla unclipped her breastplate and hung it from a shackle on the wall, then peeled off her wet undergarments.

Wilson forced his gaze towards the jagged ceiling and set about healing his weary legs and his aching back. He'd need all his strength and speed if he was going to survive a trip into the heart of Cuzco. The Inca Cube was indeed powerful, Wilson realised – it certainly controlled hundreds, if not thousands of men, and now it had pulled Hiram Bingham into its web also. Wilson tried to picture what Captain Lucho Gonzales would look like. It seemed that both he and the captain of the guard were on a collision course of some kind with diabolical consequences for them both.

All the while, the sparkling droplets of water continued to fall from the ceiling, making a splashing sound that echoed gently off the cavern's rugged walls.

49

Cuzco, Peru
1 Mile from City Centre
Local Time 11:05 pm

23 January 1908

TRAVELLING THE FOUR miles from Poroy Picchu to the ridgeline above Cuzco had taken just over an hour. For most of the journey, Aclla and her black-clad warriors were concentrating on moving stealthily rather than quickly, but there were open stretches where she ordered a burst of speed. Upon leaving the network of caves, they descended the southern side of the mountain through a sparse eucalyptus forest, eventually following a swollen stream that cut through the valley ridge and dropped away to the east where the city was located.

Cuzco was founded in a huge bowl-like indentation approximately four miles long and two miles wide. Eight hundred feet above the city on all sides was a desolate tundra plateau where little if anything grew. The trees that once surrounded the city had all been cut down for firewood, so there was no cover once the warriors went out into the open, except for the dark night and the incessant rain.

Wilson stood on the ridgeline looking down through the mist towards the few speckled lights that marked the city. Every now and again, as the clouds drifted by, it was possible to see where the cobblestone roads began and the little mudbrick houses became densely packed together. This was once the centre of the Inca Empire,

Wilson realised – the heart of the sacred puma; the place where Manco Capac, the First Inca, had thrown down the Golden Staff of the Sun God and proclaimed this as 'the naval of the world'. And that's exactly how it looked. But there were also practical reasons for locating the city inside the indentation of the valley. The soil was rich, there was ample water, and the weather was calmer – cooler in the summer and warmer in the winter.

Aclla stood next to Wilson, gazing at the city, her black cloak covering all but her eyes. 'The Inca Cube is down there somewhere,' she said, pointing the curve of her bow towards the brightest lights. 'Just exactly how will you know where it is located?'

Wilson thought for a long while before answering. 'I have a spirit connection that will guide my hand,' he eventually replied. 'A woman,' he added, hoping it would give Aclla some confidence in what he was saying. 'My spirit connection has the power to look through walls and into places we cannot. She will guide my hand, and when I discover the Cube's hiding place I will tell you where it is located.'

'There is nothing that you can say that will shock me,' Aclla replied. 'Nothing at all. I realise that you are not an ordinary man and you do not live by an ordinary man's rules. Just remember, if you find the Cube, you must not touch it. That is a risk that should not be taken.'

'I understand.'

'I pray to the gods that your female spirit can locate the Cube. It grows more powerful every moment.' Aclla's gaze remained fixed on the twinkling lights in the distance. 'We must incarcerate its power once again.'

'The female spirit will deliver,' Wilson stated.

Wilson was suddenly struck by the importance of his connection to Helena. Without her it would be very difficult to find the Inca Cube. Helena had been a strong force in his life, regardless of the limited time they had spent together. It seemed that not even a 106-year barrier of time had the power to sever the link between them.

For Wilson, so much of the last eight years had simply

been spent waiting for the year 1908 to arrive. He had gone to China to play his role in the Boxer Rebellion. A more brutal and bloody experience he could not have imagined. Once he had completed the tasks requested of him, he'd travelled to Australia in 1902 and made a home for himself in the little fishing village of Eden in southern New South Wales. He liked to fish and he fitted into the small community without standing out too much. The majority of his time was spent alone, either at home or on his little fishing boat, for fear that his presence would somehow have a negative effect on the future.

All those wasted years, he thought.

There was no doubt that being a time-traveller afforded him some amazing experiences, but the price of those stunning moments had been monumental. In the act of doing his duty he had lost the people he loved, and he had been separated from everything that he knew. Thankfully, standing here, looking down at Cuzco, he had a clear mission and a singular focus: reclaim the Inca Cube at all costs. With the help of the Virgins of the Sun he would put history on track again. The reality was, he would need to kill men to achieve his objective – he had resigned himself to that fact.

I am the Overseer, he told himself.

Aclla made a sharp gesture with her left hand and four black-clad warriors flew away into the mist like bats into the night. Aclla, Wilson and Sontane were left standing together, the summer wind blowing rain into their backs. 'If Sontane or I are wounded, and capture is imminent,' Aclla said, 'it is the duty of the other to take their virgin pair's life. You must support this.'

'Just stay out of sight,' Wilson replied. 'I'll find out where the Cube is and I'll come back to meet you. If for any reason we're separated then we'll meet back at Poroy Picchu. Is that clear?'

Sontane made a comment in Quechua, but Aclla shushed her. 'That is clear,' Aclla replied. 'If we are separated, we will wait for your return at Poroy Picchu.'

Running from the top of the ridge into the narrow

laneways of Cuzco took only twenty minutes. Just as the old woman had told them, the doors and windows of nearly all the houses and shops had been boarded up and there was not a soul to be seen in the dark streets. Heavy rain was coming down as they approached the hazy lights of the Plaza de Armas that plumed above the two-storey buildings ahead.

Aclla gestured upwards, directing everyone to climb to the rooftops via the exposed guttering. All the while, Wilson listened intently to the clatter of the falling rain and every nuance of the trickling water as it ran off the gutters then swept down the tilted gradient of the cobblestone streets. Every time his movement caused an irregular noise or the terracotta tiles creaked under his considerable weight, he was fearful it would lead to their discovery. By comparison, the Amazons hardly made any sound at all. Climbing to the highest vantage point, the rain hitting his face, Wilson eased his way up the gentle gradient on his stomach until he was finally peering down into the Plaza de Armas.

Aclla held her bow next to her, an arrow set against the twine. She gestured for her warriors to spread out. In the very centre of the plaza, about 150 feet away, was the two-tiered Spanish fountain Wilson had come to see – Pizarro's Fountain. Three smooth walkways crisscrossed the plaza from corner to corner and across the very middle, between six symmetrical triangles of grass. Directly opposite, on the other side of the plaza, was La Catedral and the two sister churches that flanked the basilica. From up here it was obvious the gradient of the land fell away to the south at a constant five-degree angle.

Wilson was thankful to see that the body of Corsell Santillana was no longer pinned to the outer wall of the main belltower. Rows of heavy sandbags had been placed around the church, the military barracks and the post office – exactly as they had been drawn on the map. There were two main gun batteries – one to the south-east and another to the north-west, each manned by three men. Both emplacements had a clear sweep across the entrance to La Catedral with their Gatling guns. A dozen oil lamps on ten-foot poles randomly lit up the vast expanse. Two soldiers wearing green, waterproof ponchos were patrolling the centre of the courtyard, walking across the middle from corner to corner, then meeting by Pizarro's Fountain every five minutes or so before going again.

Wilson counted at least a score of soldiers camped behind the sandbags in front of the church and at least another ten under the covered walkway adjacent to the military barracks. Visibility was fair for anyone with decent eyesight; Wilson knew it was going to be a real challenge to get to the two-tiered baroque fountain located smack-bang in the middle of the plaza.

Peering towards the fountain, Wilson hoped that he would eventually spot the faint shimmering light that had first indicated to him that Helena was about to appear, but as time ticked by he figured he was too far away to have a definite connection and needed to somehow get closer. The clock above the post office read four minutes to midnight. Placing his hand on Aclla's forearm, he whispered, 'I have to get closer to that fountain.'

Aclla's hazel eyes locked onto his for longer than normal. 'Be careful,' she answered. 'You must assume they will be expecting you.'

Wilson slipped backwards off the rooftop as quietly as he was able. He carefully lowered himself to the first level then jumped to the cobblestones, landing securely on his feet. Through the narrow gap in the buildings ahead the lights of the plaza cast a rectangular glow on the slippery stones. With his cloak covering all but his eyes, Wilson moved confidently in the shadows towards the sandbags blocking the end of the street. According to the map, there wasn't a guard stationed on this approach. There were eleven major streets that opened into the Plaza de Armas and at least double that number in laneways. The soldiers weren't guarding them all – it was clear they were protecting the open space, and there was plenty of that.

Wilson hoped that by getting as near to the fountain as he could, Helena would magically appear – or at the very least she would see him, move closer, and he would sense her presence. Everything relied upon one key factor – that the Inca Cube was somewhere nearby. From what Wilson had witnessed it was the power of the Cube that enabled the connection with Helena. Without it being close or having passed through this place, at the very least, there might be no connection at all.

Easing himself next to the sandbags, Wilson cautiously lifted his head and watched as the two sentries stepped across the centre of the plaza in perfect unison, rifles at their shoulders. When the nearest soldier was heading away from him he scanned the two-storey terraces to his left and right – in both directions there were covered walkways framed with pillared arches. The walkways were dark and appeared empty. He leapt the sandbags and stood behind one of the stone pillars.

Dropping to his knees in the shadows, Wilson locked his focus onto the bronze two-tiered fountain – the water had obviously been shut off and the spouts weren't flowing. As the minutes ticked past, he worried that he was still too far away for Helena to be able to connect. Wilson tried desperately to sense Helena's presence around him. He glanced once again towards the giant fountain but saw no telltale glow.

The giant belltower of La Catedral rang just once, denoting the passing of the hour. Wilson was too far away from the fountain, he realised. He had to get closer.

She'll be there, he thought.

The sudden menace of approaching footsteps penetrated the drumming rain as two dark figures rounded the far corner and headed directly towards him along the covered walkway. From the sound, Wilson knew they were military-issue boots – it had to be a two-man patrol circling the perimeter adjacent to the shops and government buildings. At the same moment, the wind began to gust and the rain began falling so heavily it became impossible to hear anything. Wilson eased himself as close to the stone pillar as he could, realising that the heavy rain would conceal the view of him from the plaza.

The two soliders were now just ten feet away.

Wilson circled behind the pillar, out into the rain, then back around the other side. Approaching rapidly from the rear, he slammed the two men's heads together with all his might. Their flat-rimmed hats muted the crack of their skulls. Wilson did his best to catch both men as they fell, but he missed one of their rifles and it tumbled end over end into the flooded courtyard.

Thunder rumbled overhead, deep and growling.

Wilson's adrenalin was surging as he grabbed the two unconscious soldiers by their ankles and dragged them into the shadows. Sizing up the larger of the two men, he set about pulling away his waterproof poncho and throwing it over his own soaking head. He grabbed the soldier's flat-rimmed hat – which was a bit small – and pulled it on tight.

Stepping into the heavy downpour, the rain striking his clothing, he grabbed the .303 rifle that was now partially submerged under the rippling surface of water. Wilson pressed the rifle to his shoulder, held his head high and marched forward into the rain. The only way to find out if Helena was actually there was to walk the fifty paces to the fountain and see for himself. It was already after midnight and, despite the danger, he couldn't miss the chance to connect with her. Too much depended on it.

50

Cuzco, Peru
Military Headquarters, Plaza de Armas
Local Time 11:59 pm

23 January 1908

THE BELLS OF La Catedral struck just once, denoting the passing of the hour. Captain Gonzales was worried sick about his family as he sat under the porch of the military headquarters and looked out at the curtains of rain sweeping across the huge expanse of the Plaza de Armas. His right leg nervously jigged up and down as he drew in another breath through his rolled cigarette then let the grey smoke stream from his lips and drift away on the soaking wind.

Gonzales was angry and frustrated, wishing he could be there to protect his wife and children in their simple home. Looking back towards the double doors of the barracks, he spotted the shackles bolted to the whitewashed wall. If only that fool Hiram Bingham had told him what he wanted to know then he wouldn't have to be here now. He needed to capture the white stranger, Wilson Dowling. He had hunted him halfway across the mountains of Peru, and so far he had not even laid eyes upon him.

I need to capture that motherless bastard!

Gonzales remembered the sadistic elation he felt as he struck Hiram Bingham's back with the donkey whip, over and over, until his skin bled through his shirt.

Reaching for the pistol on his belt, Gonzales re-enacted the moment he drew his weapon and pressed the barrel tip to the back of Bingham's head. He'd wanted so desperately to kill the American. His crying and constant complaining about needing whiskey and cigarettes had been maddening. It didn't matter to him that the President of the United States was someone called Teddy Roosevelt! The skinny man was a stupid fool who would not reveal the location of his friend. Gonzales had deemed it a perfect moment to set an example for his frightened soldiers that they would not forget. It was not the time to be soft or, God forbid, to be seen that way. And yet for some reason, as much as he tried, it had been impossible to pull the trigger. Gonzales was overwhelmed to the point of tears at the mere thought of it.

Given the chance again, he told himself angrily, he would easily squeeze the trigger without thought for the consequences. Gonzales knew it was the very same paralysis he'd experienced when he tried to lift his sword inside the church. He would have struck the bishop down if he could. He knew that the priest hungered for the flesh of his wife and children – that was his greatest fear. Gonzales hurriedly made the cross of Jesus on his chest for his terrible thoughts, then kissed his fingers.

He pulled in another drag of his cigarette. His leg was still jumping about nervously.

After they unshackled Bingham's limp body, he was dragged away to the stinking dungeon located below La Monasterio. God only knew what depraved things must have happened there. The greatest consolation for Gonzales was that Bingham would have to face the bishop on his own.

If I had killed him . . . he would have been better off.

Gonzales took another drag.

Scanning the plaza yet again, he kept a tight grip on the handle of his revolver as he mentally ticked off every location, and every man, one by one. His family's safety relied on him protecting the Triple Churches. He knew in his gut the only way to truly escape this nightmare was to find the impostor Wilson Dowling.

The wind rose and the rain began pouring down at a furious rate. Captain Gonzales was forced to stand and move away from the railing because the mist from the downpour was wafting under the covered walkway.

The roar of the elements was deafening.

Gonzales hated being here; he could not deny it.

Taking one last drag of his cigarette, he flicked the butt out into the weather and watched as it sped away on the rainwater that hurried along the gradient of the land.

Thunder rumbled above the city.

Gonzales thought about heading inside to his cot and trying to get some sleep, but he knew he'd just lie there as he always did, staring up at the ceiling, his fears gradually getting the better of him.

The downpour began easing as quickly as it had started and Gonzales wiped the water off his seat and placed it next to the railing again. Looking out at the plaza, he sat down and began checking off his men once more.

Who is the man heading directly for the fountain?

Gonzales squinted, trying to get a better look. He had not authorised any of his soldiers to patrol that area unless they were in pairs. Most likely it was one of the young conscripts from Lima, he thought.

Without fully understanding why, Gonzales stood up with a frantic lunge. Looking out at the dark figure, he was immediately certain that it was Wilson Dowling. It was impossible to know how, but he knew it. Gonzales drew his handgun, extended his arms, planted his feet securely on the wet ground and levelled the sight. This was not the moment to doubt himself. His hand was perfectly steady as he aimed for the middle of the man's chest. Taking into account the long distance and his target's quickened pace, Gonzales lifted his aim a fraction then pulled the trigger.

His gun recoiled with a blinding flash, the loud *bang* ripping through the constant hubbub of rain. The dark figure was flung backwards by the sudden impact of the bullet. The man's arms and legs violently splayed outwards like a raging bull had flattened him. He seemed to fly through the air for a great distance before landing heavily on the uneven cobblestones beside Pizarro's Fountain.

Soldiers were screaming and running towards Gonzales,

frantically trying to figure out why their captain had shot dead one of his own men. Gonzales angrily pushed them aside as he stomped out into the rain, smoking gun in hand. He knew in his gut that he had shot Wilson Dowling. Furiously yelling for his men to make a path, he pushed his way forward until he was standing over the corpse. Gonzales knelt down next to the body and ripped away the flat-brimmed military hat.

A tall white man was lying dead before him.

A sense of utter elation filled Captain Gonzales as he looked down upon Wilson Dowling's glassy eyes. It did not even register that he had shot a man – he was thinking about his wife and his children and the prospect of getting back to them as quickly as he could. Gonzales holstered his weapon and threw a clenched fist in the air.

'Our problems are finally over!' he called out. 'You men . . . take this white devil's body to La Monasterio. Finally, I will deliver the imposter that Bishop Francisco has been searching for.'

51

Andes Ranges, Peru
Chinchero Highway
33 Miles North-west of Cuzco
Local Time 7:45 am

24 January 2014

THE DARKNESS WAS beginning to fade as the twenty-seater bus accelerated up the narrow switchback to the crest of the ravine with its engine roaring. The wipers were on maximum speed trying to sweep away the constant rain that was hitting the windshield and streaming along the side windows. As the misty sky brightened, the headlights were becoming ineffective, making it even more difficult to judge the distance to the next corner.

'You'll take me to the Plaza de Armas,' Helena said the moment she climbed into the front seat. 'As quickly as you can.'

Behind her, in the first row of the empty cabin sat Chad Chadwick and John Hanna. They were both grim-faced about the erratic driving of the Peruvian man behind the wheel who was swerving around corners in total disregard for the sheer drop-offs that fell away hundreds of feet into the darkness of the valley. There were no guardrails and the road was treacherously slippery.

'Do we really need to go this fast?' Chad said as she was thrown to one side by the force of the turn. 'For God's sake!'

'Maybe I should drive,' Hanna said for the fifth time, holding the railing in front of him with both hands. 'I'm an excellent driver.'

Helena stared out the front window. 'You don't know the mountain roads as well as Naldo does. If it bothers you, close your eyes and try to get some sleep.'

'It doesn't bother me,' Hanna replied, getting thrown about in his seat. 'I love going fast as much as the next guy, I just think it would be *safer* if I drove.'

'How many times have you driven this road?' Helena asked the driver.

Naldo furiously spun the wheel as the big bus slid on the wet tarmac. He was a little fellow in his mid forties, a native Indian with chocolate-coloured skin and straight black hair. 'I have driven this road maybe . . .' he gritted his teeth with concentration as he tipped the heavy vehicle into yet another tight corner, '. . . two thousand times, I guess.' His Spanish accent was quite strong. 'That is over the last ten years.'

Helena turned around to look at her bodyguards. 'Two thousand times,' she repeated with a confident expression before looking back at Naldo. 'And how many times have you crashed?'

Naldo frowned as the bus shuddered in the middle of the turn. 'I have crashed *many times*, señorita – too many to count. This is a very dangerous road!' He took one hand off the wheel and briefly pointed up into the hills. 'What, with the rockslides and fallen trees, cars and buses. There are many terrible drivers on this road. *Terrible*. Llamas . . . I have hit a llama.'

The confident expression left Helena's face.

'Good to know . . . thanks, Naldo,' Hanna said. 'Both hands on the steering wheel would be good.'

'I have not had an accident for almost a month,' Naldo said as he gripped the wheel with both hands again. Accelerating out of the corner they headed down into the bottom of a steep wooded valley.

'Just do the best you can,' Helena said.

'I will get you to Cuzco by midday,' Naldo said. 'As God is my witness.'

Helena was pressed hard against her seatbelt as Naldo hit the brakes for a tight off-camber turn. Helena had offered Naldo five thousand dollars to get her to the Plaza de Armas by midday. If not, he got one thousand dollars. In Helena's experience, when you threw enough money at a problem you could make even the most difficult things happen amazingly quickly.

Helena had already missed the midnight deadline she'd agreed with Wilson. The road between Cuzco and Machu Picchu had not been cleared in time and she was unable to get out. In her desperation, she was able to organise Naldo's charter bus by using the hotel's satellite phone and then hiked the first ten miles of the Inca Trail in the dark and the pouring rain.

Helena attempted to convince herself that missing Wilson at midnight was not the end of the world, but the rationalisation only worked for a few minutes before she was once again lamenting her situation. Negative thoughts filled her mind and she wondered if her not being there had caused Wilson to get hurt or captured. Surely he would wait for her there, she told herself – just as she had waited for him at Machu Picchu.

'I need to get to Pizarro's fountain by midday,' Helena repeated.

'The fountain is not called that anymore,' Naldo replied. 'The conquistador Pizarro is not a well-liked man in Peru. It has been this way for many years. His fate was sealed when he murdered King Atahualpa –'

'After the ransom was paid . . . I know the story,' Helena ended the sentence for him.

'We call it the *Victory Fountain* these days,' Naldo continued. 'It was a gift from the King of Spain, Philip II of Seville, and it has been there for nearly four hundred years.'

The large bus turned another tight corner and Helena could feel the wheels momentarily slip from under them, but Naldo managed to correct the slide just in time. It was only forty miles to Cuzco as the crow flies, but on the twisting tarmac roads that zigzagged up and down the mountains, over crests and into deep valleys, it was triple that distance. The most dangerous part of the journey was at the beginning as they travelled through the steepest mountains. Hopefully, as the altitude increased and the land flattened out, they would be able to go faster.

'How am I supposed to eat my tuna with the bus shaking all over the place?' Chad muttered in frustration. 'Can't we stop for just two minutes?'

'We're not stopping,' Helena replied.

'There is no time,' Naldo added. 'We have a date with destiny.'

Cuzco, Peru
Cachimayo Highway, three miles from city centre
Local Time 11:50 am

Helena was biting her nails as the bus roared down the hill towards the outskirts of Cuzco. The rain had finally stopped and the sun was just breaking through the clouds. From the crest of the ridge they could see the urban sprawl that filled the majority of the dish-like crater the city had been built within. Under a blanket of low clouds it was possible to see the airport runway and the terminal building, as well as the two largest churches, La Catedral and Iglesia La Compañia, the Jesuit church that stood on the adjacent block. All the other buildings were humble by comparison and there was no real business district. Except for the airport, Helena decided the profile of the city looked much the same as it would have a century ago.

'The population has reached half a million,' Naldo said proudly, which was four times the number who'd lived here thirty years earlier. He abruptly swerved around a slow-moving car into the oncoming traffic. Horns blared, hand gestures were made, and vehicles went this way and that. But Naldo managed to miss them all and continue on as though nothing had happened.

Helena had been scared so many times since climbing aboard that she didn't even react.

Chad leant forward and said in Helena's ear, 'Is this really necessary?'

Helena noticed that Hanna was asleep across the seat behind her, using his little backpack as a pillow. 'Wake him up, will you?'

Chad leant over and slapped Hanna on the shoulder. 'Hey, man, you're sleeping on the job! You should be scared out of your wits with the rest of us.'

Hanna sat up with a jolt, gun in hand, eyes looking about groggily. 'I'm up!'

'I realise all this seems a little strange,' Helena said, facing her bodyguards. 'And the probability is, it's going to get even stranger.'

Both bodyguards' expressions were as stern as if they were about to parachute behind enemy lines armed with nothing but a pocketknife.

'When we get to the Plaza de Armas, I'm going to have a good look around. If I start talking to myself, don't ask any questions. If I want you to speak, I'll say your name. I expect you both to be armed and ready. If anyone bothers me, escort them away. Don't shoot anyone unless you have to. Do whatever it takes to give me the freedom I need.' She made eye contact with them individually. 'Are you good with that?'

Hanna replied with a sharp, 'Affirmative.'

'No problem,' Chad replied.

'If you think I've gone crazy, that's fine,' Helena stated. 'That's what you are getting paid for.'

The bus was doing fifty miles per hour as it raced along the busy road, then braked heavily and turned into a narrow side street. Helena checked her watch. 'You have four minutes to get me there, Naldo.'

Naldo frowned. 'We will make it, señorita.'

Hanna checked his Desert Eagle handgun and confirmed there was a bullet in the firing chamber. He made sure the safety was on before tucking it into his body holster. 'You don't pay us to judge if you're crazy,' he said over the sound of the engine. 'You know, I once worked for Mick Jagger. He had me stand guard in his kitchen for three days because he was convinced someone was eating his mayonnaise.' Hanna smiled. 'How funny is that? And Kevin Spacey was just as bad. He's obsessive-compulsive.'

'Should you really be talking about your clients?' Chad asked condescendingly.

'Most of my clients are proud of being a little bit different,' Hanna replied. 'There's no issue there. I could tell you tons of stories.'

'Please don't,' Chad replied.

The bus barged through the back streets, Naldo's hand on the horn in an effort to clear away the locals, the odd car and the donkey-drawn carts. The carts were travelling very slowly, transporting everything from vegetables, grain, wood and even loads of rocks. Most of the women were carrying packs on their backs. The men by comparison were generally walking along empty-handed, or they were smoking cigarettes, lazily driving the little carts along with a bored expression on their face and a whip in their hand.

'Seems they're not into equal rights around here,' Chad commented.

'The women's movement hasn't caught on in Peru,' Hanna observed.

Naldo turned the corner and the Plaza de Armas finally appeared. Helena's heart raced as she scanned the open space from corner to corner hoping a connection would come to her. Naldo brought the bus to an abrupt halt then pointed over at the round clock above the post office. 'We have made it, as I said we would!'

There was just one minute to spare.

'Congratulations,' Helena said distractedly. 'Chad, pay him.'

Naldo opened the hydraulic doors and Helena jumped out onto the pavement. Pizarro's Fountain was just fifty feet in front of her.

With the sun blazing through the scattered clouds, she rushed towards the fountain; the harrowing bus trip to get here was already a distant memory. Helena adjusted the peak of her baseball cap and checked that the nickel-plated revolver was tucked into the pocket of her padded vest. John Hanna walked one step behind her and to her right.

Everything in the plaza seemed familiar, which made her feel more confident.

Helena approached the statuesque black-and-gold fountain that looked like two blossoming flowers stacked on top of each other. Water spurted up generously into the breezy air, then flowed over the sides in delicate streams, between the petals. Standing in the octagonal pool underneath were four golden cherubs blowing arcs of water through their magical little trumpets.

As Helena drew closer, she prepared herself to be amazed – to once again have the ability to look through time and see the man who had changed the course of her life.

The paved courtyard glistened and there were a few people milling around, mostly backpackers with everything they owned strapped to their bodies. The ornate fountain flowed with clean, clear water, the splashing of liquid a refreshing sound after listening to the drone of the bus's diesel engine and manual gearbox for so many hours.

Helena stepped up on the retaining wall and scanned her surroundings, turning full circle. Above the rooftops she could see the rugged terrain that framed the city on all sides like a ring of mountains, but was in fact the ridge of the valley. She carefully studied the distinctive shops and restaurants with the arched stone pillars that suspended the covered walkway. She looked towards La Catedral with the two smaller churches flanking it on either side. Her attention finally shifted across to the post office and the military barracks. A feeling of dread suddenly settled over her, as if something very bad had happened here. At the same moment, the sky became darker again as a bank of brooding clouds passed over the city.

'Where are you, Wilson?' Helena whispered.

All she heard in return was the wind gusting above the rooftops and the clip-clop of a little donkey's hooves as it pulled a wagon filled with corn towards the nearby markets.

52

Cuzco, Peru
La Monasterio Dungeons
Local Time 12:35 pm

24 January 1908

WITH HIS RIGHT shoulder searing with pain, Wilson wanted to scream, but his mouth was so dry he just couldn't. His arms were stretched above his head and his hands were numb. Everything was pitch black – he couldn't see a thing in the darkness and the overwhelming stench that filled his nostrils made him want to puke. He realised after a moment that he was hanging from a wall, his full weight suspended on his wrists. He had no idea where he was or how long he had been there.

Setting his feet on the slippery ground, Wilson stood upright to take the weight off his arms. He felt like his shoulders had been pulled from their sockets. One moment he was walking across the Plaza de Armas in the pouring rain, the next he was here, the wet smell of death filling his nostrils. Taking a deep breath to settle himself, he activated his night vision. Gradually the darkness around him faded and everything came into view.

He was inside a slimy dungeon of some kind, with a low stone ceiling. The floor was shimmering wet. Immediately to his left, at his feet, he was horrified to find the decaying body of a naked woman. She had been dead for some time, more than a few days, because her bruised and battered flesh had deflated somewhat, the moisture having left her twisted corpse. The body was facing away from him, her bowels had vacated and Wilson could see that she was long-limbed with a plaited ponytail, like the Virgins of the Sun.

Looking to his right, Wilson locked eyes on Hiram Bingham shackled to the wall, suspended from his wrists also, his knees hanging just above the ground, his legs tucked behind him. He was fully clothed, leaning forward, head tipped towards his chest. It was difficult to know if he was dead or alive.

Wilson studied the lintel ceiling and the irregular rock walls. Judging by the stonework and the absence of mortar it was definitely an Inca construction. The solid wooden door had a relatively new locking mechanism with a steel latch. Glancing above his head, he scrutinised the two metal shackles securing his wrists with a heavy chain to the masonry wall. He winced as he tried to get a look at the wound on his shoulder that appeared to have been bandaged with cotton wrapping. His jacket had been removed and his shirt ripped open. Judging by the blood on his clothes, it was a gunshot wound. The distinctive odour of burnt flesh wafted through the bandage and he knew his wound had been cauterised, but for what reason he could not understand.

Thinking back, he remembered seeing a brilliant flash from across the plaza, towards the military barracks, the instant before everything went black. It made sense to him now that it had been a gun firing.

'Hiram?' Wilson called out.

Hiram stirred. 'Who's that?' he muttered as he climbed gingerly to his feet. He scanned the darkness, his pupils as wide as saucers. 'Wilson? Is that you?'

'It's me, Hiram.'

'Get me out of here!'

'I'm chained as well,' Wilson replied.

'That's just fucking great!' Hiram sobbed. 'How are we going to escape?'

'Just take it easy.'

Hiram let his head fall to his chest again. 'We're dead. I'm telling you, we're dead. You promised me fame and fortune, and this is how it ends.' He tried to yank himself free, but the chains just rattled against the stonework. 'In the pitch-fucking-black, chained to a fucking wall, God knows where. They whipped me, Wilson! Some lunatic whipped me – he was asking me about *you*! And my wrists, they hurt like hell.' He began to whimper as he continued pulling at his shackles. 'I couldn't stand up anymore, I was so tired. We're going to fucking *die* down here, I tell ya.' He finally stopped struggling with the chains and just stood quietly.

'We'll find a way out,' Wilson replied.

'I can't see anything,' Hiram sobbed. 'And the smell . . . Something's dead down here. I know that's what it is – it fucking stinks.'

Wilson looked again at the female corpse on the ground next to him. 'Just take it easy, Hiram. Let me figure this out.'

'It's that stupid Inca Cube!' Hiram continued. 'The bishop of Cuzco – the *fucking bishop* – he asked me about it. He asked me and I told him what I knew – *all of it*. I told him about you and the Amazons. About Vilcapampa. About the Inca Cube. He didn't even look surprised. Then everything went black and I found myself down here.'

Wilson could see the terror on Hiram's face.

'There's only pain and death for us,' Hiram whimpered. '*Please do something*. Use those powers of yours to get us the hell out of here.'

Unable to clench his fists, Wilson knew that the blood had drained from his hands. He needed to heal himself before he could affect his escape. On the back of his head he could feel a large bump; it was throbbing.

'Not even I am strong enough to get out of these chains,' Wilson said, rattling the metal so that Hiram could hear.

'That's just swell,' Hiram moaned. 'Just swell.'

Helena hadn't been at Pizarro's fountain, Wilson realised. A sense of worry suddenly filled Wilson's heart at the thought of something happening to her.

'You promised me fame and fortune,' Hiram muttered.

'They haven't killed us yet,' Wilson replied.

'And for what terrible reason is that? We weren't the ones who opened up the inner temple and freed the Cube! You told me we *wouldn't* be cursed.'

'Whoever controls the Cube bandaged my wound.'

'They bandaged your wound?'

'You'd do anything to get out of here, wouldn't you, Hiram? If all it took to escape this place was to touch the Cube, you'd do it is my guess.'

Hiram looked out into the darkness, his dilated pupils searching desperately for a sign of brightness anywhere. 'You said it was evil?'

'I can feel the Cube is close,' Wilson announced. 'I can feel it calling me. Can you feel it, Hiram? Can you feel it?'

There was no way of knowing how much time had passed before Wilson saw a faint strip of light appear at the bottom of the solid wooden door. He guessed that it was a few hours, but it was almost impossible to judge. The sound of footsteps, very faint at first, grew louder. It was obvious that it was just one person, walking very slowly, shuffling almost, which added to the dread Wilson felt. The irregular footsteps made a very distinctive sound that he guessed were from cobbled boots.

The strip of light under the door brightened.

A key was inserted into the lock, there was a metallic click, and the latch was eventually turned. Hiram cowered away from the light. The door slowly creaked open and the orange glow of the lamp expanded out across the wet floor to reveal the true horror of this killing place.

In total contrast, a holy man dressed in ornate papal robes appeared. He was in his mid fifties, his gaunt face creased and expressionless. In one hand he held a sterling silver hurricane lamp, in the other a large brass key. Carefully placing the lamp on the floor, he turned around, eased the heavy door closed with a creak, inserted the key and turned the lock.

The metallic sound was the trigger for Hiram to start

whimpering. 'There's a body on the floor,' he whispered. 'A naked body.'

The pitiful orange flame from the lamp illuminated the moss-covered walls and betrayed the piles of faeces, dried blood and guts. Both Wilson and Hiram stood helpless, their arms shackled above their heads, wondering what horrific fate awaited them.

The priest picked up the lamp and moved closer, his shoulders hunched, his focus entirely on Wilson. He didn't shift his gaze for even one moment, despite the mutilated body lying there.

'Do you know who I am?' the priest asked as he carefully placed the light on the floor again so that his face was half in shadow.

'Please set us free,' Hiram interrupted. '*Please.*'

'You will shut your mouth!' the bishop snapped. He was wearing the traditional robes of a bishop: a purple ankle-length cassock covered by a white embroidered rochet that reached to his knees. Around his neck hung a heavy pectoral cross, forged in silver.

'I know who you are,' Wilson replied.

The priest's expression did not alter. 'I am Francisco of Santo Domingo, thirty-third Bishop of Cuzco. I have been searching for you, Wilson Dowling. For me, this is a truly disappointing moment.' There was sadness in his voice. 'I was expecting so much more.'

'I am sorry to disappoint you,' Wilson said.

'You have a special gift of strength and healing, but that gift alone is not enough, it seems. How disappointing.'

'Where is the Inca Cube?' Wilson asked. 'I can feel its power close by.'

At that moment, the bishop's voice deepened and his words became more precise. 'Just how is it that you know of the Inca Cube?'

'I come from a place where the Cube is revered,' Wilson replied.

'*Liar!*' the bishop shouted. His booming voice set Wilson's pulse racing. 'I will ask again: how is it that you know about the Inca Cube?'

Wilson carefully considered his response – he knew somehow that it was the spirit of the Cube he was now talking to. 'I come from the future,' he eventually replied. 'I travel the pathways of time at the will of God. I was sent to this *time* and to this *place* on a mission.' Wilson threw his gaze in Hiram's direction. 'To lead this man to the lost city of Vilcapampa. I successfully achieved this aim, but was unable to leave because the Inca Cube had been taken from its resting place.'

'You travel time?' the bishop replied, seemingly unsurprised by the revelation.

'I am from the future. Many hundreds of years from now.'

'That is the source of your power?'

Wilson nodded. 'That is my gift.'

'You are tall,' the bishop said as he stepped closer, studying Wilson from every angle. 'And strong.' He didn't get close enough so that Wilson could strike out at him with his feet. 'I had the military surgeon remove the bullet from your shoulder, then cauterise and bandage the wound. The doctor was surprised the bullet did not kill you.'

'My thanks to you for saving me.'

'You are worth saving, my child. You can heal yourself. You have strength and speed beyond belief, and you can see in the dark like an owl, it seems.' The bishop paused a moment. 'Can you travel both backwards and forwards in time?'

'If the portals are open, then anything is possible,' Wilson said. 'But if the planets are not aligned then I can be stuck, as I have been stuck here for many years.'

'How long have you waited?' the bishop asked.

'Eight years,' Wilson replied.

'Where are the Virgins of the Sun?'

This was the moment when Wilson would know for certain if the spirit of the Inca Cube could read his mind or not. 'I went to Pitcos, their fortress city. But when I arrived they were gone. The meagre buildings were deserted, their possessions strewn about as if they had left in a terrible hurry. I suspected that you had sent men to kill them and they were forced to flee their pathetic outpost.'

'How many warriors did they have?' the bishop asked.

'That is difficult to know; maybe twenty warriors in all, and their families. Impressive women they are – strong and able-bodied. I imagine they would be dangerous adversaries in one-on-one combat.'

'Do you know what happens if I am killed?' Bishop Francisco asked. 'If this body . . .' he pinched at the skin on his chest, 'is lost?'

'Your soul goes into another,' Wilson replied.

The bishop nodded. 'That is correct.' He brazenly stepped forward and pulled open Wilson's shirt to look at his chest and abdominal muscles. 'You are indeed an impressive specimen.'

The bishop's proximity and the sound of his raspy voice made Wilson's skin crawl. He knew he could easily grab the monsignor between his thighs and snap his neck like a twig, but he didn't move a muscle as the bishop reached out to pull away the bandages from his right shoulder. He then prodded the wound.

'You indeed have the power to heal yourself,' he muttered. He stepped back, making him just a shadowy figure with the glowing lamp behind him. 'Maybe you have a purpose after all.'

'Please reveal yourself to me,' Wilson stated. 'I have waited my whole life so that I may communicate with the fifth dimension of the dead. You are the most powerful force in the universe. I have seen what you can do.'

'Will you be my servant?' the bishop asked.

'I could have killed that priest's body when you were close to me, but I did not. I understand your power, Great One. Reveal yourself to me so that I am not fooled into believing that this pitiful-looking man before me is my master.'

Bishop Francisco struck Wilson across the face, making a loud *crack* with the flat of his palm. 'How dare you!' Frantically reaching into his robes, he drew out a solid-silver cross about the size of a hammer and began repeatedly smacking it against Wilson's head.

Having lost his footing on the slippery floor, Wilson could feel the skin on his forehead split as the priest beat him with increasing force. He battled the instinct to defend himself, knowing it was futile to resist. Suspended helplessly from his wrists, he felt the warm blood streaming down his face, soaking his chest and clothing.

'That is enough!' the bishop called out, his voice deeper and grainier once again. He took three paces backwards and began licking Wilson's flesh from the sharp corner of the cross. 'So you want to know who I am?' the bishop asked, a smile unexpectedly rising to his blood-covered lips. 'You are in the presence of greatness.'

Wilson struggled to his feet as best he could, unsteady from his beating, slipping over twice before regaining his balance.

'You did not whimper when you were beaten,' the bishop said. 'It says something about a man that is impossible to judge in any other way.'

Wilson's face and jaw were scorching as he glared through his one good eye at the skinny priest before him.

'You are worthy and I will reveal myself to you.' A flickering of scarlet appeared within the bishop's pupils. He stood tall now as if new life had suddenly filled his frail body. 'My name is Francisco Pizarro of Trujillo. Illegitimate son of Gonzalo Pizarro Rodriguez de Aguilar. Liberator of Cuzco. Appointed Marshal of Peru in the year of our Lord 1532 by the King of Spain, Charles V. I am founder of Lima, conqueror of the heathens and the bringer of Christianity to the savages of South America. Obey me, Wilson Dowling, and your every dream will come to pass.'

'I knew it was you,' Wilson replied. 'Only the spirit of a great and powerful man such as Francisco Pizarro could have drawn me here as you have.'

'You will be my servant forever more,' he announced.

'You were murdered by those close to you . . . and you have chosen to live again,' Wilson said. 'You are indeed a god.'

'You know of my life?'

'I know everything there is to know, Great One. In

the year 1541, twenty-five soldiers brandishing swords stormed your home during a dinner party. A fight ensued. Although you were unarmed, you fought them with your half-brother, Alcantara, by your side. He was the first to die, his head cut off before your eyes. In a dexterous move, you grabbed a sword from one of your attackers and bravely struck two men down, running through a third. But as you were trying to extract the blade you were set upon and a knife was plunged into your throat. As you fell to the floor you were pierced with countless sword strikes from all sides.'

Bishop Francisco's face hardened with anger. 'They were meant to have been my friends,' he growled.

Before Wilson had a chance to respond, the deep voice continued. 'I did not whimper or ask for mercy. No . . . that is for the weak! I painted a giant cross on the floor with my own blood and called out, "Come my faithful sword, companion of all my deeds! Save me mighty Jesus, Lord of *the* world, so that I may have revenge in the afterlife! I will live again!"' The bishop was panting with rage, spit dripping from the corners of his bloodied mouth.

'Those men who killed you were traitors!' Wilson announced. 'They met a fitting end. Diego de Almargo was caught and executed, his head buried separately from his body as a warning to others to never mention his name. Without his head, he could not go to Heaven or Hell – he would forever roam the spirit world, desperate and alone.'

'You know a great deal,' the voice of Pizarro stated.

'Each and every one of your attackers did not live more than a year.'

'You know my story well. I never tire of hearing of their pathetic fate.'

Wilson lowered his head in a sign of respect. 'Great One, I will do your bidding. I will be your right hand.'

Bishop Francisco's eyes were glowing red. 'You are my servant now, Wilson Dowling. As I said on the day of my death, I will have my revenge by living again – and live again I will.'

The flickers of red vanished from Bishop Francisco's pupils, his shoulders slumped and his bony hands hung limp by his sides. It seemed that the spirit of Pizarro had momentarily left him.

'I hoped for more,' the bishop said with disappointment in his voice. 'I thought you would be the one to save me. But it seems there is no escape.'

Lifting the lamp from the floor as if it weighed a ton, the old man shuffled towards the door, unlocked the latch, stepped outside, shut the door and turned the key. The strip of light diminished as the bishop's footsteps receded, until Wilson and Hiram were left standing in the utter darkness once again.

'What the hell are you doing?' Hiram whimpered. 'Telling him that you can *travel time* . . . telling him you will be his servant. You've lost your mind,' Hiram sobbed. 'Didn't you see his eyes? That man is evil.'

'Pizarro is my master now,' Wilson replied to the darkness. 'My powers of strength and healing are his. He is the reason I am here in Cuzco . . . God has proclaimed it so.'

53

Cuzco, Peru
Hotel Monasterio
Local Time 5:35 pm

24 January 2014

THE SKY WAS noticeably darker as Helena headed towards
the hotel, which was located just five minutes' walk from
the Plaza de Armas. Utterly exhausted, it was only now
that she realised she hadn't slept at all the previous night.
The clouds had been steadily gathering all afternoon and
there was thunder in the distance. She'd decided it was best
to make her way to the hotel and get some rest before her
return to Pizarro's Fountain later that evening.

Stepping off the narrow laneway into the Hotel
Monasterio, Helena noticed the Royal Arms Escutcheon
of Spain that was carved proudly into the stone next to the
door. At one time, the Spanish marked everything owned
by the king. The impressive cedar doors were tall and
heavily reinforced with strips of interlocking hardwood
with giant brass studs. Just inside were two modern glass
doors with the hotel's emblem etched on the surface.

The rain suddenly began falling at a furious rate as the
doorman swung the glass door open. Hanna was walking
ten paces behind them and the downpour caught him for
only a few seconds, but long enough to saturate his clothes
completely.

'When it rains here, it really rains!' Hanna said as he
stepped off the street, shaking the water from his dark
hair.

Helena stood behind the glass and looked out into the rain, which was so furious that streams of water were already running down the incline of the cobblestone laneway. A sense of regret suddenly filled her at the thought of missing the opportunity to see Wilson this past evening. There was no telling what had happened to him and where he was now. She turned towards the impressive foyer and looked upon the two life-sized paintings, oil on canvas, adorning the towering walls. To her right was the resplendent Virgin Mary, to her left was the calm figure of Joseph of Nazareth; they were both wearing long, flowing robes and each had a glowing halo surrounding their heads.

The Hotel Monasterio looked a relatively ordinary building from the outside, with its two-storey whitewashed walls and bare foundation stones that had certainly been cut by Inca hands. It was only when Helena stepped into the foyer that she realised it was a grand Renaissance building covering three levels, with a huge courtyard in the middle. All the way around the inside were broad walkways on two levels with imposing arches on stone pillars that looked out upon the spectacular manicured gardens. In the very centre stood a healthy-looking cedar tree whose trunk and leafy limbs stretched upwards three times the height of the rooftop. The doorman saw Helena looking and commented that the tree was the oldest in all of Cuzco.

Thunder rumbled overhead and the walls and floor shook. Heavy rain was streaming off the angled terracotta tiles into the courtyard like a four-sided waterfall, making it difficult to see across to the other side.

All Helena could think about was how she was going to connect with Wilson again.

'The hotel manager wants to meet you,' Chad said as she returned from the front desk holding Helena's titanium American Express card. 'He wants to apologise for how we were stuck at Machu Picchu Lodge.' Two hotel staff wearing Monasterio uniforms stood politely behind her.

'I don't want to meet anyone,' Helena said curtly. 'Just get the key.'

'Ms Capriarty is tired,' Chad said, turning around. 'I will have the adjacent bedroom, and Mr Hanna will have the room on the other side.'

'I'm not sure what you're looking for,' Hanna said to Helena. 'But I know you'll achieve your objective if you try hard enough.'

'Find out where the business centre is,' Helena replied.

Hanna immediately headed for the front desk as Helena strolled into the expansive waiting area that could have been mistaken for a medieval hall in its size and construction. The stone floor was covered with rugs, which Helena assumed were alpaca. There were multiple groups of wingback lounges and sofas set in pairs and facing each other. In the centre was a Spanish colonial dining table with ten chairs. Four circular wrought-iron chandeliers were suspended between the stone archways. Above them she could see the exposed wooden floorboards of the next level. At the far end of the room was a giant fireplace neatly stacked with timber, ready for the strike of a match to set it aflame.

A teenage girl was sitting at one of the tables, drinking from a yellow mug. She was watching television on her iPhone – an American sitcom, judging by the voices.

'Do you know where the business centre is?' Helena asked.

The young girl looked up. 'Err . . . yes, I do.' She pointed. 'You go across that courtyard.' Her accent was from New York. 'The business centre is there and down the stairs. You can walk around the outside.'

Hanna approached with a booklet in hand. Helena pointed in the opposite direction. 'I know where it is. Follow me.'

The clamour of the rain was deafening and the humidity was thick in the air as they strode along the covered walkway. Hanna walked beside her trying to read the booklet and match Helena's pace at the same time.

'It says here that this hotel was built on an Inca palace.' Hanna had to raise his voice to be heard. He looked about before studying the booklet again. 'This place was once called Amaru Qhala.' He was clearly struggling with the pronunciation. 'It says this was one of the most impressive Inca buildings in Cuzco. The Spanish knocked it down so they could use the stones.'

A polished sign beside the door read 'Business Centre'. The little reception area was empty and Helena descended the carpeted stairs. The corridor was well lit, the floors carpeted, the claret-coloured walls held baroque paintings of Spanish conquistadors on horseback in full battle garb. Surprisingly, the underground corridor went for some distance and Helena concluded they were not directly under the hotel anymore. The business centre was on the left, a simple room with a relatively low ceiling, but the corridor continued on.

There were four cubicles inside the business centre, each with a wooden desk, leather chair, a computer and a printer. The room was empty so Helena strolled in and sat at the desk furthest from the door. She drew out the nickel-plated handgun from under her vest and placed it on the table beside her. With a touch of the spacebar the computer came to life with the Hotel Monasterio website. Beautiful images rotated onto the screen: the courtyard, the reception hall, the expansive hotel suites.

Helena moved the cursor to Google and typed in '24 January 1908 Cuzco', then hit the enter key. The screen flashed to life with search results:

Today in History **January 24**
Torrential rain, due to El Niño, in the Cusco area left at least 126 people dead . . .

Helena's thoughts were reeling. When she'd looked into Wilson's world, the weather had been exactly the same as it was here, so it was logical to expect that the streets here were going to flood later that evening also.

One hundred and twenty-six people dead.

That seems like a very high number, Helena thought.

She hit enter again, but there was precious little information other than the dramatic headline.

She typed 'Cusco weather'.

The results came up on the screen: '100% chance of rain, with local flooding'. The synoptic chart had a swirling low-pressure system trapped between the Andes and the Pacific coastline. It was certainly an El Niño event.

Staring at the screen for quite some time, Helena eventually typed 'Captain Lucho Gonzales', but the results only related to an Argentinean soccer player, a captain of the first division side Olympic Marseille. There was nothing that came up regarding any Peruvian soldier stationed in Cuzco.

Helena kept typing, searching every link she could think of. She typed in 'Crucifixion Cuzco', but found nothing. 'Crucifixion Cuzco Corsell Santillana' – still nothing. Then 'Juan Santillana 1908'. There was dozens of results and Facebook pages, but nothing that related to the name carved into the stone at Machu Picchu. Then she typed 'Juan Santillana Machu Picchu'. The hundreds of results that came back were interesting:

Machu Picchu | Photo

www.travelblog.org › South America › Peru › Cusco › Machu Picchu

Machu Picchu. Engraved signatures of the first two men who really found **Machu Picchu**, Jesus Vellarde and **Juan Santillana** ...

Hiram Bingham may have been credited with the official discovery of Machu Picchu, but it seemed these two *mestizos* had certainly been to the lost city before him.

John Hanna was standing guard in the doorway, facing out into the corridor, reading the little booklet about the hotel. His expression was a picture of concentration.

As Helena typed, she suddenly felt queasy. It was an odd sensation, like she needed food, or she'd eaten something that made her want to be sick. Taking a deep breath to calm herself, she placed both hands on the desk as her vision suddenly went to black. Her connection with the past was engaging.

The faint sound of footsteps echoed through the darkness around her. Helena pressed her hands to her face, trying to calm her mind. The sound was distinctive: cobbled shoes on a stone floor; a slow, shuffling gate – very slow – which only added to the dread she felt as the footsteps drew closer. A faint orange glow appeared from the doorway, getting brighter with each passing second.

Resisting the urge to cry out, it took all her effort to bring the present world and the nickel-plated handgun on the table in front of her back into view. Grabbing the gun, she walked cautiously towards the door; her visions were now flashing backwards and forwards between the past and the present.

She pressed her index finger to Hanna's chest. 'No matter what I say or do, *only* respond if I actually say your name.' She then let her vision revert to the past and peered around the corner towards the approaching light.

Hanna threw his booklet aside and drew his handgun also.

Helena's images were flitting between the past and the present, light and darkness, and it required all her concentration not to become disoriented. She could hear the footsteps against the stone floor as clearly as if they were only a few feet away. And voices. Descending the stairs was the distinctive glow of a hurricane lamp – a single orange flame. Carrying the lamp was a man wearing what looked like the robes of a Catholic priest. She could not see him clearly because his face was obscured by the shadow thrown up from the handle.

A man's voice came from further up the stairs – he was speaking Spanish. 'We should kill him immediately,' Helena could translate. It was a soldier dressed in military uniform and carrying a rifle.

'You will escort him to the church as I have requested,' the priest replied. 'If he resists, you will kill him.'

'*Vamonos!*' the soldier yelled.

From up above, a dozen footsteps clattered down the staircase. Helena stepped out into the corridor, her gun pointing towards the approaching men. Except for the priest, the rest of them were soldiers in Peruvian military uniform. Every single man was grim-faced. There was no logical reason for why Helena would point her gun at the approaching men, who were certainly 106 years in the past, but she did anyway. The problem was, her actions were freaking Hanna out and he was kneeling beside her, aiming his gun in the same direction.

The priest carrying the oil lamp shuffled slowly forward along a bare stone corridor – there was no carpet, no lights, no paintings. Pools of shiny water had collected on the stone floor.

Helena gazed back into what was now the business centre. There was just enough light to see that it had no door – the room was empty and there was mould growing on the walls. If Wilson was here somewhere, it was logical to assume that he was further down the corridor. Using the illumination of the oil lamp to guide her, Helena ran into the blackness. A few yards ahead she came to a heavy wooden door. It existed in both the past and the present. She reached for the handle and swung the door open.

In the past the door was still closed, but she was able to step right through the image.

Once again she was in total darkness except for the faint strip of light that was radiating through the gap at the very bottom. Wilson was close, she could feel it.

54

Cuzco, Peru
Hotel Monasterio
Local Time 5:55 pm

24 January 1908

SCANNING THE DARKNESS, Wilson looked towards Hiram who was slumped over again, hanging uncomfortably from his wrists. The heavy metal chains above Wilson's own head looked formidable and he wondered if he would be able to rip the shackles free from the stone. There was little doubt he had the strength to bend the steel, but his wrists would certainly break if he applied too much force too quickly.

If Hiram heard Wilson trying to escape, the spirit of Pizarro would be alerted. The Inca Cube communicated through the minds of men – therefore, whatever Hiram heard and saw, the spirit of Pizarro would know as well. That was certainly the reason Wilson had been singled out while he was walking across the Plaza de Armas. The Inca Cube could not see into *his* mind and that made him possible to identify. It also had to be the reason why Hiram Bingham was conveniently shackled to the wall just ten feet away. Hiram was an unwitting spy and Wilson needed to be very cautious about what he said and did in front of his friend.

Wilson scanned the mutilated body of the woman lying on the floor. Her decaying corpse was giving off a putrid scent and he figured that it was no accident that the corpse was here. It was certainly related to Pizarro's sick plans.

A faint glow gradually appeared through the gap under

the heavy wooden door. At first, Wilson was unsure exactly what he was looking at. The light was getting brighter and didn't have the distinctive orange glow of an oil lamp. Suddenly a figure appeared, passing directly through the wooden door like a spirit.

It was Helena, carrying a handgun!

Wilson wanted to call out to let her know he was standing there in the darkness, but he knew that anything he said would be overheard by Hiram.

'You need to remain calm,' Wilson said, his voice steady. 'I'm right here.'

Helena tried to focus on where the sound was coming from, but it was clear that she was blinded by the darkness.

'Wilson! Thank God. I can't see anything,' she replied, her voice laced with worry.

'Just stay calm,' Wilson said again.

Hiram began moaning as he climbed to his feet. 'We're gonna die down here,' he whimpered. 'My wrists hurt so much. I just want to rub them – that's not too much to ask, is it?'

Wilson looked in Helena's direction. 'This dungeon is not where we will die, Hiram Bingham. God will send an angel to save us both – a beautiful angel.'

Helena was breathing hard. 'Wilson, can you see me?' she asked, her eyes scanning the darkness.

'I can see you,' he replied.

Hiram interrupted. 'So what if you can?'

'There is a priest coming!' Helena said in a panic. 'He's leading a group of soldiers here to take you away! They were talking in Spanish, saying they would kill you if you don't cooperate!'

'I can see you there,' Wilson confirmed again. 'Hiram is shackled to the wall as I am. The body of a dead woman is on the floor. I can't escape.'

Helena's image was shrouded in a misty white light.

'How are you shackled to the wall?' she asked.

'With steel chains.'

'What the hell are you talking about?' Hiram asked. 'Of course they're steel chains!'

'Men are coming down the corridor to take you away!' Helena said desperately. 'The soldiers have rifles . . .'

A faint orange glow gradually began to appear at the bottom of the wooden door. 'Bishop Francisco is coming,' Wilson said as if he was in a trance. 'Come closer.'

'You have to escape,' Helena pleaded.

'I can't,' Wilson responded. 'Come closer.'

Hiram began muttering to himself, 'Christ, this is no way for a Yale graduate to die.'

Helena eased nearer but it was obvious that she couldn't see where Wilson was. She had to work her way around various objects so that she could move further into the room. In the future, this room wasn't empty, Wilson realised.

'The bishop is the master,' Wilson rambled. 'Possessed by the powerful spirit of the Inca Cube, possessed by the conquistador Francisco Pizarro of Trujillo.'

The orange glow was becoming brighter and Wilson knew he was running out of time to explain what was needed. 'If I am to see the Inca Cube for myself, then I will need your help to locate it. Will you help me?'

'I'll help you!' Helena replied, trying to climb over some stacked boxes. The glow of the oil lamp filtered under the door and she could now make out Wilson's image shackled to the wall with his hands above his head. She could see Hiram Bingham in chains there also. Just as Wilson had said, there was a rotting corpse lying on the floor.

A key was inserted into the lock and the mechanism turned with a distinctive wrench of metal. The door gradually creaked open and the light spilled out across the floor, further illuminating the horrors of this place.

Wilson's face and clothes were covered in blood and it was obvious that he had been badly beaten. On the floor lay the decaying carcass of a woman, her flesh was bruised and torn, her dead eyes hanging open. Helena felt her stomach rise into her mouth as she stepped forward.

Hiram attempted to cower away from the light, but there was nowhere to hide.

Bishop Francisco shuffled into the room and placed his lamp in the middle of the floor. It was the first time Helena had seen the bishop's face and a shiver ran up her spine. Diverting her vision to the present, she was standing inside the hotel's storage room. Cardboard boxes filled with paperwork and other junk were stacked three high and it was difficult to negotiate her way around.

'Hanna, watch the door and don't let anyone near me!' Helena called out as she forced some boxes aside and moved further into the room. From the look on her bodyguard's face it was obvious that he thought she was losing her mind.

Bishop Francisco pointed across the chamber. 'You have healed again, I see.' A smile unfolded on his gaunt face. 'You are quite a prize.'

Helena finally eased herself next to Wilson, her gun pointing directly at the bishop.

A soldier stood in the doorway wearing a blue uniform with gold buttons – he was obviously an officer. His clothing was soaked. Beads of water were still dripping off the wide brim of his military hat.

'Keep your men back,' Bishop Francisco ordered. 'Wilson Dowling is responsible for the horrific evils in this place. Unlock his bonds so we may cleanse him.' The stocky officer remained in the doorway, staring at the mutilated body on the floor. 'Capitán Gonzales, unshackle him!'

The bishop's loud voice finally spurred the soldier into action.

'*Capitán Gonzales!*' Helena said. 'He's the man I told you about! He's the one! According to Don Eravisto, you will murder his family in cold blood . . .'

Gonzales's expression was one of horror and disbelief as he stepped into the dungeon. His dark eyes narrowed in on Wilson. 'I shot you!' he said with acid in his tone. 'You should be dead, you unholy creature!'

'You should be at home with your family,' Wilson said to him in reply.

*

Captain Gonzales ran forward and slammed the butt of his rifle into Wilson's chest, smashing the wind from his lungs. Helena tried to intervene, but the swipe of her gun went right through the captain without making any contact. As Wilson hung defenceless from his wrists, he was struck again and again, this time in the forehead. Groaning in pain, his vision coming in and out, Wilson briefly caught sight of Bishop Francisco's face – the bastard was smiling.

'That is enough,' the bishop eventually said. 'Unshackle him.'

Gonzales was breathing heavily as he inserted the key into the latch, the pin released and the chain unhooked. Wilson fell, half-unconscious, to the stinking floor.

'You mustn't fight him,' Helena urged. 'Just lie there. There are too many soldiers outside the door for you to overcome them all.'

Gonzales clubbed Wilson in the head with his rifle again, then twisted his arms behind his back and clapped handcuffs on his wrists.

'You have to stay calm,' Helena urged.

'I am resigned to my fate,' Wilson said without moving. He turned his eyes to Bishop Francisco who was standing above him. 'Whatever you wish of me, I will obey. You are the Great Master; Pizarro of Trujillo, liberator of Cuzco, marshal of –'

Gonzales kicked Wilson in the stomach as he lay on the floor. 'Shut up, you evil creature!' He pushed Wilson's face into the filth with his boot.

The bishop pointed at Hiram. 'Bring him also.'

Captain Gonzales struck Hiram with the butt of his rifle, knocking him off his feet with one blow. He released Bingham's chains, kicked him repeatedly in the stomach then handcuffed him. Gonzales grabbed both Wilson and Hiram by the wrists, yanked them to their feet and forced them towards the door.

Wilson spat a gob of blood at Gonzales's feet. 'When I am your master, I will not forget the treatment you have given me.'

Bishop Francisco rubbed his hands together with glee.

'You seek revenge? I like that in a man. It is the measure of his conviction. But heed this warning, Wilson Dowling: if you try to escape, I will have you killed in the most painful way. Your skin will be peeled from your body, and you will be made to eat your own flesh.'

Both Wilson and Hiram were pushed along the narrow corridor between the assembled soldiers. The sweetness of fresh air filled Wilson's nostrils as he was forced up a lengthy cut-stone staircase. All the while, he was conscious of Helena's glowing brightness next to him.

She was talking, calmly and steadily. 'There are ten soldiers, including Captain Gonzales. It will be pouring with rain when we get outside. There will be flooding tonight – I've read that one hundred and twenty-six people will die in Cuzco this very evening. You can use that knowledge to your advantage.'

As Wilson was pushed up the stairs, he could hear the rain beating down outside. 'Where am I?' he whispered.

'Underneath La Monesterio, the monastery where the bishop lives,' Helena replied. 'About five minutes' walk from the Plaza de Armas. In the future, this place is a hotel.'

'The bishop will lead you to the Inca Cube,' Wilson whispered. 'Stay with him no matter what the cost. If any man touches it, he will be possessed. If a woman touches the Cube, she will die.' His voice was barely audible.

Reaching the top of the stairs, Wilson was pushed outside into the hazy light of the central courtyard. It was such a relief to feel the cleansing rain hitting his face and clothes. He hoped it would wash away the disgusting smell of death that he feared he would never forget.

'Where are you taking me?' Wilson called out.

Bishop Francisco was shuffling just ahead of him, but he ignored the question. He stepped his way through the pouring rain, across the enclosed courtyard past a healthy cypress tree whose branches and leaves were being tossed about by the powerful and chaotic wind.

'You must tell me where we're going,' Wilson said again, but the bishop did not answer.

Every few steps, Wilson was nudged forward with the stock of a rifle. Some of the nudges were so hard that they nearly knocked him from his feet. The soldiers were doing the same to Hiram and Wilson was becoming angry.

'Just stay calm,' Helena replied.

Bishop Francisco led the group through the foyer and back outside into the rear laneway. The rain continued to pour as they headed up the incline, stepping carefully from the sky across the fast-moving water that was running down the cobblestones.

Although it seemed like daylight in patches, the sky overhead was as black as ebony. The clouds were twisting into strange formations against the ravages of the wind and rain. Wilson was hit again on the back and did his best to keep his footing. He stepped closer to Hiram and pushed him along also. 'We are going to see a new world,' Wilson yelled out optimistically. 'We have a new God now!'

Hiram squinted at him, the rain beating down against his unshaven face. 'You've lost your mind,' he muttered. 'We're gonna die.'

Rounding the corner, they passed a row of sandbags with three soldiers standing guard. Through the blankets of swirling rain, Wilson could just make out that they were entering the Plaza de Armas. To his left, he saw the silhouette of La Catedral at the top of the stairs, against the brooding afternoon sky. All around the perimeter of the church were sandbags four feet high. Below the staircase, the embattlements had been washed away by the river of brown water that was ripping through the plaza from north to south. The open square was an obvious accumulation point for the torrent of mud and debris that was now gushing through the city – the roar it made was similar to that of the mighty Urubamba.

'Stay with the Bishop no matter what the cost,' Wilson whispered. 'I will find you.'

'Don't do anything stupid,' Helena replied, looking around at the dozens of soldiers with guns. 'There will be better places than this to try and escape.'

The heavy rain was thick in the air and it was difficult to

breathe. All the soldiers, Bishop Francisco included, held their hands to their faces to shelter their nose and mouth.

Thunder rumbled overhead.

A bright flash of lightning suddenly ignited the murky sky, making everyone flinch.

Mustering all his strength, Wilson ran shoulder first into Captain Gonzales, easily flattening him. Propelling himself into the air, Wilson did a spinning back kick, which collected the side of another soldier's head. The unconscious man flew against two other soldiers, arms and legs flailing in all directions, and they all tumbled down the stairs towards the torrent.

It was difficult to be smooth with his hands clasped behind his back but Wilson managed just enough grip on the slippery cobblestones to leap over the fallen men. He zigzagged left then right, then took one more giant leap and cleared the row of sandbags before flying through the air and landing on the stones on the other side. Guns fired. Bullets whizzed past him on both sides. He sucked in a deep breath and dove head first into the muddy torrent of floodwater.

Helena looked on as Wilson threw himself into the rapids. Bullets struck the water all around him. The shots were so loud in Helena's ears that she was almost stupefied by the sound. In both the past and the present, the exact same torrent of water was flowing south towards the lowest point of the Plaza de Armas. Helena's instinct was to dive into the river also, but both Chad and Hanna held her back. Wrenching herself free, she he ran along the bottom step, looking away towards the Avenue de Sol, where the brown, muddy surge was flowing.

'You can't go in there!' Chad pleaded.

'You won't survive!' Hanna yelled.

All three of them had their handguns drawn – thankfully there was no one else out in this appalling weather to see them. Helena stood on the very edge of the stairs, rain pounding her face, following Wilson's submerged body as it disappeared into the distance. His head didn't come up for air and she wondered if one of the bullets had felled him just as he entered the torrent.

Rifles continued firing, puffs of gun smoke wafting into the heavy sky. Helena raced towards the soldiers as they stood on high ground, each of them with rifles to the shoulder targeting Wilson's submerged body as it skidded away into the storm. Frantically lashing out with her fists, Helena tried to intervene, to save Wilson somehow, but her punches passed right through the soldiers' skulls. In desperation, she stepped in front of the soldiers to block their aim, just as their rifles fired.

The bullets passed harmlessly through her. No matter how she tried, there was nothing Helena could do.

Stay with the bishop no matter what the cost, she remembered.

Turning towards the church, she locked her gaze on Bishop Francisco. Thunder rumbled overhead as he angrily pointed to Hiram Bingham who was lying face first on the cobblestones. 'Get him inside the church!' the bishop yelled. 'That is an order, Capitán!'

55

Cuzco, Peru
Plaza de Armas
Local Time 6:42 pm

24 January 1908

BY THE TIME Gonzales pressed the stock of his rifle to
his shoulder, the devil Wilson Dowling had leapt over his
men, and the sandbags, before hitting the ground on the
other side. The jump was impossibly long, easily fifteen
feet from a standing start, with his hands clasped behind
his back! Just seeing the inhuman display made Gonzales
pause long enough for Dowling to find his feet, then leap
head first into the torrent that was ripping through the
Plaza de Armas.

He couldn't possibly survive the rapids, Gonzales told
himself. Not with his wrists shackled.

The fast-moving water had the consistency of mud and
it was filled with all sorts of debris that had been collected
as it gained momentum through the city. There were pieces
of wood, roof tiles, sheets of corrugated iron, small trees
– even a wooden cart shot past, already smashed to pieces
by the many impacts. Gonzales had only seen flooding like
this once before, when he was a small child. The city of
Cuzco was located inside a huge valley and when it rained,
if the downpour was heavy enough, the flooding could be
quick and deadly.

Rifles were firing as Bishop Francisco yelled, 'Do not
let him escape!' But by the time the soldiers made it to the
edge of the stairs, the white devil's body had been washed

out of sight towards the Avenue de Sol. It was difficult to know if he had been hit or not. Gonzales considered diving into the torrent also, but not even he had the courage to enter the awful muck that was moving past so quickly.

Gonzales ordered his men to head in different directions, yelling frantically to everyone he could see, including the sentries who were stationed on the gun emplacements. 'Send search parties!' he shouted over rain. 'I want him dead or alive!'

Bishop Francisco pointed at Hiram Bingham who was lying on the ground in shackles, his cheek pressed to the cobblestones. 'Get him inside the church!' he yelled.

Gonzales lowered his rifle, his mind churning with worry for his family. There was no choice but to obey. Turning away from the water, he yanked the skinny American to his feet then pushed him between the stacked sandbags towards the huge central doors of La Catedral. All the while, he was thinking about the terrible threat Wilson Dowling had so clearly made against him, saying that he needed to be at home with his family.

Gonzales's fists clenched in utter fury. *How did the white devil know that was what I was thinking?*

Bishop Francisco forced open the heavy wooden doors and stepped into the shadowy interior. 'Your soldiers will stand guard outside. You will stay with the prisoner. Drop the locking beam, now,' he ordered, then limped dripping wet towards the decorative altar that adorned the central nave.

Falling to his knees, the bishop's gaze purposely lifted to the life-sized effigy of the Nativity Virgin holding the placid infant Jesus in her arms.

Gonzales instructed his men to guard the church, then reluctantly closed the giant door, which muffled the tumultuous sound from outside. He unhooked the rope and let the giant locking beam lower down behind the door. Turning around, he noticed that the church was mostly dark, except for about twenty candles. He took off his hat and dutifully made the cross of Jesus on his chest. Normally there would have been more than a thousand burning candles setting this place aglow, but today there were very few and nearly all the alcoves were immersed in darkness.

'Please forgive me for what I have done,' the bishop prayed, his frail voice echoing up towards the vaulted ceilings. His palms were pressed together below his chin. 'I am your faithful servant.' It looked like he was sobbing to himself as he knelt there. At the same time a pool of water was forming on the smooth granite floor around him.

Gonzales nudged Bingham further into the great church, then violently shoved him to the floor on the very spot where Monsignor Pera had been brutally murdered just eleven days earlier – the discolouration of the granite still noticeable.

The bishop made the cross of Jesus on his chest. 'I believe in the Holy Spirit and the Holy Catholic Church,' he muttered. 'The communion of the saints, the forgiveness of sin, the resurrection of the body, and the life everlasting.' After a long exhalation, he turned to Hiram Bingham. 'Remove that man's bonds,' the bishop said.

'He will try and escape!' Gonzales replied.

'He will do no such thing.'

'I won't try and escape,' Hiram said. 'Really, I won't. I'll just sit over there and wait until all this –'

Gonzales slapped Hiram across the face. 'Shut up!'

'Unshackle him,' the bishop repeated.

Gonzales removed the circle of keys from his pocket. Stepping forward, he turned the latch on Hiram Bingham's wrists and the handcuffs fell to the floor with a *clank*. Gonzales kicked Bingham in the back, causing him to tumble forward and land face-first next to the bishop.

'I must go home to my family,' Captain Gonzales said. 'Wilson Dowling was swept away towards the Avenue de Sol . . . in that very direction. I must protect my family. I sense that he is a threat to them.'

The bishop stared back. 'You will wait here with me.'

Gonzales wanted to argue, but he was momentarily unable to speak. All he could do was stand there, his breath racing.

'You love your family very much,' Bishop Francisco announced. 'Your wife and three children.' He paused for a long while. 'Which of your children would you say you love the most?'

Goosebumps formed on Gonzales's skin. His hand reached for the revolver concealed within the leather holster on his belt, but no matter how he tried he could not bring himself to open the flap and draw the weapon.

'Which of your children do you love the most?' the bishop asked again.

Captain Gonzales felt weak to the knees, like all the life was being drained from his normally strong body. 'I love them all equally,' he eventually whispered.

'That is noble,' the bishop said from his knees. 'But foolish.' He wearily climbed to one knee, then to his feet. 'You cannot leave. Your place is here with me. The pathetic love you have for your family is at odds with your faith in God, the infant Jesus and this mighty Church. I know you want to reach for your gun and shoot me down, but I am not your enemy – I am merely a mirror of your faith. Wilson Dowling will be coming here, to this very church, and I will need you if I am to guard what is most precious in all of this world.'

'Let me find him and bring him here to you,' Gonzales pleaded. 'I have done it before and I can do it again.'

A perverse smile unfolded on the bishop's face. 'Wilson Dowling is a man of immense power – the Devil's power. He survived when you shot him, and I fear he will survive the rapids. He will return *here*, to this church. When he does, you will take your gun and you will shoot him.'

'If he survives the rapids, he will be near my family home.' Gonzales dropped to his knees in subjugation and looked up at the bishop. 'Please let me leave – I beg you. I pray to Jesus Christ that you will show me compassion in these dark times. I fear for my family's safety –'

'You dare to *pray!*' the bishop yelled. 'If you leave me you are a traitor to God! A traitor to the Church and everything it stands for! If you leave, your worst night-mares *will* come to pass, as God is my witness. You are my right hand – you have proclaimed it so. My right hand is needed *here*! Wilson Dowling is coming . . .'

Gonzales was breathing hard, his arms and legs shaking as he desperately tried to stand and walk away. But no matter how he tried, he was unable to move. Gathering all his courage, he looked deep into the bishop's eyes. 'Wilson Dowling said that you are Francisco Pizarro of Trujillo. Is this true, Great Lord? Is the spirit of Pizarro within you?'

The bishop's eyes flickered red.

'I am the Lord God Himself!' the bishop said with a thundering voice. His shoulders pulled back and he stood tall. 'My *will* is your bidding, Capitán! When Wilson Dowling arrives, you will shoot him. If you succeed, I will protect your family. If you fail, you will watch your children die before your eyes.' He paused. 'Look into my eyes, Capitán. What I say is the Word of God Himself. Obey me, or face His retribution.'

56

Cuzco, Peru
Avenue de Sol
Local Time 6:44 pm

24 January 1908

THE SURGING BROWN current pulled Wilson deeper. With his hands shackled behind him, he couldn't protect himself from the countless underwater impacts, other than to let his body stay supple so as to absorb the fierce blows. He collided with yet another submerged object, which momentarily catapulted him out of the brown sludge before he was quickly dragged under again. He had not taken a breath – there wasn't the opportunity – and he feared that he would not be able to survive the fast-moving torrent for much longer. He'd hoped the volume flooding would slow as it continued, but the opposite seemed to be true – the further it went the stronger the current and the undertow became.

Unable to open his eyes in the stinging mud, Wilson wondered if this was where his life would end. His senses went numb as he slammed into yet another impediment. He had waited eight years to complete his mission in Peru, and in just eight days everything had unravelled. The Inca Cube had been stolen and madness had gripped the world.

A series of random thoughts flashed through his mind as he was pummelled and tossed end over end, not even knowing which way was up. An image of Helena's face came his mind; her expression calm and reassuring. She had found him, just as she said she would. Helena represented so much of what Wilson admired most in people: loyalty, courage and conviction – relentless conviction. If he died now, he would be happy knowing that they had touched each other's lives. Their shared destiny was something that he had not expected, a constant force since he had become Overseer, and he valued it above all other things.

His lungs began convulsing, screaming out for oxygen.

He'd read somewhere that drowning was a pleasant way to die; that people who had been resuscitated claimed that when they pulled in a breath of water they felt no pain, only a serene feeling as if they were floating among the clouds. It was only when the water was flushed from their bodies to revive them that the pain began.

What will it feel like, Wilson wondered, *to drown in a river of mud?*

He thought of Hiram Bingham, a cigarette hanging from his lips, his frightfully skinny frame, the way he groaned when he didn't want to do something.

He remembered Professor Author, the genius who had altered Wilson's cerebral pathways so that he could heal his body on command, as well as engage the full potential of his strength. The funny little man was a friend and a mentor.

An image of Bishop Francisco suddenly invaded his thoughts: his pupils burning with scarlet, an evil grin creasing his face as he watched Wilson being beaten. Within him was the demented soul of Francisco Pizarro, the Spanish conquistador who helped overthrow the Inca empire.

Wilson again slammed into a submerged object which momentarily halted his forward movement. All around him the force of the muddy water tore at him, ripping away at his clothes and skin. The torrent spun him round and he was moving again, his head crunching against stone. He tried to grip at anything he could with his fingertips, but nothing would take hold.

He needed desperately to draw a breath.

Drowning is not a painful way to die, he told himself.

Wilson was suddenly whipped around against the torrent – he could feel something gripping his shoulder, then the leg of his pants! He could feel himself being dragged against the force of the fast-moving water. Objects continued to strike him as they shot past. His head was finally above the flow; he gasped a desperate breath of air. Someone was holding him, but he was unable to see. The grip was momentarily lost and he went under again, his lungs sucking in dirty water.

More hands reached out, grabbing his foot, then his legs and arms – pulling him forcefully against the current. Wilson's head emerged from the water again, the heavy rain striking his face and clearing the mud from his eyes.

He recognised the engraved breastplate pressing against him. Aclla was clinging to him, her muscles rippling.

Sontane was holding her around the waist. Four other warriors each gripped Sontane, forming a human chain. Inch by inch, the Virgins on the Sun dragged him from the powerful water.

When he was finally free from the muddy torrent, the four of them raced him along the cobblestones into a nearby alleyway. Wilson was coughing uncontrollably, goo spew- ing from his throat. In every direction he could see female warriors, their wet capes flipped back over their shoulders, bows ready, arrows drawn, watching every approach.

Two women knelt behind him and hammered away at his shackles. There were two distinct cracks of metal before Wilson's hands finally came free. Rubbing his wrists, he slowly climbed to his feet, his head tilted towards the dark sky. He let the rainwater wash out his mouth, at the same time wiping the grit from his eyes and hair. His shirt was torn to shreds and he ripped it from his body and threw it to the ground. With his muscles tensed, a loud yell escaped his lips – primal in its formation, the sound echoed ominously off the walls of the terrace houses around them.

'I never lost faith that you would return,' Aclla stated.

Wilson corralled his emotions as best he could.

'Where is the bishop?' he asked.

'Inside La Catedral. Hiram Bingham and Captain Gonzales are with him.'

'We attack the Triple Churches,' Wilson stated. He wiped his bare chest clean – the cauterised wound on his shoulder was pink and fleshy; as expected it had completely healed.

'Did you locate the Inca Cube?' Aclla asked.

'The female spirit I spoke of is here,' Wilson replied. 'The fact I can see her means the Inca Cube is nearby. Lead me to the bishop and you will lead me to her – she will direct me from there.'

'The crystal chamber has arrived,' Aclla said, pointing towards Sepla who had a leather pack strapped to her chest. 'We have the vessel necessary to transport the Inca Cube – we just need to find it.'

'When we attack, there will be many casualties,' Wilson said, looking towards Sontane and the other women surrounding them. 'The soldiers have many guns and they are controlled by the spirit of Francisco Pizarro.'

'*He* controls the Inca Cube?' Aclla asked.

Wilson nodded. 'Pizarro is a seasoned general. And the armour you wear cannot stop bullets.'

'Pizarro is a worthy adversary,' Aclla stated as if she knew his reputation well. 'Even better. We are the Virgins of the Sun – it is an honour to die in battle. We have trained our entire lives for this moment. This is an opportunity for us to fulfil our destinies and live up to the faith that Mama Ocllo and the Mamaconas have gifted us.' Rain was streaming down Aclla's face. 'We have shared much, Wilson Dowling . . . it will be an honour to go into battle with you.'

'The honour will be mine,' Wilson replied. He wanted to acknowledge her comment about what they had shared, to say something personal to Aclla in return, but Sontane was nearby and he knew it would only complicate matters.

Aclla made an abrupt gesture and the Amazons dispersed, their wet capes fanning out as they ran. Aclla pointed with her bow. 'This is the fastest way.'

Sontane handed Wilson a sword and the leather sheath to strap it to his leg.

'If the rain stops,' Aclla said, 'even for a moment, we will be exposed.'

'The rain will not stop,' Wilson replied. 'It will become even more ferocious. Of this fact I am certain.'

57

Cuzco, Peru
La Catedral
Local Time 6:45 pm

24 January 1908

HELENA WATCHED AS Bishop Francisco shuffled himself into the church. Captain Gonzales forced Hiram Bingham inside also, then pushed back the other soldiers at the door. Helena tried to scamper into the church after them, but at the last second realised that the doors in the *present* were closed. She yanked on the circular doorhandles but the entrance was bolted shut. Helena pounded her fist against the reinforced cedar in hope that someone would open the doors from the inside.

Both Chad and Hanna were huddled next to her under the stone archway as the rain poured down across the plaza. The wind was swirling and the clouds were black, making it almost impossible to see anything clearly.

'Can you believe this weather?' Hanna said. 'I've never seen anything like it.'

Chad was soaked to the skin. 'When I saw you running through hotel reception with your gun drawn, I thought someone was trying to kill you. I nearly shot the concierge by accident.' She smiled. 'You should've seen his face.'

'This is going in my memoirs,' Hanna said. 'Definitely.

Helena continued to beat her fist against the church doors. 'You must let me in!' she screamed.

'I'm not sure what's going on with her,' Hanna added, 'but she's determined, I'll give her that much.'

'You two,' Helena blurted, pointing at the door, 'shut up and help me find a way inside! I'm *not* crazy. I need you to find a way into *one of these* three churches – they are all linked together.'

Chad and Hanna traded glances.

'You go that way,' Chad said, a sense of urgency now evident in her tone. 'We'll go this way. If you find an open door, come back and get us. Understood?'

Hanna nodded and ran in the direction of the Church of La Sagrada Familia. Both Chad and Helena raced towards the Church of El Triunfo.

Running through the pouring rain, Helena worried that Wilson would not survive the torrent of mud and debris that he'd dived into. He was always taking ludicrous risks, counting on his extraordinary physical abilities to save him. One day he was going to push his luck too far and his life would be over.

Looking into the past, Helena could just make out the assembled soldiers across the other side of the plaza; they were heading north out of the city. The raging river that now cut through the Plaza de Armas had severed La Catedral from the military barracks. The soldiers would have to go some way north before they were able to cross over to this side. But even so, there were dozens of men who had already taken position around the church, their rifles resting on top of the stacked sandbags, bayonets attached.

One man against an army, Helena thought. *My God.*

She searched the rainy landscape, looking between the many buildings and along the flooded streets, in both trepidation and hope that she would see Wilson approaching. It seemed impossible to think he could get near this place with so many men standing guard outside.

What if the Inca Cube isn't here? Helena thought.

Chad approached the first of the three doors. She yanked at the huge metal latches, then banged ferociously on the studded wood with the butt of her gun. After waiting a moment, she moved on. Each door was locked and they rounded the corner to the southern side. The floodwaters were surging past adjacent to the raised foundations; the cobblestone road had been transformed into a filthy fast-moving river just like the Plaza de Armas.

Chad thumped her fist on a small door that Helena guessed was a service entrance.

'Shoot the lock!' Helena called out over the rain.

'I'm not religious at all,' Chad replied, 'but I'm not sure that's such a good idea.'

Helena pushed Chad aside, took steady aim with Don Eravisto's gun and pulled the trigger. The gunshot reverberated angrily. Helena studied the metal drop-latch which was barely dented by the impact. She took a step backwards and to the side to avoid a ricochet, then pulled the trigger three times in quick succession.

The smoking latch was now hanging open.

'No matter what happens, don't let anyone get near me,' Helena said. 'I don't care if the police show up. Make sure I have the freedom to do what I want. The fate of the world depends on it.'

Using the bottom of her foot, Helena kicked the wooden door open and stepped into the stillness of the church.

58

Cuzco, Peru
Plaza de Armas
Local Time 6:55 pm

24 January 1908

THE VIRGINS OF the Sun would provide cover from the rooftops, as well as follow Wilson in with ground support when the time was right. The outer walls of the church were easily fifty feet tall and impossible to climb without being spotted. The stained-glass windows and service entrances had been boarded up and sandbagged. That left only the main doors to La Catedral, which were crafted with heavy brass strappings and large brass bolts. Not even Wilson's great strength would be enough to break through.

When Wilson told Aclla that he'd found her sister Vivane's mutilated body in the dungeons below La Monasterio, he expected her to lose control – but she remained perfectly calm and focused, as if she knew she would have her revenge.

Against the eerie darkness, Wilson scanned the walls and rooftop of the great church hoping to see the telltale glow that indicated Helena's presence. He had asked her to stay with Bishop Francisco and it was his guess that she would already be inside. If she wasn't, he expected her luminescence to appear at any moment. He scanned the rest of the plaza, taking in the exact position of the soldiers and their fortifications.

The swirling rain was coming down at a furious rate

as Wilson waited for Aclla and her warriors to become
of 'one mind', as she called it – a kind of trance they put
themselves in. Aclla eventually tapped Wilson on the
shoulder and extended her arm, like she wanted to make
physical contact.

He gripped her cold hand and looked deep into her
mahogany eyes.

'No mercy,' Aclla said. 'We will fight until the end.'

'I'll get the door open . . . you just make sure I'm
covered.' Once again, Wilson wanted to say something
personal to her, but he just couldn't manage the words.
Men and women were about to die in battle and his
emotions already seemed disconnected.

Wilson checked to make sure the sword was strapped
securely to his left thigh. He then lowered himself to the
cobblestones and crawled on his stomach towards
the torrent gushing towards the Plaza de Armas. Using all
his strength, he took a firm handhold and carefully lowered
his half-naked body down into the raging flow. Debris and
heavy objects were striking him as he eased himself further
along, yard by yard, from handhold to handhold. Wilson
was familiar with the power and unpredictability of the
water and it took all his strength just to hold on.

Finally reaching the northern gun battery, he drew
himself out of the muddy slime like an alligator, the rain
beating down on him.

A wall of sandbags lay just ahead.

Wilson drew the short sword from its scabbard and
checked the sharpness of the blade. He took a moment to
compose himself. He would need to apply everything he
had learnt if he was to survive the next few moments. The
future of mankind relied on his ability to get inside the
Triple Churches and locate the Inca Cube.

Taking a last deep breath, Wilson felt his strength
multiply. This was a time to be ruthless.

An image of the Dead Sea Scrolls, lying there within
the glass cabinets at Enterprise Corporation, momentarily
flashed into his thoughts. It was his duty to succeed and he
would stop at nothing until he did.

Leaping from his position, he flew upwards, somersaulted and landed in the centre of the elevated gun
battery. Everything went into slow motion as his sword
cut through the pouring rain, severing the throat of one
soldier before lodging deeply into the skull of another
– blood splattered everywhere. Wilson released the
sword and spun round to grip the third soldier by the ears
and violently twist his head until his neck broke with a
crack.

Lifting the considerable weight of the Maxim machine
gun from the steel tripod, Wilson swung it in the direction of the towering church. A 500-round canvass belt
hung from the side of the weapon. Dozens of soldiers were
already coming at him from almost every direction – the
mind of Pizarro knew he was here.

A bullet whizzed past his ear.

Another grazed his cheek.

From out of the darkness, arrows began flying, spearing
flesh, as caped Amazons leapt forward in counterattack.
Wilson pulled the trigger, unleashing all hell from within
the barrel. The southern gun emplacement was decimated
as bullets and flame shredded everything before him.

Smoking .303 cartridges flew into the air as Wilson
strafed the soldiers ahead of him, their flesh brutally
ripped apart. Without lifting his finger off the trigger, he
swung his aim towards three soldiers who were running
directly for him, bayonets extended. His gunfire severed
their torsos from their legs and their obliterated bodies
were discarded to the wet cobblestones.

Amazons materialised from the darkness, their movements majestic and beautiful. Arrows were flying in all
directions. One soldier was speared in the eye, another
through the abdomen. When they were within striking
distance, the Amazons drew their swords and began
spinning and hacking away at any man in their path.

Through the gunshots and the rain, Wilson couldn't
hear the screams of death that were surely all around
him. Tracer bullets flashed across the sky. To his left, an
Amazon was impaled with a bayonet. A moment later her

virgin pair flew out of the darkness, her sword exacting the ultimate revenge.

Another woman was shot in the face.

Wilson leapt out of the gun battery, the heavy Maxim in his grasp. Oblivious of the bullets whizzing past, he scaled the stairs towards the cedar doors of La Catedral. Soldiers attacked him from all sides; Amazon warriors leapt forward to intervene. Another Amazon was killed defending Wilson, her blood spraying across the ground. He fired a devastating burst at a soldier lunging in his direction, then turned and fired again, killing another.

Sontane and Aclla were with him now, one on each side, drawing and releasing arrow after arrow from the quivers on their backs. The imposing wooden doors loomed above him now. Wilson set his feet, aimed the Maxim where he expected the locking beam to be and pressed his finger to the metal trigger.

Orange flames leapt from the gun as the mighty door began splintering.

Amazons converged at great speed of foot, doing their best to protect Wilson with their force of numbers. Bullets and arrows flew chaotically in all directions. All the while, rain continued to fall heavily from the dark sky. The Maxim gun was getting hotter in Wilson's hands. Through the smoke and steam he could see a hole being blasted into the hardwood.

Sontane went to draw yet another arrow when a bullet struck her. Her arms and legs tensed as she was catapulted into Wilson, knocking him off balance. His finger came off the trigger; he spun to see a soldier pointing his rifle directly at him. An arrow shot passed his ear, impaling the soldier through the middle of his chest.

Aclla yanked Wilson to his feet. 'Keep firing!' she yelled.

Sontane's lifeless body lay on the cobblestones, her glazed eyes wide open. The bullet had blown a hole clear through the side of her head and blood and brains were dripping out.

There were bodies and gore in all directions.

'Keep firing!' Aclla shouted again.

Wilson pressed the trigger and renewed the assault.

Aclla drew her sword, at the same time snatching the blade strapped to Sontane's lifeless thigh. More soldiers came at them. Using her incredible dexterity, Aclla avoided their bayonets and hacked away at their flesh, diving, turning and spinning away from trouble.

The canvas strap ended and the Maxim gun finally fell silent. Splinters of wood were still falling as Wilson picked up one of the sandbags. Using all his strength, he held it in front of him and ran forward at full pace. Aclla pressed her shoulder to his back and they both struck the shattered outer doors.

The sandbag crushed through the splintered wood and Wilson and Aclla skidded across the polished granite floor, smashing into the golden altar just inside. Female warriors flew in after them, turning to protect the entrance as soon as they did. Gunshots fired into the church, bullets zinging off the polished floor and shattering the inner walls. The Amazons set about toppling one of the altars and forcing it forward as a barricade.

Wilson looked up to see an effigy of the Nativity Virgin gazing down at him from high above, the infant Christ in her arms. The sight took his breath away – the serene expression on her alabaster face was in total contrast to the carnage and destruction that had engulfed this holy place.

Warriors hacked away at the gilded wood with their swords until the chancel broke free and tumbled, the Nativity Virgin and Christ going down with it. Wilson helped push the enormous wooden structure towards the entrance. Another Amazon flew in from the rain just as the altar was forced into place across the doors.

'Find the Inca Cube!' Aclla yelled.

Many of the warriors were badly wounded – gunshots and bayonet strikes had violated their perfect flesh – but there was not a look of fear or pain on any of their faces. Just the calm expression of seasoned warriors in the middle of a fight.

Polix was carrying the leather backpack with the crystal

chamber inside; she was covered in blood. Sepla had been killed and Polix had taken her place.

More and more gunshots were being fired into the church as every single Amazon took position to protect the makeshift barricade. They were sorting through what meagre weapons and arrows they had left and they were dispersing them evenly amongst themselves.

Wilson saw a faint white glow in the middle of the corridor.

'This way!' Helena called out. 'The bishop is back there!' Her words were frantic. 'Captain Gonzales is hiding at the top of the stairs, on the high altar – he has a gun. He's waiting to ambush you!'

'Where is the Inca Cube?' Wilson asked.

'It's close.' Helena replied. 'I can feel it, but I haven't located it yet.'

'You must find it, Helena!'

'First, you must stop Captain Gonzales!' Helena knelt down and drew a map with her finger on the floor, explaining to Wilson exactly where he was hiding.

'Aclla, I need you!' Wilson called out.

Helena was breathing quickly as she left Wilson and strode along the empty corridor. The church was pitch black and she was using the candlelight from her visions in the past to see where she was going. Nothing within the church had changed much over the last 106 years.

Both Chad and Hanna were complaining about not being able to see. Chad switched on the laser sight on her handgun, which at least told her the distance she was away from any objects in front of her.

Helena moved methodically along the corridors trying desperately to find out where Bishop Francisco had gone. Enclave by enclave, she searched the shadows, hoping at each turn to find him and the Inca Cube he was surely protecting.

Helena approached the sacristy chamber and glanced

inside to see Bishop Francisco standing in the middle of the floor, his hands behind his back. Hiram Bingham was kneeling at his feet with a silver dagger in his grasp.

As Helena entered, waves of nausea suddenly assailed her.

The priest called out at the top of his lungs, 'You dare to defile the House of God! You dare to bring the evil whores of the Virgins of the Sun to this most holy of places!'

Wilson eased himself into the shadows of the central nave, between the pews where the choir was normally seated. 'You are the one who defiles this place, Pizarro. You act in the name of God and yet your actions are unholy.'

The bishop began cackling. 'You think you have me trapped! You will feel the full weight of my revenge this day – I will make you pay for the futile actions you have taken against me. The revenge of God and the revenge of Jesus Christ will take their toll upon you.'

'Captain Gonzales!' Wilson called out. 'You should not protect the soul that resides within the body of Bishop Francisco. He is not a priest, he is a murderer!'

Wilson stepped out into the light.

From the very top of the high altar, above the golden balustrade, Captain Gonzales appeared, his handgun pointing in Wilson's direction.

But before he could pull the trigger, Aclla's arrow flew straight and true, striking Gonzales high on the right shoulder. He wailed as his revolver dropped over the railing. He lost his footing and tumbled backwards down the stairs. Aclla was suddenly over him, her sword at his throat.

'Do not kill him!' Wilson called out.

Helena's voice yelled from the darkness, 'Bishop Francisco is in the sacristy chamber! Hiram Bingham is in here also!'

Towards the front of the church, guns were firing more frequently and there was increased sword strikes and screaming.

Wilson called out, 'You call yourself a great man, Pizarro? And yet you hide away inside the sacristy chamber like a coward!'

From out of the doorway, Hiram Bingham ran forward in attack, his face expressionless, a dagger aloft above his head.

Wilson swept his leg, easily knocking Hiram off his feet. The skinny man's skull hit the floor with a thud and he was out cold.

'You are a coward, Pizarro! You get others to do your bidding when you should do it yourself!' Wilson could see the bishop's red eyeballs glowing in the darkness.

'I never enjoy acting through *feeble men*,' the bishop said as he limped forward into the light, his bony finger extended in Wilson's direction. 'Yours will be the next body I possess.'

Helena's glowing image called out, 'He's holding the Inca Cube!'

Wilson looked into the bishop's possessed eyes. 'The people of Peru hate you, Pizarro. You acted in the name of God . . . but you served without compassion. The moment you killed King Atahualpa your dark place in history was sealed. You murdered his wife and children before his eyes.'

'He would not accept the one true God!'

'You are a monster, and you are remembered as such.'

'I was *saving* Atahualpa's soul – so that he could go to Heaven. That is what God put me on this earth to do.'

'You are a failure, and history will *forever* be your undoing. The Inca Cube behind your back will not be enough to undo the crimes you have committed. Today you have met your match. I am immune to the power of the Cube,' Wilson stated. 'That is the reason you will fail. You cannot look into my mind and it cannot possess my body.'

'You think you are immune to the Inca Cube?' Pizarro said with a blackened grin.

At that moment, Helena sensed that Wilson had no defence to the Cube's powerful influence. 'Run, Wilson! You have to run!'

'This is something you should see,' Pizarro said with a whisper. Bishop Francisco extended his arm and opened his fingers.

As soon as Wilson's gaze fell upon the shimmering Inca Cube, he was transfixed. He wanted to touch it – he had never felt such a burning desire. The Cube was brilliant, the sharpness of its cut, the obvious weight it carried. It was like it was talking to him, taunting him, demanding that he come forward. He would be strong if he held it, he knew he would.

Aclla threw back her cape and ran screaming towards the bishop.

Seeing her coming, Wilson turned and lashed out with his fist, felling Aclla with a mighty blow. She hit the ground unconscious, her sword sliding across the floor towards the bishop's feet.

Pizarro's eyes glowed like embers. 'Come forward and you shall have it.'

'No!' Helena called out. She attempted to force Wilson back but her hands passed right through him. 'You must look away!'

Wilson stepped forward, his world a blur of lust and unbridled emotion. He wanted to feel the weight of the Cube in his hand. He wanted to feel its power.

Helena stood between Wilson and the Inca Cube. Tears were running down her face. 'You will become everything that you despise!'

Wilson's eyes were glazed over.

The bishop said with a deep voice, 'Touch the Cube and your every wish will come to pass. Together we will rule the world.'

Wilson was just inches away, his fingers extended.

It's so beautiful, he thought.

Helena began to vomit bile as the Inca Cube got close. The terrible object was no bigger than the palm of the bishop's hand. Her proximity to it made her want to run away, such was the awful power it omitted. It was only her feelings for Wilson that gave her the strength to hold her position.

Wilson was about to make contact.

He would be lost forever.

Helena hurried forward and touched the Cube first.

It seemed like a million volts of electricity struck her body. Through the obvious pain she clenched her fist and punched Wilson in the face with all her might. The impact was true and solid and he was thrown to his back, skidding across the floor.

It took a moment for Wilson to collect himself.

Helena's glowing image fell limp, as if all the life had been drained from her.

Wilson's gaze once again locked onto the Inca Cube. He climbed slowly to his feet, his breath laboured, his chin aching from the unexplainable blow he'd received.

'Come and take the Inca Cube,' Pizarro called out.

Helena was lying on the floor, motionless.

Wilson approached, step by step, unwittingly drawn towards the Cube once again. His hand extended, but this time he became aware of Helena's glowing body on the ground – she wasn't breathing.

Wilson paused, his gaze fixed on her.

'Come forward!' Pizarro said.

The figure of Captain Gonzales appeared from the darkness with Aclla's sword in his hand – blood was pouring from his shoulder, the Amazon arrow still protruding from the wound. He raised the shiny weapon to strike Wilson down.

'Kill him!' Pizarro said.

Hiram suddenly rose up, turned and plunged the small silver dagger deep into the side of Bishop Francisco's throat. The priest let out a horrific scream as the Inca Cube released from his grasp, the impossibly solid metal hitting the granite floor with the clank of an object fifty times its weight.

Bishop Francisco ripped the dagger out of his neck. Blood was spurting from the wound as he turned the blade towards Hiram. 'You dare to attack Pizarro!' he said, blood dribbling from his lip.

'*I never liked you!*' Hiram screamed back.

Captain Gonzales changed direction, threw Hiram aside,

and slashed Bishop Francisco across the chest, splitting his papal robes and cutting a deep furrow into his bony chest. He toppled and fell.

On the floor sat the Inca Cube. All three men stood above it, transfixed by its obvious magnificence. They each wanted to touch it, to hold it in their grasp, and they eased slowly forward, their fingers extended.

Suddenly, it disappeared from view.

Aclla had thrown her cloak over the Cube to conceal it.

With the spell momentarily broken, Captain Gonzales fell to the floor in exhaustion as Aclla pushed Wilson and Hiram away. The rate of gunfire increased, the sounds of death somehow amplified as soldiers desperately tried to clamber inside the church.

Wilson knelt beside Helena's glowing image. She was on her back and it seemed she was being given CPR, but by whom Wilson could not see.

Blood gurgled from Bishop Francisco's throat. 'Betrayed by one closest to me,' he said looking at Captain Gonzales. The bishop's eyes were glowing red. With a wicked grin on his face he began painting a large scarlet cross on the floor with his own blood. 'Do you know what happens if I am killed?' He laughed to himself, at the same time clutching at his bloodied chest. 'My soul goes into another!' He hacked out a watery laugh. 'I will have my revenge on you, Gonzales,' he gurgled. 'Your family will die . . . and you will watch.'

With those words, his pupils went to black.

'No!' Gonzales screamed. 'Please, no!'

Bishop Francisco grabbed at his shirt and pulled him closer. 'You saved me,' the bishop whispered. 'Thank you, my son, thank you.'

Captain Gonzales pressed his hand to the bishop's forehead. 'Who has the spirit of Pizarro gone to?' he asked. 'You must tell me . . .'

'Juan Santillana,' the bishop forced out. Blood was pouring out of his mouth and down his chin. 'He uses Santillana.' Tears formed in the bishop's bloodshot eyes. 'That is the vessel Pizarro will go to.' He gurgled once more then finally went silent.

Captain Gonzales was whimpering.

Polix ran forward with her backpack open.

Aclla pointed her finger in Wilson's direction. 'You must all look away.'

The glowing image of Helena Capriarty was still lying on the floor, unmoving. It was only now that Wilson realised she had reached across a 106-year barrier in time to touch the Inca Cube. His jaw ached from the punch she had delivered.

Aclla opened the obsidian box to reveal its glowing crystal lining. Taking a deep breath, she snatched her cloak away from the Inca Cube. Both she and Polix lifted its considerable weight with a pair of heavy tongs and carefully lowered it into the crystal chamber.

Aclla closed the lid and Helena's image suddenly vanished. At the front of the church, the gunshots immediately ceased. It seemed the fighting had stopped.

There was complete silence for a long while.

'I need a cigarette' Hiram muttered.

Wilson lifted Gonzales to his feet, turned him round and snapped off the long arrow where it protruded from his shoulder. He was pale and had obviously lost a lot of blood.

'The Inca Cube must go to Pitcos,' Aclla said.

'I need you to take it to Vilcapampa,' Wilson replied.

Aclla looked him in the eye, her bloodied sword in her hand. 'That is something I cannot do. We must take the Cube to Pitcos before the crystals burn out. There is no telling how much time we have.'

Wilson wiped the blood from his own cheek, the laceration underneath having already healed. 'I need the Cube at Vilcapampa if I am to leave this place. You know that.'

'Only the Mamaconas can grant you that privilege,' Aclla stated.

Polix locked the lid then carefully inserted the obsidian box inside her pack and strapped it to the front of her armour.

'We must save my family,' Gonzales announced, his legs were wobbling under his own weight. 'Juan Santillana will be hunting them. Please señor, I am too weak to go to their aid. You must do this for me.' His desperate eyes scanned the church for anyone that would help him.

'Can the spirit of Pizarro survive without the Inca Cube?' Wilson said to Aclla.

'I cannot be sure,' she replied. 'But the power to control the thoughts of other men is gone for as long as the crystals that surround it are active. But if the spirit of Pizarro has gone to Juan Santillana already, it is possible that he can control him still.'

'Pizarro threatened my family,' Gonzales whispered through his tears. 'You all heard it. I saved you by striking the bishop down and you must repay me. I have a wife, Sarita. And three children. Arturo is eight, Ortega is six, and my little daughter Juanita is just three years old. Please, you must help me!'

Aclla shook her head. 'We cannot help you, Capitán I am sorry. The safety of the Cube is our only priority.'

Gonzales grabbed Wilson by the shoulder. 'I live on the Avenue Pavitos, where it meets Lechugal. Not far from here. Please, señor.'

Wilson held Captain Gonzales upright. 'I am sorry, I cannot help you either.'

'You must help me!' Gonzales pleaded.

Aclla's warriors were all around her – there were only seven of them left. 'We need your strength, Wilson Dowling, if we are to protect the Inca Cube.' Aclla pointed her bloodied sword in his direction. 'You must come with us.'

'I'm going to drink a whole bottle of whiskey,' Hiram said though his obvious stupor. 'Lord knows I deserve it. This place . . .' He looked down at Bishop Francisco's lifeless body and the bloodied dagger lying on the stone floor. 'My God, what have I done?'

Captain Gonzales would not release his grip on Wilson's arm. 'You must save my family. You are the only hope I have. Please señor, my small children . . .'

'Their fate is already sealed,' Wilson replied. 'There is nothing I can do. I'm sorry, Capitán, but you will have to save them youself.'

59

Cuzco, Peru
Avenue Pavitos
Local Time 8:22 pm

24 January 1908

CAPTAIN GONZALES STUMBLED through the rain as fast as he could. It was difficult to keep his balance because of the pain he was in. The arrowhead was still lodged in his shoulder and every so often it would strike a nerve, twisting him in agony and buckling his legs underneath him. Tears welled in his eyes as he thought about his wife and family at their little home. The white stranger Wilson Dowling had proclaimed them dead already.

'Please God, let them be safe,' Gonzales whispered.

Wilson Dowling had handed him back his revolver, checked to make sure a bullet was in the chamber, then sent him on his way.

'That bastard left my family unprotected,' Gonzales muttered to himself. His fury towards the white stranger knew no bounds. 'He should have helped me!'

As Gonzales stumbled through the splintered doors of La Catedral and outside into the pouring rain, he was forced to step over the bodies of his soldiers and the freakish female warriors who had come to Cuzco to take the Inca Cube away. The cobblestones ran with blood, both male and female. The soldiers who were still alive had either disappeared into the rainy night or they were just laying there, blood seeping from their mutilated flesh.

The sudden memory of Bishop Francisco's glowing eyes made Gonzales hurry along a little faster, but just a few steps later he fell to his knees on the wet cobblestones, such was the terrible pain that was radiating from his open wound.

'I must make it home,' he whimpered, his vision fading in and out. The sky was a black void and the wind was gusting. Rain was pouring down all around, making the puddles on the roadway come alive with flickering droplets.

Gonzales once again remembered the expression on Private Ramiro's face as he told him to look after his family. 'You must protect them for me.' He had gripped the young man by the shoulders. 'I can trust you, can't I?'

'Si, Capitán, you can trust me,' the young soldier had replied.

Gonzales turned the corner to see the lights of his little home glowing against the rainy night. It was not much further. He tried his best to breathe deeply, so that he had as much of his strength as possible.

'Please let them be safe,' he whispered to himself. 'Please God.'

As he approached his home, Gonzales could see a dark silhouette of a man standing outside on the verandah. His shoulders were hunched and his head was stooped.

Gonzales limped forward through the rain just a little bit faster. He prayed that the figure in the shadows would be Private Ramiro, but he could somehow tell, even from this distance that it was not him. The rain was thrashing against his face and he attempted desperately to focus.

Gonzales could now just make out that it was a soldier; he could see the brass buttons of his jacket. If his family were indeed dead, he would take his own life, there was no other choice. Gonzales could not live without them – he had already decided that would be his fate. He lifted the flap of his holster and drew out his gun.

It was only then that Gonzales recognised the man. It was Lieutenant Capos . . . and his clothes were saturated with blood, his expression was grim.

Gonzales fell to his knees just ten feet from his property. He began to weep uncontrollably. 'Please God, why have you forsaken me?'

Capos ran forward and fell to his knees also, holding his captain in his arms.

'Please, God, no!' Gonzales wept. He lifted the revolver to turn it upon himself.

'I have terrible news,' Capos said. He glanced back towards the little house. There was blood splattered across the inside of the window.

'My God,' Gonzales muttered. He was shaking uncontrollably at the thought of what had taken place there. 'My family is dead!' he screamed. He cocked the hammer on his revolver.

'No, Capitán . . . they are safe!'

Gonzales could not believe what he was hearing. He was in complete shock.

'Private Ramiro is dead,' Capos continued. 'His throat was slashed open. Another man lies dead on the floor of your kitchen. His head has been cut off. I think it is Juan Santillana – although it is hard to say.'

Gonzales uncocked his gun and slowly inserted the weapon back into its holster. 'Where is my wife? Where are my children?' he asked.

'They are in the bedroom. They are too afraid to come out.'

Feeling his strength returning, Gonzales scrambled to his feet and ran to the door as best he could. Two bodies lay on the floor of the kitchen, one on top of the other. Stepping over them, Gonzales pushed the bedroom door open. In the darkness he could hear his children weeping.

'Papa is here!' a small boy's voice suddenly called out.

'Papa!' the little girl yelled.

Before he knew it, all three of Lucho's children were clinging to him, sobbing. His wife collapsed onto him, kissing his face and clutching him tightly. He wanted to scream in pain from the arrow still impaled his shoulder, but not a whimper left his lips. All he could utter was, 'I love you all so much. I love all.'

'A white man saved us,' Sarita blubbered. 'He burst in through the door and cut off Juan Santillana's head.' She held Lucho's face in her hands. 'You are wounded!'

'Tell me what happened,' Lucho said, his arms enveloping his family once again.

'Santillana came to kill us,' Sarita wept. 'That is who it is. He kicked open the door, his fingernails and skin were black with muck – it looked like he had been living with the pigs. He lunged at Ramiro, right in front of us, and slashed his throat open. Santillana licked away the blood from his knife, his eyes were glowing red – I swear they were – as Ramiro lay helplessly bleeding to death before us all.' Sarita was breathing hard, at the same time holding her children close to their father. 'He was possessed by the Devil,' she whimpered. 'His eyes were glowing red.' She began weeping again. 'He grabbed Arturo and threw him into the corner – to separate our eldest boy from us. That was the moment the white man came – I can only guess at the evil that would have befallen us if he had not arrived when he did.'

In the background, Capos was in the kitchen, trying his best to drag the two dead bodies out of the house and into the pouring rain.

'The white man, what did he look like?' Lucho asked.

'He was muscular,' Sarita replied. 'He was not wearing a shirt. When he saw Santillana he yelled, "Your time has ended, Pizarro!" Then with one strike, he cut off his head.' Sarita clutched at her husband. 'The white man pointed to the bedroom and told us to wait in here until you arrived. He said to give you a message; he said to tell you that the flooding caused all the deaths – the church was not responsible – that you would do your part to protect the innocent. He said you would understand.'

Lucho nodded, he knew exactly what was being asked of him.

'Who was the white man, Papa?' little Ortega asked. 'The man who saved us.'

'His name is Wilson Dowling,' Lucho replied. 'He is my friend.'

60

Inca Trail, Peru
40 Miles North-west of Cuzco – Phuyupatamarca
Local Time 11:05 pm

25 January 1908

AS WILSON CLIMBED the Inca pathway towards the crest of yet another rugged spur, he wondered if he was ever going to catch up with Aclla and her warriors. He'd been following their trail at a steady jog for almost twenty-four hours. This was definitely the route they were taking and he was surprised at just how fast they were moving. Up above, the clouds in the night sky were finally beginning to separate and flickering stars were just beginning to shine through. As Wilson breathed out, streams of condensation wafted into the frigid air.

There was no doubt that Wilson had taken an enormous risk by going back to Captain Gonzales's home. Not only had the Inca Cube been exposed in his absence, but by saving Gonzales's wife and children, Wilson had changed history – both the version that Wilson had studied and also the version that Helena had told him about – and there was no reckoning the damage that could result. But despite the ramifications, Wilson couldn't leave Cuzco knowing that the spirit of Pizarro would have his way with Gonzales's defenceless family.

Wilson remembered the moment he'd swung his sword at the neck of Juan Santillana and how his severed head had toppled to the floor. Wilson grabbed Santillana's skull by his black hair, blood pouring out from underneath, and watched his pupils transform from red to black. It was the moment the spirit of Pizarro finally left Santillana's body, hopefully to be vanquished forever. There was no time for remorse or pity for Santillana's life cut short – the man had surely been driven to madness by the crucifixion of his brother, and the perverted acts he had certainly committed at the whim of Pizarro. Wilson had chosen to strike Santillana down, although it contravened the guiding principle of the Overseer – that he should never take the life of another if it could be avoided. In this case, in these wild circumstances, he had acted out of moral duty. History was already out of balance and the damage was already done.

Captain Gonzales had not lost his family and the curse that had plagued his ancestors had been lifted. As a result, the life of Don Eravisto would be different, and there would be no cause for revenge towards Helena. Wilson surmised that if Helena had not punched him – through a barrier of time – he would have touched the Inca Cube to inevitably become a servant of Pizarro's deeds. In Helena's future, he must have committed the murders and the depravity that Don Eravisto had claimed.

And now history had been altered yet again.

Breathing hard, Wilson peered into the darkness along the stone causeway that bisected the expanse of the dry lake bed. Jagged mountains peaks looked down upon the valley from every side. With his night vision engaged, he could just make out fifteen or so caped figures against the dark terrain – it seemed the Amazons' numbers had doubled since leaving La Catedral. Wilson had finally caught up.

After leaving Captain Gonzales's home, Wilson had walked slowly through the rain towards the Pan-Am Pacific Congress. The front door was open and Wilson could see the bulbous backside of a brown donkey sticking out. He cautiously eased himself through to find Hiram sitting at his desk, an open bottle of whiskey in one hand and a cigarette in the other. Ironically, Hiram was sitting in the exact position he was in when Wilson first met him.

As soon as Wilson appeared, Hiram put his cigarette between his teeth then reached out for the donkey to pull him even closer, as if hugging him. 'It's Diablo!' he said with an exhausted tone. 'The little genius found his way back here. That's some good news, at least.' Hiram unwrapped a square of dark chocolate from a silver wrapper and fed it to the hungry animal, who quickly chomped it down.

Wilson looked Diablo over then gave him a pat on the back.

'He's survived,' Hiram muttered. '*We were worried about you, yes we were.* He's got a lucky streak, this one. We've been together a long time, Diablo and me. *I'm so happy you're alive,*' he said in a baby voice to the animal. '*Yes . . . I'm so happy.*'

Hiram unwrapped another piece of dark chocolate and held it out with an open palm. There were dozens on discarded wrappers on the floor. 'Is Captain Gonzales's family safe?' he eventually asked.

Wilson nodded. 'They're safe.'

'Thank God for that. Was there more killing?'

Wilson nodded. 'Santillana is dead.'

Hiram wearily climbed to his feet, rustled around in one of the many boxes then threw Wilson an overcoat. He pointed with the smouldering tip of his cigarette. 'All that stuff about being a time-traveller is true, isn't it?'

Wilson nodded again. 'It's all true.'

'I thought you were going mad down there in that dungeon.' Hiram let out a huff. 'I should have known better.' He took a massive swig of whiskey, then pulled in a long drag of his cigarette.

'The spirit of Pizarro could read your thoughts,' Wilson said. 'That's why I acted so strangely down there – rambling the way I did.'

'That explains part of it, I guess. But not all.' Hiram looked exhausted and dishevelled; the bruises on his face were getting darker and there were stains of blood on his damp clothing. His hands were shaking and it was obvious he was still in shock. 'Wow, what a day.' He looked up at Wilson again. 'I can't believe you're a time-traveller.'

'Neither can I,' Wilson replied.

'From now on, I'm not following you *anywhere*, no matter what you say.' Hiram paused for a moment, thinking. 'All that *death* because of one little golden cube.' He dropped his cigarette butt to the floor and stamped on it. On the table were four more that he'd rolled already. He immediately struck a match and put another one between his lips. 'You never light one cigarette from another,' he commented. 'If you do . . . a sailor dies. That's what my grandfather used to say – a sailor dies.' He paused. 'You were right when you said the Inca Cube was cursed . . . *stupid little object*.' He grabbed the bottle of whiskey and took another slug, then handed it over to Wilson.

Wilson took a gulp and felt the warm sensation running down his throat. It was only now that he began contemplating what had actually happened. Graphic images of the dead began to form in his mind – in some cases the exact moment he took their lives away – the blood and the gore, the terrible expression on their faces. Wilson then remembered the tortured feeling that engulfed him as he stepped towards the Inca Cube – all his self-control lost – and how Bishop Francisco had stood there offering it to him like it was some sort of great prize. Wilson's arrogance at believing he was immune to the influence of the Inca Cube had almost been his undoing.

Hiram grabbed the bottle and took another shot. 'The drink helps, eh?'

'You are a hero, Hiram Bingham. I realise now why you were the man chosen to discover the lost city of Vilcapampa. It's because you were the only man who could strike Pizarro down while he was at his most powerful. You acted with strength when others could not.'

'I stabbed a priest in the neck,' Hiram sighed. '*Christ*, how am I going to explain that at my next confession? What do you think my penance will be?'

'You saved us all,' Wilson replied. 'There is no penance required for that.'

'I'll probably be arrested,' Hiram muttered. 'That would be just my luck.'

'Bishop Francisco was killed in the floods,' Wilson announced. 'That's how all this will be reported. Captain Gonzales will take care of everything. That is how history will be written.' Wilson paused. 'It's time for you to head home to Alfreda and your boys for a little while. According to your destiny, you will discover Vilcapampa on July 24th 1911. I need you to wait until then, okay?'

'Three years?' Hiram muttered.

Taking Hiram's fountain pen and a piece of paper, Wilson wrote the date down and slid it towards him. 'I need you to wait until this date. It's very important.'

'Alfreda is pregnant. Did I tell you that?'

Wilson smiled. 'I know she is . . . your little boy will be called Brewster.'

'You know everything, don't you? Of course you do.' Hiram locked his gaze on Wilson once again. 'Did you know all this was going to happen?'

'The future is not fully set,' Wilson replied. 'Each of us has a destiny, but only our individual efforts create our reality. You saved the world when you struck Pizarro down – that took immense courage. You are a hero to me and to everyone else who was there. If Pizarro had succeeded, and his soul continued to transfer, there's no telling what would have happened next.'

'Did you see his beady eyeballs?' Hiram pointed with two fingers. 'I never liked the look of him – *never* did. I mean . . . I'm not a killer . . . but I never liked him.' He took another drink.

'You are a hero, Hiram Bingham. It is only fitting that you will be remembered as the man who discovered the lost city of Vilcapampa.'

Hiram lifted the whiskey bottle and had yet another slug. 'I'll drink to that.' He handed Wilson the bottle then carefully unwrapped another chocolate that Diablo wolfed down. '*I'm so glad you're safe,*' he said to the animal. '*Yes I am.*'

'Thank you for everything you have done, Hiram. And

please remember our agreement,' Wilson added. 'I was never here.'

'Don't worry,' Hiram replied. 'I'm already trying to forget the whole thing. As time passes, not even I will want to believe I met a time-traveller like you.'

Wilson ran along the flat expanse of the causeway. To the east, a crescent moon was just coming over the horizon, which lit up the terrain considerably. At this pace, it would be only a few minutes before he caught up with the Amazons.

Thoughts of Helena invaded Wilson's mind. He could not be sure if she had survived the shock of touching the Inca Cube. A grim foreboding filled his gut as he remembered her lying motionless on the church floor. It was impossible to say if she was dead or alive, but he consoled himself with the fact that her image had not disappeared until the Inca Cube was locked away.

She must have survived, he told himself.

Because of her, he had avoided contact with the Inca Cube. She had been there when he needed her, yet again, and it crystallised his feelings for her. If Wilson had one wish, he would find his way across time, somehow making it to her world, so that they could be together again.

Hearing footsteps approaching, the Virgins of the Sun separated and fell to the ground, out of sight. When they realised it was Wilson, the fifteen women rose from the shadows to greet him.

'Thank the gods that you are back,' Aclla said, a smile appearing on her normally serious face. She approached Wilson and lightly punched his chest. 'I told everyone that you would make it back to us.' She pressed her hand against his shoulder. 'The captain's family is safe?' she asked.

'They are well.'

'And Santillana?'

'His head is no longer connected to his shoulders.'

Aclla nodded. 'You did the right thing by going back.' She looked about at the Amazons surrounding them, their bronze armour glistening in the moonlight. 'Every one of us has lost her virgin pair. We are the last of our kind. According our laws, when our virgin pair dies we can no longer go into battle. The reign of the Virgins of the Sun has momentarily ended. It is our wish that you come back with us to Pitcos, so that you can help rebuild what is broken.'

Wilson looked into Aclla's dark eyes and remembered the night of passion he had shared with her and Chiello. It was an extraordinary experience, but it was not what he wanted for himself. 'I cannot go back with you,' Wilson said.

'You must,' Aclla replied. 'The Mamaconas have proclaimed it so.'

'They intend to keep me with you forever. You know this,' Wilson said seriously. 'It is my hope that you will allow me to use the Inca Cube one last time, at Vilcapampa, so that I may travel away from this place. To my world.' An image of Helena's face dominated Wilson's thoughts. 'To the woman I love. Like your sister, Vivane, against all reckoning, my priorities are with another.' He paused. 'Each of us must fight for what we believe in.'

The crescent moon finally cleared the jagged horizon and it was casting the shadows of the Amazon warriors across the Inca causeway.

'I must take the Inca Cube to Pitcos,' Aclla stated. 'I have no choice.'

From high above, the piercing screech of a condor cut across the night sky. Everyone looked up to see the giant bird's black wings swoop down, flap once, then land on the dry lake bed just ten feet away. The moonlight reflected in its eyes and they glowed white in the darkness. No one moved as the extraordinary bird fanned out its massive wings and let out another loud screech.

Wilson looked to Aclla. 'It seems that Apu is on my side once again.'

61

Andes Ranges, Peru
Machu Picchu Citadel
Local Time 6:10 am

25 January 1908

THE DAWN SKY was iridescent blue as Wilson stood on the altar of stone, at the very centre of Axis Mundi. Beams of warm sunlight cut through the taller peaks between the eastern glaciers, bathing the lost city of Vilcapampa in sunshine. This was the very spot where the most holy of Inca rituals had been conducted, including human sacrifice. The square-cut chunk of granite had a pillar of stone protruding out of the very top. The Incas called it *Intihuatana*, which meant 'hitching post of the sun'. The Inca believed this was the point where the sun was attached to the earth, holding it in place in its annual path across the sky. At midday on March 21st and September 21st, on the equinoxes, the sun stood directly above the pillar and there was no shadow cast in any direction.

High above the valley, the magnificent black condor circled the mountain ridge of Vilcapampa, its wings seemingly never moving. The bird had not been out of Wilson's view since the previous night and it was marking perfect circles in the cloudless sky as if held there by an invisible thread.

Wilson took a moment to study the overgrown ruins of Machu Picchu for the last time, laid out along the precipitous half-mile razorback ridge. Hardwood forests and thickets of bamboo surrounded the dilapidated stone buildings; every piece of exposed earth was covered with ferns, high grasses and liana vines. In the valley below, the mighty Urubamba flowed past in all its frightening glory, the roar of the rushing water leaving a steady drone in the air.

In every direction as far as Wilson could see, mountain peaks framed the horizon as if he was standing inside the open mouth of a terrifying beast, its razor-sharp fangs reaching skyward. The sight was not intimidating, however; quite the opposite, as though this was the safest place in the world.

'We owe everything to the power of the sun,' Aclla said, standing just a few yards away from him. 'That is why Inti is the most powerful of our gods. He is responsible for everything that you see around you. His energy creates all things – he warms the earth, he grows the crops that feed us, he grows the trees and grasses that feed our animals, which in turn become flesh and bone, consciousness, thoughts and will. The Sun God burns up the rain, which makes the clouds in the sky, the water then creates the rivers that carve out these valleys and great mountain ranges. We owe all this to Inti – without him there would be nothing.'

Wilson looked towards the brightness of the sun, the beams of luminescence shimmering against the shadowed depths of the forest-clad valleys below. The morning was chilly, but he could feel the warmth of Inti's power against his face.

'What will happen to the Inca Cube?' Wilson asked.

Aclla threw her cape over her shoulders, revealing her muscular arms and the brilliant bronze of her armour. 'That is not for me to say. I can only expect that the Mamaconas will know what to do. Maybe they will cast the Inca Cube into Lake Titicaca, sending it back to the very place from where it first rose up into this world of the living.'

Standing atop the countless fallen ashlars, the Virgins of the Sun were strung out across the dilapidated city, each within sight of the other. Their swords were drawn and they were alert to any approach or movement.

Aclla was given the signal and she turned to Wilson for the last time. 'The Inca Cube is in place,' she said.

'You are a great leader, and a great woman,' Wilson responded.

'I sincerely hope you find what you are looking for, Wilson Dowling.' Aclla's head dipped slightly. 'That is something I wish I could have said to Vivane.'

So many people had died in the quest to obtain the Inca Cube – both the innocent and the corrupt. It was difficult to rationalise the evil that had been committed in the name of God, but that was the way of history. God seemed to be responsible for the best in people, and in many cases His name was made an excuse for man's greatest evil.

'Thank you, Aclla,' Wilson said. 'I am in your debt.'

Wilson's gaze lifted upwards towards the black condor circling gracefully above him. The spirit of Apu, the Mountain God, had been there when needed. Looking about the ruins, he was hoping to see the telltale glow that indicated to him that Helena was near, but there was no such image. When he arrived into the future, the first thing he would do would be to seek out her history to determine if she had survived the terrible shock the Inca Cube had given her inside La Catedral.

Wilson pressed the flat of his palm to the pillar of stone beside him and took a deep breath. The ground began to shake, just a tremor at first, but soon the entire mountain ridge was moving underneath him. Wilson tensed his muscles, knowing exactly what to expect. His world was about to change yet again.

Then, with a brilliant flash, he was gone.

After eight long years, the mission of Nehemiah was finally complete.

THE FACTS

At the height of its reign, the Inca Empire stretched over 800,000 square miles from Columbia in the north, to Chile and Argentina in the south. The Inca King commanded millions of subjects within the richest and most powerful civilisation in South American history. The administrative, political and military centre of the Empire was located in Cuzco, in the highlands of Peru.

The Incas were master builders and architects, they understood the stars and the seasons, the chemistry of drugs such as quinine and cocaine, and their effects. They domesticated animals such as the llama and the alpaca; they were master weavers and pottery makers; they gave us the white potato and Indian corn, having possessed an advanced knowledge of agriculture and farming. Enduringly, the magnificent stone citadels they left behind are some of the most beautiful and well-crafted structures ever built by the hand of man.

And yet, despite the Incas being the most modern and technically advanced of all the ancient civilisations, they left behind no written language or hieroglyphics of any kind. When the last of the Incas were finally gone, they took their secrets with them to the grave.

CHRISTOPHER RIDE

THE
SCHUMANN
FREQUENCY

'Damned exciting . . . You'll be on the edge of your seat.'
THE DAILY TELEGRAPH

Also by Christopher Ride

THE SCHUMANN FREQUENCY

It's the adventure of a lifetime . . .

The Dead Sea Scrolls have revealed a stunning secret – an Overseer must cross generations to save the world. Time itself is moving too quickly, with each day becoming shorter than the last. Society is unravelling and no one is safe.

Wilson Dowling is just an ordinary man, but he's had an extraordinary offer – one that he can't refuse. He'll risk everything to see his mission through . . . but is he gambling with destiny?

Helena Capriarty fears she is losing her mind. She has an inexplicable psychic connection with a man she has never met. To prove her sanity she must find this stranger, chasing him across the globe to some of the most mysterious and ancient sites on earth: monuments that hold a secret power.

All the while, the forces of opposition lie in wait for the Overseer. And with one wrong move, history – and the future that follows it – is condemned to disaster.

So begins the quest to rectify the Schumann Frequency.

Read on for a preview of the first chapter.

Mission of Isaiah—Day One

AN INTENSE GLOW saturated the morning sky, washing it with pink, yellow and orange. The vivid splash of colours was fading quickly, just seconds away from a new dawn. Beams of gold suddenly burst upwards from the horizon as the last remnants of darkness were vanquished and the sun rapidly crested the landscape. The metropolis of Houston, the fourth-largest city in the United States, woke abruptly from its slumber. Cars and trucks filled the streets. People hurried along the sidewalks. Things moved quickly. It was just like any other day.

High on an inner-city skyscraper, an unfamiliar breeze swirled.

With a flash a time portal opened.

Two red electrons appeared from thin air and orbited each other, silently hovering above the floor. Growing in size and brightness, they multiplied into four, then eight. Over and over they doubled in number and velocity, until they swarmed together in their thousands.

ON THE THIRTY-THIRD floor of Building 1, Post Oak Towers, an office worker lowered a mug of coffee from her lips. A red glow was radiating from the roof of the skyscraper opposite. Fascinated by the strengthening brightness, she walked towards the plate-glass window and stared outside, her mouth agape. She had never seen anything like it. She squinted, trying to focus more clearly. *What is that?* she wondered.

THE MIST OF SWIRLING electrons rumbled as fingers of highly charged electricity spun from the core. A metal handrail nearby began to glow as the gusting wind reached super-heated temperatures. Everything on the rooftop vibrated furiously. Paint peeled. Scorch marks appeared on the concrete. The red electrons massed ever more closely, building themselves into a luminous tornado. The phenomenon pulsated with a monstrous energy until, at last, with the roar of a dozen thunderclaps, it detonated.

The woman watching from her office window was stunned as the heat of the explosion slapped at her face. She threw up both hands as a shield, letting the coffee mug go. Releasing from her fingers, the mug fell in slow motion, taking a lethargic path downwards before bouncing off the carpet at her feet. Boiling droplets of brown liquid—small perfect spheres—were propelled from the cup in leisurely arcs and splashed across the floor.

Everything in the city moved at one-quarter of normal speed, to the sound of a low-pitched drone.

Meanwhile, the by-now millions of red electrons were blasted thousands of metres in all directions. One by one, they swung back on a predetermined path towards the flashpoint and fused together into a molten mass. Something started to take shape. The construction—a human form—began from the inside out: marrow, bone, muscle, skin, then clothes.

With every electron finally assimilated, a man dressed in black was revealed. He was suspended in mid-air, his arms splayed outwards. The super-heated wind swirled around him chaotically, holding him aloft and whipping his hair this way and that. Yet he was unaffected by the blistering temperatures.

With a flash of golden light, the wind dropped away and the figure fell unceremoniously backwards onto the smouldering concrete. In an instant, time surged back to its normal speed, the sounds of the city rising to a familiar pitch again.

The transport was complete.

Inside her office the woman looked, perplexed, at the fallen coffee mug on the carpet. What just happened? Her focus shifted to the top of the building opposite.

The red glow was gone. She pressed her hand against her forehead—her skin was burned and blistered.

ON THE ROOFTOP, a time traveller lay pale and motionless. White smoke hovered above him in the still morning air. Suddenly, spiderwebs of electricity rippled across his lifeless body, causing his eyes to dart from side to side under his eyelids. His left hand twitched, then the right. With a mighty heave of his chest, he gasped and opened his eyes.

Wilson Dowling had successfully made a leap of almost seventy years backwards in time. He felt no pain and his breathing quickly settled into a rhythm. Numbness clouded his senses, making it difficult to think. As he lay on the smouldering rooftop pavement, Wilson stared through the smoke at the blue sky above him, trying to put everything together in his mind.

Memories slowly began connecting together. He recalled seeing GM and Jasper in the command centre, just seconds before the final transport. There was no doubt that things had become overly complicated at the last moment. *That's an understatement*, he thought. Wilson knew he was lucky to be here, in the past.

If they could have stopped the transport, they would have.

Anyway, all that mattered now was that he was *here*. The Mission of Isaiah was his new focus: completing the tasks assigned to him was the only way to get back home. Gingerly lifting his head, he gazed about. The rooftop was scorched. Hundreds of streamers of smoke wafted upwards into the motionless air like burning incense. From this perspective it was impossible to tell where 'here' was.

With his senses gradually coming back to him, Wilson began to feel the radiant heat of the concrete through his clothes. Sweat trickled from his face and a headache throbbed behind his eyes. Using all his strength, he struggled to one knee, then to his feet, and stumbled towards the molten remnants of the railing.

He was high up—very high up—on a structure of some kind.

Layers of reddish smog blanketed the skyline before him. In the distance, sunlight filtered through the rows of tall buildings clustered at the city centre. Everywhere he looked there was traffic. The pavements were busy with people. It was exactly like the old movies and photographs he had seen; exactly as his research had said it would be. Wilson felt a strange sense of comfort as he smelled pollution for the first time and tasted it on his tongue. The city was loud, much louder than anything he had ever heard before. At that moment he realised that Barton had done it. *They* had done it! This was certainly Houston—Houston early this century. The transport had worked successfully, there was no doubt about it.

A clunk echoed from the air-conditioning system as the large cooling fans on the rooftop began to turn clockwise. At the same time, Wilson's thoughts became clearer. This was potentially a hostile world, he remembered. He would need to remain composed. Remember what he had learned. Stay focused, stay positive, be in the moment. It was all quite simple, he told himself.

Joints cracking as if his body had not functioned in an eternity, Wilson made his way across the blackened concrete towards the fire escape. For some reason the situation seemed funny now. He had travelled through time—*Wilson the time traveller*. It was almost impossible to comprehend.

After taking one last disbelieving look at the smouldering rooftop, he walked down a dusty flight of steps and opened the door onto a lift lobby. There were six elevators, three on each side of the landing, and a sign saying 'Level 36'. It was a large building, he realised. Its magnetic signature must be strong. That was certainly the reason he had been recreated at that very location.

Wilson pushed the down button. A chime sounded and one of the elevator doors slid open. Soft classical music wafted out. With great curiosity, he approached a mirror at the back of the lift and carefully studied himself from different angles. His longish light brown hair was in disarray and he drew it back through his fingers to create some semblance of neatness.

The reflection he saw made him smile; nothing had changed at all. His eyes were their usual dark blue, his skin the same olive colour.

'This is all going rather well,' he said to himself. His headache seemed to be intensifying, but he chose to ignore it. A computer-generated voice emanated from the wall speaker: 'Going down.'

Wilson turned and pressed the first-floor button and waited for the doors to close. This was all too easy. Barton Ingerson was certainly a genius, he decided. It seemed the time-travel process was a complete success and there was cause to be optimistic.

His gaze locked on to the liquid crystal display above the buttons and he watched as a date scrolled past:

25 November 2012

Wilson's heart lurched, and he froze in shock. According to the date, he had arrived more than six years behind schedule.

As THE ELEVATOR DOORS were closing, a tired-looking policeman appeared from the toilets, adjusted his gun belt and plodded across the top-floor landing with a newspaper tucked under his arm. His shift was due to end in the next hour. Noticing a burning smell in the air, he stopped for a moment, gathered his thoughts, then sprinted up the dusty stairs into the morning sunshine.

Officer Frank McGuire's face went pale as he scanned the rooftop. The concrete was peppered with scorch marks and a layer of smoke hung in the air. He had only been gone for fifteen minutes. He fumbled for his gun, drew it from its holster and nervously turned full circle, searching for any sign of movement. Somehow the paint had peeled off the walls, he realised. The steel hand-rail had melted.

His plastic chair had been reduced to a pile of green goo on the ground.

With his heart pounding so loud that he could barely hear himself think, McGuire pressed the talk button on his walkie-talkie. 'This is Lookout Nine.' He turned another full circle, almost dumbstruck. 'Something's happened. An explosion of some kind ...' The radio crackled in his hand.

'This is Base. Repeat your transmission.'

'Lookout Nine!' he repeated more emphatically. 'An explosion of some kind! On the roof!' He struggled to stay calm. 'I don't know how. I can't explain what happened!'

'Lookout Nine, did you see anyone?'

'I'd have been killed if I'd been up here,' he gabbled. There was a moment of silence, then the radio crackled again.

'Lookout Nine, hold your position. We're scrambling a response unit. Repeat: hold your position.'

WILSON STARED AT the date scrolling past every few seconds. The soft music played on the background as the elevator began its descent. Wilson took some deep breaths and tried to work out whether arriving six years late would affect his mission. The Schumann Frequency would probably be higher, but what would the ramifications be? He concluded that, genius or not, Barton had made a critical error. The temperature of the transport pod must have been too low.

Unexpectedly the elevator halted. Wilson glanced at the display panel:

Level 24

The doors slid open. An armed security guard stood in the foyer outside, staring intently in Wilson's direction. The man was chunky, with a thick neck and bulging jowls. His pale green uniform clung to his barrel chest and his black pants were a little too short for his squat legs, revealing a pair of white sports socks.

There were badges on the man's shirt—'Security' and a company name. His freshly shaven skin and neatly combed hair suggested he was just beginning his day.

Wilson looked away, trying to appear relaxed, but he could feel the man's gaze still locked upon him. *The elevator doors will close*, he told himself. *It'll be okay*. A revolver was strapped to the security guard's belt and Wilson stole a brief glance—it was the first time he had ever seen a handgun close up. Inadvertently his eyes slid upwards to the guard's face and then to his eyes.

'Going down' echoed from the speaker.

The sound was a trigger.

Without provocation, the guard leaped through the doorway in attack. There was no room to manoeuvre, no way to escape.

Barton's words echoed in Wilson's head: 'You'll have a weakness after you've travelled through time. Your eyes will make you vulnerable. This is very important. You must wear your contact lenses, otherwise you will be attacked.'

The guard's full weight hammered Wilson into the back wall of the elevator with a crunch, smashing the wind from his lungs. Wilson gasped for air as he tucked himself into a ball to deflect the frenzied onslaught of punches and kicks. In some way he felt like a spectator; it was impossible to conceive that this was actually happening to him.

Both men tumbled to the floor between the closing elevator doors, which sprang open in response. As if awakening from a bad dream, Wilson suddenly began to fight back. Clothes began tearing, muscles quivered. He clumsily struck out, but felt a heavy blow to the head in reply, then another. The pair groaned with exertion as the inelegant melee continued. It was primal combat in its simplest form. Spit flew from the guard's mouth as he repeatedly drove Wilson's head into the carpet.

The guard was too strong!

In response Wilson forced a command from his lips: 'Activate Overload.'

A familiar chill quaked through him as a mixture of adrenaline, testosterone and endorphins flooded his body. Feeling his strength multiply twenty-fold, Wilson effortlessly flung his attacker out of the elevator into the foyer. He expected the guard to retreat at this sign of newfound strength, but that was not the reaction. The man merely regained his balance, snarled and charged fearlessly once again. Wilson hurled him away, this time with such force that the guard was slammed into the elevator doors on the other side of the foyer and fell in a heap on the floor.

But in just moments, the guard gathered himself yet again, as if possessed by an unstoppable compulsion, and sprinted forward, screaming at the top of his lungs. In one quick movement, Wilson leaped into the foyer in counter-attack, grasping his adversary in a headlock and holding him tight. The solid man thrashed about, scratching and trying to bite, but Wilson's grip was like a vice. Seconds ticked by and the guard's struggling inevitably gave way to unconsciousness.

Wilson concluded that the man's reaction had certainly been caused by an optical trackenoid response. It had to be. His contact lenses—worn to prevent this very effect—weren't working.

A pair of dark sunglasses protruded from the guard's breast pocket. Wilson snatched them up, realising they could mean the difference between life and death.

The doors slid closed and he was once again in the confines of the elevator. Calm music continued to play in the background in total disregard for the situation. It was almost annoying. Stretching his shoulders from front to back, Wilson felt profoundly tired. The after-effects of the Overload command were coming. He was filled with dread—he had always likened the feeling to having his spine ripped out of his body with all the nerve endings attached. First, there was a cold sweat, and his body began shaking. That was the easy part. Then the excruciating pain began, like acid flowing through his veins. He clenched his teeth and suppressed the urge to scream.

It was difficult to know how long the pain lasted, but

it always felt like an eternity when in reality it was only seconds. Wilson took a moment to compose himself and assess the situation. Checking himself in the mirror, he realised his clothes were torn and saturated with sweat. He was so weak he could barely stand. Blood was trickling from his bottom lip. The only good news was that his headache had gone. He looked at the dark sunglasses in his palm; they were his only hope of avoiding further confrontation.

The elevator suddenly stopped again. The panel read:

Level 14

'Oh no,' Wilson whispered. Slapping the sunglasses over his eyes, he straightened his clothes, wiped the blood from his mouth and nervously backed away to the far corner of the compartment. If he was attacked now, he certainly wouldn't have the strength to fight.

The doors hissed open and an office worker loomed just outside. Of average height and wearing a white shirt with a blue tie, he gave Wilson a cursory glance before shifting his attention to the ream of papers in his hand. The man stepped into the confined space and jabbed a button on the panel. The elevator doors closed and they descended a floor. The doors hissed open again and he stepped away without incident.

To Wilson's great relief, he was alone again. The glasses must be working, he surmised. But how could he be sure? He watched the red digital numbers descend one by one. When the doors eventually opened on level 1, a murmur of voices filtered towards him. An impressive marble atrium spanned the building lobby. Bright morning sunlight beamed through the glass ceiling. The air was warm, heated to an uncomfortable temperature.

Wilson cautiously made his way towards the railing. Below, at ground level, an endless stream of workers poured in through the double doors, making their way towards the elevators. *Hundreds of people, all potential killers*, he thought.

Walking with a slight limp now, Wilson wound his way down the white marble staircase towards the crowd. The situation made him anxious, but there appeared to be no negative reactions to his approach. Strangers bumped and jostled him as he made his way outside, but it was nothing out of the ordinary. Stepping into a sunlit forecourt, he felt the cool morning air on his face and breathed a well-earned sigh of relief.

But a high-pitched chirping sound snatched his sigh away.

Police sirens echoed off the walls as four squad cars simultaneously screeched to a halt in the car park, roof lights blazing. A gaggle of smartly dressed officers jumped from their vehicles and raced from street level up a single flight of steps towards him. Wilson didn't immediately understand what was happening, but he instinctively turned back towards the building, moving with the flow of the people. Nothing about the situation made any sense. It had only been moments since the incident with the security guard—surely not enough time for the police to arrive in these sorts of numbers.

The officers bustled past and took up position at the entrance.

'No one is allowed inside!' one of them bellowed.

'Everybody move back!' yelled another.

The growing crowd was forced away and Wilson was herded back down the steps with the throng. Two more squad cars appeared at either end of the street as all local traffic was diverted away from the building. Sentries, carrying rifles, were now posted at each corner. The operation appeared well organised.

An unmarked sedan with tinted windows stopped next to the kerb and a policeman uniformed in black hurried to open the rear door. Seconds later, a giant of a man with red hair climbed out. He was enormous, easily dwarfing the officer beside him. Wilson stared at him, then looked around—everyone in the crowd, police included, appeared to be distracted by his presence. They're frightened of him, he eventually realised. Sensing the opportunity to slip away, Wilson dashed across the street into a narrow alleyway.

HIS EXPRESSION STERN, Commander Visblat stared towards the rooftop. He was the most senior law enforcement officer in the city. Almost two metres tall, he was an imposing figure in a loose-fitting black suit. Aged in his mid-forties, he had a full head of distinctive wavy red hair and an overbite that magnified his strong jaw. His skin was pale and he was dark around the eyes from habitual lack of sleep.

Visblat carefully studied the building. *So it happens here*, he thought to himself. Scanning his surroundings he momentarily caught a glimpse of a shadow stencilled on a wall in an alleyway across the street. One second it was there; the next, it was gone.

A voice suddenly interrupted his concentration, 'This way, Commander.'

Visblat stared down at the man next to him.

Officer Benson pointed in the other direction. 'The entrance is this way, sir.'

'Have SWAT gone to the roof?' Visblat said in a gruff voice.

'Not yet, Commander. They're on their way. We were the first to arrive. Apparently it was an explosion of some kind. I've requested the bomb squad attend.'

The last thing Visblat needed was the bomb squad, but it was of no consequence. His quarry was close—he could feel it. 'No one in that building is to leave here until they've been checked against the identikit image, do you understand?' He gestured imperiously across the street. 'Get that alleyway checked out. I think I saw something over there.'

'Yes, Commander.' Officer Benson immediately directed one of the sentries to investigate.

Visblat stared at the crowd. 'Quarantine the entire area. I don't care how much they complain. No one is to leave. This is the terrorist we've been waiting for.'

'Yes, Commander.'

'I want to see the trooper who was assigned to watch the rooftop.'

Officer Benson leaned closer. 'I've given orders to keep Officer McGuire isolated, as you requested.'

'I want to see him, *alone*,' Visblat said under his breath. 'Not a word to anyone about this. Do you understand?'

'Yes, Commander.'

Visblat waited at the top of the stairs as a group of uniformed men dutifully surrounded him, three deep. He gave orders left and right: 'Get that crowd further away. *You*, check the loading bay.' Armed men set off to complete their tasks. 'I want a one-mile checkpoint perimeter from these doors.' Visblat waved his arm in a giant circle.

An officer raised his hand and spoke, 'Commander, there are dozens of streets and laneways. We don't have the manpower to cover everything.'

Visblat gave him a burning gaze. 'Just do the best you can.'

The sight of Visblat's eyes made the officer's skin crawl. 'Yes, Commander,' he said compliantly.

Visblat stood tall. 'Men, this is the moment we have been waiting for. Find the fugitive and bring him to me. *Move it!*' The remaining officers scurried in different directions. Visblat looked once more towards the alleyway, pondered what he thought he had seen, then entered the office building.

WILSON'S PACE SLOWED. He needed more time to think. The failure of his contact lenses would have cost him his life if not for his Overload command. How could Barton have made *such* a critical mistake? And the police, why were there so many? Could they possibly be looking for *him*?

At the end of the alleyway, a steady stream of cars rumbled past towards the city.

The security guard's furious expression flashed into

Wilson's mind once more. Wilson had never been in a fight before, let alone suffocated someone into unconsciousness. The Schumann Frequency was seriously out of balance here—the ferocity of the security guard's reaction was testament to that. Wilson felt sick in the stomach; the thought of being set upon again was playing on his mind.

The sound of running footsteps unexpectedly filled the alleyway behind him. Wilson turned to see a policeman approaching at full pace, gun drawn. It took a moment for Wilson to react—he just couldn't process what was happening.

'Police! Stop right there!' the officer yelled. 'Stop!'

Stunned into action, Wilson sprinted for the end of the alley. If his sunglasses were removed, which would surely happen if he was caught, he was in even more trouble. The traffic was moving quickly and he ran the full length of the street waiting for the opportunity to cross without slowing. The Overload command had stripped much of his energy and he was going as fast as he could. Seeing an opening, he threaded through the traffic, dodging a car that came within a fraction of ending his escape.

But even so, the officer was still behind him.

A shop doorway was open and Wilson ducked inside. The smell of fresh doughnuts filled the air. Customers reeled as he dashed past them. He jumped the serving counter, bolted to the rear and out the back door. A wooden fence. Wilson launched himself over. A steep embankment. He hurled himself down. Another tall fence, chicken-wire. He scaled it, landing heavily on the other side. A bustling freeway lay before him like a river of moving steel that defied being crossed. Vehicles swept by in both directions, four lanes each side, moving at insane speeds.

The policeman had made it to the fence. He was puffing. 'Stop ... right ... there! I mean it!' he yelled as he awkwardly poked his gun through the wire.

'Why ... are you ... chasing me?' Wilson spluttered, raising his hands in the air.

The officer coughed, trying to catch his breath. 'Get down

... on your stomach! Hands ... behind your head!'

Wilson was aware of the incessant drone and whoosh of traffic hurtling behind him.

'I said ... lie down!' the officer yelled again.

With only one hope of escape, Wilson turned and ran along the freeway apron. There was suddenly a gap in the traffic. Taking the opportunity, he sprinted across the smooth pavement. Horns blared. Tyres squealed. A fender almost collected him. Someone screamed a curse from an open window flashing past.

The police officer scaled the fence and landed on his feet.

Wilson made it to the relative safety of the guard rail in the middle of the road.

A torrent of vehicles continued in either direction.

'Stop, or I'll shoot!' the policeman yelled, at the same time taking aim through the traffic.

Wilson jumped the waist-high rail to the other side. One lane at a time, he told himself. The city-bound traffic was more heavily congested—seemingly moving even faster. A car streaked by only centimetres away. The rush of air nearly knocked Wilson from his feet. Car horns blared. He shuffled forward. Vehicles swerved by on either side.

The officer sprinted forward, making it to the guard rail.

Wilson took yet another step. The sound of screeching tyres suddenly dominated his senses. A white sedan was bearing down on him. There was nowhere to go. A side mirror clipped his lower back, catapulting him into the air. Strangely, the impact was painless. With a crunch of steel on bone, the police officer was simultaneously struck down just behind him.

Glass shattered. Metal splintered.

Wilson found himself face-down on the freeway, out-of-control vehicles almost upon him. A series of images flashed through his mind: the magnificent Rembrandt in the Enterprise Corporation boardroom—a painting of a sleeping baby, so peaceful in his crib, being watched over by his mother. Faces of friends: Professor Author, Jenny

Jones, his grandfather. Another image: the ominous Dead Sea scrolls, each and every parchment so impressively spread out in custom-made glass cabinets. Then another: the view from Mount Whitney, a series of mountain ranges of ineffable beauty, white puffy clouds sweeping past, high above. Barton Ingerson was there, looking like a god. He was wearing his Mercury Team labcoat, telling Wilson how important his mission was.

'There is no room for complacency,' Barton said. 'If you fail, *this* reality will be gone forever.'

At the point of impact, Wilson's mind suddenly went blank.

And with him went all hope for the future